A KISS OF
DAGGERS

CHRISTOPHER D. SCHMITZ

TreeShaker Books

TREESHAKER BOOKS

Special Offer

Stay up to date on the world of Arcadeax... you'll get access to a bunch of special freebies, bonus content, and the author's newsletter. You can unsubscribe at any time.
To get access to this exclusive group, just follow this link:

https://www.subscribepage.com/duelist

and add your email to be added immediatley!

CONTENTS

Prologue   VIII

1. Chapter 1   2

2. Chapter 2   22

3. Chapter 3   36

4. Chapter 4   48

5. Chapter 5   63

6. Chapter 6   76

7. Chapter 7   90

8. Chapter 8   109

9. Chapter 9   136

10. Chapter 10   151

11. Chapter 11   171

12. Chapter 12   190

13. Chapter 13   210

14. Chapter 14   229

15. Chapter 15   250

16. Chapter 16   273

17. Chapter 17   295

18. Chapter 18   310

19. Chapter 19   332

20. Chapter 20   351

21. Chapter 21   373

22. Chapter 22   386

23. Chapter 23   396

24. Chapter 24   407

25. Chapter 25   415

26. Chapter 26   422

Epilogue   429

Also By Christopher D. Schmitz   433

Glossary   434

Fullpage Image   438

Fullpage Image   439

Acknowledgments   440

About Author   441

PROLOGUE

L OVE ACROSS SPECIES WAS forbidden, but that had not stopped Remington Keaton.

Remy, *a human*, dared to love an elf.

Remy clutched the bit of silver jewelry in his hand and examined the scars on his flesh, there. They crisscrossed his forearms and snaked down to his digits and he grinned darkly as he touched the marks of raised skin that chronicled his life from one struggle to the next. He made a fist and stared at the earring. *Her earring.* Jewelry owned by the one he loved... The elf woman who had kept him sane in a world that hated him.

Acceptance did not come easily to those few humans trapped in the fey realm of Arcadeax. Most men and women, sons and daughters of Adam, were happy just to survive.

Not Remy. His thirst for vengeance and discovery made him ambitious. It birthed a desire in him to overcome the odds, whatever the cost.

Remy turned to the elf who he'd given his heart to. He grinned at her, a glint like metal alighting in his eye. "Do you remember that day... How we met?"

He didn't expect an answer, but his hand dropped to the knife at his side: a ceremonial dagger forged in the fires of adversity. A blade given to him by the very nature of Arcadeax, from the gods themselves, when he'd awoken in Arcadeax all those years ago. None quite knew how a human boy had acquired a dúshlán in the first place—but like all the mystic daggers, it was linked to Remy's need for revenge.

Remy had fought for every scrap he'd ever earned. He harvested pain where he'd not planted.

The human looked over his shoulder and again at his lover. Years had passed since they first met, but she remained as youthful and as beautiful as ever. "I do still desire children with you—despite the risks..." He trailed off. "What shall we tell them about how we fell in love?"

Remy waited in the silence and then winked at her. He answered on her behalf, "I think we must start where it all began... In the ditches beyond Cathair Dé."

CHAPTER ONE

R EMY DROVE THE SHARP end of his tool into the soil where it made a familiar, gritty *schirk, schirk* kind of sound. He blinked away old memories of all the times in his past when he'd dug holes instead of ditches and then dumped bodies in them, filling secret graves in the dead of night.

"Just a couple more weeks and we'll be in the city," said his friend, Thoranmir. Thoranmir chatting instead of working did not surprise Remy. They'd known each other for a while.

Pausing to push locks of hair behind long elven ears, Thoranmir continued. "I've been trying to get back to Cathair Dé ever since, well, you know."

Remy worked his pick axe in silence. He seldom spoke of his past.

Finally, he wiped the sweat from his brow and rested his pickaxe over his shoulder. It was made of form-poured cupronickel; Iron was illegal to own. Something about its elemental properties reacted violently with the fey, but iron was only one of many available metals.

Thoranmir tossed him the water bladder they shared. Remy took a deep drink from it. He poured a small amount of water to crown his head. It dripped down his hair and pooled at the bandanna's base, which held down the bulk of Remy's wild, mussed mane.

Together, Remy and Thoranmir slaved away to dig a run off ditch that would connect to a road culvert at the edge of a rural noble's property. His fruit orchards had been flooding lately and the oversaturation of water threatened the health of the grove.

Remy and Thoranmir were lucky enough to have secured the back-breaking work. They'd been at it a couple of weeks and were almost done. Hopefully, it would pay enough to afford some decent lodging in the city of Cathair Dé, which had been Thoranmir's home before a chain of regrettable decisions led him away.

An elf maiden with brown, loose curls of hair walked the road and passed the diggers. She appeared close to their age. The maiden glanced at Thoranmir and then she smiled quickly, blushed, and turned away. Then she turned into the orchards and cut through the trees, heading toward the main estate.

"What was that about?" Remy asked.

Thoranmir flashed him a goofy grin. "None of your business."

But the infatuation was obvious. Remy had watched the bumbling flirtations for a few days already, but he left his friend to it.

Remy began to dig again, while Thoranmir still watched the lovely elf's backside as she ambled toward the main house where the noble lived. She'd come initially from the small woodland village of Vail Carvanna, where Remy and Thoranmir had purchased their digging equipment. On most days, they saw her walk to the lord's house. They'd deduced that she was the governess for the noble's precocious daughter.

Still staring into the trees, Thoranmir asked, "Do you think Odessa looks much like the child she plays nanny for?"

Remy grinned. "So, it's Odessa?"

Thoranmir smiled broadly. "Odessa Cócaire. We had a chat the other night when I found her on the way to the village."

Remy laughed and ribbed him. "I wasn't aware you knew how to talk to girls."

"I haven't always been a homeless drifter, you know." After one last glance, Thoranmir returned to work.

Together, the pair moved soil for several hours until the heat arose and the sun crept toward midday. Thoranmir collapsed to his butt in the shade, panting for air and splaying his shovel beside him.

Remy, the stout one of the pair, remained on his feet. He was considerably thicker in the arms and neck than most sidhe, the elven fey of Arcadeax. Remy's stout frame was often reason enough for employers to give him labor related work.

As they rested, Odessa walked near and called to them. "Thoranmir? Have you or your friend seen a child, an elf girl? The lady of the house sent her to pick some flowers."

Thornamir suddenly possessed the energy and prowess of two Remys as he stood to his feet, puffing out his chest, trying to impress her. "No. We've been out here working so hard that we don't see much else. I suppose it's possible that she…"

"There she is," Remy said, and pointed.

An elvish girl picked flowers on the opposite side of the road, just a short jog away. She plucked them one by one; some she placed in her flower basket and others she wove into the wreath of wildflowers that adorned her flaxen head. Her utilitarian dress made her exact age a mystery.

Because she was so young, perhaps eight years old, she could have been the child of the noble or of any of the house staff. Only a fool would try to force a child into the gaudy clothes worn by those in high society, that is, unless they were attending a formal function. But Remy could see what Thoranmir had said earlier; the child bore a remarkable resemblance to Odessa.

Remy and Thoranmir watched the girl work for a few moments, jealous of how light her chores were. Picking blossoms and weaving chaplets were far easier tasks than trenching furrows.

Thoranmir turned back to flirt with Odessa, and Remy was content to allow it. They were ahead of schedule and could afford a break.

Their employer's estate bordered the public road, and that made the noble responsible for the highway's upkeep. As loathsome as some of King Oberon's taxes and rulings were to the lowest castes, at least this requirement meant Remy and Thoranmir had work, and more importantly, wages. And that meant they could eat—even if the fruit of the noble's orchard was off limits.

"I could take a nap right now," Thoranmir said, stretching in the sun, practically inviting Odessa to join him.

"You always want to take a nap," Remy said. "We've got to finish this ditch, though, or we'll fall behind."

Thoranmir stared at the callouses that had developed on his hands. "I don't know that I like this kind of work..."

"Or any other," Remy quipped.

That made Odessa laugh. Thoranmir furrowed his brow at his friend and looked wounded.

"I mean, I ought to just be wealthy. I do hate this kind of toil."

Remy frowned. "You should have thought of that before you decided to be born to poor parents."

"And in the heat... Why can't we do this sort of work *after* the hot part of the day has passed? I'd much rather do this sort of thing in the evening. I'm something of a night owl, you know. How about you, Odessa?"

"I don't mind staying up late... Depending on my company." She smiled. They chatted quietly between themselves.

Remy rolled his eyes. He knew how his friend would stay up all night prattling about big ideas, but Remy guessed they meant something else entirely. Thoranmir's late-night conversations often kept him awake when Remy just wanted to sleep so he could be rested and ready to labor in the morning. Thoranmir treated every night as if they were young cousins roughing it during a holiday. The two had a small camp in the forest wilds where they hung a couple hammocks tied between trees and buried a locker to hide their tools and valuables within—an attempt at saving toward a better life.

"Oh, I know. But day is much easier to work in than night," Remy reminded him.

Odessa curtsied slightly. "I should report the girl's whereabouts to my lady. She ought to be done soon." She winked at Thoranmir and then turned back into the orchard.

Thoranmir sighed and watched her go. "I'd rather be up all night and sleep all day, I think. Maybe Odessa would care to join me?" He grinned at his friend.

Remy shook his head and ignored him.

"I hate when it's hot, especially at the height of summer. Maybe I was meant for the unseelie..."

"No," Remy insisted with a serious tone that shut down Thoranmir's conjecture. Only those who had never been to the unseelie lands spoke lightly of that hell. Remy knew it firsthand.

Thoranmir shrugged and stretched on the comfortable ground. And then he snapped his head toward the forest.

Remy heard the sound a moment later and spotted the carriage blazing through the gate as if its driver were desperate to arrive. Four horses galloped, pulling an open carriage with four elf men. The chargers' coats glistened with a frothy sheen as the vehicle careened forward.

Remy saw the girl absentmindedly dawdling, a basket of flowers looped around her forearm as she concentrated on weaving her flowers together. She paid no mind to the traffic and wandered toward the road on a certain course for collision. The child would be little more than a mushy bump in the road next to the horses and cart.

Dropping his pickaxe, Remy sprinted for the road while Thoranmir sprang to his feet. The elf waved his hands over his head, trying to get the attention of the driver.

Indifferent, the driver paid no mind to poor folk on either side of the road. He cracked the reins, urging the horses onward and at a greater speed. They galloped harder, curving around the gentle bend in the forest road and onto the straight shot that spanned two leagues before turning away again.

Remy roared a warning, trying to get the girl's attention—warn the carriage driver, *anything!*

The little girl looked up and froze, directly in the path of the speeding horses. She dropped the small bouquet she had carried and gasped, standing stiff as a board.

The clapping hooves of the chargers thundered as they bore down on the elf child who stood riveted to the road: helpless.

ONE COULD SEE A great deal from the mezzanine high atop the Suíochán Naséan, the wizards tower, which rose eighty cubits from dirt to peak. From its top floor gallery one could overlook the city of Daonra Dlúth which formed a circle, skirting the capital of the seelie realm, or one could turn and look inward at Faery Cairn, the home of the Summer Court and Oberon, king of the sidhe, the elves, and also the rest of the fey in his domain.

Suíochán Naséan provided views not afforded to any except for the wizards with rights to access it: the mavens, politically aligned spell casters who governed their factions of magically gifted citizens.

However, the wizards were not in the top of the Radiant Tower. But with the assets at their disposal, they could see a great deal *more* even by remaining in the basement of the Suíochán Naséan.

Seven mavens—all of them elves—sat upon seven simple chairs, each at the point of a seven pointed star, the heptagram called the fairy star, which was inlaid upon the floor with precious metals. A chair bore a maven seated at each sharp vertex.

The mavens' attendants, political successors, and apprentices, stood around the walls.

Footsteps echoed from the stairwell that led deeper still into the earth. All eyes turned expectantly and a mature, silver-haired elf ascended, fixing them with eyes that were somehow older than his body appeared. He was dressed in robes, like the other mavens and the sigil embroidered upon his chest seemed to glow with white threads. Additionally, he wore a silver pin upon his breast denoting further political authority in the Summer Court.

Calithilon the White took his place at the center of the star and the remaining members of the maven council stood simultaneous, pushing chairs back with their legs. Their attendants retrieved them and stowed them out of the way of the proceedings.

"I have consorted with our... guest," Calithilon said. "She has verified what rumors some of you have heard in your districts. I remind you that we must treat this information with caution. So few have the talent to predict futures—and it is a potent gift, filled with symbolism and subjectivity.

A female maven with a violet emblem on her chest muttered, "If Oberon knew that we had a seer…"

"Enough, Amarthanc," growled Calithilon with a steady voice of authority. "Each one here is sworn to secrecy on that matter and has taken the vow in the olde tongue." He switched languages to intensify his point. [Words in the olde language are binding and cannot be violated without great consequence.]

Amarthanc was the youngest of them, and most prone to breaking the council's internal protocol, but a stern glare from the high maven was usually enough to keep her in line. Her smug expression wilted. She bowed her head, letting Calithilon speak without interruption.

That the mavens held a kidnapped seer hostage in the bowels of Suíochán Naséan was no matter to jest over—or even to allude to outside of immediate company. Too powerful was such a gift—too potentially dangerous to the gilded throne. Even despite oaths of fealty and unequivocal loyalty, the fact that the mavens possessed one with future-seeing abilities would be viewed as a threat by Oberon.

After a moment of silence, Calithilon turned to address each of the seven members of the council under his authority. "Days ago, Oberon sanctioned an amateur dueling contest in the barony of Cathair Dé. It was recorded as one of our duties to attend to in keeping with the maven office."

Nods circulated the gathering. It had been a minor discussion point during the last assembly and was barely worthy of note. Far more pressing was the coming cataclysm. There had been signs that doom was coming for the mavens. Arcadeax was shifting—and it had little to do with their unseelie enemies on the other side of the world.

"What does some inconsequential city have to do with fulfilled prophesies?" asked Tinthel who wore an orange sigil that spanned her breast.

"Nothing. Everything," said Calithilon. "We need to know who it is that brings this doom to our doorstep so we may prevent it, as we have done in every cycle of prophecy. We do not know where this one comes from or who it is. We must consult every source."

"Last time, it was a dragon," said Glirien the Blue. "Is it a dragon again, perhaps still young and disguised as a common sidhe?"

Calithilon frowned. "Doubtful. The Pendragon, the ruler of their kind, resides in a sister realm beyond the reach of Arcadeax, and she has quite forgotten who she is. That makes her a lesser threat. No, the old grudge has passed. This is something new."

Mithrilchon the Red spoke. "Cathair Dé's duels are under my sanction. What must I know. What did the seer tell you?"

"Merely that whoever wins must be watched—and closely. The winner, whomever it is, threatens the very structure on which we all stand upon. Whether by greed, stupidity, or malice, she could not say, only that his or her actions spell a certain end," said the white maven. "The maven council, and the power they represent, is in grave peril."

"Our answer is a clear and easy one," interjected Adlegrion the indigo. "We send assassins to work down the roster. Kill them all in one fell swoop."

Calithilon shook his head, scattering his silver hair. "We cannot for two reasons. First, Oberon has provided sanction and already delivered the prize: Dagda's Kiss. Violating the mystic sanctions is unthinkable, but it could be done. However, the seer has seen some special protection. A tremendous higher power sponsors this herald. Some kind of eldritch force, perhaps a ward, safeguards him or her. Until it is removed, it may prove perilous to use magic against the person."

Such wards were capable of reflecting back upon a magical attacker with equal weight or more. Worse, they were sometimes known to transfer a curse to the person murdering him or her even if taking non-magical measures. There were many sources of such wards; the most likely culprits, since they could rule out any sort of special ancestry or natural arcane immunities based on the targets' species, was some kind of magic artifact such as an amulet. They could not take preventative measures until they knew the type of mystic protection being employed.

"Person?" asked Mithrilchon.

Calithilon the White narrowed his eyes and made a severe look as he made a clutching motion to summon the members of his cabal to take a closer step. The mavens all did as indicated and closed the gap so that their chief could cast a spell which would envelop only those in their circle in a bubble; only they could hear his words.

Not even the mavens' apprentices were allowed to know Oberon's business.

"One of the contestants is the stolen child from the world of man," Calithilon said.

The mavens traded glances.

Tinthel asked, "I thought the boy was taken by orks in the unseelie?"

Calithilon nodded. "He was. But he's since made his way out, and is perhaps more dangerous for it."

Amarthanc squinted, looking confused. "What are we speaking of?"

"A political gambit made years ago, before you were taken onto the council," said Fimion the Green. "The less you know, the better."

"This complicates things," Mithrilchon noted. "He must not know why he is here—there are many humans in Arcadeax—none of them truly belong, but especially this one."

Calithilon nodded gravely and then relaxed the spell.

"Is there a favored outcome?" Mithrilchon asked, tugging at a stray bit of embroidery on the semi-circular crimson circle at his chest.

The highest maven nodded. "It is widely believed the champion from House Vastra will sweep the contest."

"Then we shall surveil this elf," Mithrilchon said. He looked back to his apprentices, Agarogol and Loitariel, who both wore red symbols that matched his own. They both bowed their heads in silent agreement.

"And what of the *other* problem," Amarthanc finally spoke again. "Power has leaked from the dark gate. We have all sensed it. Infernal energies at work in Arcadeax."

Calithilon frowned, but was grateful that she did not press the point. The white maven's job was to guard the Black Gate. If any power or force had passed through that sealed portal and into Arcadeax, it could not happen without the white maven's knowledge or complicity.

"Nothing has passed the infernal gate for six thousand years. The way is shut, and nothing can force it open." Calithilon met each set of eyes, almost hoping one of them would challenge his words and scry the gate. It would only prove the truth of Calithilon's words.

But some dark force *was* at play in Arcadeax, though few outside the circle of mavens could understand that darkness, evil, barely existed. The maven council had named their positions after ranks of the light spectrum, but all those who had power and truly understood it saw the world more in shades of gray than as black and white. The mavens understood the stakes and the game—that seemed to indicate that, if any force was drawing power from the infernal realm, a potent source of magic that was *truly black*, even as the mavens saw things, it was probably someone intimately familiar with their ways. *An excommunicated maven, perhaps?*

Calithilon said, "Be ever vigilant. There are other sources of magic in this realm. And all of it is possible to be misused." Calithilon dismissed them.

Mithrilchon bowed deepest, and then collected his apprentices. "We shall depart at once," he told the high maven.

The white elf's face remained grave. "Stick to the shadows. Whatever is at play threatens more than just Suíochán Naséan. It could bring down even the gilded throne."

Mithrilchon nodded. He headed for the stairs with his apprentices in tow.

RIGHT BEFORE THE HORSE hooves could smash her apart, Remy flew across the road and tackled the child, scattering petals skyward like threshed chaff. They landed in a rolling heap, safely in the ditch nearby.

She screamed, but her cries were quieter than the thundering hooves that rushed past them. Wagon wheels crushed the flowers into fragrant paste upon the packed earth of the highway.

Remy and the child rolled to a stop on the grassy heather, flattening the wild flora beneath them.

The carriage didn't falter. It sped further away and into the distance. One of the men in the open cart looked back at them with an amusedly callous grin.

Thoranmir arrived right after the carriage had gone. He cursed at the wagon. "Bastards. Typical upper-class prigs. I bet they'd have had us prosecuted if a horse had gone lame while trampling us."

Shaking his head, he checked them over. Remy and the child appeared no worse for wear, besides a few scratches on their cheeks where stubbly stems and low bracken bit their flesh.

Remy rubbed the girl's back while she bit back tears and coughed. He'd tackled her quickly, and the move had knocked the wind from her lungs. "Not likely," he said. "I mean, you might be right *if they were upper class.*"

Thoranmir furrowed a brow.

"They weren't nobility," Remy explained. "Just assholes. The carriage wasn't nearly posh enough for them to have been affluent, but they looked just wealthy enough to afford what they need-ed—a hurried ride somewhere. Wherever they were going, they had some urgent purpose behind it."

Remy turned to the child. "Are you okay?"

She gasped and sucked in a deep breath, the raggedness from her breathing finally leveled out. "Yes... and thank you. My name is Donnalia," the girl said, nursing her bruised ribs. Her eyes lit up when Remy adjusted his head covering. It had broken free and exposed his tousled hair that hid his ears. "Y-you're a human?"

For a moment, he almost panicked. But the child didn't seem to harbor any resentment for his species. *Hatred is usually cultural and has to be learned.* Remy retied his bandanna.

"Yes," Remy said matter-of-factly. "That's not terribly uncom-mon, is it?" He adjusted the sleeveless jacket that he had wrapped around his tunic.

"But it is," Donnalia insisted. "I know there are some around, but I've only ever seen one other... and *you're a duelist, too?*" She whispered the last part reverently.

"No," he said, quickly tying the folds of his garment to cover the telltale handle of the dúshlán knife that he always kept sheathed at his hip. It was one of the few possessions that he'd kept for all of his life... at least all that he remembered.

Parts of his story were a mystery even to him. It began back when he was about Donnalia's age, when he'd awaken in the unseelie realm.

"If I was a duelist, I wouldn't have to dig ditches now, would I?" Remy asked.

"But you have a dúshlán. It is a dúshlán, isn't it?"

Remy sighed with resignation. "Yes."

"Why would you have it if you weren't looking to duel the person who it is keyed to?" the girl asked. "Don't you plan to kill whoever the dúshlán is linked to? I mean, why else keep it?"

"I just... are little girls your age always this clever?" Remy asked.

"Just not clever enough to watch the road for traffic," Thoranmir joked, prompting Donnalia to turn and kick him in the shin. Thoranmir yelped, but her brassiness at least confirmed that she was a child of the nobleman. No commoner's whelp would dare such a thing.

Donnalia crossed her arms. "Maybe not *all little girls*. But Daddy says I'm smart, even if he doesn't want to show me off..."

"I'm sorry," Thoranmir said, doing the intelligent thing and appeasing her, in hopes she'd both forget to mention to her father that one of the ditch diggers was a human and simultaneously praise them for saving her. A good report could be worth a few coins to the master of the house. "Now might be a good time to run back home, where it is safe."

"I can take care of myself," she began. Though her words had a certain kind of lisp to them.

"I'm sure you can," Thoranmir said, "but—"

"I want to know more about the human." Donnalia tried to get a better look at Remy's ears, her words still sounding a little odd, but she masked it well.

Remy didn't let the inquisitive child bother him and returned to the ditch. "Your parents hired us to dig this nice ditch and offered us such a meaningful and generous wage," he said, his words bordering on sarcasm, which luckily went over her head.

"Please?" she begged. "I've never seen ears like that. Not up close."

Remy stared at her, incredulous.

"Don't be such a little hob," Thoranmir insisted. "Now run along so we can—"

"She's just curious." Remy sighed, untying the fabric around his head. He knelt on one knee so she could see.

She ran her fingers through his hair, not minding the sweat from his labor. Finally, she exposed the blunted tops of his ears. "Ewww! It's disgusting," she whispered like a child exposed to something both fascinating and borderline pornographic.

Remy made no reaction. *She's only a child... knowledge and exposure drive out fear.*

A shrill, mechanical whine buzzed in the distance and Donnalia stood. "Got to go," she yipped, as if suddenly aware that it was improper for a young lady in training to fraternize with ditch digging crews.

Donnalia sprinted back across the roads and into the orchards in the direction of her family home. Her now empty flower basket flailed in her grip as she disappeared among the fruit trees and she linked up with Odessa, who had come in search of her.

"Cheeky little goblin," Thoranmir said as his human friend retied his hair up to hide his ears again. He watched Donnalia and Odessa turn and stroll back home.

"At least you didn't pretend like you were suddenly now learning about my ears when the kid found out... *again*," said Remy.

They both watched as a single horse galloped out of the forest. It pulled a fancy carriage, which was the source of a low whine.

The buggy was likely twice the weight of the previous one and carried at least as many folks, but the horse seemed barely burdened. The carriage boasted a mechanical hover device on its bottom which glowed with an orange hue. There, ampoules of mystic energy pulsed, powering the levitating contraption.

Collecting akasha into those batteries was an expensive endeavor, but machines powered by the mystic energy had become more and more popular among the richer class. Few knew the secrets of how the akasha was collected or stored, but folks assumed it was done by the Aes Sídhe—those with the capacity to cast spells. What folks *did* know was that the stuff was expensive, volatile, and effective.

"Now *that's* what I expect an upper class carriage to look like," Remy told his friend as they watched it pass.

"I dunno. It looks like a flagrant waste of money if you ask me," Thoranmir said.

Remy wasn't paying attention. His eyes were fixated on the riders seated within the extravagant vehicle.

The ride had a retractable awning which had been pulled down so that the passengers could enjoy the open air. An older couple dressed in fine clothes rode with their faces pointed to the rear and with their backs to the driver. He looked like a simple footman; he sat atop their stacked luggage.

At the rear sat the most beautiful elvish maiden Remy had ever seen. She looked around with eager eyes, her golden hair swept back by the breeze. She seemed to appreciate the beauty in the landscape of the seelie countryside in high summer, smiling at the emerald grass and violet blossoms as much as at the dusty ditch diggers.

She locked eyes with Remy and blushed as the carriage passed by. It continued down the highway with the driver oblivious to anything outside of the road.

"Did you see that?" Thoranmir asked. "I think she fancied me."

Remy only grinned, his eyes still fixed on her. "Sure thing," he said, even as she glanced back over her shoulder and briefly met Remy's gaze again. *Her eyes are electric.* Remy didn't know how the alchemists harvested the akasha that they used to power the mechanicals, but he felt infused by it in that moment.

"That's what I want," Remy whispered.

Thoranmir had already returned to the ditch with his shovel, turning the earth. "What's that, mate? A fancy carriage?"

Remy touched the handle of the blade at his hip, caressing the dúshlán. "Her... *her life*... a life of ease alongside a woman like her. Or better yet, *her*." He stared a moment longer.

"Rich and famous with a beautiful bride? Do you want to eat cake every day and shit gold, too? You need a different dream, my friend. That one's already taken. You can't have my dream," Thoranmir said.

Remy ignored his friend. He was used to hard work. He'd fought his way out of the unseelie. He'd never met anyone else capable of that, though he'd admit his circle was small. But still, Remy was willing to work to achieve his goals. "I'll get my dream. Someday."

He turned back to his job and hefted his pickaxe. Remy swung it down into a mound of dirt and the air seemed to detonate with the thunderous sounds of an explosion.

CHAPTER TWO

S TILL CARRYING THE PICKAXE, Remy sprinted toward the scene of the carnage. He dashed up a stony outcropping and climbed to a vantage point as he ran toward the sound of the explosion. He knew that Thoranmir followed at a distance. The elf had stood there, blinking. The human sprang into action without hesitation.

Remy could not blame Thoranmir for lacking the quick reaction time Remy possessed; he'd developed his out of necessity. In the unseelie part of the world, one learned to be quick in order to survive. The rules were different on the other side of Arcadeax, but regardless of whether one was in the seelie or unseelie kingdoms, or even in the faewylds, failure to remain vigilant often resulted in death. Remy was a survivor above all else.

He kept low and clambered up the ridge, masked in the underbrush. Just down the embankment stood the four elves who had nearly crushed Donnalia. Remy spotted their carriage and team of horses hidden in the trees some distance past the road.

The lone horse from the wealthy folks' carriage that had passed them lay dead in the street. Its midsection lay busted open, with internal organs exposed to the sky. Flipped onto its side, the anti-gravitational carriage smoldered where some kind of explosive device had been used to aggressively halt the vehicle.

Remy stealthily bypassed the assassins as he sprinted toward the fray. He looked back to where Thoranmir hurried to catch up and flashed him a few hand signals.

Then, Remy darted down the slope and used his added momentum to launch himself at the four attackers. Remy used both hands to swing the pickaxe at the first assailant who he caught unawares.

The spiked side of his tool impaled the first of them, cracking ribs and vertebrae before bursting through. With his lungs rupturing, the elf collapsed to the dirt with a thud, wrenching the tool free from Remy's hand in the process.

Remy used his forward progress to launch his form into the next elf, who'd turned to address the noise behind him. The fighters collided in a heap of limbs. Remy had the foresight to lower his head. The top of his skull smashed into the enemy's nose.

With a yelp, the elf fell over, blood gushing down his chin.

At the front, nearest the road, the assassin's leader howled, "Stop! Stop this at once. This is a sanctioned duel. We are registered duelists on a private contract!" Like all duelists, he wore a pin on his breast as a mark of his license. It bore no ribbons of honor or inset gems, which would indicate how long he'd had it, so that meant he was new to the dueling profession.

His announcement halted Remy's progress. Remy staggered to a stop. Killing duelists on a valid assignment was punishable by death. Remy was not a duelist, which was the domain of gentlemen of wealth and stature, but everyone knew the legalities of the job.

Remy frowned, standing and splaying his hands to show that he was not a threat. There were rules to dueling, and one of them was to announce yourself prior to the engagement to give the target an opportunity to provide a defense.

Many wealthy individuals kept a duelist on retainer to defend them if a sanctioned charge came against them, and many universities even offered dueling classes so that new graduates could hold their own if a duelist took a private commission. It had created a whole class of young business-minded folk with a passion for dueling.

"That's not true!" a voice called from behind the overturned carriage. "There was no announcement of a duel—you attacked us!" An older gentleman with long ears poked his head up from behind the wreckage to find that his rescuer had downed half the duelists already.

"Is that true?" Remy asked, eyeing the duelist. "It looks like you are breaking protocol."

"None of them are dead, or even wounded." The duelist rolled his eyes. "I am here to execute a private contract for a duel against Fuerian Vastra." He held his sword in hand , pointing it at the toppled carriage. With his free hand, he brandished a marker to prove his orders. "Outside of special circumstances, dueling rules mean to fight to first blood unless the target demands a fight to the death… and rumor has it you'll choose the latter," he yelled to the elves hiding behind the wreck.

"You foolish child," the older elf spat from his hiding place. "Fuerian is not riding with us. He took a private escort back to Cathair Dé, far ahead of us."

"You're Harhassus Morgensteen, are you not? Fuerian is betrothed to your daughter, Jaira?" The duelist's confidence faltered.

"Yes," hissed Morgensteen. "And Fuerian is. Not. Here," he stressed through gritted teeth.

The duelist blanched. If he had followed protocols properly, he should have known that. His shoulders slumped for a moment and his eyes darted as he considered options.

Remy knew the elf duelist's choices were limited. As a duelist, he'd just attacked an innocent bystander while breaking protocol. He had no protection from the duelists guild and would be stripped of his rank and license. He'd possibly stand for attempted murder as well, if the attacked party chose to press the issue.

And from the sound of Morgensteen's voice, he certainly wanted blood.

The duelist's posture straightened. Remy recognized the dark decision reflected in the attacker's eyes.

Without any witnesses to the crime, none would be the wiser, Remy thought. *It would go down as a random act of violence on the highways beyond the city of Cathair Dé.*

"Get him," the leader snarled.

The thug at his side slugged Remy across the face and sent him reeling just beyond the grasp of the elf with the busted nose, who scrambled back into the action.

Remy spun toward the nearby trees, in the direction of the four horses and the coach he'd previously spotted.

Dashing past a thick tree, a loud *clang!* echoed as Thoranmir smashed a shovel in the face of his pursuer. He'd stood exactly where Remy suspected. This was not the first scrape they'd faced together.

Turning on a dime, Remy barreled around the tree and flew straight into the elf with the broken nose. The flying tackle knocked the elf into a tree, where his head collided with a sickening crack, like sundering wood in the hands of a swamp troll.

His enemy slid down the tree and onto his rump with a twisted neck. Remy didn't bother to check if he was unconscious or if his neck had broken. These brigands had murder on their minds: self-defense was justified.

"Grab the horses," Remy barked.

Thoranmir nodded and sprinted deeper into the thicket while Remy whirled back to the road. He snatched his pickaxe up as he hurried past the first of the dead elves.

The duelist chased them around the busted remains of the hover car, trying to corner them. Already Morgensteen's valet lay dead with a jagged slash across his neck. Red blood mixed with loose scree where the body lay.

"Get back here and face me," the elf with a sword yelled to his prey.

Using one arm to keep them back, Morgensteen protected his wife and daughter as best as he was able, blood running down his face where the elf's blade had nicked him. It appeared that he would die first, and then the killer would eliminate the rest of the witnesses.

The criminal's blade slashed down at Morgensteen but stopped just short of cleaving flesh. Remy's pickaxe blocked the sharp edge, and he grinned at the duelist.

"What? How..."

"*Your* friends aren't as resourceful as *my* friends," Remy growled, using a foot to shove the elf backwards. His enemy recoiled, staggering to keep from falling to his rump.

The foliage behind them suddenly shook and burst apart as Thoranmir urged the chargers through. He angled the carriage toward Morgensteen and his family. It arrived within moments.

"Get out of here!" Remy yelled at the family he was rescuing.

They wasted no time; the wagon didn't even come to a full stop as Morgensteen leapt in. He helped his wife inside while Remy practically tossed Jaira, the daughter, all the way into the carriage.

Thoranmir cracked the reins and sent the horses into a frenzy while Morgensteen clung to the back, only half aboard. His wife and daughter clutched the elf's fine clothing, half tearing it as they dragged him aboard. The violent jostling of panicked horses threatened to toss them all from their seats.

Roaring, the duelist charged at Remy, who spun to meet his enemy just in time to block the blade with his digging tool. The sword hacked a deep groove in the pickaxe's haft. Remy worried that it wouldn't last long against the metal edge of the weapon.

Remy pressed his attack, charging and swinging his tool. The duelist's first block lopped the head off the pickaxe. Unrelenting,

Remy swung his haft like a club, which the duelist also blocked, severing it again and rendering the club useless.

Remy ducked below the sword stroke that the duelist thought would finally end the interloping ditch digger. Remy popped back up inside the duelist's guard and yanked his dúshlán from the sheath hidden in his jacket. He plunged the dagger upwards and into the enemy's midsection.

The duelist staggered back two steps, freeing his torso from the short blade he'd never known was present. His eyes filled with surprise and his mouth filled with gurgling blood. He fell dead.

Remy stared at the bloody dúshlán knife, still in his grip. The runes inscribed within the blade's grooved fuller did not glow. He frowned. "Pity." He wiped it clean and sheathed the knife before Thoranmir could return with Morgensteen and his family.

Already Thoranmir had turned the carriage in a tight arc to redirect them from Cathair Dé, the city still several leagues in the distance.

Thoranmir pulled back on the reins. The carriage slowed to a stop near the wreckage. Morgensteen helped his wife and daughter out of the wagon.

Jaira stumbled slightly and Remy stepped forward to catch her. He squeezed her hand, and the two locked eyes. Something like lightning passed between them, stronger than any akashic jolt.

Morgensteen thanked Remy, cutting in between them and taking his daughter's hand. He didn't seem to appreciate her being helped by some low-class ditch digger, however helpful he had proved himself. "I thank you, sir," Morgensteen said, turning to address Remy. "You've saved the lives of myself and my family."

"I just did what anyone would do if he or she wanted to act rightly," Remy said, hedging to one side to try and get a better look at the beautiful girl who had so enthralled him.

"Well said," Morgensteen commented, looking over the young men who had helped him.

Remy and Thoranmir stood shoulder to shoulder, covered in dirt that had turned to ruddy mire where the attackers' blood mixed to form a mirey cake. No two folks had ever looked more as if they belonged in the poor farms which existed to help house and feed those in abject poverty than those two did.

In truth, they'd just left the poor farms a few months ago. Deep-seated prejudices thrived among the most poverty-stricken, who saw any public aid to a human as thievery—particularly if those resources could have helped elves instead.

Remy adjusted his headband to make sure his ears remained concealed. Not that it mattered much. Morgensteen barely looked at Remy.

Morgensteen nodded his head and grumbled something to himself, which sounded like a question regarding his rescuers' moral statures.

"I'm taking my family back to Cathair Dé," Morgensteen told them. "We'll inform the authorities and they'll send an investigator out to look into this and clean up the road." The look he gave them was unmistakable. It communicated something deeper: *if either of you are wanted by the law, you should leave before they arrive.*

"Thank you," said Remy with a curt bow. "But we're just two simple tradesmen, working a small job nearby. I am Remy Keaton and this is Thoranmir Shelton." He held up the pieces of his ruined pickaxe for the elf to see. "Of course, it'll be more difficult to complete our job without our tools."

"Yes. I do suppose we can at least help in that regard," Morgensteen's wife insisted, fixing her husband with a firm gaze.

"Yes, Daddy," Jaira said, peeking around his frame to make eye contact with Remy again. Her eyes sparkled like the facets of precious gems when they caught his gaze—and not from the frantic endorphin rush of the murder plot. There was something *more* there. *Attraction?*

Morgensteen sighed. "I suppose it would be my civic duty." He emptied his pockets and turned over a fistful of coins, including a few gold pieces, several silvers, and enough coppers to replace the pickaxe and buy a week's provisions for them both. It was nearly as much as their employer had promised for their work on the ditch and drainage system.

"Thank you," Thoranmir said, slightly in awe.

"Very well then," Morgensteen concluded, hurrying his family back into the wagon. "We must make all haste back to Cathair Dé. If Fuerian has enemies looking for a duel, let us hope there is too little distance between here and the city for others to make such a foolish error."

The father climbed into the seat, looking unfamiliar enough with the reins for Remy to assume it had been many years since he'd driven a carriage. He urged the horses forward, and the wheels turned, carrying the elf family toward Cathair Dé.

Jaira turned back and looked into Remy's eyes as the ride whisked her away.

"You're sure that's what you want? All the pomp and circumstance and the stress of high society and duelists?" Thoranmir asked. "I mean, it sure seems terrible having so much disposable income... You're fine with all that?"

"Absolutely," Remy said, never taking his eyes off the elf maiden as the distance grew greater between them.

"Yeah," chuckled his friend. "Me too."

HYMDREIDDIECH THE BLACK KEPT his hood over his face to mask any distinguishing features. Without something to allay attention, he would be noticed in a crowd. That fact had made him good at veils, illusionary magic, from a young age.

But Hymdreiddiech was not content to study the arcane arts and excel where he had gifts; he had delved ancient texts and discovered darker paths. While his peers aspired to be recognized as talented wizards and hoped to someday be invited into the council of mavens, Hymdreiddiech made a pact with outsiders: creatures of power who existed beyond the arcadeaxn realm.

Creatures who elevated me from the unseelie gutters and amplified my magic enough that I can destroy my foes, especially the maven council!

While the mavens had ordered themselves along the spectrum of light, Hymdreiddicch accorded himself as *The Black*. He knew what he was, and what powers he consorted with. Order, balance, everything that the mavens worked to achieve were antithetical to his goals. Hymdreiddiech was a force of pure chaos; he was the *Black Maven.*

Hymdreiddiech had plotted his revenge for decades. Steeped in the rage that consumed him and fed him at the same time. His patience had finally paid off.

The time to strike verged on the horizon like a burgeoning dawn.

The black maven was used to waiting.

Presently, he sat in the comfortable shadows. A fine, leather chair creaked slightly below his weight. Voices echoed in the hall.

The door of the darkened chamber opened and a finely dressed he-elf entered. His hand pushed the button on a wall and lights illuminated the room. They were powered by the mystic power of akasha, as were so many of the baubles and toys within the home.

Hymdreiddiech's mark was a wealthy elf who he'd watched for years, and this elf had a notable penchant for investing in new technology. Most of his estate had connection ports for akashic devices. Machines that used the arcane power to keep food cold, light lamps, and power contraptions.

"Greetings, sir," Hymdreiddiech rasped as he turned in the comfortable chair.

The elf stood straight, surprised by the intruder and jammed a hand into a fold of his clothes and produced a small contraption made of metal and crystal. He pointed the jagged glassine object and shouted. It lit up momentarily and fired an enormous, crackling arc of lightning at the black maven.

Hymdreiddiech erected a mystic barrier, tweaking his spell as the jagged lines of blue energy danced all around the bubble that protected him. He shifted the properties of his magic sphere so that it absorbed the energy, drawing in all that the lightning rod produced.

Then the lightning stopped.

"A wand?" Hymdreiddiech raised a brow, momentarily wondering if the elf had eldritch abilities. However, Hymdreiddiech quickly realized the wand was an akashic device, and not an actual wand. The lightning had run its course when the battery had depleted.

Hymdreiddiech held up a hand before the homeowner could try another tactic. "Stop. I am not here to cause you harm."

The elf didn't listen. He rushed towards a ceremonial sword hanging upon a wall.

"I come with a bargain, not with violence," Hymdreiddiech said. "I come to both reward you and to collect a debt you aren't even aware that you owe."

That finally got the elf's attention. He paused by the sword, rather than drawing it. "I am listening." He leveled a gaze at the sorcerer.

"I can see you have no lack of wealth… but I come offering something worth far more than gold or jewels. I am offering you *power*."

"What kind of power?" the elf strode confidently to his desk and sat at his chair, motioning the intruder to join him.

Hymdreiddiech followed. "Not mere magic or political influence, neither is it purely financial. What I offer is the culmination of those things and more. It is real thing: control. Authority. Enough that even Oberon would be fearful to challenge you."

"But there is a catch?" The savvy business trader leaned across his desk. "Before you say more, what is the cost?"

"Small in comparison," Hymdreiddiech watched the elf's eyes. They obviously did not believe him. *He is a smart sidhe, then.*

"What I want is rooted in my desire for satisfaction against old enemies. I trade in the arcane and subterfuge. I am aware that you have your own shadowy business dealings. Connections to specific crimes against your own kind." Hymdreiddiech watched the elf bristle at the reality that he had knowledge of criminal activity. "But this is not blackmail. I could not care less about the dream hallow and the actual business done by your company, Stór Rúnda. I am here to show you the next step… to partner with you and achieve something unthinkable. I need one who trades in legitimate business, and you need one who trades in arcana."

The owner of Stór Rúnda cocked a listening ear to the black maven. With a grin he said, "Tell me your plan."

Hymdreiddiech did… at least, he told the elf what *his* part would be.

The elf paused as he thought it over. "This all sounds well and good, but I am uncertain how you knew so much about me and my operation. Tell me your name. Who are you?"

"You may call me Hymdreiddiech."

"Hymdreiddiech... that is an unseelie name?"

The elf nodded. "I am the Black Maven, the hidden one. Usurper. Devourer. And much more. *But who I am?* Two years ago you received a parcel with detailed instructions on how to create the dream hallow." Hymdreiddiech grinned. "I am the one who sent it to you."

CHAPTER THREE

R EMY DROPPED THE PICKAXE next to the shovel at the campsite he shared with Thoranmir. Located a short distance off the main road, their tents were not difficult to locate and they were situated close enough to their work site for the camp to be convenient.

Thoranmir walked past the smoldering coals, and collapsed into his hammock. It stretched between two trees barely adequate to hold his weight and bounced precariously. He greedily pushed a small cake into his mouth.

For the last couple days Donnalia, under Odessa's watchful eye, had delivered pastries she'd swiped from the family's cupboards and wrapped in butcher paper. It was too good to last; they had just finished the ditch and would soon find themselves in need of work again.

Remy held his head close to a copper water bucket and splashed his face and neck, trying to wash the grime away from his neck. He removed his headband, soaked it, and used it to wipe the heat away from his clavicle.

With his collar still dripping, a feminine voice cleared a throat. "A-hem."

Thoranmir nearly fell out of his cot and Remy whirled to find the source of the sound.

Jaira stood demurely near the remaining empty hammock. She radiated her typical beauty. Behind her, a tall and regal looking fey stood. He had a serious face and hard eyes framed by his dark hair and brow. Pointy ears protruded barely past his coiffed hair.

The he-elf nodded measuredly as his eyes scanned the two ditch diggers like a predator sizing them up; they lingered a moment on Remy's ears. His hand remained on the hilt of his sword as he addressed them. "I am Fuerian Vastra. Thank you for rescuing Jaira and the Morgensteen's the other day. The attack was meant for me. Rest assured that I would have dealt with attackers in a similar manner, though perhaps with a cleaner kill." Fuerian glanced amusedly at the new pickaxe laying nearby.

Remy nodded, hoping that their impromptu guests would not take note of his ears. Or at least, wouldn't take offense. It took great effort for him not to turn and bask in Jaira's beauty, but did not want to risk offending Fuerian, who he recalled was Jaira's fiancé.

He looked over at the elf newcomer. Fuerian looked every bit like the new class of wealthy fey produced by institutions of higher learning and supported by rich nobles, the richest of *that* caste were called the méith. Because of their prevalence in dueling culture, their customs had become chic in the last few generations.

Universities had begun allowing its students to train under masters they employed so the wealthy class could properly engage in their own defense. The middle class found employ and wages beyond their ken as duelists, and a whole culture of dueling enthusiasts developed for those who looked at the activity like a sport... a sport where one's honor was at stake, often including their lives.

Fuerian wore a brooch fashioned to look like a lamp, and there was some kind of amulet around his neck which bore the Vastra family crest. Remy recalled the symbol on his lapel and knew that the Vastra family made street lamps and they contracted with cities to keep them lit.

Remy also noticed Fuerian did not wear a duelists pin, but that was no surprise. Those who were registered duelists, as some wealthy elves were, could not deny the challenge of another duelist. At least, not while within designated zones. Those were typically in a city, or in the village square if the setting was more rural. Because of the non-refusal rule, many of the elites trained to acquire the skills of a duelist, but declined to enroll in a dueling house roster.

Dueling had come to be integrated into Arcadeaxn law, at least on the seelie side. On the other side of the world, rules, if they could still be called that, were much less of a concern. The seelie also lacked businesses that printed the yellow rags to advertise who gained or lost honor because of a sanctioned bout or who fell out of displeasure of the mavens, the ruling court of duelists who formed a political caste.

Jaira stepped forward with bright eyes and dispelled the creeping tension that burgeoned between Remy and Fuerian. "I wanted to bring this to you personally." She held a neatly folded envelope pinched between her fingers. "It is an invitation."

Remy noted the effort it took for Fuerian to keep his face placid. Remy allowed himself to focus on the girl and he accepted the letter. "An invitation to what?"

Thoranmir grinned, glancing from Fuerian to Remy to Jaira. Tension welled thick between them. Thoranmir joked, "An invitation? Where is mine... you know, Remy could've been skewered if I hadn't arrived in time."

"Oh," said Jaira, momentarily flustered. "Of course, you are welcome to participate as well, Thoranmir."

"Excellent. We accept," Thoranmir said excitedly.

Remy's eyes scanned the folded paper. "You might wish to retract that," he said. "Sir Morgensteen is hosting a dueling contest. The winner will receive sponsorship and dues paid into a dueling house of his or her choosing."

"The chance to change your stars," Jaira said eagerly. "The rules are standard as prescribed by the mavens," she insisted, to assuage any fears.

Standard rules meant that duels were decided by drawing first blood unless the wounded party chose to escalate the stakes and demand the contest end in death, but such a scenario was rare. Duelists were not assassins.

"Truly it is," Remy noted. Skill in a fight was only one component required for a duelist. He'd have attempted it much sooner if he'd had the ability to pay the required fees for a guild membership; the initial outlay was considerable without a sponsor.

She looked at Remy. "My father allowed me to make a few of the invitations since I have a hand in awarding the prize. I can think of nobody I'd rather choose than my rescuer. We were, in fact, just returning to Cathair Dé from Faery Cairn, where King Oberon sanctioned the competition."

Thoranmir raised a brow. "Oberon... the prize?"

"It is tradition," Fuerian informed him. "The winner of such a contest is always recognized with a kiss, bestowing the Blessing of the Dagda. It will be awarded by Jaira, whose father is the sponsor." He leveled a hard gaze at the ditch diggers. "That is why I am also entering it: so that my betrothed lips touch none but mine."

Remy's jaw cocked into an amused grin. "Something worth fighting for, surely," he said. He didn't care about fey religious observances or traditions surrounding the elves' god-like Dagda figure.

But a kiss from Jaira?

"Oh," Jaira said, turning to face him. She wore a hoop earring on either side of her head and they framed her face with a glint of filigree silver. "I thought you said this contest was beneath your skills or desire to—"

"I know what I said, but now I say that I am competing. Your father gave me that right," Fuerian snapped, cutting Jaira off.

Thoranmir and Remy both watched Fuerian's nostrils flare. He and Remy would have a laugh about that over the fire later in the evening.

Fuerian offered additional comment. "You have made your intentions clear enough with your pledge to Oberon a week ago."

Remy studied them.

"I made a vow before the king in the high tongue," she said. "No lips will touch mine until the contest is decided." Jaira's eyes flitted from Fuerian to Remy and then settled on Thoranmir as if to explain that she'd preferred to opt for such a pledge rather than kiss the elf who would one day become her husband. "Such words bind me to my oath."

Thoranmir leered at Remy, though. He'd obviously noted the way her gaze lingered on the human and guessed she would have welcomed Remy's lips, regardless of his shortness of ears. Remy wondered if she'd even noticed them yet.

"Come along," Fuerian insisted. "Your invitation is delivered. Let's get out of this... let's just get you back to Cathair Dé," he chose his words carefully so as not to offend.

She made a pouty frown, but a futile look of resignation took over. "You will come to the contest though, won't you?"

"I do not have a sword," Remy began.

"Oh, do give him a sword, Fuerian?" she asked.

Fuerian looked at him with dark eyes. "My dear, if he comes to the competition, you have my word that *I shall give him my sword*." He took her by the hand in order to escort her away. The double entendre seemed to go over Jaira's head, and she looked relieved.

Fuerian paid them no mind and turned his back to them, taking his betrothed back to Cathair Dé and steered Jaira's shoulders to keep her feet moving away from the unwashed workers.

"I've actually still got the swords from those elves who attacked you before," Thoranmir said. "So I think we've got it covered. I hid them in the bushes just in case... you know... maybe we'd need them."

Remy looked back, directing a menacing look at Remy.

In a fleeting moment, the wordless gesture said more than words ever could have. *Come to Cathair Dé at your own peril.*

O<small>DESSA STOOD OFF TO</small> the side, hovering a step back from Donnalia as she laughed and snacked on some of the treats she'd brought the two workers. The daughter of the noble elf had dared to venture out as far as the diggers' camp this time since they'd finished the project earlier in the day.

The governess kept close to her ward, but knew well enough than to get in the way of a strong-willed child who would become a lady soon enough. After a few days, however, the workers had proved themselves as safe folk to take a child around. And Odessa seemed appreciative of the opportunity to continue her chats with Thoranmir.

"Show me again?" Donnalia asked Remy with the odd lilt she spoke with, and then she popped a small cake into her mouth.

"Little gremlin, always harassing my poor human pet," Thoranmir ribbed Remy.

Donnalia turned her head and cocked it, trying to catch what he'd said and make sense of it. "What?" she finally asked, watching his mouth more closely.

Remy finally understood the child's struggles: why she'd not heard the carriage a few days prior, why she spoke oddly. "Donnalia, are you deaf?"

The child's composure threatened to break at her discovery. She nodded slightly. "I can hear. A little."

She reached out and touched Remy's smooth ears. "Yours are ugly, Remy... but they work." Her words belied what each of the adults suspected. The child had developed the distinct symptoms of a crush on the human who had saved her, but none were bold enough to address it.

Odessa frowned. "It will be hard for her when you two are gone. I've not seen her this happy in ages."

"In a couple years, she'll forget all about us," Thoranmir said. "She'll be off to see the court and meet other noble ladies... and men."

Odessa shook her head. "Because of her herring, Lord Fyndrolker has adamantly refused to let her have anything to do with high society."

"Still, we cannot stay," Remy said as he tied a cloth strip around his head again. "We must head to the city after the lord pays us."

"So soon?" asked Donnalia with a pout.

Odessa looked equally sad as she gazed at Thoranmir. But despite the sadness on her face, there was a glimmer of hope in her eyes.

"Remy's got an invitation to some big dueling contest," Thoranmir boasted. "He's going to win a pile of riches and the heart of a pretty lady."

Donnalia's brow darkened, as if she'd already staked a claim on Remy, though he was a decade older than her. Age would matter less in another ten years, but it was a weighty difference currently. She sighed. "Do be safe."

Bracken and reeds snapped as they broke behind the ladies, and Lord Ylamenor Fyndrolker pushed his way into the small campsite. He looked angry. "There you two are," he accused, as if he'd walked in on something improper. "You should not be fraternizing with low folk like these."

Odessa and Donnalia practically melted. They bowed their heads and took a verbal lashing. Luckily for Donnalia, her averted eyes meant she'd miss most of the nastiest words.

Lord Fyndrolker turned to the laborers. "And you two. Get off my land. I'm not paying either of you a cent. I don't care *what* you are." His eyes lingered on Remy. "Yes. I've heard rumors about you... son of Adam."

The lord turned back to the girls. "And you, Odessa *Cócaire*," Lord Fyndrolker used her full name to remove any thought of familial grace. He narrowed his gaze at her, and she wilted beneath it. "You should know better. I forbid you to have any more contact with these men."

Odessa nodded and wiped her cheek. She took Donnalia by the hand and retreated, heading in the direction of the estate.

"The job is complete, sir. We'll be gone by morning," Thoranmir spoke diplomatically. "But we've worked your land almost two weeks now. We do insist that you pay what you promised us."

"Not tomorrow, not ever will I give you coin. And you'll leave now, not in the morning. I did not pay you to entertain my house staff and crippled daughter." Lord Fyndrolker's eyes blazed with anger. "I heard you quit the job and ran off during that incident a few days ago. So far as I'm concerned, you abandoned the job site."

Remy met them with an equally steely look. He held the lord's gaze and Thoranmir swallowed and stepped back so he wouldn't be caught in the crossfire.

"The work is done, sir. Who do you think dug your ditches?" Remy started, taking a half step forward.

Fyndrolker matched the man's hard glare. "I do not know. It could have been anyone—I did not supervise the work directly. Perhaps it was a band of brownies or a hob. I don't care... I only know that a *human* could never accomplish such craftsmanship. Leave now and I won't summon the constable and charge you freeloaders rent."

Remy pointed. Through the trees, one could barely see the stone boundary markers on the other side of the road. "Your property line ends over there. These are Oberon's woods, sir. Do you contend that you might steal them from the king of the seelie court?"

Fyndrolker sniffed as if he thought they must have been stupid because they were laborers.

"Because these are Oberon's woods, we are entitled to sleep here," Remy insisted.

"Be that as it may," Fyndrolker spoke with a rage he barely held in check. "Accidents are known to happen in the wilds."

Remy held the elf's gaze and searched his eyes; he saw what information he sought. The lord would not back down. "We shall be gone in the morning," Remy said, keeping his tone equally in check.

"See to it that you are." Fyndrolker turned and left.

"But what about our pay?" Thoranmir asked Remy.

Remy sighed. "An elf like that... I'm not sure he was ever going to pay us. But we've got the coins from the Morgensteens still, plus our savings. And we can sell whatever else we have in the village before we head towards the city." Remy stared into the distance, imagining Jaira rewarding him with a kiss. "I've got bigger fights ahead of me than some country lord."

"We," Thoranmir corrected. "I was invited too."

Remy nodded. "*We've* got fights ahead," he chuckled. "We probably won't ever remember any of this," he sighed and then reclined in his hammock.

He touched a finger to the dúshlán at his waist and frowned, knowing his words had been a lie.

Remy remembered every time he'd been a victim... every time except one.

CHAPTER FOUR

⸺ ✦ ⸺

T HE BUILDINGS OF CATHAIR Dé loomed around them as
if they were the jaws and teeth of a leviathan capturing a
ship adrift. Remy scanned the denizens of the city with wary eyes,
assessing threats, but Thoranmir practically skipped with joy.

"Isn't it grand?" Thoranmir asked, grinning from ear to ear as he
recognized the familiar sights. It had been over two years since he'd
last been home. "Come on, don't look so sour. None of these elves
are trying to kill you, Remy. They just want to make a coin or two.
I could even tell them what you are and none would care—at least
not in this part of the city."

Remy glanced around and watched a crowd made up mostly of
elves, each walking on journeys of their own. Aside from the elves,
a few of the little folk and an occasional ogre wandered past. Those
who stayed tended merchant stands or greeted folks at storefronts.

He sighed, knowing Thoranmir was right. Remy had seen many
cities, but he'd steered clear of them after his mishaps in the unseelie. The lesson he'd learned there was simple: avoid cities at all
costs. But the urban areas in the seelie kingdom had a much less
treacherous bent.

Swallowing the nag in the pit of his gut, Remy followed his guide, knowing that, in fact, *everywhere* was treacherous. But Cathair Dé's dangers were less "knife in the back" and more "have I got a deal for you."

Remy ignored a crier who promised his luck charms would make him Arcadeax's greatest lover and put his eyes forward, keeping his free hand firmly upon his purse strings. He wasn't sure if he preferred the seelie city's masked friendliness or those folk of the unseelie realm. At least there he knew who and what wanted to kill him, which was typically everyone and everything.

Braided copper wires sagged overhead as they stretched from roof to roof. Shake-topped cottages belched steam where they hid mechanical contraptions within. They'd come in on the cheap side of the city where the industrial buildings mixed with the flea-ridden residential district.

The fey were not without technology. In some homes, machines burned fuel which powered contraptions to supply light, give life to simple machines, or provide warmth. Others chose to utilize the akasha, and still more prided themselves on the natural, like burning wood for heat and foregoing any of the finer services as they became available, such as the aither. Most in Arcadeax distrusted the new advances in tech or regarded them as mere curiosities. Only the Aes Sídhe, those born with an innate skill in magic, or those with education in the arcane, could craft spells, meaning it was usually easier to find a tradesman magi to accomplish mystic tasks. Except for the aither and the akasha.

Anyone could use the aither through the technology that had become available in the last generation. However, low-end users could only skim the surface of possibilities. Mages were accessing it for thousands of years with a kind of astral projection. But without a more permanent kind of enchantment only capable of casting by true masters, what they had accomplished and placed in the aithersphere in generations past disappeared into oblivion when they died.

Now, wealthy folk had built empires within it, stored whole worlds there, and that translated to strongholds within the aithersphere.

Remy knew very little about the aithersphere except that he'd once traveled there in a spirit walk after eating hallucinogenic fungus in the unseelie. It was there that he'd learned how to escape into the seelie realms of Arcadeax. He'd always been grateful for that experience.

"We're coming into a designated dueling zone," Remy told Thoranmir as he followed his friend through an arch and into a market square.

Thoranmir shot him an askew look and Remy pointed to a warding post with a duelist's symbol upon it.

They stopped near it. Remy pointed to the other two posts that were visible in the distance. "You'll need to learn what those are if you're serious about going through with competing."

Thoranmir gave his friend a grouchy look. It was obvious that he still felt hurt that Remy wouldn't take him seriously as a contender.

The market was much like any other. Carts filled with fruit and vegetables sat parked with their vendors announcing wares. Collapsible tables were arranged in loose rows and larger stands acted as endcaps. Some were shrouded with colorful sheets to act as draping, while others did the same with tapestries and rugs they displayed for sale, giving the area a maze-like appearance.

Despite the carnival atmosphere, men and women seemed on high alert. Remy noticed the sidelong glances they shot him. Folks watched with both their eyes and their peripheral vision for thieves and duelists. While public duels in the sanctioned zones were rare, when they occurred, they were horrendously showy and shut down the markets for hours at a time.

Remy noted three elves standing near the edges of the sanctioned boundary lines. They hovered close enough that they could move out of bounds, enabling them to refuse challengers if they came. While inside the designated bounds, they could not refuse a duel.

Peering at their lapels, Remy's suspicions were confirmed. They wore swords at their hips and also the duelist pins, but only one wore a ribbon. He was young, as were the others, and his ribbon was yellow with a red stripe. It indicated that he'd won a duel in a public challenge zone and drawn first blood for victory. Had it been a black stripe, it would have meant the duel was fought to the death.

Remy met that duelist's eyes and felt the elf's gaze search him for a lapel pin. Not wearing one, the ambitious fighter moved on, assessing other potential threats.

"Come on," Thoranmir muttered, tapping him on the chest. "Cafe Mil is around here. I'm sure of it."

"We can't afford to eat anywhere nice," Remy reminded him.

"We can't afford it *yet*," Thoranmir assured him. "Our fortunes are going to change soon. I can feel it. Besides, it's only a short distance away from my sister's, so we've got to go that direction anyway."

With a sigh, Remy followed his friend into the gathered crowds who perused the market wares or shopped for their basic needs and sundries. A young boy or girl on the corner of every other endcap cried out headlines from the gossip papers and held up printed copies of the local journals they were selling.

Before Remy could take a look a commotion broke out ad a group of sidhe hollered a bunch of anti-human insults. One of them held up the news flier one of the young elves were selling.

"They are letting a human enter the dueling contest. A *human!*" He whipped the locals into a frenzy over the notion and Remy adjusted the wrap that hid his ears as the vocal opponent called on his acolytes to protest the move.

Thoranmir leaned closer. "The Frith Duine," he told him. "Local human hating group." He made a sour look. "They've been gaining popularity lately, growing all the way into the heart of Faery Cairn."

"Something to worry about?" Remy asked.

"Mostly just a bunch of loudmouths," Thoranmir said. "They're all talk, as far as I know... I mean, keep your bandanna up, just in case though."

Remy nodded and tuned them out. He picked up one of the thin, folded sheets the criers were selling. The weeklies were yellow rags printed regularly with all the local elf news. The headlines often involved a mix of serious, newsworthy information and tabloid headlines about lost honor and other such scandals. Typically, these included a duel. The whole dueling industry was fueled by the weeklies.

Flipping through, Remy shook his head when he spotted paid advertising. He wondered how often anyone who had an advertisement account was reported on by the tabloids. He'd bet money it was seldom, if ever. The center fold advertised the upcoming contest hosted by the Morgensteen family. Its primary prize was sponsorship, with full membership's fees paid to the dueling guild of the winner's choice.

"That'll be a copper, sir," came a tiny voice.

Remy blinked and looked at the child. He was a boy, perhaps a year or two older than Remy was when he awakened that first cold night in the unseelie. The paper boy's ears stuck out too-big and ungainly below his cloth derby cap.

Remy frowned. "Excuse me?"

"For the paper," the boy told him.

Remy handed him both a copper and the journal. "Here. You keep the coin and sell the paper. I got what I needed from it." He left the boy behind and tailed after Thoranmir.

Slipping through the crowd, Remy encountered the pungent aromas of musk and unwashed flesh as he hurried after his friend. Spices and herbal odors swarmed his nostrils. Some of the more exotic ones niggled at his recollection; he'd encountered them many years prior in memories which he could not quite place—perhaps from the times before he'd come to Arcadeax.

Thoranmir seemed to slide through the crowd with subtle grace as they burgeoned in knots that thickened the deeper one traveled between the market rows. Remy hurried to catch up, his broad and muscular shoulders having a difficult time navigating the narrow channels. Just as he thought he'd caught up, Remy found his feet affixed to the ground. His eyes locked onto the sight of Jaira Morgensteen.

Her perfume caught his nose like a hook and he found himself transfixed. She hadn't seen him, as she had turned to face the other direction. Remy was certain it was her.

Fuerian was at her side, escorting her through a market visit. He had another man with him, a protector who wore the dueling pin. Its ribbon appeared purple and the way he glanced around the area and then back at Fuerian indicated who his ward was; the ribbon indicated who he had successfully defended in a private challenge.

Remy stared at Jaira, who mingled with folk. He noted that only one of her ears wore jewelry this time. She was missing the mate to her silver earring on the one side. He recognized those engraved hoops anywhere after admiring them the previous day.

A shimmer of light caught his eye in the dirt nearby. Remy stooped to find the missing earring. He bent to snatch it up. As he stood again, he caught a sidelong glance from Fuerian, who wore a displeased look upon his face as he pushed his betrothed through the crowd and away from Remy.

Only a moment later, a severe-looking elf stepped in front of him. He barred Remy's path and blocked his view of where Jaira and Fuerian went. It was the elf who wore the dueling pin and purple ribbon.

"You are lost, sir," the duelist insisted, shooting a look that practically pierced through Remy like daggers.

Remy defended, "What? No, I just found this..."

The duelist's hand fell to the pommel of his sword. "I said *you are lost.* Go back the way you came."

Something about the stern demeanor and the threat of violence made Remy take a step back, dispelling the tension between them. Remy slid the missing jewelry into a pocket and nodded, slinking backward into the crowd and letting its hustle and bustle absorb him.

A split second later, a pair of hands clamped onto him like a vice. "Remy! There you are," Thoranmir exclaimed. He dragged him a short distance into an area where the crowd lessened into lighter numbers and then pointed. "Look, I found the bistro. Isn't that grand?"

Remy caught his bearings and nodded. "Yes. Yes, of course." He wasn't sure why the elf duelist had rattled him so. But he planned on being ready next time, though he was still working out in his mind exactly how he should have reacted.

One thing was certain for him: Remy did not like Fuerian Vastra. Certainly the dislike was mutual.

"Follow me," Thoranmir insisted. "We'll soon be at my sister's. Anya is going to love you—you'll see."

A N ALLEY WOUND BETWEEN tall buildings that stretched overhead making Remy and Thoranmir feel small as they traveled through. Something about the dinge made Remy's skin crawl. The quality of their surroundings grew progressively worse as they walked.

At the mouth of the alley, where it had connected to the public square where Fuerian's zealous duelist had threatened them, trash receptacles were arrayed neat and orderly. Here, derelict bins lay overturned with their contents strewn and rummaged through.

Remnants of small fires lay charred and broken, sometimes smudged up the sides of walls where the flames had licked up the sides of the structures. Broken glass and busted crates were scattered here and there, growing more common the deeper they ventured into the vein.

"Are you sure we're going the right way?" Remy asked.

He expected Thoranmir's reassurance. *Yeah—it's a shortcut. I know my way around these parts,* Remy had expected. But Thoranmir said nothing. His friend walked instead with grim determination.

A confluence of alleys formed a kind of grimy, urban glen where the circuits intersected. Remy spotted a few makeshift tents and other structures assembled out of rubbish. He spotted a foot sticking out from below a collapsed lean-to. It twitched and then pulled back inside the trash heap.

Remy did not feel unmoved to the plight of the homeless, he counted himself among their number, but when he caught a set of hollow, dispassionate eyes peering up at him from a nearby hovel, his heart set like iron.

The denizens of this place where not merely down on their luck, they'd *chosen* this life. He'd seen it before in his time in the unseelie. There were creatures there that could enslave the mind even as they gave pleasure, trading unwary folk chunks of their life for the enraptured bliss they could produce in the vulnerable.

These people are victims.

Sliding his hand to the hilt of his dagger, Remy nudged his friend. "If this is not on the way to your sister's we should not be here. And even if it was..." he trailed off, watching the scene warily.

Thoranmir gulped and set his jaw. He took a half step away from Remy and held aloft a few coins. They did not amount to much, but Remy knew that the pitiful, greedy eyes peering out from their hiding places would not care. The hunger that blazed in them might have made them willing to kill for such paltry offerings.

His first few words warbled, but then stiffened as Thoranmir found his voice. "I am looking for someone. These coins to whomever can give me answers."

A grubby elf wearing tattered rags emerged wholly from behind a crate. His ears bore unwashed blisters where they tapered to points and he was missing several teeth.

"Do you have a name, friend?" he asked.

Remy gritted his teeth, recognizing something in the tone of how the elf said "friend." The elf would put a knife in their bellies for those coins if he thought he could get away with it.

Remycurled his fingers around the hilt of his weapon with a loose and ready grip.

Thoranmir shot his friend a brief, apologetic look which admitted he'd made a planned detour. "I am looking for an elf named Eldarian. He would be about my age and skin color. Darker hair, perhaps. He might have some skill with the arcane so he might be telling fortunes or doing some other menial spellcraft in the city?"

Remy raised an eyebrow as he put the clues together.

The inquisitive, homeless fey took a step forward and rested his hand on a busted crate. Remy could see the busted, jagged plank he'd set at the ready. It was sharp enough to impale a person and blended in perfectly to the dilapidated scenery around them.

Remy shot the elf a hard look and rattled his blade in its sheath for just a moment. He met the creature's vicious eyes and felt him size up the two intruders. Remy flashed him a dangerous glint of the eye to warn him back. But the elf did not seem to care.

Another dirty elf emerged from his hovel, and then another. A third poked his head out and struggled to his feet on uneasy knees. "Do you have another name?" the elf asked. "I know two Eldarians."

The dangerous elf relinquished his hold on the spike and faded back into the stacked crates. He shot resentful glares at the other residents of the alley. *Even if he* could *kill us for a few coins,* Remy

understood, *he'd have to murder all the rest to claim them as well...
there are probably more present than just these.*

Thoranmir shot his friend a sheepish look as he spoke. "Eldarian
Cócaire," he said. "He has family nearby who are searching for
him."

The old elf tottered back and forth on uneasy legs. "I... I don't
know any Cócaires." A look of sorrow crossed his face; telling
the truth had cost him something. He brightened, "But I *do have*
information you may find useful."

Thoranmir looked at him inquisitively.

"You say this Eldarian has some mage skill... if he has gone for
schooling recently, he may have been taken."

That caught Remy's attention. "Taken?"

"Yes, yes." The elf agreed. "Someone has been kidnapping students from the academies. Few are talking of it, and the schools
deny it is happening, but *it is*. They say it is part of the secret wars
between the unseelie and the Oberon."

Remy kept his face neutral. The information could not be accurate. He knew the unseelie and how they thought. Young mages
without proper training were little threat to them.

"We live in strange times," the elf insisted. "Open war is coming
again after so many centuries... Why else would the forces of winter
hobble Oberon's spell casters?"

Thoranmir's face mostly remained impassive, but Remy spotted
marks of disappointment on it. He watched his friend hesitate, as
if he might not pay for information of dubious reliability. But then
Thoranmir tossed him the coins.

The elf gathered them up with glee and officious praise for his benefactor.

Thoranmir sighed and turned to search for the best path away from here.

Before they could go, Remy withdrew another coin, one worth half what Thoranmir had delivered, and found those eyes near the crates which still glowed balefully with anger that it had not earned.

In the pit of his gut, Remy knew the elf would kill the informant for those coins. *He'll probably wait until their owner and the rest are asleep and then put a shiv into him.*

He addressed the spite-filled elf while brandishing the cash. "What you are thinking of doing, do not." Remy flicked the coin to him and the hard elf caught it without ever breaking the gaze with Remy. "If I hear of foul play I will return and demand recompense plus interest."

The elf narrowed his gaze, but nodded slightly at the veiled threat. *The interest paid would be in blood.*

Thoranmir watched the tribute exchange hands. He'd stiffened as if only suddenly realizing how dangerous the situation had been.

Remy tapped his friend and gestured for him to lead the way. "Your sister is still waiting."

"Oh. Uh, yeah," he broke from the reverie and turned towards the mouth of one of the alleyways.

Before speaking, they took a few steps so their conversation would remain private.

"Did you get the information you need?" Remy asked.

Thoranmir scowled and shook his head. "No." He sighed. "El-darian wasn't taken. From what Odessa knew, he'd..." Thoranmir trailed off and shrugged.

Remy knew what he meant. *He had chosen this life.* Whatever substance the residents of the alleys were addicted to, it had its hooks into the brother of a girl Thoranmir was smitten by.

Remy clapped a hand on his friend's shoulder. "We'll keep our eyes open. It's maybe all we can do."

Thoranmir nodded and they walked towards the alley's exit. "Remy?"

Remy glanced at his friend.

"Don't tell my sister?"

Remy's brow knit. "I think she ought to know. Maybe she could—"

Thoranmir shook his head. "Someday. But it's my secret to tell, not yours."

Remy pursed his lips, but nodded. Thoranmir was right. Remy had to respect his wishes.

They walked a few steps more until the quality of the passage improved. Thoranmir asked, what do you think he meant about the two major kingdoms going to war, I mean the seelie and un-seelie?"

Remy returned a tight lipped glance. The human played it close to the vest that he had intimate knowledge of the unseelie, but Thoranmir had seen enough to know about his friend's familiarity. "I haven't formed an opinion," he spoke softly. "Not enough facts to do so."

Thoranmir offered a measured nod.

A voice broke nearby.

Both Thoranmir and Remy whirled on their heels.

"Whatever a young man carrying a dúshlán blade has to do with disappearing arcana scholars and the warring children of Father Olbion, it certainly cannot be a good omen."

CHAPTER FIVE

R EMY REGARDED HER COOLLY as the old she-elf pulled
back her dirty hair to better address them. The hair was a
faded brown, but Remy could tell it was shock white wherever it
remained clean closer to the hat she wore. Her ears were thick and
had plumped near their tips as a sign of unhealthy living and her
face was a network of crags on her nearly olive skin.

The old crone who'd spoken to them sat on bent knees upon a
tattered blanket with a few wares spread out before her. She did not
have much for sale beyond a few trinkets and her blanket extended
barely beyond the mouth of the alleyway where she'd be barely
visible to passersby in the market where they'd come from earlier.

Still, a fire lit in her eyes as she splayed her hands over her wares
and Remy could tell that this woman was no beggar—she sold
items—and direct or implied charity would be unwelcome.

"Father Olbion must be truly displeased with his warring children," she groused.

"But there is no war," Thoranmir reminded her. "Only rumors
of it."

She shrugged. "Not openly, perhaps, but the father of the courts never intended for this." She clucked her tongue with dismay. "And he never intended for the younger brother to be deposed by that spider."

Thoranmir shot Remy an inquisitive look.

"The current ruler of the court in King Wulflock's absence," he explained quietly.

"Olbion was just an elf," Thoranmir shrugged, as if to argue with the old woman, not a god.

Her eyes twinkled as if rising to a challenge. "Of course that is true," she said. "But he was favored by the Dagda." Her gaze fell back to Remy and his knife, "Much like your friend, here. But I *knew* Olbion, back when I had the favor of the court, and I had the eye of Oberon, even." Something in her voice indicated soreness on that point.

Thoranmir curled a lip in disbelief.

"Hazhimon was known as a great beauty in her day—and not this pathetic figure you see before you. And I see all that goes on in Cathair Dé," she insisted conspiratorially. "My beauty may have been stolen, but that has only served to make me invisible."

"Stolen?" Remy asked.

Hazhimon nodded.

Remy knelt licked his thumbs, and wiped at the skin of Hazhimon's forehead. It remained the same faded green and was not discolored as her hair was. "You are no mere elf," Remy noted, meeting her gaze.

She'd watched him in kind. "And neither are you," she chuckled, "child of Adam."

Remy stepped back away, gritting his teeth to keep his composure. He reassessed her for a moment. "You are a hamadryad?"

Hazhimon bowed her head, admitting to her heritage as a tree nymph. Her life force was tied specific tree somewhere, and that tree was unwell, as evidenced by the paleness of the greens of her skin and her age ravaged body.

"I am Remy. This is Thoranmir," Remy said, and then asked, "Shouldn't you be dead, if your tree has been destroyed?"

"The Dagda favors me," Hazhimon told him. "Perhaps differently than with you—though I find a dúshlán in the hands of a human to be a curious thing. But who am I to question the will of the Dagda who creates such gifts for purposes their wielders can scarcely understand. It will be the Dagda who remedies the discord between Olbion's children, not war."

"Hazhimon," Thoranmir interjected, "you have seen many things. I am looking for someone, a young arcanist. I believe he is in the city. His name is Eldarian Cócaire."

Her wrinkled face twisted in a gnarl of deep thought, and then she shook her head. "Apologies. I am good with names, but I don't know any Eldarians. Does he wield great power or is his ability with magic more middling?" Her eyes locked on Thoranmir.

The elf's cheeks tightened revealing how little he knew about the elf he searched for. "He is about my age and of no major repute, so I have to guess that he is not any sort of prodigy."

Hazhimon chuffed darkly. "Then he is likely in one of the academies that cloister themselves between Cathair Dé and Daonra Dlúth. And those places have been... unsafe, according to rumor."

Thoranmir shook his head. "I am told he is in Cathair Dé."

She shrugged. "Equally unsafe, perhaps even more so. Untrained spell crafters are seldom found in the city these last two years. You'll be hard pressed to find a soothsayer or reader even, unless they are of advanced skill already."

The two travelers exchanged odd glances, trying to ascertain that cause.

"Something is stealing young spell crafters," Hazhimon suggested.

"And you think that, whatever it is, it's taking them from both the countryside academies *and* the city?" Remy asked. "You think they are related?"

Hazhimon nodded gravely. Then she hedged back from the decision with a shrug. "Welll... It is uncertain," she said. "And whatever is the cause, it is a less urgent problem than the shadow men."

Thoranmir cocked his head. "Shadow men?"

Hazhimon indicated the alley they'd emerged from. "Those folk who have become shadows of what they were. Some new poison stupid or bored elves have begun taking it for recreational purposes. It leaves them happy, blissed out of their mind, and thinking they can access the aither, even. But it makes them into slaves and they turn violent to get more."

Thoranmir pressed in on the topic and Remy took note of his interest. He pressed her with questions, but Hazhimon knew little else about what the drug did, or where to get it. "Most of these kids all look the same," the hamadryad admitted. "Certainly *after* they imbibe the stuff: all hollow eyes and detached looks."

He described Eldarian to her, but she shrugged again. "I am sorry I cannot be more helpful."

Remy recognized the mettle in the woman. If she had useful information she would have given it freely. She wanted to help, with no thought of how she could twist the situation to her advantage, and she hadn't cared about Remy's parentage.

The human bent down and laid a few coins on her weathered quilt and picked up a leather strip with a few beads on it. He knew he overpaid, but that had been on purpose.

"Blessings of Dagda upon you... doubly so," Hazhimon said as Remy threaded the material around the sheath of his dúshlán. "And if you ever wrest my tree away from that bitch Queen Titania," Hazhimon spoke with words that bit like a winter wind, "I shall grant you such a boon as not seen in a century."

Remy and Thoranmir nodded to each other. They departed back into the market before meandering back onto the main thoroughfares of the city.

"You think Eldarian is hooked on this... drug?" Remy asked.

Tight lipped, Thoranmir shrugged. "His sister thinks so. The rest of her family, though, insists he would never do such a thing. They are adamant that he is still away at an academy, learning the ways of arcana."

"And is just too busy with his studies to write home?" Remy suggested.

Thoranmir tilted his head in agreement. "Odessa knows better. I said I'd try to find him."

They walked a short ways further in silence.

"If you're going to get wrapped up in this—or even just with this girl," Remy said, "I still think you should tell your sister. She might be able to—"

"Duly noted," Thoranmir cut him off.

Remy let that stand and did not press further, even if he thought it an unwise decision. If his friend got into trouble, he might need more help, or help of a different sort, than Remy could provide.

After a few turns through the market, they came to a familiar spot again.

"Come on," Thoranmir said, clapping his friend on the shoulder. "No more delays. We'll arrive soon. I'm sure my sister is going to love you."

"I DON'T PARTICULARLY LIKE you, Remy Keaton," grumbled Anya Shelton once the two were alone. "You seem to have gotten my brother mixed up in some dangerous business."

The elf's homecoming had been filled with hugs, and wine, and plenty of stories from the last couple years. Most of them seemed exaggerations to Remy, and he played a role in many of the tales, as told by Thoranmir. Each had seemed to draw a look of skeptical disapproval from the sister.

Thoranmir had gone to take a scalding shower and wash away the last few weeks of toil and grime. He promised to save some hot water for his friend. Neither of them had had the opportunity to enjoy such a privilege for a long while, but Anya's first-floor apartment, modest as it was, possessed several upscale amenities.

Thoranmir's shower left Remy alone with her.

Remy bit his lip and tried not to stare at the elf woman. She wore thick, glassy bifocals on copper rims and sat in her akasha-powered wheelchair. Anya lost her legs in the accident which had claimed hers and Thoranmir's parents, and the mechanical contraption was her best means of mobility. It hissed and belched tiny burps of steam when she used the joystick to operate it.

Tiny wires attached to leads where they pressed into ports on her skull and dangled like gossamer threads. As an aithermancer, she was connected to the network and maintained a near-constant presence there on behalf of her business contacts, acting as secretary, manager, and security for many wealthy contractors.

Because she no longer needed to operate her legs, the parts of Anya's brain that would normally have controlled those motor functions now contributed to her ability to parse the aither.

Remy didn't understand any of it, but he didn't need to. Still, something about the way she fixed him with those dark, lens-covered eyes unnerved him.

"I am sorry, and I agree with you. I don't think Thoranmir should enter the competition. He is... he's not..." Remy struggled to find words that would make his friend sound weak or dishonor him.

"Weak? Inept? Going to die if he has to fight? That's what you were going to say, right?" Anya accused.

Remy grit his teeth. Thoranmir had not warned him how blunt his sister was. "I, um..."

"Well, it's true. He's always thought he was more capable than he really is. And I warned him not to run off with his so-called friends on the last business venture, and now here we are." She brushed the wire leads out of the way, laid them over her shoulders like locks of hair, and crossed her arms.

"You can't let him fight in the arena," Anya insisted. "If you're a true friend to my brother, you can see that. He's always had a bigger opinion of himself than the rest of us."

Remy nodded. He kept his voice low as he said, "I have tried to discourage him, but once he's set his mind on something..."

"Yeah. I know my brother. I guess we'll just have to *unset* his mind."

Remy rubbed his face, unsure how they would go about that.

"We'll just find something else that he wants more," Anya said as the nearby door swung open. Thoranmir emerged with a towel wrapped around his waist.

"What are you guys talking about?" Thoranmir asked.

"Oh, you know," Remy said. "Just getting to know each other." He narrowed a gaze at the letter Thoranmir had sealed with a wax signet. "A letter?"

"Mind you own business," his friend said, yanking the parcel out of sight and stuffing it into a pocket, but not before Remy glanced the scrawled name it was addressed to: Miss Odessa of Vail Carvanna. Thoranmir slid the three coppers he'd been carrying to post it back into his pocket, too.

Remy held up his hands in defense. "Just making small talk," he said, standing. "But I'll leave you two alone to catch up. I need to stretch my legs. You want me to drop that with a courier?"

Thoranmir's cheeks reddened, but he withdrew the letter and handed it over.

Remy nodded, then turned on his heel and departed.

R EMY LEFT THORANMIR AND his sister to catch up, giving himself an opportunity to explore the city—this time on his own.

After an hour meandering through the streets, he felt a disquiet in his soul. The constant sound of voices and turning wheels muddled with the smells of the urban area: aromas of lantern oil intermixed with a leather tannery and suffused with wisps of exotic foods cooking somewhere on a street vendor's cart. It made the overstuffed sense of the place loom larger. Without taking the time to acclimate, and having never been to Cathair Dé before, he felt out of sorts.

The structures nearer the center of the city were behemoths: shining bastions that gave glory to their builders. The further Remy wandered from them, the worse the conditions of facilities became, until most of them were one or two-story things, sometimes with a lean-to or shack built upon its top by a late owner. Whether they were coops for fowl or used to house lowly dregs of the city, Remy didn't know.

Copper strands snapped and sizzled overhead as wires transmitted connections and power to homes or businesses. In the cheaper parts of the city, the insulated holders sometimes failed momentarily to crackle with akashic energy and wisps of ozone. Others did the same, sparking with whatever the aither was made of. Pipes moved steam and micro-fissures leaked hot air and vapor. Remy headed for the city border, hoping to walk again in the trees and set his mind at ease.

The city faded to a haze behind him as he walked away from it, but the trees were too manicured. There was no wildness to them. Remy could always tell when something felt off. After walking half a league, he realized why.

The outskirts beyond the city were largely dominated by estates crowned with regal manors where nobles and wealthy families dwelt.

Remy did not want to have any hounds released upon him for trespassing, and the tamed wilderness was not what he sought. He returned to the road until he finally found the dense, unchecked growth indicative of nature. There, he plunged into the thicket.

There had been so much noise in the city, and the woods on the wealthy estates were optimistic imitations of nature—quiet, manipulated versions bent to their owners' whims. The untouched forest brought his soul some sense of relief, and he found himself able to concentrate on his thoughts.

Remy had always intended to eventually make his way into the city. He'd always had a plan: gain enough wealth to make his way in this world, acquire either prosthetics or surgical enhancements to hide his true nature, and live comfortably enough until he found out the mystery behind his dúshlán. *And then extract the vengeance demanded by the blade and be at peace,* he thought.

A smile tugged at the corner of his lips. *And then, there was Jaira.* She had changed everything. With just one glance from her, he'd forgotten the entire plan.

Remy's neck reddened as he thought of it. He put a hand into his pocket and wrapped his fingers around her misplaced earring.

In that moment, he consciously acknowledged what he'd already decided in his heart: he would abandon his dúshlán quest for her, if she would have him.

Remy's foot tangled in a snarl of thorny vines that threatened to trip him as he walked through the wild wood. Removing his leg from the bracken, he sighed and frowned when he remembered Jaira was already betrothed, although she didn't seem as fond of Fuerian as perhaps Jaira's father did. *Was there room to pursue her?*

How would her father react if he knew Remy wasn't of Arcadeaxn origin?

The human sat on an old stump to try to sort out the discord between his heart and head. Below him, the disintegrating birch crumbled slightly under his weight, softened by years of weather. Moss and lichens released spores into the air as Remy disturbed them and then all was quiet. He felt the silence close in around him, as he'd hoped. But the circle did not fully close. A strange and pleasant song filled the distance faintly.

Remy turned his ear and listened. He could not quite make out words, but there was an inherent beauty in the tune. Finally, he made his way toward its source, walking softly through the trees and keeping hidden. As he walked, he spotted sparrows and a rabbit that had paused and inclined its ears as well.

For a moment, Remy wondered if he'd been entranced by some kind of sirine. But there was not enough water nearby to sustain such a creature. He crept further and then peered into the clearing, where a small woodland glade opened. Upon the verdant carpet, he saw *her*, dancing as she sang.

It was Jaira. She sang with strange words: that of the olde tongue. Remy knew that it was the formal language of the elves and the official language of the seelie court; *high speech they call it in the political courts*. Spells, when cast by verbal components, were often used uttered in it as one of the tongues of power. It had a cadence and energy about its flow that harnessed eldritch energies.

Remy knew the ancient language passably enough—learning it was just one key to surviving Arcadeax. He listened to her tune. It was about a captive woman who waited for her true love to come lest she die of a broken heart.

He watched her in secret for many minutes until her song finished. His hand remained in his pocket, his fingers curled around the jewelry.

Jaira paused. "I am here often." She turned to look directly at the foliage where Remy hid. "I do hope you'll come and hear me sing again."

A moment later, she moved to the far side of the glade, to where her horse stood tethered at some branches. She called back to Remy. "And perhaps next time, you can return my earring to me." Her lips quirked into a smile, and then, she mounted her horse and guided it into the wooded trail that led to her home.

"I will dance here again soon," Jaira spoke aloud, just before her mount disappeared into the foliage. "I will tell you when," her voice came through the leaves like a song.

Remy watched her go, grinning from ear to ear. *Then she is not Fuerian's... not yet.*

CHAPTER SIX

⸺ ◆ ⸺

F UERIAN STOOD NEXT TO an old friend outside the dilapidated building in a section of Cathair Dé known as The Haunts.
Most buildings in The Haunts were caving in on themselves, partially burned out, falling down, or in one kind of major disrepair
or another.

The Haunts were a multi-block section of the city that had been
mostly abandoned and avoided by any citizens with any common
sense. Though, that also made it the perfect draw for other sorts of
folk. The down and out, the anonymous, and all manner of those
engaged in illicit trades used The Haunts as their own.

Naz Charnazar, Fuerian's duelist and bodyguard, glared from
one elf to the other. Fuerian looked at the distressed surroundings
with indifference.

The other elf, named Gareth, was similar in age to Fuerian, taller,
and boasted a paunch around his midsection. He came from one
of the ambitious families that Naz was barely familiar with and
which was on the cusp of the elite circles that the wealthy ran
in. Whether Gareth's family had been prominent in the past and
fallen from grace by two pegs or had continually clawed their way

up from middle class, Naz could not recall. He only knew Gareth and Fuerian had attended university together.

"I'm telling you there's mad amounts of potential money in this," Gareth insisted.

Fuerian tilted his head in a subtle tell that was familiar to Naz. Gareth had his ear, despite the fact that, if they were in The Haunts for it, it was either illegal or grossly distasteful. Perhaps both.

"You've just got to see it to believe it," Gareth said, motioning for them to go inside the husk of a building nearby.

Naz fixed Fuerian with a hard look and held up a hand. His employer gave him a barely perceptible nod and the duelist whirled on his heel, hand dropping to the pommel of his blade, and then he stalked towards the hovel.

It was a two story structure that looked like it might fall over at any minute. Some kind of rot in the center made one corner crumple with its roof tilting precariously, like an ill placed hat ready to slide off at any moment. The stairs creaked beneath the duelists weight as he climbed. The door opened with unexpected silence and smoothness of motion.

Naz stepped through the entry and was greeted by a wave of sickly sour aroma. The smell of unwashed bodies and chunky, liquid sick hung like a thick miasma within the building. His nostrils flared and the duelist pressed ahead, stepping with cautious, catlike nimbleness.

Crumbling furniture adorned the edges of the rooms he passed through and heaps of moldering fabrics, perhaps old tapestries used as improvised blankets, made odd lumps at random intervals.

He finally arrived at the places main antechamber where he found half a dozen elves of mixed gender, alongside a few other fey creatures.

A faun lay nude, with his eyes rolled back in his head. A goblin huddled in the corner shaking as if fevered. The elf folk were in similar states.

Naz observed them cautiously for a few moments and then decided they posed no significant threat. His hand rested on the handle of his sword. *If they* became *threats, they'd fall quickly and disappear into The Haunts like so many others.*

The duelist returned to the front entrance and motioned the all clear for Fuerian who was still in deep conversation with Gareth. They walked inside the place and gave barely any thought to its condition, or the odor, and strolled as casually as if it were a library.

Gareth led them to the room with the bodies and motioned as if he were a proud rancher showing off prized stock.

"See? What did I tell you?" he grinned at Fuerian. Gareth gave a shove to one of the filthy elves who sat cross legged and barely breathing, as if in a trance.

The elf fell hard, but didn't respond to the assault. Gareth even gave him a little kick in the small ribs, eliciting no response except for heavy breathing.

Naz stood aloof, letting his employer have a conversation, but he remained tense. His hand rested at his weapon, ready to intervene as Fuerian knelt to look over the elf on the floorboards.

Fuerian checked him over, and then the others. He spent an uncomfortable amount of time checking the responsiveness of a female elf in the circle. She looked as if she might have once been pretty, before coming to The Haunts.

Finally, he stood. "Show it to me." Fuerian held out a hand and Gareth placed a small, glass vial into it.

Fuerian held it up to the dingy shaft of light that broke through the window, half choked by whatever sepia lace rags the moths hadn't yet devoured. He tapped the container and granules of the white powder shifted in place.

"Dream Hallow," Gareth said, pointing to the blissed out denizens on the floor. "These ones lost control of their habit, but it's very posh with aristocracy right now. Or at least, with their kids. Mainly academy hopefuls. Some a little younger."

"And it just... makes them happy. Out of their mind... puts half their mind in the aither, according to some folk. Lets one do what they want, go where they want, be who or with who they want," explained Gareth. "Leastwise, that's what I've heard."

"You've never tried it?" Fuerian asked.

Gareth pinched his fingers close together. "I only dabble. I don't want to blow out the pleasure centers in my brain... but it did make me feel great. I see the appeal," he pointed to the goblin, "but I've never seen that one in any state but this."

Fuerian cocked his head.

"They say overdosing can sever the cord between body and spirit when the dream hallow sends it to roam the aither," Gareth said.

"Who are 'they?'" Fuerian asked.

"The guys I see selling it. And that's what I've been saying. They are idiots, some low level thugs. So much potential to earn some coin, long term. We find out who they work for, or else how to make it, and then run the street. I've got the manpower, and you've got the know-how and capital," said Gareth. "And look at these sods. It's not like they're going to quit buying anytime soon."

A reserved grin crept across Fuerian's face. "I forsee a few beneficial uses for the stuff."

He made for the door. Naz followed.

"Get me the info we require to follow up on this lead. It could be lucrative," Fuerian called over his shoulder. He and Naz departed.

"**W**HERE IN THE FEY is Remy?" Thoranmir asked his sister. He'd looked all over for him, hoping to find him but couldn't spot him anywhere. "I wanted to take him down to that little cafe..."

"Cafe Mil?" Anya asked.

"Yeah but..."

"That place is disgusting."

Thoranmir scowled. "It's been my favorite, like, forever. Do they still serve those spiced apples and mead?"

Anya fixed him with a stern glare. "Those apples had maggots, and the mead was weak. Only you ever liked that place." She turned her wheeled chair and rolled toward the door. "Now, come on. We're going somewhere that *I like*."

"But what about Remy?"

"He can get his own supper. Besides, he left so we could talk about our lives and get each other back up to speed," Anya said, leaving off the part that Remy and she both agreed she could better make a personal attempt to discourage Thoranmir from the dangerous competition.

Thoranmir followed his sister, but he paused at the door. She threw an inquisitive glance over her shoulder at him.

Her brother fidgeted nervously.

"What is it?"

He frowned with a kind of half shrug. "I dunno. It's just... I don't think I've had supper without Remy in probably two years."

Anya took a gentler approach and waved him to follow. "I'm sure he's fine. But I haven't had supper with you since before you left *over* two years ago."

Thoranmir bobbed his head to acknowledge her words, understanding her point. His sister's mechanical chair thrummed and whirred as she drove it through the urban streets. They traveled through the nicer part of the city and came to a private club where a man at the door granted Anya access.

"He's with me," she told him, pointing to her brother.

The guard, a burly elf with broad shoulders and missing half of one ear, nodded. He turned over a waiver for Thoranmir to sign before entering. The newcomer scanned the agreement, which threatened to chop off his hands and castrate him if he told anyone outside the club's membership what he saw inside.

Thoranmir signed the form and the sentry let them pass. Inside, the hallway and other rooms gave off a posh vibe, which Thoranmir readily absorbed. A large sign read *Thistle and Barrel Club*.

"How are we here?" Thoranmir whispered, amazed that his sister somehow had access to one of the most upscale private clubs. It was a well-known house for amateur duelists, both the elite and wealthy kind. Members valued their privacy and personal company above all else.

Anya grinned at him. "The club hires me to do their work in the aithersphere. And membership has its perks, including access to the clubhouse and an amazing chef." She led the way to the clubhouse, keeping only to small talk. Anya knew that she couldn't push her brother one way or another on his most recent fantasy of becoming a duelist. But she *could* lead him to places where he'd become better informed.

The legless elf waved to an attendant who stood on the far side of the lounge. The elf wore fine clothes and a detached look. "Chechey, I brought my brother for a visit. Can you prepare whatever the special is today and put it on my tab?"

Chechey gave her a stiff bow and disappeared behind a couple of doors to pass on the order. His muffled voice barely carried back to them.

A few elves milled about the lounge. The lighting was comfortable and the furnishings might as well have been made of gold and rare animal skin. Everything about the Thistle and Barrel reinforced the exclusivity and excess of its clientele. And Anya, Thoranmir observed.

On the far wall, a slate board had been hung with a number of names and columns to show its members' standings. All the data on the board was highly illegal: it was a ranking system for amateur dueling, which was technically against the law.

But the sort of folks who could afford memberships at the Thistle and Barrel could afford bribes to stay above the law.

Besides, Oberon had made it a point to turn his eyes away from the amateur houses, and there were a number of technicalities about it that allowed them to operate outside the sphere of law. They only happened on private grounds and between cocksure fighters, with nothing but pride on the line. Typically, they were pissing matches between wealthy men and women who had studied the combat arts in universities and wanted to engage in sport or settle disputes with their peers, but not be vulnerable to the open challenge areas in public places. In a word, it too was *exclusive*.

Chechey returned with a drink for Anya and Thoranmir. He nodded and then mixed a cocktail for one of the members at the table nearest them.

Thoranmir sipped the drink, his taste buds melting. It was the best mead he'd ever had, and he couldn't help but sigh with pleasure. The edges of his mouth defied his concentration and turned up at their corners.

"Better than the Cafe Mil?"

He flashed her a begrudged look, shrugging. "It's all right, I guess."

Anya chuckled and shook her head. She sipped from her glass and watched her brother from her peripheral vision.

Thoranmir's eyes caught sight of the ranking board. The first column had a duelist's name, followed by a win and loss column. Perhaps more important than those numbers were the purple hash marks after a few names. They likely designated the same thing a duelist's purple ribbon would: whether they successfully defended a private contract. One did not need to be a licensed duelist to defend a contract, though one had to be a professional fighter in order to take one on. A few names had one behind it, though one name had *two* purple marks. One name had six: Fuerian Vastra.

He'd successfully defended himself six times against professional duelists... six times that were recorded, at least.

Thoranmir gulped as he mulled that fact over.

Fuerian's name was at the top of the rankings and he led by an impressive majority. The haughty elf had only three recorded losses with seventy-four wins. Under his name, an elf named Deohecha was scribbled with two purple marks trailing it.

Thoranmir's thoughts were broken by two elves talking loudly, as if they'd had just enough to drink that they forgot their volume. Both had a young and affluent look about them. They threw darts at a corkboard affixed near the rankings.

"It's ridiculous, Fenemos," griped the elf at the throwing line. "The under-mavens decided Fuerian's victories at the upcoming competition could count on the board."

"Stop your mewling, Aerendyll. If you had enough talent to climb any higher on the board, you already would have."

Aerendyll snatched Fenemos's dart. "I'm good enough to hit your name off that board," he challenged and then threw his opponent's dart. It sailed wide and high, lodging in the wall well beyond either elf's reach.

Fenemos sighed and shook his head. "They've got good precedent, you short-eared bastard. Now go get your darts. It's my turn and you've got to let me use yours now."

"Precedent?" Aerendyll scoffed.

Fenemos nodded. "We get to count purple ribbon challenges, so why not others? Besides, if he loses, he's got to count those, too."

"Yeah right," said Aerendyll. "Like Fuerian's gonna lose. He's only entering this contest because it's going to pad his numbers. He'll be uncatchable now."

"As if you were going to catch up," Fenemos laughed, quaffing a drink. "Besides, I heard it was for a wholly different reason. But you're probably right—Fuerian doesn't lose. Those few times he has, I think, were on purpose. And none of those competitors that got invitations are going to put up much of a fight. It's all theatrics. Fuerian doesn't want to go professional, and this way, the Morgensteens don't have to pay out."

Thoranmir caught Anya's sidelong glance as she drank from her mead cup.

Aerendyll shook his head dourly. "Purple hashes. Those shouldn't count either. They're really only a mark of how much other people hate you. And Fuerian's an unseelie prig."

Aerendyll chuckled as he collected the darts after Fenemos threw. Then, he threw a trio of his own. "It's no wonder he's scored so many purples. You know, I heard he's killed at least two people he's dueled."

Fenemos raised a brow. "I'm fairly certain the two you mentioned had their memberships here expire because they moved to different cities…"

"No, really. I heard it from a mutual friend who helped bury the bodies and settle all the person's affairs. When is the last time you heard from Glenric?"

About that time, Chechey returned with a plate of sizzling rabbit dusted with fragrant spices and a dish of stuffed mushroom caps over greens drenched with berry vinaigrette. A few moments later, Fenemos and Aerendyll took their darts and left, apparently finished with their game.

"…definitely placing a big bet on Fuerian winning the whole contest," said Aerendyll as he walked past Thoranmir and Anya.

"Payoff is better on an unknown fighter. I can bet smaller," said Fenemos. "I don't know who I'd pick, so I'll maybe throw a dart at the names. I'd advise you to do the same, but you'd never hit one."

And then they were gone. Afterwards, the room went mostly quiet.

Thoranmir took a few bites. The food was delicious, but he mostly picked at his food, his appetite withered. His eyes kept flitting back to the slate board and the rank standings for the Thistle and Barrel.

J AIRA'S CHEST FLUSHED RED and her face filled with elation as she closed the door to her family's home and then leaned against it. Her breaths came ragged, but less from the dancing and more from her nerves unwinding as the tense energy tapered off. That strange energy coursed through her whenever she was around Remy.

She looked up and spotted a pair of greedy eyes watching her. Vennumyn, one of the family's maids, watched her as if recording Jaira's every move.

The much older woman shifted aside and into the shadows as if she could sneak away unseen. A sense of indignation rose up in Jaira and she walked into the adjacent room, anticipating Vennumyn's movements. She bypassed the staircase and walked into the next room circumventing the route.

A moment later, Vennumyn stepped in through the smaller servant halls. The self-pleased look fell from the maids face once she realized her cleverness had been sabotaged.

Jaira stared at her with arms crossed and a raised eyebrow.

"My lady?" Vennumyn asked, pushing a little more respect into her voice than she usually gave the youngest Morgensteen. "Do you need something from me?"

Jaira let the request linger in the air a moment longer as she stared Vennumyn up and down. She was a middle aged elf with silver streaked hair pulled in tight locks. Her dark eyes were slightly too close together, but her bent back had never shied from work. Still, she'd always seemed untrustworthy to Jaira, even if her parents liked her well enough to keep on as house staff—though never well enough to promote to head maid.

"I am concerned that you may be overly interested in my affairs, Vennumyn," Jaira said flatly.

Vennumyn tilted her head, and finally answered, "Is it not your intention to marry Fuerian Vastra?"

Jaira's lips pursed in annoyance before she got it back into its carefully rehearsed mask of placid neutrality. "He and I are betrothed."

"Many are eager to see two great houses unite," Vennumyn said. "Surely the newest married couple in Cathair Dé will need an experienced staff for their home."

Jaira ground her back teeth together. *Not over my dead body.* "I am concerned that you might think you see things as something that are either more, or less, than they really are."

Vennumyn bristled. She almost crossed her arms indignantly, but then relaxed them into a practiced, nonthreatening stance and let them dangle at her sides. "So I did not see you dancing in the glade for that street urchin who somehow gain entry to the dueling contests?"

It was Jaira's turn to bristle. She nearly lashed out at the maid, but Vennumyn continued.

"I hear things, you know I hear things. Rumors travel faster than the aither on a windy day, they say. I hear he's a *human*," she said conspiratorially.

Damned gossip, Jaira cursed to herself. She set her hands on her hips. "Why would you even think I as entertaining him?"

"I saw him sneaking away from the woods as you were coming up to the house."

Jaira narrowed her eyes. She said nothing, but knew that the only way she'd have spotted Remy was if Vennumyn was outside and near the glade enough to spy on her. The woods were too thick for her to spot him from anywhere else, and for her to see him leave the woods for the road, she'd have to have been clear on the other side of the Harhassus estate to have enough of a visible angle around the wooded bend.

I'll have to keep my eyes on this one, she thought.

"I'd certainly love to work in one of the Vastra's homes," Vennumyn said. "They pay very well. Or so I hear."

Jaira cursed beneath her breath and then turned, too disgusted with the greedy servant to remain in the same room. *I'll have to watch her close, indeed.*

CHAPTER SEVEN

R EMY SHOVED THORANMIR OUT the door of Anya's apartment. The streets were quiet aside from the occasional
pedestrian ambling by as the morning light burgeoned on the city
skyline.

"Ow, ow, ow!" Thoranmir complained as Remy twisted his arm
and forced him into the small courtyard between the road and
where the building's entrance began.

Remy hooked a foot under a long stick that lay on the ground
and used a foot to toss it to the elf. Remy snatched a broken rake
handle that leaned against the building and motioned for his friend
to attack him.

"Come on, man, I don't want to fight you," said Thoranmir.

"It's not fighting, it's training, and if you're adamant that you're
going to exit the tournament, then you're going to need to be
better prepared," said Remy.

"Yeah, well, how come you get the good stick?" Thoranmir
griped.

Remy shook his head at the juvenile complaint, but decided to let it go. "Fine then, we'll trade." He tossed his practice weapon across the yard so his friend could grab it.

"Ha!" Thoranmir flashed him a roguish grin. "Now I have both swords. And you thought I haven't learned anything about fighting in all our travels."

Thoranmir leapt forward and pressed the attack, wielding both of the sticks with more efficacy than Remy would have thought.

"I guess so," Remy said, chuckling. He dodged, pivoted, and put some space between them. "Fine. Have it your way, then." Remy took another step back near the stoop to the building and putting up a hand to forestall the attack while he set down his pouch and a few loose items so they would be neither lost nor damaged as they sparred.

With gentle care, he set Jaira's earring down atop the leather pouch that had only a few coins within which Remy assumed he might need in the course of the day. His dúshlán remained in place, though Remy had no cause to need it; it's presence on his hip had become second nature to him. Remy could bend, twist, and roll without it impeding his movement.

Remy turned back to his friend and squared off, motioning that he was ready.

Thoranmir lunged at Remy, swinging with his dominant hand.

Remy sidestepped and waited for Thoranmir to swing with his weaker side. The attack came, slightly slower, and more predictable. Remy ducked and swiveled in a smooth motion, popping upward with an open hand strike that knocked the stick free and into the air where Remy caught it.

"I'll take that, thanks," Remy said.

Thoranmir snorted blast through his nose and then doubled his grip on the rake handle before swinging.

Remy assumed his friend put a lot of stock in the milled stave being stringer and he swung hard, probably hoping to break Remy's stick and then exploit the resulting advantage.

It's a good tactic, Remy thought. *As long as he can sunder my stick before I whack him.*

Remy blocked a low slash and then grabbed Thoranmir's forearm as they pressed their rods together. Thoranmir did the same, trying to replicate the move that had given Remy back his weapon in the first place.

As they locked together, with each vying to knock the other person's sparring weapon from his hand, a hooded street urchin darted from behind the shrubbery nearest the apartment building and snatched Remy's purse—*and Jaira's earring!*

"Hey!" Remy shouted as the thief whirled on his heel and dashed away.

The urchin's hood fell back revealing a young sidhe in a flatcap. He was barely into his teenage years.

Remy turned to face the engage the thief. Thoranmir had been so focused on their engagement that he did not notice the burglar and seized upon the sudden opportunity.

Before Remy could utter another word, Thoranmir flung the stick from his friend's hand and whirled with the rake handle. A meaty *crack!* thundered as Thoranmir whacked Remy across the rear of his leg and toppled his friend.

Remy reached down with a gasp and clutched the welted hamstring and shot an icy look at Thoranmir who, suddenly realizing what had happened, too late, dropped the dowel with a sheepish grin.

He shot past his friend who had barely hobbled to his feet. "Come on," yelled Thoranmir in pursuit of the thief. "He's getting away!"

"NO NAMES," FUERIAN TOLD Gareth again as the enclosed carriage rolled slowly through the narrow roads where middle class buildings rose above their foundations, reaching upward with the same ambition present in their tenants... tenants who the elite caste knew would never rise beyond their humble moorings without a sponsor. Centuries worth of noble breeding and inter-family agreements had assured such an outcome.

Fuerian fixed the ambitious elf in his gaze. Gareth was exactly such an elf, and if Gareth and his family were to break into the upper circles of nobility, he needed Fuerian and the Vastra name. And that sponsorship came with a certain amount of debt.

"Well, what should I call you, then?" Gareth asked.

"Boss. Chief. Vengeful sidhe spirit. I don't care." Fuerian leaned back into his seat as the narrow passages broadened at an intersection. And then the vehicle crept to a stop between two buildings.

"Chief it is, then," Said Gareth. "I'll be Cú Chulainn, like from the—"

"It'll just be Gareth," insisted Fuerian.

Gareth turned and flashed a wounded look.

"No names *for you*," said Fuerian. "Nobody knows who you are. You don't have a reputation to protect... yet," he added for the sake of keeping his flunky's spirits high.

It had the desired effect and Gareth brightened.

The nearest structures made up half of a cluster of four towers. They were not overly large, but reasonably tall, and though their faces were maintained to look appealing and retain a modicum of civility, the four passages between them pierced to a dark heart hidden behind.

The service alleys were just wide enough for a refuse wagon and led to a joint utility court where dumpsters and maintenance access for all four would be found. Bundled wires dangled too low before they branched off to connect to individual apartments where they delivered an akasha drip and a thin tube bent into a V angle where someone had tried to hang off it and nearly kinked shut an aither connection that terminated somewhere in one of the buildings.

Gareth pointed to the obscure quad. "That's where the Dream Hallow sellers run their operation out of."

"Your guys are ready? You know, in case your negotiation skills reflect your grades?" Fuerian asked, recalling their time together at university.

"Hey," Gareth said, mocking wounded pride, "I did eventually pass that class... and *yes*. My crew is ready." He handed Fuerian a metal cylinder.

Fuerian cocked a brow. "What's this?"

The tube gleaned, made of polished cupronickel. A single push button raised on one side and the bottom had a twist off compartment for an akashic battery and a union connection for the smallest kind of aither port.

"If it goes poorly, the button will signal the cavalry. It sends an invisible signal to summon anyone with the receiver. I figure it makes no sense coming in heavy and making them defensive. Maybe they'll see reason," Gareth suggested.

"Dream Hallow pushers?" Fuerian chuffed. "Not likely, but this plan does show a certain amount of foresight."

Gareth beamed at the compliment, and then stepped out of the carriage and strode confidently into the dealers' den. Fuerian and Naz walked a pace behind him.

The quad was big enough for the refuse collector to do his work comfortably and there was ample room for him to even turn his wagon if need be. The cobble floor was reasonably well maintained and the backside of the four buildings each had a descending hive of metal ladder work in case of emergencies. The system of wolfranium lattice affixed to the exterior walls and hung just high enough that someone could pull him or her self up from the ground.

For a moment, Fuerian thought he saw movement at the top of one building. When he looked closer, he saw nothing. *Motion must have been a bird.*

Fuerian rubbed his eyes. *It's nicer than I assumed,* thought Fuerian, noting the metal. Wolfranium was extremely common, but he had expected builders to go with something cheaper like vantadium, which melted at a much lower temperature. Fuerian momentarily imagined the lower casted residents fleeing an inferno only to have their escape route collapse and dump them to their doom.

He shook away the thought when activity responded to their presence.

A surprisingly high quality lean-to was erected where one of the dumpsters used to reside before being moved adjacent one of its peers. One elf, finer dressed than the others—though still sporting the trappings of middle class, remained inside while a trio of his underlings emerged. Another elf stirred in each of the fire escapes' lower levels.

The gang had the distinct look of street ruffians, but their clothes were of a quality make and they each seemed to obey expected hygiene norms. .

I don't suppose you want addicts in charge of the supply if you want a business to succeed, Fuerian mused, looking them over. The dealers may have peddled the dream hallow to others, but these fey were not users. At least, they did not over-indulge. These elves were entrepreneurs, much like Gareth sought to be.

None of these were low-casted urchins and all appeared to be still youths, likely living nearby and still with parents who had no idea of their children's activities, or that their kids probably earned far more than their parents due to the illicit activity

Glancing around, the leader of the trio unclasped a latch on his belt pouch. He lifted it enough to display a collection of stoppered phials similar to the one Gareth had showed his partners in The Haunts.

"What you need?" the dealer asked Gareth.

Gareth tried to look past the frontman and signal the elf still remaining below the awning. "Lemme speak to your boss."

The boss didn't respond, but dealer's two friends tensed and the four additional thugs clambered down from their perches on the metal fire escapes and hemmed them in.

"Nothing you can say to him that doesn't go through me first." He jiggled his pouch. "Now, are we doing business here, or not?"

"I have a business proposition for you," Gareth ignored him, calling past the vendor.

Fuerian grinned at his friend's gumption. These elves may have been hungry, growing fish in a relatively small pond, but Fuerian owned the pond.

The vendor clicked the pouch shut and turned it so that its precious cargo rested out of the way and at the small of his back. His knuckles cracked as he balled his hands into fists. "I don't think you heard me—and I think we're about to have a problem if you don't vacate immediately."

Gareth continued, "It would be financially lucrative if you heard me out on this. I represent an interested party."

"Who's that? Is that him?" the thug angled his head at Fuerian.

"I represent the Chief—"

"Chief Cú Chulainn," Fuerian told Gareth.

Gareth gave him an annoyed look, but Fuerian flashed him a smile. *Cú Chulainn was a more creative name*, Fuerian admitted to himself, and Gareth sometimes had a flare for the dramatic.

"And what does this Cú Chulainn offer?" the thug asked.

Gareth smiled. "You get to keep doing what you're doing—but you're going to work for me. Unless you want to limp back home with nothing."

The elf under the awning chuckled and shook his head.

"Get him," the first thug shouted, and they all rushed Gareth.

They pummeled toppled Gareth and pummeled him with their fists. Curling up to shield himself from the blows, the very surprised Gareth called for his friends to help.

Fuerian cocked his head and watched for a moment.

After a few seconds stretched long, Naz reached for his weapon and took a half step forward. But Fuerian put a hand up to stay his protector. With a sigh and an eye roll, Fuerian thumbed the button on the emergency signal. A puff of amber mist emitted from the handheld device, but it made no other signal that it had worked.

Fuerian shook it and put it to his ear, but it was quiet. He did not know how, or if, it had worked.

A moment later, open wagons pulled up and blocked three of the four alleys and Gareth's hired enforcers poured from them: six elves from each.

The gang of dream hallow sellers looked up, startled. They realized the game was over and whirled to flee down the remaining path. The elf below the makeshift canvas structure snatched a pair of lockboxes and clamped them shut before joining the rest.

A fourth wagon pulled in just late enough to herd the gang into a choke point as Gareth's troops fell upon them. The thugs fell upon the dealers, producing saps, leather wrapped clubs that were typically less lethal than their alternatives, and knocked them senseless. Some of the more scrappy elves were dragged to the ground by Gareth's ruffians and their peers bludgeoned them, overwhelming them with numbers.

Gareth, back on his feet, stalked towards the leader with his closed and locked boxes. Taking a sap from one of his underlings, Gareth cornered the elf against the alley wall and cracked him across the face, knocking him prone.

The young elf dropped the boxes and they bounced to Gareth's feet.

"I *said* you all work for me, now," Gareth hissed. He glanced back at Fuerian and then at his foot soldiers. "Your timing could have been a little better." He wiped a trickle of blood from the corner of his lips and smacked the elves' leader again.

Gareth's victim cried out. "We *can't.*"

"Why not?" Fuerian asked, finally stepping into the scene once all the dream hallow dealers had been knocked prone. "My friend here wants very much to get involved in your trade. Who makes the dream hallow?"

"There's only one supplier. And we don't even know who."

Gareth pressed a foot to the elf's throat and used a gentle pressure to choke him. "How do you get it, then?"

The elf gasped and gurgled until Gareth let up. "I don't know anything, I swear! Wagon from Stór Rúnda drops it off weekly... a rural egg supplier, I think—that's all I know."

Fuerian rubbed his chin and mumbled. "It sounds familiar, but it's not a company I can think of."

Gareth tapped his friend. "Let's get out of here."

Fuerian's brows remained knit. "But Stór Rúnda..."

"You don't remember it?" Gareth asked, "Because I sure do, and you *should* if you were any sort of a decent student in your academy days."

Fuerian and Naz followed Gareth as he led the way back to their carriage and explained, "I know the businessman who's responsible for making the dream hallow. And if you think real hard, so do you."

REMY AND THORANMIR SPRINTED after the thief whose speed ticked up a notch when he noticed the pursuit—and that they were gaining on him.

The thief was lean and wiry, and he should have been able to outrun them, but his speed flagged. Remy guessed he was just a youth and had never had any real reason to build the endurance necessary to sprint so far so fast.

They hadn't gone too far from Anya's section of Cathair Dé when the thief took a sharp turn between two buildings. Only a narrow alley separated them and when Remy looked closer, a matching pair were behind as well, making four identical apartment complexes.

Remy slowed slightly. The thief's shadow jostled between the steep walls and then moved indecisively, finally picking a path and slipping out of sight.

"Careful," he told Thoranmir. "Go slow, and make sure to yell if he runs out the other side. We can't lose him in the crossroads."

Remy made a hand motion to communicate that he was going to dash around to the other side and come in at a right angle. They'd be able to see which way he ran if they flushed him out one side or the other before apprehending him.

Thoranmir nodded and crept into the alley at a slow enough pace to let Remy circle around to a flanking position.

Remy and Thoranmir moved with the kind of speed and tactical sense of each of other that wolves and other pack creatures exercised. They converged at the same time in the center of the quad.

The thief spotted Remy first. The human was larger and he moved more quickly to make up for the extra distance he'd had to run. Whirling on his heel, the thief turned to exit on a different vector, bur Thoranmir flew out of the shadows and tackled him.

Together, the two elves rolled in a flailing storm of arms and legs until Remy fell onto the heap and wrapped the thief in a restraint, hauling him to his feet. Thoranmir yanked free the stolen satchel and jewelry to return to their friend.

"Help! You guys gotta help me," the thief yelped in a too-highly pitched voice to be much beyond puberty. He struggled against an arm lock and his flatcap fell to the ground.

Remy and Thoranmir turned their heads to see a small gang of ruffians. They looked already worse for wear, as if they'd just lost a tailteann game, and clustered mostly beneath a canvas lean-to where a dumpster should have been. Most of them sported fresh bruises, scratches and scuffs, and a few even leaked blood from recent wounds that hadn't had time yet to sufficiently clot.

"Is this one of yours?" Remy asked, shaking the teen.

"He's not ours," said the gang's leader, but they wearily poised themselves for a fight, anyway.

"Come on, guys, it's me," the thief wailed. "You said if I—"

The leader silenced him with a menacing glare. "Like I said. Not ours. Do to him whatever you want."

The gang took a slow step towards the intruders. They evidently planned *something*, and were bad liars as far as the young thief was concerned.

"I'm thinking we retreat?" Thoranmir asked.

Remy shrugged, more with his facial expression than his body, which was currently locking the kid's arms.

"I mean, we can totally take them," Thoranmir insisted, "but I already beat your ass with that stick earlier, I don't need to assault a bunch of kids, too. Besides, we got what we came for."

The intruders took a cautious step backwards, heading for the exit.

"Kid? I ain't no kid," roared the young elf in Remy's grip. He twisted his bony arms enough to wriggle momentarily free. He snatched his cap and then he sprinted to a dumpster, leapt to grab a metal bar, and then clambered up a fire escape.

Before melting out of sight in the maze of metal stairs, he yelled down. "You guys are a bunch of assholes. I didn't want to sell your shitty dream hallow, anyways."

The kid vanished.

Remy noticed how Thoranmir's feet planted and his heart sank. "Dream hallow, you say?"

Remy shook his head at Thoranmir and motioned for him to disengage.

"Listen," said the gang leader. "I'm not in the mood."

Thoranmir's head tilted ever so slightly. Remy knew exactly what the motion meant. "Yeah. That makes two of us."

Thoranmir flung himself at the elf, who already had a black eye, and dragged the drug peddler to the cobblestone path. Thoranmir fought his opponent's arms for control, gained an angle, and threw punches, shouting down ancient insults and newly invented profanities as he did.

The elf's friend's moved to intervene, but half of them were already so badly injured from some previous altercation that they couldn't engage. The remaining three rushed for Thoranmir.

Remy got between them and kicked the legs out from under the first of them. He came to his feet in a practiced maneuver and leapt into the second, bringing his knee to bear between his enemy's legs and simultaneously butting the top of his head into the elf's nose.

He released the dispatched elf just as the third reached Thoranmir. Remy surged to his side and body checked the thug. They both sprawled to the ground.

Remy scrambled and reached his feet as the first elf darted towards Thoranmir. The enemy had recovered and grabbed a wooden rod from a nearby refuse pile. It had probably been a broom handle at some point in its earlier career, but as a stave, it could've made the difference in Thoranmir's remaining success.

Thoranmir had his opponent face down on the ground, an arm around his neck. He'd early choked the drug dealer into submission when the thug ran towards them with his wooden pole.

Remy yanked his dúshlán blade free and stepped between them, blocking the elf's strike. The edge of the dagger bit deep into the wooden dowel and Remy controlled the business end of it, pinning it to the ground. He stomped on it, snapping it in two.

His opponent let go and Remy snatched the shortened rod and lunged forward, cracking the elvish thug across the side of the head.

The elf collapsed as if his legs had turned to liquid and Remy turned to face the remaining enemy who had climbed back to his feet. The enemy spotted Remy's weapon and noted that the engagement's stakes had just escalated. He turned tail and ran.

Remy turned and gave a threatening leer to the remaining, injured members of the gang. They all found surreptitious exit paths as well.

"Now, are you gonna talk to us like a gentleman, or am I going to have to beat the answers I want out of you?" Thoranmir asked.

MITHRILCHON, THE RED MAVEN, sat patiently. His primary apprentice, Agarogol remained relatively relaxed, mimicking high maven. One of the eight magi of the maven high council at Suíochán Naséan, he tried all times to portray to his two under-mavens exactly what it meant to be a maven of such a station.

The Radiant Tower, what lay persons of various species often called Suíochán Naséan, was a symbol for power. In Mithrilchon's mind, its very existence brought peace to the seelie folk.

He was glad that at least one of his students had so thoroughly tried to emulate his example—what he thought an Aes Sidhe should be. There were many wizards among the Aes Sidhe, those capable of magic, but the mavens held themselves up as the highest of standards—they had the endorsement of the Gilded Throne. All Aes Sidhe had great power, and Mithrilchon had maintained that power must always hold itself in check lest it become abused. Loitariel, by contrast to Agarogol, paced back and forth on the rooftop and exuded a nervous kind of energy.

Her frequent patrols kicked up the pigeons which tried to roost there, potentially giving away the fact that intruders had camped out on the building's roof while doing their surveillance. She frowned and retreated to the center of the building where the other two mavens waited.

The pigeons returned. Mithrilchon whispered a sleep spell, lulling the birds into a deep slumber. He knew Loitariel would return to her nervous pacing at some point; the maven knew enough to be prepared.

Agarogol asked her, "You are certain of what you felt, Loitariel?"

She nodded. The maven was not a seer, but she had a gift for seeing when important points in history converged. She could sense significant points in the fate of the realm. While seers saw the potential tangents in a more prognosticative way, she could sense when things were about to happen, or which events and decisions disqualified the *potential* visions of a seer and narrowed down the true path. Without direct access to a seer it was a less effective gift, but it fit their purposes.

"There," she pointed over the ledge of the flat roof and to a carriage as it approached. "Here is one of the points that will converge in this area."

Agaragol and Mithrilchon joined her and they spied on the carriage as its owner exited. Fuerian Vastra, accompanied by one of his underlings.

The elves entered the alleys connecting a common utility area to the surrounding streets. Fuerian, ever observant, looked up at the roofline and directly towards them.

Mithrilchon muttered an obfuscation spell he'd prepared and then nudged a bird. The pigeon took flight to add misdirection to the magic.

Fuerian paid them no mind and returned to his business below. The mavens watched with passive interest until another group of elves showed up and a small gang war broke out below. Fuerian's forces won the altercation after boxing them in. He and his thugs savaged the group of misguided sidhe youth before leaving.

Mithrilchon and the others watched the events with cold detachment. Once the event had passed, he noted, "Somehow these... children have gotten their hands on dream hallow." He tapped a finger to his chin thoughtfully. That certainly seems significant to what the seer has foreseen about the downfall of the Suíochán Naséan... how anyone else outside the tower discovered the means to make the stuff certainly bears investigation." He mumbled something unintelligible as he ruminated.

"You... suspect a traitor?" Loitariel asked.

Mithrilchon licked his lips, declining to comment specifically. "It's significant and should be mentioned in our report to the high council."

Agaragol withdrew a bound journal he carried and jotted it down. "Duly noted."

"More," interrupted Loitariel. "The next part of the convergence."

A young elf dashed down the alley with two others pursuing. Another elf and Remy, the human mentioned by the seer, began a second altercation with the recently abused apothik peddlers.

"His name is Thoranmir," Agaragol identified Remy's partner.

Together, they beat up the same crew as Fuerian. The thugs may have been wounded already, but Remy and Thoranmir were only two.

"I think the seer may have been wrong. At least partly," Loitariel said.

Her two companions turned to look at her.

"It's Thoranmir," she explained. "The seer had no mention of him specifically, at least, not according to Calithilon the White. But Thoranmir is certainly touched by destiny. I can sense it. The convergence of those significant events—it centers on him. He is some kind of tether between the human with the dúshlán and Fuerian."

Mithrilchon cursed below his breath. He, like many other mavens, disagreed with the Radiant Tower's rule that only the white maven should have access to a seer. Were it any different, they could parse one threat from the next, and know exactly who it was that would cause this supposed cataclysm. Then they could eliminate the threat before it could fully gestate.

"Damn it," he finally mumbled. *If Calithilon could be wrong about this, what else could he be wrong about?* With their potential doom on the line, they could not afford to take any chances.

CHAPTER EIGHT

———— ❖ ————

T HORANMIR DRAGGED THE DEALER to a chair beneath the canvas awning and hurled him against it. It rocked back against the brick wall, but held the elf's weight and he slumped into a defeated, seated pose.

Remy raised a brow. He'd never seen his friend like this before and pulled him aside. "Are you okay? I mean, did you even know the guy you're looking for?"

Thoranmir's lips tightened and he shook his head slowly. "No. But his sister... I like her. I really do, and she's so worried about him. When she was young, when she didn't have much else as a... an outcast child rumored to be bastard, her brother was the only one watching out for her. Now she's doing the same... and I'm watching out for *her*."

Remy bobbed his head, and then flicked his wrist and pointed the tip of his knife at their hostage's neck.

The dealer sat back from where he was edging forward, trying to set up an opportunity to flee. He held up his hands. "Hey guys, I just sell low grade pharmaceuticals for people looking for a good time."

"What's this crap do, anyway?" Remy rummaged through the nearby table where goods were lined up in neat little rows of glass containers. He lifted a clear, stoppered jar made of thin, fragile glass and looked at the granules of whitish crystals. They looked like bleached out beach sand.

"They just make you feel good. Really, really good," the dealer claimed. "Some folks say it'll send you into the aither, all on your own without any need for a connection. They call it dream hallow."

Remy retrieved three more of the containers and opened them. "And it's all perfectly safe, right?"

"Yeah. Yeah, of course," the dealer said, unconvincingly.

Thoranmir grabbed his jaw and held it open. "Then you won't mind us making you feel great."

The hostage squirmed and fought as Thoranmir held him down. Remy carried over the bottles and tipped them precariously close to spilling into the elf's mouth. He held off just before any of it dumped out.

"I already know what too much of this stuff can do. You're going to tell me all that I need to know about one of your customers... or else my friend is going to make you feel amazing for *the rest of your life*," Thoranmir said, letting the implications linger.

The dealer made an agreeable noise.

"Who's your supplier," Remy asked, before Thoranmir could ask about Odessa's brother. "Someone's got to be manufacturing this stuff."

"I already told those other guys. I don't know. I've never seen anyone in person. I just move the product on the streets."

"Other guys?" Thoranmir asked, but then he let the subject pass. "It doesn't matter. I just want to know about one elf in particular. I need to find him. He's male, about my height. His name was Eldarian Cócaire. He didn't grow up in Cathair Dé. He's from the rural towns."

The dealer replied with a confused, worried look. He clearly understood that his future relied on providing a satisfactory answer. Clearly, the elf wished he could give Thoranmir the answer he wanted.

"I—I'm sorry friend. But I don't know anyone by that name."

Thoranmir roared and flipped the table over, obliterating the bottles and ruining the dealer's product supply. He picked up one of the two wooden lock boxes and flung it against the brick, exterior wall. It smashed apart and broke into a heap of cracked planks, glass shards, and busted nails. The shifting sands of freed dream hallow leaked through the ruined cracks and poured to the cobblestone ground where Thoranmir kicked and scattered it.

"He would have been about your age," Remy insisted. "Perhaps a couple years older at most... before Cathair Dé, he was a student at one of the arcana schools—"

"Oh! *That guy?*" Recognition spread across the dealer's face. "I mean, I know *of him.* He used to buy from one of my dealers out by the slums... The Haunts, they call it. Last I heard, he was in deep. Got a bad habit. Started buying a cheaper version from some gutter punk who cut the product with busted glass, sand, whatever he gets. Makes dosing hard to figure; usually leads to users overdoing it."

Thoranmir growled and hurled the second lock box at the wall. It was heavier and splintered open. The dealer winced as it fell to the ground, spilling coins all over.

"Where is he, now?" Remy asked, more than happy to play the decent side of *good elf, bad elf* for once.

"I dunno. Haven't heard about him in weeks," the dealer said. "I don't even know him personally. We'd never met. I just remember kooky stories about him."

"Such as?" Remy asked.

"I—I don't know... that he made wild claims. Said he was kidnapped and sent to the unseelie. Said that the akasha was evil... hated the stuff, was terrified of anything that used it, but couldn't leave the city 'cause he couldn't get dream hallow anywhere else. Hooks were in deep, I'm sure."

Thoranmir picked up a satchel and emptied it of any personal belongings. Then, he stuffed the coins from the dealer's broken container; they were mostly a mix of very low and extremely high value amounts where they'd been traded in at a coinery. He grinned at the dream hallow pusher's worried response.

"I'm guessing this money belongs to whoever supplies you with the stuff?" Thoranmir guessed.

The other elf nodded.

"Good," hissed Thoranmir. "Let this be a lesson in what it feels like to have so much taken from you, and still owe more. *That* is how your junkies feel. Good luck repaying it all," he whistled as he estimated the amount. It was no small sum.

Thoranmir turned his back and began walking back home.

The dealer stood, as if to complain, or maybe make a play for his stolen cash.

Remy leveled the tip of his dúshlán and his opponent strained, poking himself slightly in the neck. It barely nicked the elf, drawing only a single drop of blood and dropping him back into the chair.

"No. He's walking away, and you're going to let him go." Remy bent until he was nearly nose to nose with the sidhe. "I want you to know that I've never seen my friend like this, so count yourself lucky that he did not kill you. I know killers, and he was prepared to cross a line today."

Remy stared at the bloodied and bruised young elf. Defeat clouded his face as much as the grays and purples around the elf's orbital and cheek bones; this kid was no killer—even if he *was* a thief of life in other ways.

"No more business in this part of town," Remy insisted, fixing him with cold, hard eyes: eyes that implied the severity of disobedience—the eyes of a killer. Eyes that had survived their most vulnerable years in the unseelie. "Tell all your pushers. If we chance across them moving dream hallow, you'll lose more than your apothiks or your money. It'll cost your life."

The elf's eyes burned and his jaw was set, but he nodded.

Remy turned and jogged to catch up with his friend. They neared the end of the alleyway. As they did so, Remy whispered, "Go right, not left."

Thoranmir glanced sidelong at him, but did as told. "That's not the way home."

"I know. But you just made a powerful enemy. I don't see anyone I can pick out as a spy, but you don't want one following you home—getting Anya involved in this—do you?"

"Oh gods... oh *gods*," Thoranmir said. His voice warbled plaintively and his legs buckled with a slight hitch as the weight of what he'd done evidently landed.

"Don't worry," Remy said. "I have a plan to allay any eyes from Anya, but you should be more mindful moving forward. You just kicked a hornet's nest."

They walked a block in silence and the distance made Thoranmir stand straighter, more resolute. "But we got some info, right? I didn't do all that for no reason, did I? Odessa's brother..."

"Yeah," Remy said. "You got something. You got a clue."

FROM THEIR ROOFTOP PERCH the mavens watched Remy and Thoranmir abscond the scene.

"How many potential cataclysms have you lived through, master?" Loitariel asked, her eyes still fixed on the human who fled the scene.

"This is my second since attaining position on the high council," said Mithrilchon.

"And the last one involved a dragon?"

Mithrilchon nodded. "A young one, but yes."

Agarogol suggested, "What percent of these almost-cataclysms involve creatures not native to Arcadeax?"

Mithrilchon cocked his head. "Who says dragons are not native to our realm? They are native to *all* realms in fact... but I get your meaning. I have not studied the particular histories, but I am inclined to guess that the majority involved them in some way or another. Unseelie interlopers also make up a significant percentage. And at least one of them was instigated by a traitor within the maven's ranks."

Agarogol balked. Mithrilchon didn't think it possible for the pale elf to get any whiter. He'd always suspected some sort of ailment in his apprentice, but it had never affected Agarogol's performance, and his demeanor inclined Mithrilchon to put his apprentice up as his replacement if the worst should ever happen to him.

The fervor below had finally died down and the twice-thrashed street gang finally dispersed. The mavens watched them go and a quiet fell over the connected alleyways where they'd spied.

"Fuerian is a capable duelist, especially considering the records we have on him through the amateur duelists guild. But I had not expected such prowess from the human." Mithrilchon tapped a forefinger to his lip. "Our involvement in this matter must remain secret. Whatever actions we are motivated to perform in preservation of the high council must not come back to damage their reputation."

"Our ends will justify our means," noted Loitariel.

"But the populace rarely understands the weight of taking such difficult measures. They cannot see beyond their own immediate needs," Agarogol fired back.

Mithrilchon bobbed his head. "That is why we have need of some muscle. I should hire a mercenary, especially given that options involving magic have already been ruled out by the council. Getting caught triggering a ward would only send up a signal that the mavens are involved."

Loitariel bowed in agreement. Agarogol raised a hand and disagreed with her again—and with his master.

"Do you think that the wisest? I agree that we need mercenary help. But hiring one with the prowess to contend with two potential duelists—and on such short notice—seems a difficult task. Plus, any that are that capable might prove difficult to control," Agarogol explained. "Their minds might prove resilient enough to overcome any limits we might place on them."

"Your point?" asked Loitariel. "We cannot *do nothing*."

Agarogol remained unflustered. "My point is that mercenaries tend to have loose lips. I am suggesting you let me take care of it... no—I am not so physically proficient to handle our quarry, at least not anything beyond that Thoranmir fellow. But in my studies I have learned how to make a loyal minion from a body of one fallen. A thrall who should prove strong, tough, and fully controllable."

Mithrilchon raised a brow and turned fully to his apprentice. "You are suggesting necromancy, the creation of a sluagh. That is a magic not looked upon favorably by the council."

His apprentice cocked his head. "But it is not illegal. And the source of the power does not flow from the black gate, though it *is* unseelie of origin. The White Maven has assured us that the way to the infernal realm and all its power remains sealed ever since the revolt after the last Hell Tithe."

Mithrilchon continued to hold his gaze.

Agarogol continued, "I know that the White Maven himself uses this spell to puppeteer corpses whenever activity would bring one into contact with cold iron—a necessity for gathering Foil Milferra."

Mithrilchon could not suppress his frown; he turned and stared at the wreckage of the dream hallow. His apprentice was right. *Had the disbanded elves from below been braver than Calithilon? They would have had to risk pain and poison from the ferrous mineral in order to collect enough of the rare reagent to collect the dream hallow... unless someone connected to Suíochán Naséan stole it for them.*

The red maven looked at Agarogol. He nodded once, resolutely. "Do it."

"I shall need some time to prepare. And a corpse—not too old or it will remember itself, but it not yet be fully decayed," said Agarogol.

"Then depart to your duty," Mithrilchon said. He called his apprentice back before he could climb down the metal ladders at the building's edge. "But Agarogol—"

The pale elf paused and inclined his ear.

Mithrilchon gave him a sharp look. "Only the one sluagh. A personal bodyguard you might call it. If it is discovered, the last thing we need is for a scared sidhe populace thinking that the Aes Sidhe—and the mavens, too—are raising an army of undead. Nothing would shift the political winds against Oberon more quickly."

Agarogol agreed. Then he slid down the ladder and out of sight.

Loitariel waited until he was gone, and then spoke. "I have always been suspicious of that one."

Mithrilchon turned to face her. "I am aware that you two have something of a rivalry. It was intended that way. The proper amount of antagonism brings out each of your strengths."

"So you have no reservations about Agarogol raising the dead?"

"*Animating* the dead," Mithrilchon corrected. "There is a difference."

"Semantics," Loitariel said flatly.

"Important nuances," Mithrilchon said. "Do you have more to offer than a complaint against your peer?"

"I do. I don't disagree with the wisdom behind enlisting some help. I am merely voicing my concern. I've never claimed to trust even my fellow red mavens."

Mithrilchon smirked. "And how about *me*, Loitariel—do you trust *me*?"

Her face remained indifferent. "Master, you've already noted a willingness to pit my talents against Agarogol's, even as we work to mutual ends. That does not particularly instill trust. If I may say that I respect you, would that be sufficient?"

"As long as you still have something to contribute to the Radiant Tower's mission."

"I do," said Loitariel. "You know that we can take no chances. Leave no loose ends. Risk nothing to chance."

"Agreed."

"Then we should pursue a magical solution as well as a physical one." Before Mithrilchon could voice his objection, Loitariel raised her hands and sought a chance to explain. "We are Aes Sidhe. We are magical creatures, those beholden to Suíochán Naséan. We are the mavens, and our magics are our strength—even when wards are involved."

"Then you have a plan?" Mithrilchon asked with mild amusement.

"I do. The Kiss of Daggers."

Mithrilchon raised a curious brow.

"It is a fairly simple curse," Loitariel said, "but also a powerful one. We already know that the human carries a dúshlán. He is not alone in this world. A dúshlán is a powerful magic: vengeance magic borne of rage and of need and birthed by Arcadeax itself. That makes it a fetiche, a magic older than that of the Aes Sidhe.

"The curse of daggers is the same. It is powerful and ancient fetiche, powerful enough that it will take hold even in the presence of a ward that would redirect or dispel other magics. It is a subtle curse, not likely to be detected. And it is a curse I feel competent enough to evoke such a fetiche."

"Fetiches are intensely personal magic," Mithrilchon said. "You would have to touch the target of such a spell. How will you do that without exposing us?"

"I could find my target sleeping or unconscious. I feel confident in my abilities. Also," she said, "I would not be targeting the warded party. I would target *her*. The prize."

"Hijack the Dagda's blessing?" Mithrilchon rubbed his chin as he thought it over for a few moments. *Even if the ward existed and the fetiche was weak, the she-elf would take the arcane backlash, and not the mavens.* "I like this plan. But I want you to work together with Agarogol to enact it. The time for conflict between my apprentices has passed and the time to ply magics in concert is here."

Loitariel gave a stiff nod.

"Then we are agreed. We shall pursue both plans, yours and Agarogol's. We have too much at stake to put all our trust in any one plan."

The apprentice bowed and allowed herself a small smile, not content to be outdone by her peer. "And Master Mithrilchon, I *do* respect you."

"Good," said Mithrilchon. "Now you'd better research this curse of yours so that it goes off without a hitch. I don't need to tell you what could happen if you bungle such a powerful magic."

Loitariel bowed, and the two made for the rooftop's exit.

F UERIAN SAT ACROSS FROM Gareth and nursed his beverage. He looked up to his name on the competition board and noted his healthy lead. Few places were as safe for a wealthy elf as the Thistle and Barrel and so he'd released Naz for the evening.

Gareth had two empty mugs before him and the third arrived had just arrived when he grinned at his friend. "Still can't remember?"

Fuerian took a sip and let the name ruminate in his mind. *Stór Rúnda*.

With Gareth chortling in the background, something finally clicked and the memory unlocked. A local business professional had been a guest lecturer in an academy class. He'd come every year and given a variant on the same speech.

Fuerian remembered that he was no fey of high repute. He did not have title or name, but he had respect and wealth, especially among the non elites. The lowest castes all wished they were méith, and the middle class all believed that entering the méith would be possible through hard work and ingenuity.

Stór Rúnda demonstrated the opposite was true—the méith, the true elites, knew that a certain breeding was required, or a title, at least, if the bloodline was not there.

An elf of Oberon's court sponsor a family or person and grant them access to the upper class, even a permanent appointment, much like Gareth had hoped to receive from House Vastra. Sometimes, depending on the mood of the Summer Court, a position could be created for a new friend of the court. *Often,* however, a méith house was de-elevated and replaced with another.

Fuerian tapped his lips thoughtfully while Gareth continued to subtly cajole him in his playful yet bumbling way.

"Mister smarty-elf can't recall what it's from…" Gareth trailed off and then chuckled into his mug as he slugged back another mouthful.

Fuerian turned to regard his friend with narrow, calculating eyes. A look that made Gareth stiffen; the elf had seen Fuerian give that glare before.

Gareth's eyes turned up to the name with so many hash marks on the dueling leader board. Around the middle of the ranked list sat the name of a cantankerous fey who'd given Fuerian endless grief. *Glenric's name.* Gareth, and a few other friends, had helped dig Glenric a shallow grave; Glenric hadn't survived long past the duel.

"Of course I remember," Fuerian said coolly. "From our days at the academy."

Fuerian hadn't given any new information beyond what Gareth had already shared in the alleyway, but Gareth shut up and nodded as if accepting that Fuerian had practically named the elf.

Gareth is a toady, Fuerian recognized, hoping he would still be up to the task of a joint venture to take over the dream hallow trade. He needed someone he could manipulate like a marionette, but who was also strong enough to operate without strings.

Stór Rúnda meant Secret Store *in the high speech,* Fuerian reflected.

Like the guest professor who had taught that lecture, Stór Rúnda was obscure. *Secret.* That teacher remained in the background, doing business and earning wealth, which was exactly the sort of connection Fuerian desired if he was to pursue trading in the dream hallow.

Perhaps that is why he has not sought to become méith? One has greater freedom in the darkness if he has never been in the light.

Through the course of the lecture, the guest speaker walked through the steps of building an unknown company, *Stór Rúnda,* and then, once all the pieces were prepared, aggressively overtaking the competition, subverting the market, and branching out until the secret store became a household name.

But Stór Rúnda had never been a real company, Fuerian mused. He'd checked, long ago. *But it is now... and if its doing business in the apothiks then it would be wise to invest in the startup phase. Silently, if possible.*

"He always used the same company name, each year he gave the lecture," Fuerian said.

Gareth looked at him with recognition that Fuerian *did* in fact remember.

Fuerian named the elf and Gareth nodded with quick, shallow bobs.

"It was his hypothetical company for the same talk he did annually." Fuerian threw back a big swig from his mug, feeling that he'd earned it. "I need you to run out to the academy and find out how to contact him."

"And then what?" Gareth asked.

"Set a meeting. Mention dream hallow if its necessary to get his attention, but I want to sit down with him," Fuerian insisted.

Gareth threw back the remainder of his drink, turned and headed for the door.

J AIRA POKED HER HEAD around the lashed poles that a market vendor had used to construct her simple booth. The stall's sidewalls draped sheer panels and boughs of bound fabrics that partly obstructed the busy square. The smells of smoky tandoori cooked meats permeated the airs, doing its best to mask the sour odors of unwashed bodies of the lower casted elves and the musky aromas of those fey creatures who were not of elven descent.

She sifted through fabrics and other sundries as she glanced around, hoping she was not so clearly hoping to chance an encounter with Remy in the market. She had company. Her father had insisted she take Vennumyn along if Jaira was planning on going into the city today.

Vennumyn the snitch, she accused, without saying the words allowed.

Earlier, her father had insisted that she go to retrieve some sundries that the house staff failed to receive, earlier. The Morgensteen estate usually had a delivery wagon at least once per week, but some of Harhassus's vendors seemed to be regularly slipping and failed to deliver their goods.

At first, Jaira had feared the worst, that the family had welched on a debt, and creditors were withholding goods from them. But Harhassus was not an elf to let his word be smirched. Jaira soon realized that their spotty deliveries were all related to perishable foods.

Even now, she watched Vennumyn argue with an egg vendor at his wagon across the aisle where it was parked below the signpost marking the zone as a boundary for duelists with its emblematic sigil. The she-elf shook an order ticket at a cantankerous farmer in bare feet; his ears drooped as Vennumyn berated him.

Poor farmer... nobody deserves to be forced into Vennumyn's company. Jaira was smart enough to realize the source of ire from her father's contractors: Harhassus Morgensteen had a penchant for innovative new toys, gadgets like the hovering carriage the Morgensteens had lost when Jaira first met Remy.

Harhassus'd recently had installed some kind of new system in the estate's stock room. A buried line provided an akasha drip to power a cooling chamber that kept everything stored there at a frigid temperature. It reduced the waste and overage in addition to extending the time foods could be kept. Her father had figured it would pay for itself within a couple years—but he had not expected his suppliers to be so angered by his forward thinking.

Despite the dull roar of the crowded market, Jaira's ears twitched at a kind of metallic, grinding sound. The steady murmur ceased and then whirred as some akashic device adjusted nearby. Then it fell silent again.

"A-hcm," a female voice cleared her throat very close by.

Jaira turned to find a legless elf seated in her chair. She had folded her arms and waited for Jaira, clearly desiring to speak to her.

The disabled elf looked strikingly familiar to Jaira who blanched at her appearance. Jaira stiffened as if pierced suddenly by the Gaoth Sidhe—the chill wind of ill omens. *I have seen her before... in my dreams.*

Jaira refused to think about her dreams, and for good reasons. Instead, she concentrated on the chair-bound elf's face.

Her skin was darker, and some features of the woman's face made her think of Thoranmir. Jaira blushed and only just realized she must have been his relation. She cocked her head and recalled a name for the she-elf. *Anya Shelton. She handles my family's interests in the aither.*

Jaira asked, "Are you Thoramir's—"

"He is my brother, Miss Morgensteen," Anya interrupted, making Jaira raise her eyebrows.

Jaira nodded, stepping closer so that their voices would not carry to spies. *Well, to Vennumyn, at least.*

"How can I help you, Miss Shelton?"

"Just Anya is fine." She adjusted her volume accordingly. "I saw you in the market and thought to engage you in conversation."

"And here we are," Jaira said.

Anya tried to smile, but it came across as unfriendly. "You know that your fiancé is a killer?"

Jaira's eyebrows rose a moment. She shrugged, surrendering the matter. "I know what he is... and I know why it is that you fear Fuerian."

Her eyes began to cloud with a kind of misty opaqueness, like a window frosted by winter's chill. It seemed to come on without her intention, and then Jaira trembled and then shook it away.

"Y-you're a seer?" Anya whispered. Arcanists gifted with future-sight were the most sought after—and they were often taken, forced into service, and sometimes abused. Their prognosticative gifts were so precious that they had to remain hidden for their own safety, even from the remainder of the spell-casting community. That often meant they lacked the proper training, and sometimes had poor control.

Jaira opened her mouth to dispute Anya, but she remained silent. She looked across to see Vennumyn still bickering with the vendor, though the chaperon did cast furtive, suspicious glances at Jaira and her new friend.

Dropping to one knee, Jaira took Anya's hand and made a serious decision. "I am entrusting you with this secret. You know what it could cost me if this were known—it would dangerous."

Anya nodded slowly and suggested, "Even more so than consorting with a human."

Jaira agreed with a mirthless grin. "Far more so." She sighed and resumed the conversation where they'd left off. "I know why you fear for Thoranmir, but I also know that *only Remy* stands a chance of beating Fuerian."

"You have seen this outcome?" Anya whispered.

"Yes," Jaira whispered in an equally quite tone. "But I only scc potential futures, like broken images of a mirror, distorted by angles at each fracture point. I only see things that *might be*... and only when the sight takes me... I... I don't control it."

Anya fixed her with a hard, cold stare. "Your visions. You've seen my brother." It was not delivered as a question.

Jaira tilted her head with acknowledgment.

"Tell me what you have seen."

"I can not," Jaira whispered, insistently. "I can not tell it all. And I know not which is his end."

Anya snapped her head to Jaira. Her words confirmed the aithermancer's fear: *his end*.

Jaira's eyes welled up. "I know only the *potential* futures."

"Tell me."

Jaira's eyes reddened and she crossed her arms, hugging them to her body. "Some of the futures I've seen for him are extraordinary. One is painful. Brutal and tragic."

"For you or for my brother?" Anya asked.

Jaira shook her head, not providing an answer. She bit her fist to close off memory of what she had seen. "There were many outcomes. So many. And in every one of them *you* are there. For better or for worse, in both the best and the worst of the outcomes."

"And my brother?" Anya asked.

When Jaira did not answer, Anya asked again, but louder, "And my brother?"

"He remains in only one of them... one of the more extreme outcomes," Jaira said, trying to sound convincing and hopeful.

It was Anya's turn to fall silent.

"Portents are not written in stone," she told the elf she'd entrusted with a secret that could damn the only heir of the Morgensteen house. "Please. You've got to understand that—"

"Revoke my brother's invitation," Anya interrupted again.

Jaira regarded her as if the legless elf had slapped her. "I can not."

"Sure you can. You're family are the ones putting this whole thing on. Just dis-invite him, or whatever."

"I have seen futures where I tried. He will not accept it if I force him out of the contest," Jaira said. "I've seen it. He might seem like a sidekick, but Thoranmir is very stubborn," she looked down at Anya, realizing the family resemblance went beyond mere facial similarities.

Jaira held her breath, hoping Anya would accept her answer, hoping she would not call her bluff.

She'd seen many futures. Safe futures. Outcomes where Fuerian won and Thoranmir was safe. In none of those was Remy present, or likely alive.

In some visions, she was Fuerian's plaything, in others she fell under his thrall, and in others her mind and soul had been hollowed out by some unknown force leaving her a shadow of her self.

And looking forward even further, she saw her final destination: the shadow elf. Some terrifying figure who plagued her dreams—but she refused to let that potential end haunt her dreams and she pushed it out of her mind.

Regardless of the shadowy elf, Thoramir's safety means the end of me—it is the only guaranteed outcome. She bit her lip. *Every other result leads to Fuerian... and that brings me one step closer to the villain.* She was not certain that the elf who terrorized her visions was *not* Fuerian. And right now, it did not matter.

"Damn it. He *is* a stubborn sidhe," Anya flashed Jaira a stern glare. "But I'll see he finds his way out of the contest on my own, then, without *you* doing anything. The visions you talk about all mention extremes; so I hope you have a very mediocre future. Good day, Miss Morgensteen. Regardless of outcomes, your secret will remain safe with me. I know what it is to be different."

Anya thumbed the control stick on her mobile akashic contraption and the wheel sprang to life, pivoting her and carrying her away before her stern mask could crack.

Jaira only started to call after Anya when a loud voice pierced the sky. A challenge rang out in the market. Nearby, one duelist flung aside his cloak where he'd been keeping to the shadows and waiting for his opportunity. He bellowed his right to demand the contest to another duelist who stood, blinking with surprise. The attacked fighter was just trying to get something to eat as dinner time neared.

The surprised elf wore a pin with a single green ribbon for completing a private contract. The challenger boasted six short, yellow ribbons with a thin, red stripe beneath his dueling marker.

Both elves were young, about Jaira's age, faces flush with youth and naivety.

Metal rang as swords were drawn. The crowds cleared and a woman screamed as the space cleared rapidly to make room for the fight.

Jaira rolled her eyes at the challenger. "Damn honor flag hunters." She had little respect for elves who waited around, hiding in the hopes of poaching relatively easy victories so they could boast more ribbons, and thus, create prestige and then upcharge for their services.

Vennumyn hurried through the crowd and snared Jaira and tugged her away from the battle as blades crossed. The fighters thrusted and parried clumsily.

"Things're getting dangerous in the market. No place for a lady. Look at you—pale white as if you'd been munched on by the cail-leach. Now come away, we must return to the house," Vennumyn insisted.

Jaira continued watching, even as the maid dragged her away. But her eyes were not on the combat. They were on Anya, whose wheeled chair belched a trickle of glittering akashic steam as it moved.

And then the crowd, thirsty for blood, obscured the elf and her chair.

Finally, Anya turned and went with Vennumyn.

REMY QUICKENED THEIR PACE as they emerged in a nicer part of town. Buildings here were taller, and of a better construction, more statuesque. This part of Cathair Dé appealed to the eye, as much art as it was function. Streets were better, green-space broke up medians, and aither wires and akasha delivery lines were hidden along sight-lines or buried to keep the view of the sky uncluttered. It was a place even elites could feel comfortable in.

"You seem in a hurry," Thoranmir noted.

Remy let his friend catch up so they were shoulder to shoulder and walking lockstep. "We're being followed."

"What? You're sure?" Thoranmir lost a half step while turning his head.

"Now is not the time to gawk," Remy insisted. "Where is the nicest inn nearby?"

"Gawk?" Thoranmir seemed to take personal offense. "I thought you said we'd lose any pursuit a borough ago."

"We should have. You didn't notice them?" Remy asked. "Three pairs of thugs. The first two gave up when I'd thought. The one still tailing us is more persistent. They have more at stake. Now where's the inn?"

Thoranmir pointed to a large, stone structure with architectural flourishes. He looked back and spotted the pair of elves. One had a bruised and misshapen cheekbone and the other boasted a dried trickle of blood from scalp to neck. They both looked familiar—and had come under the duo's fists.

Remy grabbed his friend and keep pace. "It's personal for those two."

"What does that mean?"

"It means they intend to kill us," said Remy.

They passed a large fountain in the courtyard of the pristine lodging house and hurried up the stairs. At a landing, worked stone statues of dvergr make flanked them. One figure was of Oberon, long-time king of the Summer Court and the seelie kingdom. The other depicted his brother, the once and future unseelie ruler: Wulflock.

"What—*kill us*?" Thoranmir complained, but was cut short when an elf with a rapier stepped outside.

Clearly tasked with security services, he watched Remy and Thoranmir take their final two steps up to the entrance.

Remy withdrew a coin from his purse while simultaneously slipping Jaira's hoop earring around his smallest finger so he wouldn't misplace it again. It was the largest denomination he had, but he had to put on an air for his plan to work.

"We're just checking in for the night," Remy told him, circumventing questions by placing the coin in the elf's hand and guessing it was customary to tip for service in this part of the city. He wasn't watching earlier and so he wasn't certain how much coin Thoranmir had taken from the dream hallow sellers, but Remy hoped it was sufficient to cover the lodging costs.

The sentry nodded measuredly as he opened the door for the guests, but his eyes remained suspicious of them and burned a hole in the back of Remy's neck as they walked.

"You've got the cash," Remy whispered as they approached a businesslike she-elf at the front counter. "Get us a room overlooking the front."

Thoranmir nodded and secured the room, prepaying for it in exchange for the key. He jested about a rough travel schedule and rigors of the road to allay any suspicion for their un-wealthy appearance despite such an opulent venue.

Moments later, they were inside their room.

As Thoranmir locked the door, Remy peeled back the draperies and searched the courtyard. His friend joined him seconds later and they spotted their pursuers: two wounded young elves sat on the fountain ledge, just waiting for their opportunity. Watching and waiting as darkness fell.

CHAPTER NINE

━ ✦ ━

FUERIAN DISMOUNTED HIS HORSE after Naz gave him an hand sign indicating the scene was safe. Gareth followed suit on the horse behind him.

"You're sure this is the place?" Gareth asked him.

Fuerian shrugged. "You're the one who provided me with the address for Stór Rúnda. I merely arranged our invitation."

Stór Rúnda was an egg farm on the outskirts of a rural village a short ride south of Cathair Dé. Long rows of crude, slat buildings stretched into the distance and the unmistakable, pungent scent of poultry hung heavy in the midday air. Worse yet, low casted elves walked from the laying buildings to the storage facility with baskets filled with eggs in each hand.

Naz nodded his nose towards the main office, a squat bungalow removed just far enough that the smell was likely lessened there. He approached, and before he could knock, the door swung open.

Naz entered and then an arm motioned for them to join him.

Fuerian and Gareth hurried to the door and were promptly greeted by a dozen elves holding crossbows at their faces. Another mercenary held a blade to Naz's neck. Beyond that, a familiar looking elf sat in an elegant looking wingback chair.

"Come on in," he said, placing a finger to his lips to indicate they should not speak. "The air inside is so much better."

Gareth grimaced, but Furian kept a calm demeanor. He had half expected something like this.

The party entered. Once Naz had finished disarming himself, he was allowed to stand with the others.

"Greetings, old friend," Fuerian said. "The air *is* better in here. No odor at all," he noted.

The elf had aged slightly since their last meeting on the academy grounds. But aging for the sidhe came much different than it did for humans, or for other members of fey species for that matter.

"I have a *very* talented mage at my disposal for such things as a mystic sphere to keep the stench at bay." Their host continued, "You are wise to have abstained from using my name," he said. "These elves have orders to shoot you immediately if you use any other name than the one I will give you. None of those under my employ know my true identity—so I was quite shocked to have received a letter from you noting the connection to my secret business ventures."

"What shall we call you, then?" Fuerian asked.

"Nhywyllwch shall suffice. It is the name my employees know."

Fuerian nodded, but Gareth asked, "If we made the connection, is it possible that others will as well?"

Nhywyllwch shook his head. "You and your peers were the last to have heard me speak of Stór Rúnda, so that outcome is very unlikely."

Fuerian narrowed his eyes, noting that Nhywyllwch gave away nothing to his forces. They had no information with which to betray the elf. *Playing very close to his vest, indeed.*

Nhywyllwch signaled for the others to lower their weapons and the crossbows pointed to the floor instead of to the gangster's guests. "You demanded this meeting, Fuerian Vastra. So speak. Tell me what you want."

Fuerian winced at the use of his name. The irony was not lost on him that Nhywyllwch treated him much as he treated Gareth.

Straightening and smoothing out his coat, Fuerian reached into a pocket and produced a tube of dream hallow. He turned it between his fingers with amusement. "A remarkable product with many designer applications. It could be used recreationally, or as a tool to relax the chastity vows of young maidens. I have half a mind to ply it upon my fiancée in order to gentle what I suspect will be an overbearingly obstinate she-elf."

Nhywyllwch offered him a half smirk in response. "I am familiar with the Morgensteen family."

Fuerian continued, "We know that you are the source of the dream hallow. A remarkable product, and one with a huge potential. It is fairly new, or at least its presence is somewhat recent in Cathair Dé. When asking any local apothecary about it, none of them have any inkling how to make it." Fuerian gave his best business-like grin. "You have a product with high potential demand and a clamoring repeat sale."

Nhywyllwch looked unimpressed. "Yes. And?"

"When Gareth first convinced me there was a huge market for this, that the potential profits could be substantial, I did my market research. You do not have market penetration, my friend. Dream hallow is only available locally and in a few neighboring towns. *You need distribution—someone to take care of the ground-level operations,*" said Fuerian.

"So you want in on my operation?" Nhywyllwch chuckled, leaning forward. "I do remember you, Mister Vastra. And you always did strike me as an ambitious little shit, you know that?"

Fuerian shrugged sheepishly. "Probably true, though you're perhaps the first with enough audacity to say as much aloud."

Nhywyllwch stood, pushing the chair back with his legs. "But that ambition might serve you well in certain roles where you might prove useful. That is…" [If we can come to a formal agreement,] he shifted into the olde tongue to reinforce the point.

[Certainly, that can be arranged,] he responded. "I have ideas. Plans for how an injection of money could stimulate the movement and sale of the dream hallow into other communities. I just need a little time to get the capital together. You know, I'm to be married soon, and it will be easier to draw on certain accounts once the wedding is concluded."

"I don't want you money, and I have little time or desire for the trappings of the sidhe upper castes," said Nhywyllwch.

"If you don't want money or influence, then why push the dream hallow at all?" Fuerian asked, wondering if Nhywyllwch did it for pure recreation—if he was a user himself. *If that's the case, we could never do business; he'd prove far too unreliable.*

"You will see, young Mister Vastra," Nhywyllwch looked down his nose at his guests. "There is something I want far more than money. And you're going to help me get it."

MORNING HAD BROUGHT A renewed sense of optimism for Thoranmir. Not only had Remy's plan to throw their pursuit off the trail of Anya's home worked, but he'd slept in the most comfortable bed ever designed. Nevermind the tossing and turning one generally experiences when a drug addled street gang wants to murder you... but aside from *that*.

He sat up and yawned. He turned so his legs touched the floor when he spotted Remy at the window.

Remy surveyed the courtyard with wary eyes like prey approaching food when predators roamed nearby.

"Are they still there?" Thoranmir asked.

"No," Remy said, finally letting the curtains fall back to cover the view of the fountain. "I saw them finally leave last night. I think they realized how conspicuous they were in this part of town."

"As if we're any better?" Thoranmir quipped.

Remy shrugged. "But we're hidden, laying low in a private room... plus we can ring a concierge and have them deliver us some clothes so we'll blend in."

Thoranmir wondered aloud, "Do you think they'll try again?"

Remy shook his head. "No. I think that gang took probably took the warning to heart. These two idiots let their pride get in the way and once a little time had passed, they probably thought better of picking a fight with the two guys that had already kicked their entire group's collective ass." A moment passed. "The darkness."

"Pardon?" Thoranmir asked, not understanding.

"Darkness has a way of doing that—making you feel small and alone. Vulnerable. It bleeds the hubris out of the cocky and makes them second guess themselves. I won't say we've seen the last of them, but they aren't likely to come looking for us, at least. But be on guard near your sister's home, for sure."

Thoranmir rubbed his chin and agreed. A broad grin spread wide on his face.

After staring at his friend for a long moment, Remy asked, "What's so funny?"

"A tenday ago we were breaking our backs for bent coppers, and *now?*" Thoranmir stood and grabbed his purse, upending it and dumping the coins upon the bed. They bounced, and clinked; several bounded onto the floor and rolled in spinning loops.

Remy whistled.

It was no small amount.

"*They* might not chase us down, but whoever they owed this money to might come looking for us," Remy warned.

Thoranmir imitated a sad face. "So much for those fancy clothes," he said. "So what do we do with all this money?"

"First, we split it up, I guess. Like we've always done," Remy suggested. While they made two even piles, he asked, "Can you think of anything you said that might let the gang know who we are?"

"No," Thoranmir shook his head, pausing to search his memory. "I don't think I said your name aloud at all." He hoped his memory was correct. "That thief might have been watching and waiting during our sparring session, though."

Remy thought it over, and then ruled that out. "No. He was just a kid. It wasn't a planned job—he saw my purse and snatched it as a crime of opportunity. Classic grab and run. If he'd have watched us for more than a few seconds he would have known enough to leave us alone."

Thoranmir nodded, seeing the thread of logic. He tossed the last remaining coin into the air after an odd count. "Heads its mine, tails its yours?"

Remy snatched it mid-flip. "No. Tip the housekeeper." He tossed the coin onto the dresser drawer set.

Thoranmir shrugged. He was suddenly unworried about a spare coin, coincidentally valued at a full day's wage of a ditch digger. The Thoranmir of one month prior would have been worried by that fact. It wasn't enough of a sum to consider himself rich, but it could buy a fresh start. It was more like gaining a sudden inheritance than becoming wealthy and affluent overnight. It would not give Thoranmir access to a life of méith... but he could pretend for a day or two.

"So what will you do with your half?" Thoranmir asked.

"I have plans."

"So do I," said Thoranmir. "Big plans."

FUERIAN RODE ABREAST OF Nhywyllwch as the entire party from the egg farm traveled the road. Aside from the ever watchful glower of Naz Charnazar, there existed little tension in the group.

Gareth rode a half a stride behind Fuerian, lagging slightly, but he was not a critical part of the conversation, which did not touch on their business in the slightest.

Nhywyllwch had promised they would return to that topic as soon as they arrived at their destination. He wouldn't divulge *where* that location was, or *what* it was, either. That provided reason enough to give Naz the ulcer it appeared he was giving himself.

"Then the fool hit the tree branch while trying to come after me. Smacked him right in the face!" Fuerian laughed.

"You agreed to this fight without even having a weapon?" Nhywyllwch laughed. He seemed to hang on every word. He was a true dueling fan and admitted at the outset of taking the road that he followed all the standings. But he was especially interested in the more local area rankings than in the high end status seekers tracked by the guild of mavens who oversaw the king's interests in sport dueling.

Fuerian nodded vigorously. "Yumiah was a huge fool, and an even worse swordsman. Carried this rapier with a massive and gaudy basket hilt. When the branch hit him in the face, he dropped the thing, so I stepped on the handle with one foot and grabbed Yumiah by the ears and pulled him to me, running him through on his own blade."

Nhywyllwch winced at the thought. "He died?"

Fuerian nodded. "No. He got lucky. But the idiot never dueled again. Stopped coming to the Barrel and Thistle altogether, even. I hear he's running customs at the river port... and he's apparently an even worse accountant than he is an amateur duelist. But his father holds a title so he is méith. He could burn the place to rubble and ash and he'd keep his job because of that."

The kingpin elf grew quiet and stared ahead a few moments, as if evaluating exactly how valuable an alliance with the future head of the Vastra House might be to him. Fuerian knew he was building a strong case.

After half a day's ride they came to an ever more barren scrap of land where the highways were broad and visibility stretched for leagues in any given direction. Hot winds had eroded patches of ground and exposed thin tubes of copper that stretched perpendicular to the road.

Ahead of them, in the distance, was the crossroads: a junction of four major highways. Each one led to a city. Near the junction, the copper lines rose out of the soil and lifted high into the air where they were mounted on T posts so that the tubes crossed from all four corners and fed into the single building at the distant intersection.

"That is where we are going," Nhywyllwch pointed.

"To the pump station?" Gareth asked.

Their guide nodded.

"You must first see, in order to understand."

Heading west on the highway, a team of mules pulled a long trailer. The load was settled on akashic repulsors so that the cargo, a massive cylinder nearly twice the length of a large house, rode behind the mules. The repulsors were the same arcane machinery that was built in Harhassus Morgensteen's now destroyed carriage. Without wheels, it meant the cargo created no friction with the road; once it was in motion, it took very little to keep it in motion allowing for weighted loads far heavier than in previous centuries.

Fuerian squinted. "Is that an akashic tank?"

"Yes," Nhywyllwch informed him.

Fuerian tried to calculate the value of the tanker's contents. The fillers were rare and well defended. Guards stood atop the cylinder. They were outfitted with tower shields that had arrow slots cut in place and were welded onto place for mobile defense.

How akasha was produced was a crown secret, another resource under the purview of Oberon's mavens: the governing body of spell casters. However it was made, the supply had finally increased enough that the Summer Court began running supply lines to cities so that everyday fey had access to the wondrous technology.

Before they arrived at the pump house, the massive freight hauler had come to a rest outside its doors. Workers opened a trapdoor in the cylinder and bled its contents into a drainage grate. Fine granules of amber and gold fell like someone had unloaded a desert dune made of pixie dust; the silty flume glowed with the raw energy that it contained.

Nhywyllwch led them into the main building. The aromas of cleaners, lubricants, and solvents filled the air and pulsed stronger with each wave of the *whoosh, whoosh* of the massive bellows system that was central to the facility.

All of the security team that Nhywyllwch had hired remained outside except for two. Naz chose to follow Fuerian and Gareth.

Nhywyllwch pointed to the systems of tubes and connections. A pressure valve connected to a tank and it's needle bobbed slowly and in cadence with the *whoosh, whoosh*. "It is an impressive system, is it not? Paid for off the taxes and duties owed to the Summer Court—built on the fortunes of the working and upper castes... except for the méith, of course. They are exempt from taxation."

He led them to a huge set of tanks. Between them, a large counterweight dipped below the floor and then rose again, rotating on an axis that allowed the derrick to maintain its perpetual motion and continue drawing up the contents of the akasha lines and maintaining pressure that sent the mystic fluid up and through the copper tubes which exited through the roof and then stretched away and to the smaller pumphouses in the cities.

"The raw akasha is stored in the bins below our feet," Nhywyll-wch said. "It mixes in the fluid tanks over there. The stuff doesn't *need* to be wet, but it helps move the final product through the distribution tubes and deliver it to the taps installed in homes."

Nhywyllwch looked around at the various systems with won-der-filled eyes. "It is all so very impressive."

Gareth finally interjected, "Yeah. Okay. It's all very neat, and all, but what does this have to do with dream hallow?"

Nhywyllwch turned to face the pudgier elf. "Very little. Hardly anything at all, in fact."

Gareth growled and turned away in frustration. Fuerian kept his eyes focused on the Nhywyllwch.

"This is not some eccentric interest for you," Fuerian recognized. "'Not much' is significantly different than 'nothing at all.'"

Nhywyllwch grinned. "Perceptive. Follow me to our next desti-nation."

He made for the door when Naz called after him. "This isn't another half-day trip for a ten minute tour is it?" The duelist shot Fuerian a skeptical glance, wondering how much time his employer wanted to waste on something that increasingly looked like a fools errand.

"A quarter hour, perhaps. Supper will be provided there, and sleeping quarters. The return trip is best taken in the morning," Nhywyllwch said.

Fuerian followed. Naz rolled his eyes, but he went too, leaving Gareth to bring up the rear.

J AIRA PINCHED THE BRIDGE of her nose and sat at the chair in her family's drawing room. Sometimes, when she tried to abstain from seeing a vision, her head would pulse and pound, giving her a migraine.

She rolled up the top on her desk and set a fresh piece of paper before her. She withdrew a charcoal stylus and began sketching. Having something else to concentrate on always gave her respite from the pain.

She would rather endure the sharp ache behind her eyes than see another potential variant on the same vision. Jaira could often tell which potential future she was seeing before it took full hold of her psyche. This one was the end of Jaira Morgensteen.

Jaira had seen it hundreds of different ways through the years. Many elements were always the same: a pale elf dressed all in black seized her, dragged her away. And then she saw nothing but an endless prison of glass.

In some versions, the dark elf hunted her and she was alone. In many, she was turned over to him by Fuerian—and in each of those she wore jewelry marking her as a Vastra—Fuerian's wife. And still in many others, a human protected her.

Whenever she had the human variant, she could never see a face, but she could sense in that dream state that she loved him. And he loved her.

When she first glanced Remy on the side of the road just outside Vail Carvanna she knew it was him in an instant.

She'd seen the visions before, and she had no desire to relive them again. One of them she'd have to live for real. Instead of dwelling on her thoughts, she sketched. Jaira drew happier things, hopeful outcomes. Pretty things.

Her sketch began as a figure in the woods. It's outline took shape and form, and then another body developed. The second one became a woman under her guidance, and the first figure transformed into a man. They embraced. As it took greater and greater detail, Jaira could clearly see it was her and Remy. She blushed at the image and the intimacy the two of them shared in the sketch.

After completing it, she set it aside and withdrew another sheet of paper and then set an ink and quill nearby for writing.

Remy. I have been thinking about you. Us. I cannot seem to dislodge you from my head, and I hope to see you again soon, though guardians in my life seem opposed to it. I shall be singing in the glade again at the same time on the day after tomorrow. Perhaps I will dance for you again?

Jaira folded the letter into a neatly folded parcel and noticed that her headache had disappeared.

She addressed the message to Remy using Anya's address and wrote a date upon it. She slipped her sketch inside the folded paper and took out her wax stamper which marked it as coming from her.

Jaira stood and went into the estate's main entry. Inside, a small scarsella set back from the entry making a kind of booth where a credenza sat for messages incoming and outgoing. A finely crafted stand held her father's messages meant to go out and she shuffled through the stack of them.

She checked the nearest timepiece and noted that a delivery boy would be along in less than an hour. Jaira slid her letter in amid the bundle so nobody would be the wiser, and then she slipped away, heading deeper into the estate.

Out of the shadows crept Vennumyn who leaned out from the apse to make sure Jaira could not see her rummaging through the evidence. The maid paused, finding Jaira's letter addressed to Remy.

A serpentine grin crept across her face, and she slid the letter into the pocket of her apron. She slipped away as if she'd never been there.

CHAPTER TEN

— ❖ —

R EMY AND THORANMIR STOOD together inside the long
hall made of polished stone. The entry to the chamber was
warded with anti-magic spells that gave the air a slight tingling
sensation. Various sized doors lined the walls in neat rows and rows
like a finely trained regiment of soldiers.

Thoranmir stared at his open door and the tray which he'd
pulled out from the storage box. He'd dumped his stockpile of
riches inside and stared at it longingly.

"I can't even live like a king for *one day?*" he complained to Remy.

Remy shook his head. "Not without drawing suspicion."

Thoranmir frowned some, but slid the coin-filled container
into the locking receptacle and then locked the door. He lashed
a leather lanyard around the only key to the safe box and slid it
around his neck.

Remy placed a small pouch of coins into the much smaller
unit he'd purchased. His was on the opposite wall and barely big
enough to put a fist inside, but it served his purpose. Remy had
a long, memorized list of places he'd stashed emergency supplies.

His formative years in the unseelie had taught him the value of preparation.

Funny thing, Remy scratched his head. *I remember every cache, and if I put a weapon in it—but not how much coin I have lying about.* Aside from when his stomach growled at the aroma of a restaurant or street vendor, Remy had seldom put stock in the value of money to accomplish his needs. *But a blade?*

He locked his box and slid the key into a pocket with Jaira's earring.

Thoranmir glanced at the bulging purse laid against Remy's hip. "Really? You're just going to hang onto all that coin?"

Remy shook his head and adjusted the headband which hid his ears. "I said I had plans." He motioned for Thoranmir to follow.

They walked the streets for a short while until the neighborhood lessened in quality, and then Remy stopped a patrolling constable to ask for directions.

A short while later they arrived at an orphanage. It was a run-down dump of a building which looked as if it might have once been a palatial and ornate structure. Several of the nearby buildings bore the marks of long-since faded glory indicating that this might have once been the local seat of former elites. These were undoubtedly former homes of méith elves.

Remy and Thoranmir walked up the steps, which had been thankfully preserved by some stone mason who didn't want the entrance to the place to fall off.

Within the tall doors they met a wiry elf with sallow skin and lanky hair. He wore a long robe similar to a school headmaster and he watched as a row of unwashed fey children walked single file through the atrium on their way to one activity or another.

The elf lowered his voice mid-scold as the duo entered, and then turned to greet them. "Hello gentlefolk... can I, uh, help you?"

Remy could feel the elf's eyes scan him in the mid-sentence pause. He sensed the elf judging whether or not the unannounced visitors were worth the time to bother with.

The orphanage's representative gave an almost imperceptible kind of shrug and then called to the children. "Go with Ehchai. She will lead the next lesson until I return." He returned his attention to Remy and Thoranmir.

"I am Dennariuh," he introduced with a shallow bow. "How can the Otannuh Orphanage be of assistance?"

"I'm looking into homes in the area, orphanages in Cathair Dé." Remy's eyes scanned the fey children as they passed. He noted they were mostly elves, a random dwarf, sibling fauns, and a trow draped in a heavy cloak so that the sunlight could not cause the dark elf pain. The trow child kept a hand on the elf in front of it who guided it through the hall.

"I do see you serve many, here?" Remy asked.

Dennariuh nodded. "We have one hundred and thirty-six children in our facility. Are you here considering adopting a child?"

"No. I'm just looking to do some good with an inheritance I came into suddenly," Remy responded.

"Ah! A sponsorship," Dennariuh said excitedly. "As you can see, our building is in great need of some basic repairs and, of course we always need—"

"Where are the human children?" Remy interrupted.

"Ahhhh," purred Dennariuh as if he'd ascertained Remy's true intentions. He lowered his voice a few decibels. "You have a wish to purchase a ddiymadferth. We have none in stock in the moment, but perhaps if you—"

Remy surged forward and slugged Dennariuh in the midsection, doubling the spindly elf over with a gut shot that nearly broke him in two. He ripped his bandanna off his head and let Dennariuh get a good look at his ears as the elf gasped for air and tried not to puke.

Dennariuh finally gave in and fell to his hands and knees. He puked all over the floor.

"Where?" Remy demanded. "Where can I find human children?"

With a shaking finger, Dennariuh pointed north. "Th-three blocks," he managed to choke out. Another center. Th-they have ddiymad—children of Adam there," he corrected himself.

Replacing his headband, Remy whirled on his heel and stormed out with Thoranmir chasing after. After following Dennariuh's directions, they arrived at the next facility.

Remy and Thoranmir found a staff member as easily as they had at Otannuh.

"Do you serve human children, here?" Remy asked bluntly.

The female staff member shrank back slightly and tried to get a read on Remy.

Remy slid his headband down and the she-elf nodded slowly and kept her voice quiet. "We do. But for their protection we try not to advertise that." A hopeful look crept across her face. "Are you here to find out why humans are disappearing in this region?"

He shook his head. "No. I am sorry, but I know only rumors about it."

"I wish they were mere rumors," she said. "I've not seen anything personally, but I know other orphanages will sometimes collect and sell human children. An elf came, a real nasty sort, and asked if he could purchase all the non-fey we had, as if they were cattle." She made a sickened face. "Ever since, we only tell human folk that we have any of their kind."

"Do you know what purpose they had on them?" Thoranmir asked.

She shook her head. "I can only guess slave labor. Maybe sexual deviancy? *Or worse...* he could have been anthropophagi."

Remy nodded dourly. "Thank you, you and your kin, for your service." He handed over the purse with his remaining coin. "For the continued support and protection of the children."

He replaced his head covering and left as the orphanage worker opened the satchel and gasped at its contents.

As they hit the streets Thoranmir asked, "Do you think there is some connection between the local abductions of those with spellcraft talents and someone taking humans?"

Remy screwed up his face. After a few moments thought he responded. "I don't see a link. Humans are rarely gifted with arcane abilities, we're just not built to be compatible with them."

"Well I don't know about that," Thoranmir said. "I've known people to be augmented by spells and have wildly unexpected results with magic, especially in the faewylds."

"Have you spent much time in the feral lands beyond the seelie and unseelie realms?" Remy raised a brow.

"Well, no. But I've heard stories."

"They're just stories," Remy said. "But even famous human wizards like Myrddin only achieved his power because he was a half-blood."

"Myrddin was a changeling?" Thoranmir asked, excitedly.

"No. Not half fey," Remy said. "He was a cambion."

Thoranmir shuddered and paused, losing a step. Demon incursions upon Arcadeax were not historically unknown, and keeping the denizens if the infernal realm at bay was the job of those who held thrones. Chiefly, it was Oberon's primary task to safeguard the realm, ever since the king's brother, Wulflock, had disappeared, apparently abdicating the unseelie throne.

"But Myrddin was from the earth realm, where demons have an easier time penetrating the veil between worlds," Thoranmir said, catching up.

"Exactly my point. I can't see what missing humans has to do with missing Aes Sidhe."

Thoranmir stroked his chin.

Remy knew his friend well enough to guess his thoughts. "I don't think it's a mystery you'll be able to solve. Bad stuff happens. Pick your battles."

"Well, *somebody's* got to make Arcadeax a better place," Thoranmir insisted.

"You can't take on every bad guy in Arcadeax, not even with my help," Remy said. "You already picked a fight with the dream hallow pushers. Now you want to investigate this too? Maybe you should just assume that evil is a problem everywhere and focus on what little good you gather to yourself."

"Maybe you're just a cynic."

Thoranmir's words rocked him and Remy stood straight, stopping. *Isn't that what I'm doing with my donation—helping make this world better?* He swallowed and then composed himself. *But maybe I could do more?*

"You might be right," Remy told him.

His friend looked Remy in the eye. "What good is it to gather a cluster of goodness around yourself if a larger, evil world is waiting to tear it apart?"

Remy looked at his friend. Deep down, Remy knew he was physically stronger than his friend who had the world to live for, but hadn't had to do the things Remy did. He'd been made a monster in the unseelie. He'd killed people, even as a child. Remy had been called Aderyn Corff: *the Corpse Bird*—a shadowy assassin who'd been molded into a killer by the orc warlord who had enslaved him and transformed him into a weapon of terror.

Aderyn Corff had died in the unseelie—Remy had left that world behind, but he'd felt dark thoughts return to him when he'd held his dúshlán against the neck of the apothiks dealer. *That part of me will always be there,* he swallowed the lump in his throat as he looked at his friend: a more innocent and optimistic creature who'd never had to snuff the life from another. Remy's skills had been honed to precision before he'd escaped the winter court and fled to the seelie. They were deadly skills, but necessary.

In his mind Remy heard Thoranmir's appeal on behalf of all who were weaker: *please, defend us.*

He nodded, knowingly. "Fine, fine. I'll keep my eye out for abandoned children and kidnapped mages. But let's not go looking for trouble. It's unwise to poke a sleeping cú sidhe without an escape plan—or a very good weapon."

Thoranmir nodded.

Remy knew he only appeared to let it go. His friend was committed to solving the mystery.

"Oh, hey," Thoranmir suddenly exclaimed. "Is this way back to Anya's? Are you taking us home?"

Remy nodded. "I think it's safe. Maybe. *I hope.*"

SCRUB BRUSH PROTRUDED UP from the cracked soil where the twisted bracken tried pushing leaves skyward. But in the absence of any ongoing irrigation, the greenery withered and died, like everything else on the farm. Fences were broken and posts often laid horizontal, busted at their base.

Sparse patches of grass carpeted old pastures where cattle used to graze, but most of it was now burnt away by harsh rays and the small, two story farmhouse stood in disrepair. A corner of the foundation sank noticeably and the porch roof sagged like an old man slouching uncomfortably; several rows of plank siding hung loose or were missing entirely. The cattle barn looked to be in the same condition.

Someone screamed inside the barn: roars of pain broken intermittently with babbling pleas for mercy.

Nhywyllwch led the party to the stock house and his henchmen opened the sliding doors, exposing the darkness within to the late afternoon light. A long aisle of poured masonry stretched into shadow, mirrored on either side by head restraints for holding cows in their stalls for milking. Some farmer of ages past used the aisle for easily feeding his heard from one central access.

Now, a tall elf in a black, hooded robe stood there, waiting for them. Only the pale skin of his chin was visible below his hood. His hands dripped blood.

Behind the darkly clad elf, a lone sidhe was trapped in the cattle stall with his head locked tightly in the neck restraint. He'd sunk to his knees and his face was purple and swollen. A cut leaked red over one eye and his lip had split open. The prisoner shuddered as he blubbered, fearful of what an audience meant when a single handler had beaten him beyond recognition.

"This is Hymdreiddiech. My partner and expert on all things arcane."

Fuerian bowed with a curt greeting, assuming it had been Hymdreiddiech who cleared the air at the egg farm.

Hymdreiddiech returned the gesture.

"He is an academy student?" Fuerian asked, looking the prisoner over. He wore the stole and robes of one studying mystic arts at one of the spell casting academies.

Nhywyllwch nodded. "Yes." He looked to the dark-robed elf, tossing a small pouch to his accomplice. "Show him, Hymdreiddiech."

Hymdreiddiech opened the drawstrings and produced a kind of fungus from inside. He pinched the stuff between his fingers and then grabbed their captive by the jaw and forced the contents inside his mouth, using a finger to ram it down the victim's throat before snapping the mouth shut with a loud *clack* of teeth.

He coughed and spluttered, but Hymdreiddiech held the mouth shut, even when the beaten elf vomited. Hot string of puke leaked from his lips in thin tendrils, but the poor creature kept the fungus inside until he'd swallowed everything in his mouth.

Moments later, he shook with seizures and his eyes rolled back. Hymdreiddiech released his head, but ripped the student's robes and stripped him of his clothes. The subdued student-mage fell into a trance and sweated profusely. And then he began to glow. His perspiration generated its own luminescence.

Fuerian approached cautiously, realizing what had caused it. He reached down with a finger and wiped the creature's skin. "Akasha?"

Nhywyllwch nodded silently.

"What was the stuff in the bag?" Fuerian asked.

"Foil milferra," said Nhywyllwch. "It is the necessary reagent to force the transformation."

With a head movement, a pair of Nhywyllwch's mercenaries draped a sheet below the victim to catch the raw akasha as it fell from the entranced elf. It poured out like sweat from an exhausted athlete as he shed the dust-like stuff in fine sheafs. "It is a very rare fungus. It sends one into a kind of trance much like entering the aither, only uncontrolled and filled with emotion, rather than a spiritual journey filled with order."

"The beatings help," Hymdreiddiech growled. "Terror heightens the response and the akasha production. Once the elf is on the brink of dehydration, we restore them. Hydrate them. Then we can begin again. The shedding process takes only a few minutes." He grinned smugly at the victim. "It's just a shame he wasn't a seer. You should see how much greater the production is."

Fuerian stared at the creature and Gareth stepped forward. The elite elf sensed what his partner wanted to know, but he stayed Gareth with a hand, sensing they were about to learn something significant. He did not wish to push their hosts. Instead, he asked, "How much more?"

"It can only be measured in degrees of exponents," Hymdreiddiech said.

Nhywyllwch waved the notion away. "But capturing someone with the ability to parse the future has always proved the challenge, and so we are not relying on that for my plans."

As he spoke, the henchmen took away the sheet and its pile of akasha which glowed like bioluminesent pollen. Hymdreiddiech turned the elf over and forced a waterskin into his mouth, forcing its contents into the captive until he retched.

"But this is what your friend is so cager for," Nhywyllwch pointed to the vomit. The foil milferra had crystalized inside their victim during the shedding process.

Retrieving the glassine rock, Nhywyllwch dropped it onto the hard floor and crushed it beneath his heel.

Fuerian and Gareth stared at the results once Nhywyllwch removed his boot. The pulverized shards made up the dream hallow.

"You want the dream hallow, Mister Vastra? You can have it." Nhywyllwch locked eyes with Fuerian and shared an unyielding gaze. "I have my aims set upon much bigger prizes."

"But the money," Gareth said. "There's a fortune to be made in—"

Nhywyllwch interrupted him. "That coin is a drop in the bucket when weighed against the akasha; it will soon be routed to every major seelie city in Arcadeax. Imagine how much more valuable that product is than compared to whatever coin a bunch of junkies can muster.

"While selling some dream hallow has helped generate some seed money and pay some bribes, it will not buy me access to what I need for my larger plan." He whirled to Fuerian. "You know my true name. But you might not know that Harhassus Morgensteen has an intense dislike of me. A hatred that dates to our mutual days at university. I must acquire only one thing." Nhywyllwch held the gaze with Fuerian, searching him to see if he'd figured it out.

Fuerian had. "Foil Milferra?"

Nhywyllwch nodded. "Harhassus owns a failed mine. It's a squat piece of worthless land, but he will not sell it. Not to me, anyway. But as the son-in-law and heir, you will inherit it."

"I've heard of his mine. He quit operations because of all the iron ore. Nobody would work the mine... stuff makes the skin burn like nettle-oil."

"Worse, actually," Nhywyllwch shuddered. "But you're right. And in the absence of workers, the foil milferra bloomed. It grows only upon iron, something no fey can touch."

Fuerian narrowed his eyes. "Then how will you harvest it?"

"Leave that to us," Nhywyllwch said.

Hymdreiddiech came to his side. "Plans have already been in motion for quite some time."

"Fuerian will provide you with access to the foil milferra and you will give us the dream hallow trade?" Gareth reiterated.

"Plus twenty percent on the akasha profits," Fuerian interjected, not wanting to give away what he recognized was an enormous amount of money he could siphon from the coffers of every city in the kingdom at no cost to himself and through a completely legal manner.

Nhywyllwch raised a brow as he laughed. "You take your business to heart, I see. It's a wonder the Vastra clan has not yet ceded authority to a better-headed entrepreneur. I hear your family is—"

Fuerian cut him off, not wanting to discuss his family politics. "My time is coming. And soon. But the deal? Twenty percent?"

Hymdreiddiech slid his hood back, revealing his face and his empty, disturbing pink eyes and clear hair and eyebrows. The elf was an albino. And now that they'd seen his face, Fuerian knew they would not escape this farm alive if an agreement was not reached. "One percent," he growled.

Fuerian looked at the elf. He was definitely a mage, and likely of considerable strength. Fuerian knew that others rightly considered the heir of House Vastra to be a dangerous person—but even Fuerian's blood ran cold at the thought of fighting a spell caster. He'd already seen what Hymdreiddiech was capable of with the young prisoner in the milking stall.

"Ten percent," Fuerian said, stiffening his inner resolve.

"Every percent you take cuts into my share of profits." Hymdreiddiech bared his teeth. He countered, "Five."

Nhywyllwch interrupted, "You'll not do better than seven and a half, Vastra. I suggest you take it."

Fuerian grinned. "We have a deal."

Nhywyllwch bowed. "Then we shall be in touch soon. Meanwhile, you might avail yourself of the farmhouse. Supper will be provided, and you can return home at dawn."

Fuerian looked face to face from Gareth and Naz; neither were comfortable here. "We'll leave now, if that's acceptable. We'll be home late, but I'd prefer to stick close to Cathair Dé. I have something of a human infestation right now."

"By all means," Nhywyllwch motioned to the road.

Fuerian bowed and exited politely. He and his companions climbed into their saddles and made all haste back home, knowing that their arrival would be late, and even then, they'd have to push their mounts.

The ride was long, and wearying. Fuerian's mind turned over with countless machinations as he traveled. But there would be time enough to revisit them later, across a table instead between saddles. And he could use a night's sleep, first.

He rode his horse directly up to the apartment he owned in Cathair Dé. Gareth peeled off and headed to his own home.

Traffic was light at this hour, except the handful of courteseans who made it a point to pass by the apartment; it was no secret to the beautiful women of Cathair Dé that Fuerian often paid for companionship.

A small cluster of painted ladies parted to reveal a woman with whithering features and a scowl that seemed permanent. She wore the robes of a lady's maid.

Fuerian stopped his horse and dismounted. Naz did likewise and took the reins of both horses, leading them to the stables. "Vennumyn," Fuerian greeted her.

Vennumyn hurriedly bowed. "Mister Vastra. I have news." She held out the opened letter.

Jaira's sketch fell to the ground and Fuerian snatched it up.

He examined it with a snarl, shredding it and throwing it into the gutter. Fuerian scanned the note. "Thank you for coming to me with this." He deposited a few coins into Vennumyns hands and then gave her back the letter.

"See that it gets to where it is going," he ordered.

"My lord?" Vennumyn wilted beneath Fuerian's gaze. He did not like her questioning him. "I will see it done."

Fuerian watched her go. He had a plan. Fuerian was a dangerous elf. And he intended to press that very point on the morrow.

Anya wheeled over to her brother as soon as he and Remy walked through the door. She grabbed him as if urgent, and pulled him close, practically melting against him. Thoranmir tugged away after a moment, but Anya only held on tighter.

"By the Dagda, Anya. I was only gone one night. You'd think I had left forever," Thoranmir said.

Anya peered past him with eyes that moistened at their edges, they locked on Remy. She finally released him. "I know," she did a mostly passable job of keeping the worry from fraying her voice. "But you left before..."

"I said I'd be gone a month," Thoranmir said.

"And you were gone more than a year. I'd feared the worst," she said. "I... I don't know what I thought. Your friend's crazy girlfriend said that..." She trailed off, noting that she could not explain what prophecy Jaira had seen—and if she tried, her brother's doom was guaranteed.

"I'm just—just so..." She finally sighed to clear her exasperation. Anya tweaked her chair so that it turned to Remy. "I'm sorry. I didn't mean to speak ill of Jaira."

Remy offered her a warm smile of understanding. "I only wish that what you said was true."

"That she is crazy?" Anya asked.

"That she was my girlfriend. You know Jaira?"

Anya shrugged. "The Morgensteens are a client. I bumped into her the other day and... well, I think my mood got the better of me. There's been a suspicious elf hanging around outside all day. It's had me kind of spooked."

Thoranmir stiffened and sank back against the wall while Remy hurried to the window and peeled back the draperies to check the visibility. Thoranmir mouthed the words to Remy, *Dream hallow*.

A knock broke the dense silence that had fallen inside the apartment.

Anya's chair burped a toot of akashic exhaust as she adjusted its angle and then steered it towards the door. She glanced back to the two males in her apartment as if angry for the drama that they'd brought to her doorstep.

Remy had tensed to strike if need be. Thoranmir tried to hide behind a piece of furniture. *Surely to get the element of surprise*, she gave him the benefit of the doubt.

She pulled back the door and then relaxed her grip on the handle. She chatted in a dull murmur the others would not be able to hear. The curiosity bought them over and they peeked at a finely dressed man.

He looked a little surprised to see the two others there, but regarded Remy with curiosity. "You are Remy Keaton?" he asked.

Remy nodded, and then the elf produced a folded parchment sealed with a smudged wax seal, but dated and addressed to him.

"Apologies, it seems to have stuck to some legal documents that were delivered to me today. Wet wax, and all. Sometimes that happens."

Remy squinted at him. "You are a lawyer?"

The elf nodded. He wore a goofy, curved hat and fancy clothes. "And I've been waiting here most of the day to catch you." He handed the envelope over.

The letter was addressed to Remy Keaton at Anya's address and the lettering was in a flowing, feminine script. She muttered a few barely intelligible words about being a halfway house and visitors receiving post at her address.

As the lawyer sized up the man, he spoke mostly to himself. "Remy Keaton... so you're the human they decided to let in to the contest?"

He turned his eyes to Remy, hoping for some kind of interaction when Anya barked, "Good day," and slammed the door in his face.

"Well that was a little rude," Thoranmir noted. "And he wasn't strange. He was dressed like a wealthy, successful practitioner. "

"I know Count Fohmin," Anya groused. "There's only one reason a wealthy elf was doing a mail delivery—and it's the same reason he was overly interested in Remy. I've seen records on him. Huge gambling debts. He was interested in seeing if the underdog human competitor might make it past the first round of the tournament so he could hedge bets."

"I'm the underdog?" Remy asked with surprise.

Thoranmir shrugged. "I'd bet on you."

Remy sniffed the letter's inside after breaking the wax stamp. He smiled.

It's from Jaira, Anya decided.

"She sent me a letter," Remy confirmed with a broad grin spreading across his face. "I'm going to see her tomorrow."

"A letter," Thoranmir said, tapping his lip thoughtfully as he peeked out the window at Count Fohmin as the lawyer walked away. He glanced back to Anya and returned to the previous conversation. "Strange... indeed. I kind of fancy the look," said Thoranmir. "Someday I'm going to be wealthy and successful, and I'm going to look the part, too. Floppy clothes and all."

Anya stared at him a long moment. "I hope so. I really, really hope so."

CHAPTER ELEVEN

T HE NIGHT HAD COME and gone. An industrious printer delivered local news in the early morning hours, leaving the folded papers on doorsteps. Bound within, at the center pages, was the leaflet most of Cathair Dé's populace cared about: news regarding the dueling contests.

Remy had cooked a small breakfast, not expecting Anya to dote on him—especially after the dangers he'd brought to her house. The empty plates had yet to be cleared from the table. One plate still had food on it; the biscuits had gone cold and the thin gravy with salty meat lumps had congealed. Remy and Anya had watched it thicken as it cooled.

Thoranmir had not arisen for breakfast yet.

"Thank you for the breakfast," Anya said quietly. Something clearly bothered her and it was written all over her face. "Do you remember what you'd promised me—that you'd get my brother to drop out of this foolish duel?"

Remy's brows knit, but he nodded. That hadn't quite been the way of it—Remy didn't make promises that he wasn't absolutely sure he could keep—but he understood her meaning, and the tension in her voice revealed how important it was to her.

"I do," Remy said.

"He's got to back out soon, I think," Anya said. "Have you asked him about it yet?"

Every day, he wanted to say. But Remy hadn't overtly pressed the point. "I will speak with him today."

A melancholy smile spread across Anya's face. She seemingly knew that conversation was going to cost Remy something. "Thank you," she said.

Remy noted the desperation in her eyes. He knew that dueling was dangerous, deadly, even. Thoranmir knew it too. But Anya seemed to feel the effects of the worst possible outcome. *Could she be a seer? Maybe some talent developed or accessible within the aither?*

He put the thought out of his mind. Seers, *real* seers who could see the future, were extremely sought after—and hinting that you possessed the gift was a dangerous proposition. Remy didn't think Anya liked him enough to entrust him with such secrets.

A few minutes later, Anya rolled over to her work station and set a contraption on her head so that she could enter the aitherspphere and do the work which she had been contracted for.

Remy returned his attention to the newsprint. He glowered at the block print of Fuerian. Some talented artist had taken license to make the elf, well, good looking. Remy scowled at the paper, suddenly somehow jealous of ink, paper, and lies.

A door opened and Thoranmir finally emerged from his room, though not disheveled and zombie-like as one might have expected from an over-sleeper. He came out chipper and spring-stepped, and eager to chat.

Remy finished the article he was reading about preparations for the upcoming dueling contest. It was mostly an unabashed love letter from a reporter with a crush on Fuerian, anyway. It made good points, though only touching on how many of his past opponents never competed again. *Fuerian had a habit of permanently injuring opposing competitors.*

Thoranmir munched away on the breakfast, barely noticing it had gone cold and stale. He had promised to show Remy his old haunts today. He'd insisted, actually.

With a mouth full of biscuit, the elf chattered on about the places he wanted to drop by and see. Dried crumbs rained down on his shirt as he adjusted a dagger on his belt.

"This sightseeing tour wouldn't have anything to do with your search for Eldarian, would it?" Remy asked.

Thoranmir shrugged. "It wouldn't hurt to turn over a few stones while we're out and about."

It won't hurt, unless we get jumped by dream hallow peddlers, that is. Remy checked that his dúshlán was tight in its sheath, and then followed him to the door.

J AIRA BRUSHED HER HAIR with a smile and then stretched, loosening her back and the muscles at her hips. She was eagerly awaiting a reunion with Remy in the forest glade, later, and had dressed in an outfit that was perhaps a little more revealing than she might have normally wore.

No sense in subtlety, especially so close to the duel... and to Fuerian's anticipated wedding.

If Jaira's recurring visions had informed her of anything, it was that her window to avoid any fate with either Fuerian or with the shadowy elf—or both—meant that she needed Remy to fight for her. But that didn't make Remy only a means to an end.

She liked him—she knew what he was. And she'd seen the way he looked at her and thought the feeling was mutual... was more than *just a feeling*. Her visions had shown her that they were happy together.

But she did need the human champion to fight on her behalf. Jaira had to anticipate the worst of the scenarios she had foreseen that involved Remy—and what some of those hypothetical Remys endured meant that he had to feel more than just *like* towards her.

Jaira looked at the time piece and knew that it was almost time to sneak off towards the glade. She descended the stairs in time to see a familiar carriage pulling up the drive.

Shit! Of all the worst timing...

The Morgensteen's butler announced the arrival of an unexpected guest. "Mister Fuerian Vastra to see Lord and Miss Morgensteen," he announced in a basso voice.

Jaira whirled around the newel post and tried to duck out the back, but ran almost directly into her father who approached through the hall to greet their visitor. He gave a disapproving glance at his daughter, clearly catching her in the act of trying to run away and escape Fuerian before she could be seen.

"Greetings, Fuerian. To what do we owe the pleasure? We were not expecting you," said Harhassus.

Fuerian inclined his head as he entered the home, his bodyguard in tow. "No, Sir. I was in the area, meeting some friends. I thought I would drop by. I had a few minutes to spare and thought to invite myself in. I have to meet with them for only a short conversation, but perhaps we could discuss some business, after?"

Harhassus's eyes sparkled. He was eager to talk business and already had plans he'd hoped to implement once House Vastra and Morgensteen were formally aligned. A fresh injection of cash would do wonders for the Morgensteen's ventures, not that they were ready to disclose any of those particulars until after a wedding had been consummated.

Jaira scowled at the interloper. She'd been polite up until now and obeyed all social convention, but she didn't want to even *imagine* consummating vows with the Vastra.

"Oh, certainly," exclaimed Harhassus, who had practically dragged Jaira over to stand with them. "Let's grab a drink, and perhaps you will stay for supper."

Jaira rolled her eyes and stood silent, half a step removed from the two he-elves.

"Certainly a drink," Fuerian said. "We will see about supper. It will depend on my business."

Harhassus poured them each a dram of golden liquor from into crystal tumblers.

"Let me just have your butler inform me if my contact arrives. I'll see him privately. You likely know Gareth Morass?"

The older elf nodded. "Yes. It's a shame how his family wasted such position."

"I've known him a long while, since before my university days," said Fuerian. "House Morass might someday make its return. But for now, Gareth works in my employ on some of my special interest projects, of which I have many."

Harhassus's eyes twinkled. "I know how that goes. One cannot be successful long-term without looking to the future."

Fuerian nodded and stood. "I'll just be one moment."

Jaira watched as he stepped towards the entry and gave instructions to the butler and to Naz, his duelist on retainer who waited in a chair near the exterior door. Before he returned, Vennumyn slid into the hall outside the Morgensteen's sitting room with all the grace and silence of a viper hunting prey. She tried to minimize how visible she might be, but Jaira spotted her in the reflection of a picture.

Vennumyn slid a scrap of paper to Harhassus Morgensteen's guest. Fuerian nodded a silent *thanks*.

No doubt she's giving him a record of all my recent deeds, Jaira surmised. *Probably keeping a record of my bathroom schedule, too.*

She gave up any hope of meeting Remy that night and snatched the tumbler meant for Fuerian upon his return. Her father cocked an eyebrow at her, but she threw the stiff liquor back in one gulp and then set the empty glass down.

Locked in the house with my father and Fuerian Vastra as the two males decide my future?

She was going to need all the help she could get to survive the night without having to bite off her own tongue just to stay polite.

T HORANMIR HAD DRAGGED REMY all across the city that day, showing him the sights. Remy followed his friend as they toured. It gave him them both a chance to look for signs of the thugs who had been pushing dream hallow.

The tour mostly brought them through the parts of Cathair Dé that many others might have avoided. But they were simply the forgotten and local parts, the behind the scenes areas that visitors might have went past, rather than the dregs.

The places weren't particularly dangerous, but were generally uninteresting: narrow, utilitarian alleys, districts two or three blocks off main thoroughfares, specialty shops, and places that didn't bother advertising to folks outside their usual clientele who knew where to look for them. Unlike Thoranmir, the places the elf best remembered had very little personality.

In their absence, Thoranmir seemed to forget about the gang of dream hallow sellers. Though he made it a point at almost every stop to ask locals after any sign or memory of Eldarian.

Remy noted that his friend refused to give up on Odessa's brother. Still, Remy refused to discourage his friend, even if he thought it was a fruitless endeavor. He'd already promised Anya he'd try to dissuade Thoranmir from the contest. He very well couldn't take *all* of his friend's pursuits from him.

At least the dream hallow thugs had taken their warning seriously. There was no sign of them in the neighborhoods they visited.

Thoranmir seemingly took pleasure in pointing out many of the locations he remembered from a young age. Even though Remy had little interest in a fountain where little Thoranmir used to splash or where teenage Thoranmir found a peephole at a bathhouse and had seen his first naked female breast—actually, Remy *did* find that one intriguing—he followed his friend dutifully.

The day pressed ever forward. Remy knew he still had to talk Thoranmir out of competing. A convenient opening to the topic refused to present itself and bringing it up bluntly might crush the poor elf's pride. And so, Remy suffered the city's most boring tour ever as he looked for a relevant opening to the discussion.

As Thoranmir chattered away, Remy grinned and nodded. They still stood by the aforementioned peephole: a knot hole in the plank wall set on the back side of an obscure building and the location in an alley hid any curious watchers at the rear-end. Wisps of steam leaked from small opening.

"So, you ever..." Remy wriggled his eyebrows and made a lewd gesture with his finger, sticking it through a loop made with his fingers.

"What? I..." Thoranmir stammered. He laughed. "The hole's too high off the ground."

Remy squinted at it. "It is terribly small. Waaayy too small. I mean, I could almost get my fist through it, sure, but..."

"Wait a minute. *That's* small?" Thoranmir looked obviously uncomfortable and self-conscious. "H-how big is it supposed to be?"

"I'm just kidding," Remy said, playfully shoving his friend. "Or am I?" He checked the sun's position in the sky to get an estimate of the time. His heart thumped eagerly as he recalled Jaira's dance from the last time he'd seen her. "Oh. I need to get somewhere."

"The contest is in a few days," Thoranmir said. His voice brimmed with tension as if he'd wanted to talk about it for a while—also hoping for an organic turn in topics. "You probably want to see the arena still, right?" He motioned him to follow. "I know where it is. I wanted to see it, too."

"Listen, Thoranmir," Remy began, but his friend moved too rapidly. "I'm actually not heading for the..."

Thoranmir stood in the street like a statue. His sudden shift in mood caught Remy off guard and the two friends practically spoke over each other. "Remy, I've decided not to compete."

With his back turned, Remy didn't need to hide the look of elation at the sudden news. "Does Anya know?"

Thoranmir bobbed his head, shrugging. "I think so. Maybe." He turned to look at Remy, who tried his best to hide his relief. "She showed me some stuff a few days ago and tried to discourage me. But I just, I dunno... I think I have to find Odessa's brother. If I get hurt or distracted from the search he might never be found. I mean, no one else is even looking."

Remy frowned. "Anya does not know, but she worries for you. You should tell her straight away."

Thoranmir narrowed his eyes. "You're just trying to get rid of me. You weren't going to the stadium at all, were you?"

Remy's lips crooked in a half smile. He admitted, "No."

"Well, where were you sneaking off to?"

Retrieving the earring from his pocket, he held it aloft and showed him. "Back to see Miss Morgensteen again." Remy's eyes twinkled. "I do think Jaira is teasing me. She dances in the forest in such a way that..."

Thoranmir repeated the lewd motion this time. "Oh yeah? You ever stick a little something between the leaves and, uh..."

Remy shot him a screwy look. "This is real, Thoranmir. I'm going to use her father's contest to make the people respect me. I'll win a future—and rescue her from that lout, Fuerian."

Thoranmir kept his expression neutral, even though his voice warbled slightly. "Fuerian is a dangerous elf, Remy. I've... heard things. Just trust me. He's a scary piece of shit. And he's rich enough to make his way through someone's intestines and still come out looking like a polished gold nugget. Just be careful."

Remy nodded, deciding not to argue. "Regardless. *I will win this.* For her. And so, I'm relieved that we will not have to face each other."

Rummaging a hand through his hair, Thoranmir sighed, "Well, I'm glad I won't have to face Fuerian." He shrugged. "But who knows how it will go? Maybe you won't have to, either."

Remy smiled; he adjusted the special knife at his belt, and then glanced to the sky again. He took another parting step and pointed back toward Anya's apartment. "Tell your sister about your decision. She'll be so pleased with the news."

Thoranmir gave a short bow. "I will. Tell Jaira I said hello, and that she better not break your heart. Oh and," he made a motion as if he were adjusting an imaginary head dress, "remember to keep those under wraps."

As they departed, Remy turned toward the edge of Cathair Dé, where the Morgensteen estate was, and the woods where Jaira danced. He adjusted the headband, which kept his hair over his ears and obscured his heritage.

Remy rounded the corner and Thoranmir ventured further into the alley, taking the cross-town shortcut that he knew, stopping only momentarily to peek through the knot hole and chuckle for old times' sake. He leveled an eye and was greeted with the sight of a three naked he-elves of an elderly persuasion sitting spread eagle in the steam where the place had been converted into a males-only sauna.

"Nope," Thoranmir stepped back, blinking and trying to rub the image away. "Nope, nope, nope... too much has changed since I left." And then the elf turned and headed deeper into the alley.

Neither Remy nor Thoranmir saw the small cluster of elves that emerged from the shadows and stalked Thoranmir as he went.

R EMY WALKED ACROSS A short, moss-covered stump and stole over a tiny stream before entering the forest. In a few moments' time, he came to the glade where he had seen Jaira dancing previously.

He did not see her there, but her horse's reins were tethered in the thicket on the far side where the creature stamped impatiently. The human caressed the circular form of the jewelry in his pocket and then stepped forward and into the opening.

"Jaira? Jaira, I am here." He spoke at a normal volume, not wanting to broadcast his presence to the entire Morgensteen estate. Besides, she knew to expect him.

"Jaira?" he asked again.

Whistling came in the distance, then. The tune was lilting and bird-like, happy and optimistic.

Remy imagined her dancing and walked further toward the sound, thinking she was teasing him. He saw the slender figure of an elven maiden in a dress walking between willow fronds that hung down like verdant drapery. "Jaira?"

The woman turned with startled eyes and before Remy could react, four thugs leapt from the bushes and apprehended the human. A fifth elf emerged from the wild growth and called back to the elf, "You may return to the estate now. And bring Jaira's horse with you. Naz will see you get there safely."

Fuerian.

Remy saw the embarrassed lady head back for the mount and realized she was some kind of maidservant or worker in the house. Fuerian must have pressed her into service.

Now, the arrogant fop stalked toward him like a snake toying with a mouse.

The woman avoided Remy's as she struggled to untether the horse's reins at the edge of the clearing.

Nearby stood the duelist Fuerian kept on retainer; he'd warned Remy away days ago, and that warning now seemed justified. The elf glanced once at Remy with flinty eyes and then turned to escort the maidservant back to the house.

No need for him here. Besides, fewer witnesses to worry about, Remy thought, guessing at Fuerian's motives for escorting the duelist.

"I see you brought a few friends along this time," Remy managed, despite Fuerian's goons choking him as they held him firm. Thoranmir's earlier comments echoed in Remy's mind. *Fuerian is a dangerous elf.*

Fuerian grinned. "I've got little need of assistance when it comes to confrontation, *ddiymadferth*," he puked the word with an accusatory tone. "Humans are barely worth my notice."

"Then call them off."

The elf tsked. "If I did that, you'd want to escalate this until I had no choice but to kill you. And then I'd have to waste time burying your body and covering it all up for Jaira's sake... seems like a big waste of time."

"Escalate? What do you mean escalate?" Remy said with a hoarse voice as a thug pressed on his neck. "We're just old pals talking, right? I'm not even armed."

Fuerian raised a brow and then reached beneath the folds of Remy's coat. First he checked the pockets; the elf's hands bypassed the earring but withdrew the safe-box key where he had stashed the bulk of the funds after he and Thoranmir shut down the dream hallow traffickers. Then, he drew the dagger from Remy's hip. It was the length of a forearm and razor-sharp.

"That... is not... for you," Remy rasped, straining against the choke hold and hoping he was right. The blade's engravings did not glow. If it was meant to kill Fuerian, the runes would be blazing right now with ancient magic fueled by Remy's need for vengeance.

Fuerian's eyes locked on the blade. He realized which item Remy was talking about, and he tossed the key into the tall grass. It was immaterial to their quarrel—or its resolution.

"He's right, boss," said one of the elf's companions. "That's a dúshlán knife. I mean, he *could* use it. But it's generally bad form to..."

"I know what it is, Gareth," Fuerian snapped. He tucked the blade within his own belt for safekeeping, turning back to the human. "And I'll give it back just as soon as this short-eared bastard drops out of the contest. It's of little value to anyone else."

"Are you afraid of a little competition, Fuerian?" hissed Remy. "Or are you more worried I'll beat you in a fair fight? Or are you jealous that Jaira prefers me?"

"Hold him, Gareth," Fuerian said. His friend, a slightly overweight elf, held Remy firm, clutching a fistful of the human's hair.

Fuerian slapped Remy across the face, hard enough to snap his head aside, even with Gareth holding it. "Then I'll just see that you're eliminated from it properly."

A trickle of blood and saliva dripped off Remy's lower lip. He risked a defiant, bloody smile. *Haven't been slapped like that since Rhylfelour, the unseelie orc warlord who trained me... well, tormented me, a decade ago...*

Fuerian glared daggers at the human, outraged by the blatant insolence.

Remy knew exactly how it had turned out for Rhylfelour. And the orc had been far stronger than Fuerian.

Remy's grin twisted into a sneer. "And when I win? After I take Jaira from you, you'll willingly return my knife?"

"It's a dúshlán," Fuerian's friend reminded him. "It's honor bound to him."

Scowling, Fuerian barked at him, "You think I'll take a man's life without a care, but still worry about things like honor?"

The other elf nodded with a grave look on his face.

Fuerian's lips curled into a snarl, but he said nothing. In his silence, Remy could tell his enemy agreed. Even Fuerian could not permanently steal the blade and risk a curse inherent of the Arcadeaxn magics which had formed it. "Damn it, Gareth," Fuerian hissed.

"If I win?" Remy repeated.

"I doubt that very much," Fuerian scoffed. "Especially if you actually face me. You'll have no use for a vengeance blade after I'm through with you. My sword always penetrates deep, and I'll be sure to thrust it carelessly into your flesh when I open your veins. There will be little left for any doctor to do but produce a death certificate." He narrowed his gaze. "*Doctor...* or a veterinarian." He spat and cursed, again using the obscenity, "*Ddiymadferth.*" It was an ugly word, a derogatory unseelie term used to refer to vulnerable prey—but which had come to refer to humans.

The elvish rake sneered. "I'll let Jaira visit your grave after I take her as my wife and—willing or not—put my heir in her belly."

Remy trembled with rage, angered by the rake's flippant attitude toward Jaira and Remy's dúshlán. He leaned into the restraining elves' hold, which squeezed his throat and lowered his voice a whole octave as they tried to keep him from Fuerian.

"Swear it," Remy growled through his choked windpipe. He bared his teeth as he insisted. "Swear it in the olde tongue. Promise to return it to me and leave Jaira alone once I've beaten you."

Fuerian's eyes wilded at the human. The olde tongue was the ancient language of the fey. Agreements spoken and deals made in it, if spoken aloud, had a kind of binding magic to them. All Arcadeax itself would enforce the contract. Not even mighty Oberon could defy such magic.

Fuerian sneered. But then, he spoke aloud in the words of the ancient ones, which were typically reserved for spell craft and functions of the high elvish court.

[I shall return your dúshlán blade when either you exit the agreed upon dueling contest or I do. And if you beat me in a fair duel, I shall leave Jaira Morgensteen to your care.]

A kind of hush fell over the glade when he finished the pronouncement, like the silence that followed a thunder peal. Fuerian reverted to the common tongue. "Satisfied?"

Before he could answer, Fuerian locked eyes with his minions and barked an order. "Work him over and then dump him in the river."

"With pleasure," said Gareth. And then he and the other elves in Fuerian's crew began. They took turns pummeling Remy with their fists while their peers restrained him.

Fuerian walked away, heading towards the house in the distance—Jaira's house—as the thugs beat the human.

Remy watched his enemy depart; with every blow that landed, the rage within him intensified and promised future retribution. He refused to cry out as others pounded his face and body with their fists.

And then, the husky ruffian slipped a soldered band of titanium around his fingers and seated them at his knuckles to make his blows land all the harder. Remy's body was not nearly as resolute as his voice, and Gareth's next stiff roundhouse landed against his temple, knocking Remy out cold, and back into dark dreams of his harsh childhood at the hands of an orc warlord.

CHAPTER TWELVE

— ◦ —

"**Y**OU KNOW I'VE NEVER been fond of your plot to marry me off to Fuerian Vastra," Jaira told her father plainly. She stared out the large window, upset at being sequestered for some kind of purposeless meeting. She'd had other intentions for the evening, and voiced her objections to a suitor coming and occupying her time without advance warning. "And why you're keeping me in the house against my will is an outrage. I am old enough to make my own decisions. Including my refusal of Fuerian's proposal."

Harhassus Morgensteen blinked at his daughter, incredulous that she would say as much so openly and with company present.

"You know I am standing right here," Fuerian said on the other side of the room, easily within earshot. He and Harhassus had been sharing drinks in the antechamber of the Morgensteen mansion. "Besides, I thought I saw a predator out there in the trees." Something about the look on Fuerian's smug face communicated exactly who that "predator" had been.

Jaira caught sight of Vennumyn who blanched with recognition at the quip before she faded into the background. The maid's eyes lingered just a moment too long on Fuerian. Jaira knew that Vennumyn was in cahoots with him.

They must have found Remy... it means he came—but I won't be seeing him tonight.

"I just don't care that you're standing there," she finally said, pouring herself a goblet of red wine.

As soon as he'd left, Jaira had guessed that the Vastran snake knew that her plans for the evening had involved a rendezvous with Remy.

"Come now, daughter," Harhassus intervened. "You know this family merger is important to our business. For both of our businesses," he added, motioning to Fuerian.

Jaira rolled her eyes. "I'm glad that I'm so politically expedient. I'm sure that for a small sack of gold, you could sell my body parts to the anthropophagi."

Harhassus grimaced at the thought. "Well, exactly how much gold are we talking about?" he jested.

Jaira threw him a scathing look. "I'm being serious."

"No. You're being over-dramatic."

"It's because she's got a new crush," Fuerian said, sipping from his cup. "Someone a shade nicer and far more heroic than I."

Harhassus sighed through his nose. "Remy Keaton."

Fuerian nodded.

Jaira put her hands on her hips. "So what of it? Aren't I allowed to like whomever I want? Since when is my romantic life the subject of your business arrangements?"

"Of course you are allowed to love whoever you choose," said Harhassus. "Just so long as it's Fuerian Vastra. Or any other Vastra, I suppose. I don't think you understand the significance of joining our family lines."

Jaira swirled her finger through the vermilion fluid in her goblet. "I understand, Daddy. But I don't care. I want more out of my life than to be someone's political prop. I want what you and mother have."

Harhassus's cheeks flushed. "Not every one of us gets to marry for love, daughter. Perhaps if she had been able to have a son, or more daughters, you'd be free to do the same. But that is not the Arcadeax we live in."

"I should get a say in my life," she argued.

"And you will," said her father. "But it's my job to make sure you say the right things up until you're beyond my roof. And the *next roof* you'll live under will be grander. What roof can this ditch-digger provide, except twigs and canvas?"

Pouting, Jaira pushed her cup away from her with enough force that the wine sloshed over the side and spilled onto the table. She fixed her eyes on Fuerian. "I can handle the difficulties of life, Father. But I do not like *him*."

"I think I do not compare well to the poor boy from the road, at least not in her eyes," Fuerian said. "But I am an elf of means and stature. I've caught the eyes of many elf girls since coming of age," he bragged. "Though I lack, perhaps, this Remy boy's swarthy neck and arms. Perhaps you'd be even more attracted to a subterranean dvergr—at least then you'd be bedding a fey. They may be a little shorter, but I'm sure their girth would make you moan with pleasure." Fuerian sipped his glass, but kept his eyes locked on Jaira over the brim.

Jaira's face burned red and her nostrils flared.

"That's quite enough," Harhassus barked at Fuerian, shooting him an icy glare at the elf before his daughter could issue a violent, escalating retort. The marriage was an arranged one, like many among the elite class often were. But transactional though it was, Harhassus was still Jaira's father, and some lines could not be crossed.

The younger elf raised his hands in surrender and then set his glass aside as if the drink and not his nasty personality had been what caused him to so deeply slander Jaira. "My apologies," he quickly corrected.

Jaira fumed, not believing for one second that he meant it.

Harahssus, however, seemed placated by it and turned to Jaira calmly. "You can't possibly like this boy," Harhassus said. "He's a simple laborer. He comes from no money, or standing. He'll never make a name for himself inside Oberon's court. Not unless he dupes some wealthy old dame on her death bed."

"I am sure Remy is *not* simple," Jaira defended.

Fuerian tilted his head. "He digs ditches. That is a job for the simple minded who supply simple solutions for the problems of their betters."

Harhassus raised a glass. "Simple solutions are the frequent paths of vagabonds, I always say."

Fuerian grinned, knowing he had the older elf's support. "He's more than that." Fuerian shot Jaira a manipulative look. "Or actually, *less than that*, I should say."

She glared back at him. Her eyes almost pleaded for him not to tell the secret... Harhassus did not know what Remy really was.

Fuerian ignored her silent request. "Remy Keaton is a human. Even if Oberon might tolerate them, Titania would never allow such a one in her presence—can you imagine how the Morgensteen name would be ruined by such association?"

Harhassus nearly spit his drink out. "He's a—he's a what?" The older elf's eyebrow twitched uncontrollably as he whirled to stare at his daughter. "No. Out of the question. I forbid it."

"Yes, Daddy," Jaira said, staring at Fuerian with a glare that was sharp enough to kill. "A human saved your life. And mine. And mother's. All humans deserve our scorn."

He glowered at his daughter, unsure exactly where the sarcasm started. "I absolutely forbid you to have anything to do with him. Do you know how many humans there are in Cathair Dé?"

"I do, Daddy." Jaira wilted. Her father had worked up a full head of steam and would not be slowed any time soon. She had to let his anger run its course.

Fuerian grinned at her, victorious. If he'd had a Thistle and Barrel style scoreboard, he'd have marked a win in his column.

"Nearly six hundred. *Six hundred!* That's almost half a percent of the population, and they're destroying our fine city."

"Yes," Jaira sighed. "So I've heard you say before."

"It's a wonder Oberon hasn't had them all wiped out. It's only a matter of time. But there's no way that *my daughter, or any Morgensteen,* is getting caught up in their schemes. Is that clear?"

"It is clear, Father," she said, with her eyes downcast.

"Good—now," Harhassus said. He sighed and smoothed his shirt and waistcoat, which had gotten bunched up in his exasperation. "Not that I'm anti-human. But let's be serious and put this all behind us. Fuerian. Another drink."

Fuerian poured Harhassus a new cup and handed it over. The older elf obviously needed it to calm his nerves.

"You've got blood on your hands there, Fuerian," Harhassus said, putting a finger on the younger elf's wrist. "No. Just on your cuffs."

A crimson stain had seeped into the lace ruffled at base of Fuerian's sleeve. He dabbed at it with water from the nearby serving bowl. "Oh. Yes. My apologies." He winked as he tried to clean it away—it was still fresh from the moments leading up to Fuerian re-joining them at the estate.

"You have been doing some extra-curricular dueling again, I see. That must have been your meeting with Gareth?"

Fuerian shrugged. "You know me. I'm just preparing for my upcoming competition."

Harhassus put a hand on his future son-in-law's shoulder. "You must preserve your strength, my boy, if you wish to win that kiss." He looked directly at his daughter.

Jaira growled something unintelligible and then stormed out of the room.

#

Thoranmir walked a circuit around the perimeter of the coliseum which would host the upcoming duelist's contest. It was an impressive structure capable of holding tens of thousands of fans, which was a point of pride for Cathair Dé.

Compared to the cities closer to Faery Cairn, Cathair Dé was only a small barony and practically rustic as far as those closest to the inner sanctums of the Summer Court were concerned. The fact that Suíochán Naséan, the home of the council of Mavens who oversaw the dueling guilds, had agreed to send mavens to oversee the proceedings had given the city a shot of prestige.

Cathair Dé's stadium walls towered above most of the establishments that surrounded it and they appeared to scrape the sky clean of the clouds overhead as Thoranmir stood near the base of the main gate. The place's interior was an open-air field with seating that surrounded the central area; it was used for a variety of events, including sports, orations, and other major activities—typically the kind events where admission could be charged.

Presently, Thoranmir's route brought him around the massive structure and in search of the office, where he could find the game master the Morgensteen family had paid to assemble their sponsored competition. At its core, the coliseum was a business and operated as such.

He finally found the office entry and there Thoranmir met with a secretary. She passed him up to three workers beyond her in the chain of command until he met with an aged and frumpy elf who looked more like a clerical officer than an event promoter.

A name plaque listed him as Adawar Mynthane. He was rail thin and sat almost hidden amongst rows and rows of freshly printed handbills which had just arrived from the printer. They'd been stacked all around the elf's office.

Thoranmir made his case and explained that he could no longer go through with his commitment to compete. The game master muttered grumpily to himself, and then unloaded on the former contestant.

"Do you know what it's going to cost me to change that? I just had all these printed." Adawar stared down his nose at Thoranmir.

"I... uh... I'm sorry?"

The promoter glowered, but started crossing out Thoranmir's name on official looking rosters and tournament charts. He refused to look at Thoranmir.

"So I... I'm gonna go, then," Thoranmir said as he slipped out of the office, leaving the promoter to angrily scratch his name off wherever it was listed.

Thoranmir leaned against the wall and gave a big sigh, knowing he'd been officially struck off the roster took a huge weight off of him. He hadn't realized how tense he'd become with all the recent mounting pressures.

Now without a concern in the world, Thoranmir whistled while he headed back for his sister's apartment. He left Adawar behind and exited the building and the day seemed so much brighter, brimming with hope and new possibilities.

He walked, wide-eyed, and marveled at how much Cathair Dé seemed to have changed in the few years since he'd been here last.

His carefree mood made him oblivious as the four elves who had followed him from the alley grew closer.

As Thoranmir left the more heavily populated part of the city, he ventured back toward the shortcuts he knew. They crossed through the less savory parts of the city, but he'd never had any serious altercations using them, and they hadn't seen any sign of the dream hallow gang since the night at the hotel—and they'd been looking.

He didn't notice as two of his four stalkers peeled off and hurried to unknown destinations.

Thoranmir quickened his pace as he came to a long and narrow alley. It cut a direct path back to the wider roads and would take him back to Anya's. He hurried into the corridor when something rushed out from the dark and slammed into him, knocking Thoranmir off his feet and sending him sprawling through a wall of paper-covered studs, meant only to keep out the riffraff and insects as laborers worked inside.

The place was empty, however. There hadn't been workers within for years.

Thoranmir skidded to his side within the relative darkness and found himself in a gutted building that looked like it had once been a storage facility. Nearby, a cloaked figure—presumably the same one that had tackled him—lay sprawled out on the ground. A second elf, dressed the same, leapt through the breach and locked eyes on Thoranmir.

"Ah crap," he muttered, scrambling to his feet. Thoranmir recognized a setup when he saw it. *I guess those street thugs found us after all! But I'm not giving any of that coin back—and I won't let them keep poisoning this community.*

Thoranmir noticed the mugger's dress—the drug vendors had all been dressed like modern elves in the middle caste... like bored university students. *This was not them;* he breathed a sigh of relief.

He hoped that this threat was some down on his luck fey, or even a human, who was desperate for a quick score. Thoranmir understood that he might have looked like a tempting target: walking alone through a dark alley and without paying much mind to his surroundings... *maybe some detoxing dream hallow users needing a fix?*

As Thoranmir got to his feet, he bellowed loudly, "I don't have any money or valuables on me. I'm a worthless target and not worth the risk." He put up his fists and tried to look as intimidating as possible, hoping to deter a desperate mugger.

His first attacker slowly rose from the ground with a kind of menacing articulation which focused on Thoranmir. The attacker was an elf.

Thoranmir looked more closely at the elf's companion. Both thugs both wore scarves that crossed over their nose and chin, concealing their identities. But their eyes remained visible, and the murderous gleam in them indicated that they were far more than the desperate ruffians he'd hoped for. They wanted blood, not money.

These are not your normal street thieves or addicts! His heart plunged into his guts with icy momentum.

"Behind you!" Thoranmir pointed to something in the distance to try and throw up a distraction. His attacker's didn't even flinch.

Thoranmir turned, and bolted.

#

Jaira stormed out of the room and Fuerian watched her go. He admired her back side and the swish of her hips as she went.

They were betrothed, but with her disposition set against him, he'd never had the opportunity to have her... not in the way that would give Fuerian pleasure. But he had plenty of imagination, and no shortage of other local opportunities.

Good thing Madam Holworth's bordello is near my apartments.

Fuerian was under no illusions that any affection he might receive from her in the future would be strictly mechanical and out of marital obligation. That didn't bother him in particular. He had no intention of changing his arrangements—now or after his marriage—with the female guests he entertained at his place.

Harhassus winked at Fuerian, likely misinterpreting his thoughts. "Now that she's gone, we can chat about that business you'd requested we talk about."

Jaira's father looked introspective for a moment as he thought about his daughter's relationship to the Morgensteen's business ventures. "She does have a good business sense about her. She's warned me off from a few bad investments in the past... prevented more than one future tragedy for me."

Fuerian raised a brow and rubbed his chin. "Oh, really?"

Harhassus nodded. "But this isn't really a strictly business thing you wanted to talk about, is it?"

"No." Fuerian shook his head, letting go of whatever it was Harhassus meant about Jaira. He wanted to limit her involvement in this particular transaction as much as possible. "I wanted to discuss the mines you own well outside of town."

"The *iron* mine?" Harhassus guffawed, spitting the words as if they were poison. To the fey, they *were*. Iron inflicted pain in arcaeaxn creatures—pain like nothing else. It harmed them skin to soul, with blistering efficacy. Iron was perhaps the only thing worse than fire, and pain inflicted by it bore a permanent mark in a victim's psyche. One never forgot the severity and intensity of the wounds the toxic metal inflicted. It was like a brand that hurt when pressed to flesh, but which also never subsided.

"Yes. That mine."

Harhassus raised an eyebrow. He leaned forward. "The mine went dry of titanium years ago, and none of the fey can hardly go inside any longer. You have some ulterior use for it?"

"I do."

"Okay. Spill it. What do you have in mind?" Harhassus asked."

Fuerian shook his head. "I'm sworn to secrecy on the matter."

Harhassus stroked his chin thoughtfully. "Well, you can't be mining the iron. There's no money in it since Oberon has made it illegal and there's no legitimate use for the ore and using it to harm the fey carries a death sentence... that only leaves something *new*. You've got some kind of new discovery you think can make the mine profitable again?" An eager gleam sparkled in his eyes.

"I hesitate to confirm anything. This venture is more likely than not to be a big dud... but if I could acquire the with little risk and then take a chance, it would create some opportunities to turn something of no value into a boon."

The older elf grinned wryly. "And you hoped to get the mine at a price better than market?"

Fuerian laughed. "Market price? It's riddled with *iron*. The mine's a liability and toxic. It honestly has a negative value. I was hoping to see if you'd deed it to me after the marriage is consummated and our houses are aligned. As I mentioned, the risk is extreme, but there may be future opportunities in business if the new advances pan out."

Harhassus sized up his daughter's suitor, and then took out his quill and a parchment. "I'll give it to you right now, provided you agree to never sell it or lease it to a few competitors. If the mine can be made profitable again, well, all the better for my grandchildren, eh?" He winked at Fuerian.

"I'd sign that in a heartbeat." The younger elf smiled... certain he knew exactly which names Harhassus was listing on a transfer deed.

Harhassus's pen scratched as he drew up documents.

He thinks he's unloading a garbage property—a negative asset—to House Vastra. Jaira could be kidnapped by unseelie raiders, effectively ending our houses mergers, and he'd still think he came out ahead with giving it away.

"You're too kind," Fuerian stated as he signed the bill of transfer on a copy that Harhassus would have recorded.

Harhassus turned over a copy for Fuerian. "The mine is yours," he smirked. "Now you've just got to get my daughter to root for you too... but something tells me *that* might prove a more difficult challenge than making a failed mine profitable... even one filled with iron."

#

Thoranmir whirled on his heel and dashed deeper into the facility where his attackers had pushed him. He searched frantically for an exit door as he plunged deeper into the darkness of the building which was under construction.

Who are these guys? Fuerian and some of his friends, perhaps? That thought compelled him to a greater pace. *Whoever they are, they're heavy hitters and they mean business!*

The sounds of footsteps chased him in the shadows and Thoranmir turned around a corner, crashing directly into the chest of a third brigand, similarly clad to the two he'd run from. They tumbled to the floor in a tangle of arms and legs.

Thoranmir rolled away as quickly, disentangling himself and launching himself to his feet. He hoped to escape, but he found himself surrounded by the enemies.

A fourth elf entered from the far side. He moved lethargically and wore a similar face covering, but his eyes were like vacant, dead things, somehow still burning like hot coals. *The strangely stiff and slow member of the group.*

"All right. You want a fight, then? You'll find I'm not as easy as the next elf." *Gods, I hope that's true... I wish Remy was here right now.*

Before waiting for the enemy to make the first move, Thoranmir went on offensive, punching with one arm and grabbing for the nearest elf's chest. He tried to get a fistful of fabric so he could land repeated blows to his opponent's face. *I have to take out one or two of them right away if I hope to actually stand a chance... of escaping—no way I can take them all.*

His opponent was not unskilled and bobbed his head enough that the blows landed with little effect, mostly glancing off the thickest part of his skull and bruising Thoranmir's knuckles. But the elf's scarf tore free under the twisting movements. Thoranmir's hand ripped through the clasp on the elf's cloak and jacket, exposing his tunic.

Thoranmir paused for a moment, dumbfounded by the sight. The fabric was made of a fine material and two sets of interlocked stag's horns had been embroidered in red to make a circular shape. He thought he recognized it but couldn't be certain—whatever it represented, it looked like it could be somehow attached to Oberon's court. *Maybe a duke's house or something?*

His enemy smashed a fist down and broke Thoranmir's grasp. Another of the elves kicked his feet out from under him. Thoranmir landed flat on his back and the rear of his skull cracked on the ground with a liminal flash of light.

Before Thoranmir could react, a dagger pressed against his throat. He stared into the cold, unflinching eyes of the elf with the crimson embroidery.

"Do not move," he growled.

Thoranmir barely risked gulping against the keen edge of the knife. He composed his wits and held his hands open to show he was no threat. He knew they were not thieves, but he hoped he could still play dumb and find a way out of the situation. "I seriously don't have any money."

With Thoranmir cowed and at his mercy, his assailant wiped a trickle of blood away from his lip and relaxed the pressure he held against the blade. "I am not here for your money, and I don't particularly want your life. I am here for one thing and one thing only."

"H-how can I help?" Thoranmir asked, trying to get a look at his attacker, but the shadows still concealed his identity.

The elf restored the sash that covered his face. "Remington Keaton must not win this contest," he growled.

"You work for Fuerian Vastra, then? Remy really *does* have him scared."

The three laughed, genuinely amused. The fourth stood stone quiet. Thoranmir realized that at least one of them was a female by the pitch of her voice.

"We do not care about some local contest or a pissing match between an elf, even one of the méith, and some random human," the leader insisted. "But we must do our duty and prevent the son of Adam from ever learning his true origins. Under threat of death, he must never be allowed to clamber out from the ditches."

Understanding washed over Thoranmir.

"You know how he got dropped into the unseelie as a child? You know something about the dúshlán blade he carries," Thoranmir said. And then, he clamped his mouth down, biting his tongue. As he said it aloud, he realized the revelation made his captors much more likely to kill him.

Thoranmir wilted beneath their gaze after his admission. "Um. Maybe you could just ask Remy nicely?"

His captor pressed the knife harder against his throat. He pushed with just enough effort that a single drop of blood seeped from Thoranmir's skin. "You must not tell Remy, or *anyone* for that matter, about this."

"But I'm sure that I could convince him if I just..."

"No."

"Well, maybe just mug him and tie him up, or detain him. Kind of like you're doing to me right now."

"There is a powerful force preventing us from direct interference with the human," the leader admitted. "*But not from torturing or killing others who he cares about.* Perhaps Anya Shelton, the cripple?"

"No!" yelped Thoranmir. "All right, all right. You made your point. How do I cooperate?"

"Simple. Get Remy Keaton to quit this contest, or ensure that he will not win by some other means. Kill him for all we care, but he cannot claim a victory in the arena. The human must not rise above his station."

"I thought you knew Remy," Thoranmir argued. "How can I get a guy like that to quit a contest like this? Winning is the only way to get what he really wants—the girl he loves. And you won't even let me tell him to drop out. How am I supposed to do that?"

"You will figure it out," said his attacker. "If you don't, your sister will pay a price." He tapped his ears. "And we'll know if you speak of this to your friends."

Thoranmir realized the significance of him being able to speak of it. If he told Remy any of this, it would be one more puzzle piece fitting into what his friend knew of his mysterious past. The more pieces that came together, the more likely Remy came to recovering whatever secrets bound him to the dúshlán.

The female member of the group traced a sigil on Thoranmir's forehead and it momentarily tingled with a burning sensation. He'd been marked with some kind of observation spell.

"Just remember, we're always listening," she told him, and then the attackers slunk away into the shadows.

Thoranmir cursed before picking himself up off the dusty floor of the abandoned warehouse. He made his way back to the alley, hurrying to his sister's home. *How am I supposed to do what they want of me when I can't even talk about any of this?*

He grumbled, mostly to himself as he exited the long lanes that stretched between buildings. Thoranmir had fallen deep into thought, surrounded by alleys that no longer felt safe as they had previously.

A voice called to him, "Thoranmir... young elf," Hazhimon said, startling him.

Thoranmir turned to find the withered, old hamadryad assess him with her shrewd eyes. It took him a moment to recognize her and then he remembered she'd claimed to be good at remembering names.

"You look like garbage... and you're alone." Her voice shifted to take on a hint of worry. "Is your human friend okay?"

"Oh. I, uh, think so," Thoranmir said. "Are you looking for him?"

Hazhimon shook her head. "No, no. I am looking for you. I have a lead."

He tilted his head.

"You were looking for information on your friend. You wanted to find the elf, Eldarian Cócaire. You still want to find him, correct?" Hope brimmed in her eyes as if she'd banked on receiving some kind of reward for procuring the information for him.

"Yes," Thoranmir said, still rattled by the assault in the alleyway. But he compartmentalized it the best he could and shifted mental gears to focus on whatever she'd discovered. He fished a hand into his pockets and located a what sparse few coins he had on his person and then delivered them to Hazhimon.

"You found him, Eldarian Cócaire... you're sure it's *him?*"

Hazhimon pointed vigorously. "I am certain. I was given the name from a transient who sought shelter at the Havnell Mission near the north entrance to the Haunts. Do you know it?"

Thoranmir nodded. It was a kind of urban poor house which boarded able-bodied adults who were down on their luck, but attempting to right their lives. The mission was not terribly far from the orphanages which he and Remy had visited earlier.

He thanked her again, meeting her brilliant eyes, and knew she was telling the truth of it.

Thoranmir turned and headed for his sisters. He had a lead on Eldarian, but didn't know how long it would be good for. He'd need Remy's help for that, and he still didn't know how to deal with the red circle bandits and how to force Remy out of the competition.

Thoranmir raked a hand through his hair. "This is just getting worse and worse."

CHAPTER THIRTEEN

"WHERE IN THE FEY is Remy?" Thoranmir cursed, pacing back and forth in Anya's apartment. His sister shot him an annoyed look from the side of her eyes.

"He's with the girl?" Anya's words were more of a statement than a question.

Thoranmir nodded.

"He didn't come home last night." She folded her arms across her chest. "Little brother, do I *really* have to explain where he probably is and what he's probably been doing?"

Thoranmir's brow furrowed. He wasn't concerned for Remy's safety. Thoranmir was annoyed because he'd wanted Remy's help that morning following up on Hazhimon's lead. But he didn't want to tell his sister that.

Anya pressed her point. "Don't you have some girl you are sweet on? The one with the letters?"

Thoranmir stiffened, wanted to argue with Anya, but then paused. He surprised himself and instead of trying to keep his relationship with Odessa a secret, he started babbling on and on about her. The fire went out of his anger as he told his sister everything.

"It sounds like you really like this girl."

He smiled sheepishly. "I do."

"Then why didn't you stay there with her in Vail Carvanna?" she asked. "Was it because of Remy—you wanted to help him win this contest?"

Thoranmir shook his head. "No." His face darkened somewhat, "A big part of me actually hopes that he loses," he confessed. "But I still want him to get his girl." Thoranmir clamped down his lips, realizing that even that may have been saying too much.

He sighed, "But to answer your question, Odessa has a brother who is in trouble. I promised her that I'd find him for her."

Anya leaned forward. "And did you?"

Thoranmir shook his head. "No. But I got a lead last night and I wanted to go out and look into it."

Anya placed her headset on her brow. "Tell me this brother's name."

"Eldarian Cócaire."

She closed her eyelids as she stepped into the aither and Thoranmir could see her eyes flitting back and forth behind their veils. And then they stopped.

"I see him. Just in passing... mentions of enrollment in a mage's academy. Is this the one?"

"Yes," Thoranmir nodded.

Anya frowned. "It looks like he just... disappeared." She opened her eyes and looked at him. "Why would a promising mage, despite the fact that he has very little family or other connections, just disappear?"

Thoranmir looked his sister in the eye. "A bigger question is if this is an isolated incident or if this has been happening a lot, lately."

The blood drained from Anya's face.

"What do you know?" asked Thoranmir.

She sighed. "Not much. Just rumors, same as everybody else."

"But you're an aithermancer. You can get at information most people don't usually see."

Anya nodded. "Yes. I've got a trail of information I've been collecting in my personal aitherspace. I just... it doesn't show me much more than what... nevermind."

"Anya. No. Out with it. Why can't you tell me?" Thoranmir asked.

She tightened her lips. "The thing is, the people who are spreading the rumors about human kidnappings and disappearing mages and are asking questions are all... well... they sound crazy. Most of them are lunatics, living on the fringes of society and in places like The Haunts."

At mention of The Haunts, Thoranmir grew serious. "Are they crazy?"

Anya's face hardened. She said quietly, "No. There's something—someone—out there doing things. Bad things."

A moment of silence passed between them.

Thoranmir's face softened when he realized why she was so passionate about researching the disappearances. *She thought I was a victim... she was looking for me all these years since I'd left the city.*

"And Odessa's brother is caught up in it." Thoranmir turned to the door. "I can't wait any longer. The tip I got last night pointed me towards Havnell Mission, right outside The Haunts. Eldarian is there—or *was*."

As Thoranmir strode towards the door, Anya called out. "Hold on. If you're insisting on going, I'm coming with you."

Thoranmir wanted to protest, but then thought better of it. Even if it might be true, he couldn't tell his sister that she might slow him down. He was uncertain if there was any real danger, but telling her that would certainly piss her off.

Instead of arguing, Thoranmir held the door for her and they both headed in the direction of The Haunts.

JAIRA SAT ON HER bed, feeling like a prisoner in her own home. After insulting Fuerian the previous day, her father had confined her to the house unless accompanied by an escort. Her fiancé had told Harhassus that he'd spotted Remy lurking on the grounds prior to coming in for drinks and kindly sent the human away with a stern warning to not return.

At least her father had asked, with at least a hint of worry, if Fuerian had killed Remy. But Fuerian claimed to have only disarmed him and sent him away, and Fuerian now wore Remy's distinctly recognizable knife at his hip.

Fuerian is a liar. He's done something. That explains the blood on his sleeves.

Worry lodged deep in Jaira's gut and made her heart sink. She argued against it with her head. *Remy is a fighter. He is more than capable of handling himself– even against Fuerian.*

Someone knocked at the door and it opened slowly and with a slight creak. Lady Eilastra, Jaira's mother, poked her head in to check on Jaira. Seeing her there, Eilastra entered the room.

Their eyes met. Jaira made no attempt to hide her frustrated indignation. She sighed and flopped backwards on her bed, letting the pillows half bury her as the fluff of air tousled her hair over her face, forming a mask she could hide behind.

Eilastra sat next to her and parted the locks.

"Most girls my age are treated like adults. They aren't imprisoned in their own homes, you know," Jaira accused. "They're off finding love, marrying, and having babies of their own."

Eilastra grinned sympathetically. "And many of those girls would claim that their newly domestic life was just another kind of prison."

Jaira glared at her mother. Eilastra was the more reasonable of Jaira's parents and had a way of slapping sense into her with simple words. But that didn't mean Jaira had to like it.

"You know that your father is just trying to—"

"I don't care what his purposes or motives are, Mother. What he is doing is *wrong*. He's forcing me to marry someone I detest," Jaira seethed.

Eilastra sat in thoughtful silence for a moment. "You know that your father had the opportunity to marry for love? He and I—"

"Yes, yes," grumbled Jaira. I've heard this story before."

Her mother shook her head slowly. "No. You haven't. Not all of it, so hush, child."

Jaira pouted, but something in Eilastra's motherly tone made Jaira sit up and hug her legs to her chest as if her mother was telling a bedtime story.

"With wealth and stature comes certain comforts and privilege. Your uncle, as the oldest brother, was set to inherit the dragon's share of your grandfather's wealth, leaving your father with very little to live off of aside from his determination and grit." Eilastra smiled faintly at the distant memory of the Harhassus from her youth.

"This same disadvantage is what allowed him to marry for love. He had hardly any wealth. Though he had the Morgensteen name, without being the heir he had none of the position or favor in Oberon's court. Your uncle very nearly ruined that name as he and his wife squandered his inheritance with foolishness and frivolity."

Her mother's lips tightened thin for a moment. "Your grandfather was great at many things, but making smart matches was never a skill he possessed. You've only met your aunt in passing, but she is... *was,* a wasteful she-elf. Extravagance for the sheer sake of pride. She squandered their wealth."

Jaira blinked as she watched her mother. She'd never heard either parent speak ill of her aunt or uncle; they were shopkeepers who eked out a meager existence at a store they owned and living in their modest apartment in Daonra Dlúth, much closer to the king's court.

"Your father made his fortune by working hard and making smart investments where others could not or would not. He made hard decisions... found land for his company and mined where nobody else dared."

Something about that last detail came out oddly, as if there were more details there, uncomfortable details. But Jaira let it go and focused on her mother's story.

"In the midst of all that, he met me. *But I won't tell you* where." Eilastra looked out the window, suddenly carried far and away with the revelry; she stared for a few moments, remaining in the memory. Then she smiled and looked down, transported back to the present.

Eilastra continued. "Eventually your father purchased back the Morgensteen estate, which had been his family home and the seat to the House's heir for generations. That act allowed your uncle, who was on the edge of financial ruin, to start a new life: the life that should have belonged to the younger brother. But because your father claimed the Morgensteen title and estate with the purchase that makes you its only heir. With that comes certain duties and responsibilities."

Jaira sighed through her nose. This part had been drilled into her over the years.

Eilastra kept the same even, motherly tone, which, like sugar, helped the medicine go down easier. "Your father is aware of your fascination with this..." Eilastra's mouth made a shape to indicate she'd almost used the vulgar word to describe Remy. *Ddiymad-ferth*. She said instead, "This son of Adam."

Jaira acted like she wanted to protest that as a mere rumor, but she could not betray her feelings for Remy. Instead, she said nothing.

"Your father is trying to shield the Morgensteen name from ridicule," Eilastra said. Her face softened. "And even more than that, he is trying to protect *you*. *Your name*, so that you can return to polite society after you've..." She trailed off a moment. "Rumors are difficult things to kill, daughter."

After what?

"They—they're saying things about me?" Jaira asked. "What are they saying?"

Eilastra swallowed hard, as if preparing to deliver difficult words. "That you are going through a *curious* phase. That you have taken a kind of erotic fascination with humans—that you've taken a human lover. It's a fantasy your father hopes you will soon out-grow, before it disqualifies you from any standing in the Summer Court."

She believes these rumors!

Jaira was incensed by her mother's lack of faith... and then slumped her shoulders and admitted they were *not* just rumors. They were at least partly true—and certainly Eilastra had seen it all play out before her very eyes.

Instead, Jaira hissed, "Titania," as if the name were a curse. She had set the precedent for the seelie fey's persecution of humans.

Eilastra nodded. Oberon's wife famously hated humans. Certainly the collection of bastard changelings, what they called half-blood children of fey and human origins, at court were the only ones tolerated within arcadeaxn society. And changelings who Oberon had fathered were never spoken of. Recognizing them for what they were placed attention on them, and that drew the ire of Titania who'd never shied away from punishing a messenger for any bad news they delivered. Without noble connections, Changelings were hated at least as much as humans.

"Who's saying these things?"

"It doesn't matter *who* says them," Eilastra said, "because at a certain point, it only matters *how many* are saying it."

There she goes with her clever words again, Jaira thought, refusing to acknowledge their deep wisdom.

"Just remember that your father and I love you very much," Eilastra said.

Before she could control her mouth, Jaira said, "Well, he has a funny way of showing it." She grimaced as her words bubbled to the surface. "I mean, *Fuerian Vastra*, of all elves."

"You'll see... someday," Eilastra said. "Not now, or even soon, but some day you'll see how he is trying to set you up for greatness, daughter."

Jaira squinted quizzically at her.

Eilastra explained, "House Vastra has been a prominent family of Cathair Dé for generations and a stalwart fixture in the Summer Court. They represent the best alliance for your future. For your children's future."

Jaira had not given much thought to how her choices would impact any children she might someday have. *Any child of Remy and I would be a changeling...*

Eilastra said, "Someday soon, not likely during *your* age of potential breeding, but probably in your children's, Oberon's son will finally settle down and claim a wife."

Jaira sighed and frowned as the wheels of her mind turned. She finally understood what her mother had implied.

Harhassus's decision had more to do with responsibilities as an heir to a title than it did with family. But that did not mean she had to like it. If she could, Jaira would reject any titles, fortunes, or estates—and the strings that attached to them—if it meant she was free to love and free to live.

But this... this wasn't even about *her*, she acknowledged, or even about allying Houses Morgensteen and Vastra. Harhassus Morgensteen was making a play at allying his family with an heir of royal blood.

"It may not feel like it in this moment, but your father cares for you far more than you can understand. If something ever happened to you, I don't know what he would do—*that* is why I believe your father has made the best choice. And how I know you will be capable of uniting ours and House Vastra... if your father thought it would damage you in some permanent way, he would never forgive himself for arranging it."

Jaira stared at her bedspread in the burgeoning silence that followed. Not daring to meet her mother's gaze. *Consequences be damned.* Despite her father's wishes and her mother's words, Jaira still had every intention of marrying for love—even if it tarnished the Morgensteen name.

Eilastra squeezed Jaira's hand and then stood to leave Jaira to her thoughts.

"Mother?"

Eilastra paused at the door.

"If there was another choice—a better choice than Fuerian, and one who I approved of, would you support me in that choice?" Jaira asked.

Eilastra's eyes glimmered, and she tilted her head in subtle agreement. "If it could bring about all the things your father wants for you, then I would... even if that choice was a human."

So long as Queen Titania remains in control of public opinion, chances at that are slim...

Eilastra's eyes sparkled with a faint glimmer of rebellion, a nature that Jaira always knew her mother had possessed, and held carefully in check.

Her mother backed out of the room and clicked the door shut after her.

F RIGID FINGERS GRIPPED REMY chilling him deeper than the frosts he'd felt in those years in the unseelie. In addition to the cold, a strange sensation like floating gripped him. *Is this the aither? No... maybe I'm dead.*

Then, he felt himself choking. He awoke with a gasp and lifted himself from the river where the current had turned him against the wooden post of an old river dock and pulled his head under.

How long have I been floating? It was evening when I was supposed to see Jaira dance!

The sun was on the wrong side of the sky and neared midday indicating that he'd been unconscious at least through the night and morning. Remy grabbed a hold of the dock's moorings and dragged himself onto the shore, coughing up water and vomit.

Remy thought he even saw the greens of algae and tiny water shields as he hacked his guts out onto the banks.

How much did I suck in? I'm lucky to be alive!

His eyes shifted between focus and a range of blurs, but he saw a pair of boots and thick legs standing before him. Remy's chest heaved in sucking gasps and as his sight cleared, he found nothing there but scrubby brush near the boat launch.

Oxygen deprivation, he assumed, double checking that he was, indeed, on land. Remy checked all of his senses to make sure they were accurately reporting data, and then touched his head. His bandanna had slipped down around his neck but his unruly hair matted down over his head and pasted to his scalp, concealing his ears from any passersby.

Once he'd gotten enough air, his memory returned to him. Fuerian and his pals had jumped him and stolen his dúshlán before beating him unconscious and dumping his body.

Panic suddenly struck and he reached for his pocket. The earring was still there, and curiously, so was the key.

Gareth, the big elf, Remy remembered, *he was superstitious about the knife and the high speech... he probably put it there in case there were any rites or curses attached to it.*

Remy touched the part of his face Gareth had struck him with the metal knuckle band; it left an angry welt that throbbed to the touch. *Too bad he didn't feel similar about physical violence.* He'd compelled his enemy to form an unbreakable vow, one that the magic nature of Arcadeax, and the gods themselves, would enforce. Because of that, Remy felt he'd gotten the better end of his bargain with Fuerian.

Water shed off him as he stood. Remy winced. His torso and stomach hurt almost as much from the violent puking as from where Fuerian's goons had worked him over. He flopped a few steps like a half-drowned mouse. Then he caught sight of two deeply yellow orbs that glowed beneath a nearby stone bridge where a broad road crossed.

Remy squinted and then made out the shape of the creature that did its best to stay out of the light. He asked it a question in the language of the unseelie:

[Friend, how far is your bridge from Cathair Dé?]

Remy could make out the thing's large, gnarled hands. He'd dealt with enough trolls during his years in the unseelie to know how much the creatures hated the sunlight. It could kill most breeds of the species.

The day was overcast enough that it might have allowed the troll to emerge. He probed the light with a long finger to see if it was safe to come out, and after a moment, the finger hardened to stone. The troll grumbled at the test, but not angrily. He snapped off the petrified digit and then flicked it casually aside as if it had been little more than a stray booger.

After the stone finger splashed into the river, the troll's booming voice chortled, as if amused to hear its own tongue spoken so far from its home. It said, [A half day's walk by road. Shorter if by horse.] Licking his lips, the troll looked around with hungry optimism and asked, [Do you happen to *have* a horse?]

[Sorry. I do not.] The human gave the bridge troll a stiff bow. [But happy collecting, friend troll.]

Remy spotted a fat toad waddling in the grass nearby and snatched it. [I've neither crossed your road nor have coin for your toll, but you look hungry and though the sun is not bright, it is high.]

He threw the toad into the shadows near the beast. It croaked when it smacked upon the dark stones. The troll scooped it up and slurped it down.

[Thank you, friend Adam.]

[Your nose is keen,] Remy said. He smiled and shook out his hair before removing and wringing out the bandanna which he'd replace once it had dried. [I am called Remy.]

[I am Skreekuzz. Tell me, what news from the unseelie?]

[No news that you would be interested in,] Remy said, knowing the question that all trolls asked—but especially those scattered outside the reach of the Winter Court. [The brother is still lost. Wulflock has not yet returned to rule the unseelie.]

"Hrrmmph," the troll growled like a great pouting dog. He blinked his round, glowing eyes and bobbed his head with a wave.

Remy waved back cordially, departing. He was not a particular friend of trolls, but it never hurt to try to remain on cordial terms with creatures powerful enough to smash you to goo without effort. They were terrifying in battle, and most of the race had been excommunicated from the central parts of the unseelie, forcing most of them into hiding; many even took refuge here in King Oberon's domain. The trolls had sided with Oberon's brother, Wulflock, during an overthrow of his Winter Court and been thusly banished.

The trolls and their allies looked forward to Wulflock fulfilling his vow to someday return and reclaim winter court's Rime Throne. In the wake of his absence, every half decade or so a new ruler overthrew the previous, except for the last thirty-eight years where Anansi the Spider Queen reigned, though she'd gone through consorts at approximately the same speed as overthrown rulers.

Whatever happened to them in the end Remy preferred not to wonder about. He'd known Anansi, and he'd escaped her webs and had little desire to return to her lands.

He shuddered, glad he'd been able to escape the unseelie. Not all the humans he'd known there had been as fortunate. Remy started down the road and walked back toward Cathair Dé.

Once he'd dried off enough that his legs would not bind in his pants, walking the road came easier, but he knew it would be hours before the city's silhouette would rise in the distance. His stomach grumbled and twisted; he hoped to arrive in time to find some food.

T HORANMIR STOOD ON THE stops of the mission and turned to catch his sister's gaze. He shook his head.

She sat in her mobility chair at the bottom of the steps; there was not any way for her to follow.

"I'm sorry," explained the she-elf at the front gates. She produced a bound pad of papers and her fingers were stained with charcoal. "I knew Eldarian. He was here for several days."

"His sister sent me to search for him on the family's behalf," Thoranmir said. "Please, if he's gone somewhere, the family—his sister Odessa, in particular—is desperate to know what happened to him."

She bit her lower lip as she flipped through the pages and turned over the sketchbook where she'd recorded Eldarian's likeness. "He was so sweet. But he was... *broken*."

Thoranmir stared at the portrait. "How do you mean?"

"He was not lucid... not usually. He had some demon in him—an intense fear and a hunger, seemingly all at once, whenever he was in his right mind," the artist said.

Thoranmir cocked his head. "Like, a literal demon?" A jolt of fear ran through him. Myths of Oberon's forces sealing the gate to the infernal realms had long since entered legend.

"No, no," she said. "I mean it figuratively. But something broke his mind."

"Do you think something happened to him at the academy?" Thoranmir asked.

"I do. Whatever happened to him there destroyed his mind."

Thoranmir bobbed his head for a few moments longer. "You're sure he's not here?"

"I'm sorry. I don't know where he might have gone." There was both sorrow and sincerity in her eyes.

"Can I take this?" Thoranmir held up the sketch.

She nodded and tore the page free for him.

Thoranmir descended the stairs and met his sister on the road.

She leaned out of her chair to peek at the image of Eldarian. "I only caught part of what she said. Is your lead dead?"

"Yes."

Thoranmir paused as he thought it over, and then he shook his head. "Not exactly."

Anya gave him a screwy look

"She said he had a demon in him... some kind of need. I'm pretty sure she's describing his need for the drug, probably the dream hallow. If that's the case, I think I know where he went."

With his sister's chair riding hot on his heels, he walked along the path leading into The Haunts.

Thoranmir turned and faced the corridor of road that lead to the increasingly dilapidated structures in the most dangerous part of Cathair Dé.

CHAPTER FOURTEEN

L OITARIEL DID HER BEST to eavesdrop without looking like she was, but it meant standing near the creature that Agarogol had created with his distasteful kind of magic. The dead-eyed elf did not look right, or smell right, and everything about it unnerved her. She swallowed her distaste and breathed through her mouth as she turned her ear to the conversation nearby.

Calithilon had sent Tinthel, the next lowest ranked maven, to check in and bring back an update. She and Mithrilchon spoke in hushed tones, but the two council members spoke with enough insistent that Loitariel could hear them without much struggle.

"Have you ascertained which contender is warded?" Tinthel asked.

Mithrilchon scowled. "I wish I had a simple answer for you. The member of House Vastra bears a charm that provides him some protection. It is a family heirloom and honors his position as the successor to the line. I doubt he even knows its significance."

Tinthiel's eyebrows rose. "It seems a good indicator of who is responsible for the coming cataclysm."

"It is not," Mithrilchon argued with her.

"The human, by some strange miracle, bears his own dúshlán. He is marked by some strange magic, perhaps a special destiny that has been arranged by a god."

Tinthel chuffed, "A confused god, it must be, to give a dúshlán to a ddiymadferth."

"Be that as it may, it is the fact you may report to the White Maven. And besides, you know as well as I do what actions were taken at the aphay tree." Mithrilchon's eyes flitted back to his apprentices to warn Tinthel that their conversation was not perfectly secure.

Loitariel did not know the contents of Calithilon's secret conversation with the ranking mavens. She could surmise, however, that it had something to do with the human, Remy Keaton.

"We have also not checked every other contender to see if they, to bear some protection that the seer had noted in her visions," Mithrilchon said.

"And what prevents there from being more than these two?" Tinthel's voice took on an irked ring.

"We could waste time running down every competitor, but that would be a foolish waste of time when we can narrow it to two and prepare a plan for each," Mithrilchon explained. "We can not possibly respond to every potential scenario. What if a last minute contender is added to the bout and he or she is the cataclysm bearer? We can only set plans against so many potential scenarios, and with each one we risk exposing ourself and then invalidating the seer's visions."

Tinthel frowned, obviously unhappy. There was not more that could be done, but any maven with an ounce of historical knowledge knew that they'd tipped their hand once before while over-relying on a seer. It had led to catastrophe during the Infernal Wars.

"The very thing that provides Remy Keaton his protection will be his undoing. One of my apprentices will deliver an ancient curse, a fetiche. *The kiss of daggers.*"

"And you think you can deliver it securely?" Tinthel asked.

Mithrilchon nodded.

"You have a plan for the human. Then what? What is your plan to deal with Fuerian Vastra?"

Their voices sank just low enough that Loitariel could not hear them. A few moments later she heard the red maven's call.

"Loitariel," Mithrilchon summoned his apprentice.

She hurried over to him and the maven placed a finger below her chin and lifted her to stand straight. He thrust a hand below her skirts, surprising her with a sudden grope.

Loitariel stiffened and her eyes widened with surprise. Her master had never made sexual advances or taken any license afforded by his position of power—even though she'd tried to use her body to gain favor earlier in her career.

"You are not unattractive," Mithrilchon said, "and I know you want to serve Oberon through the Suíochán Naséan. How deep does your loyalty lie?"

"It is complete," Loitariel said.

"Even if it requires your flesh?"

Loitariel nodded, undid the clasps of her robes and her clothing fell to the floor. She stood her there, fully nude and at Mithrilchon's complete disclosure.

Mithrilchon turned to Tinthel.

The female maven raised her brow and admired Loitariel's body, still in its relative youth. "She'll do."

T HORANMIR STOPPED A THIRD fey, an elf of tylwyth teg descent. She looked like any other she-elf, though perhaps wilder somehow, perhaps feral. The tylwyth teg had longer ears which ended in sharper angles than seelie or unseelie sidhe; they were wildfey: independents. Their people had sided with neither the winter nor the summer courts in the wars between Oberon and his brother.

The wildfey studied the drawing Thoranmir had shown her. Like the others he'd interviewed, her eyes wore that same kind of vacant expression which indicated some kind of substance abuse.

Her willowy arms and gaunt features might have been normal for the tylwyth teg, but Thoranmir wasn't sure. He'd not met with many of them in his life. Political dispositions between the seelie and unseelie being what they were, most of the wildfey remained in their own lands, the faewylds, and they rarely made homes where they would fall subject to Oberon's laws.

Finally, she nodded, making her dreadlocked hair sway with the motion. The tylwyth teg pointed. "I saw him this morning, seeking an escape to aither."

"In that building?" Thoranmir asked.

She shook her head. "The alley between. It is a dead end. He's maybe still there."

Thoranmir hurried towards it even as the tylwyth teg began to beg for money as some kind of payment. He and Anya both ignored her, assuming she'd only use any coin to do further self harm.

The entrance to the alley created a long chute that looked like a ravine blasted by miners. Both buildings on either side had succumbed to the ravages of time, active disrepair, and vandalism.

Anya paused at the edge, uncertain the wheels of her chair could handle the rough terrain. "Be careful," she called.

Thoranmir grumbled a reply that he'd heard her, even if he moved too quickly to actually follow her advice.

Ahead, he spotted a pair of feet sticking out from behind a half-collapsed garbage bin. Thoranmir yelped and hurried forward.

He rounded the edge to find a figure clad in dark robes crouched over the babbling form of Eldarian Cócaire. Whatever the thing was, it was dressed similar to the four elves who'd attacked Thoranmir after he'd dropped out of the dueling contest.

It shrieked with an animal-like sound when it spotted Thoranmir and then seemed to explode like a cloud of smoke. The concussive force of it blasted Thoranmir with a gout of heat and nearly knocked the sidhe from his feet. He shielded his eyes and then, a moment later, turned his view back.

The thing, whatever it had been, was gone.

Thoranmir ran to Eldarian's side and crouched to his knees. "I've got him, Anya! I found him. *What's left of him,*" Thoranmir muttered.

Whatever, whoever, the cloaked thing was, he was feeding Eldarian from a glass tube which had been discarded nearby. Thoranmir examined it. It was broken, but there were still a few of the white crystallized granules within. More were stuck to the side of Eldarian's face where they'd poured from his mouth.

"Eldarian! Eldarian?" Thoranmir shook him and the elf's tongue lolled out of his mouth. More crystals clung to it and Thoranmir brushed them off as best as he was able.

"I can't get through," yelled Anya, shaking her chair with frustration.

Thoranmir looked back at her, not wanting to leave his sister unattended in such a dangerous place. He glanced from her to Eldarian, and then back. He set his jaw and then picked up the unconscious elf who babbled in unintelligible words.

Eldarian writhed with limp, dying-fish motions as Thoranmir tried to carry him back to the street. Thoranmir nearly dropped him twice until he repositioned, locked his hands around the too-thin elf's chest, and then dragged him in reverse.

Huffing and puffing, he finally laid Eldarian to rest at the entrance to the alley. The unconscious elf began to shake and bubbles formed where his lips barely parted.

"He doesn't look good," Thoranmir said.

Anya's face was grim. "No he does not. What's wrong with him? I didn't discover information about anything at all similar when I looked into those disappearing sidhe."

"Have you heard of dream hallow?"

She shook her head, and so Thoranmir told her what he knew about the stuff.

"Gods cursed alchemy," she muttered. "I should have expected as much. For millennia there have been a lot of different ways to reach the aithersphere. Very few are safe, most involve a lot of discomfort, a little magic, and toxic flora. Technology and aithermancy have been the only safe and reliable way to get there—but we don't do it to *escape*. Whatever this is—the compulsion to get there—it's eating away his soul."

As if on cue, Eldarian stiffened. His back arched like a contortionist, and then he relaxed.

Thoranmir nodded and then pressed a finger to his neck. "Oh, no you don't!" With an angry smack of his fist, he slammed it down onto the elf's chest.

ELDARIAN GASPED AND WENT rigid for a moment before he started mumbling nonsense phrases at varying volumes. But at least he was breathing again as Anya's brother administered aid.

"Stay with us, for your sister's sake," Thoranmir shouted at him.

"Why are you doing this?" Anya asked Eldarian. "Why do you take the dream hallow?"

"B-black night... unseelie paradise... like stars in the sky..." he babbled.

"I've got to know," Anya insisted, crawling out of her chair and onto the dirt where she could sit with the elf. She positioned her mangled stump legs so she could be near the victim. "What happened to you? What happened at the academy?"

"The demons... my stomach—oh, my stomach... fireworms inside me..."

"He's not making any sense," Thoranmir said. "We've got to get him somewhere they can help him."

Anya caught her brother's eyes. "Look at him, Thoranmir. Do you really think he's going to survive this?"

Thoranmir tightened his jaw and refused to answer.

She pulled some equipment from her chair. "If this dream hallow garbage does what it sounds like, then he's a goner for sure. His body might live, but he's about to fade out."

"Fade out?" Thoranmir asked.

"The toxins I mentioned... there are certain plants in nature, especially in the faewylds, that can send one to the aither. It elevates the mind and spirit... almost like making one immune to gravity." Anya fixed her gaze on her brother. "What would happen if you became so light that you just floated away?"

"Like, if I just floated up and into the stars?" Thoranmir asked.

Anya nodded as she climbed into her chair and affixed a headset to her brow. "That is exactly what is happening to him. Quickly," she pointed to a nearby building that looked somewhat functional. "Drag him there."

Eldarian babbled words that neither could understand while Thoranmir did as requested.

On the exterior of the house was an aither port and Anya jacked into it with a cable splitter and then withdrew a backup set of equipment as her brother deposited Eldarian.

She tossed him the headset. "Put that on him."

"But he's not an aithermancer," Thoranmir argued. Anybody could use the aither, but only few could parse the strange world of soul-matter and information well enough to not use an interface.

"He's not cogent enough to use the tech... and he's already *in the aither*," Anya insisted. "If I can find him there... maybe I can..." She trailed off, not wanting to give her brother any false hope.

"The crystal... the crystal," Eldarian mumbled over and over again.

Thoranmir put the headset onto Eldarian who offered no resistance.

Anya closed her eyes and sent her consciousness into the aithersphere. She found Eldarian easily.

Eldarian, or Eldarian's spirit form to be exact, cowered behind a giant crystal that protruded from the ground. She'd spotted several of them in the aither, and intrinsically knew which one Eldarian had meant... he was calling for her—for help.

In the aither, Anya had legs. Here she was not crippled and her body was strong—far stronger and tougher than even most stout elves I the real world.

"Eldarian," she reached down a hand. "Let me help you."

He looked around, skittish, and horrified out of his mind. But he took her hand and stood on weak knees, barely able to balance on his feet.

"What happened to you?" she asked. "You were at the academy. Were you one of the students who were kidnapped?"

He nodded.

"What did they do... where did they take you?"

"Eggs... Stór Rúnda," Eldarian shouted with a mad cackle.

Anya cocked her head, trying to understand.

His head turned aside and his eyes focused on something that was not there. He moaned, "Vomit terror... the beatings... raw emotion. Hot... I'm so hot... it—it's coming!" His voice rose to screams at the end. His fingers curled in on themselves like green reeds cast onto hot coals. His skin cracked and began falling like clumps of autumn gossamer.

"No, no, no!" Anya howled. She clutched him, trying to hold him together, but the more she tried to help him, the more he crumbled apart, as if Anya was trying to knit together a moldered crochet blanket.

"Who did this to you?" Anya asked, hoping for a name or a lead she could scour the aither for.Moments later, he collapsed in pieces. The chunks of him disintegrated as his terror-filled eyes stared into the sky.

There was nothing she could but let Eldarian fall apart. The high dose of the dream hallow severed his spirit's tether to its body, and his mind evaporated into the aither.

Sinking to her knees, Anya stared at her hands which smoldered as the last remnants of Eldarian broke apart into mist. She wept for only a moment, and then she returned to the real world with a jolt that made her sit up.

"He... he's gone, Thoranmir."

R EMY'S STOMACH GRUMBLED AGAIN and he realized it had been almost a full day since he'd eaten anything last. Somewhere in the distance somebody was cooking. The oakey smell of campfire and sizzling meat wafted towards him, tantalizing him with tasty promises.

He tried to ignore the aroma and pressed forward on the road, hoping to outpace it and hurry back towards Cathair Dé. *Maybe I can get back in time for supper,* he hoped.

The further he walked, however, the stronger the smell of the food came. It's source was somewhere up ahead and Remy had take care not to drool. He tried to ignore it, but his nose identified baking, breads, and someone pouring fat drippings over venison.

Remy nearly staggered off the beaten road and towards the woods where the aromas came from. He paused when he stepped into the grass, inexplicably lured towards the pleasant aromas and the promise of food.

If someone is cooking in the woods instead of the open, its probably a trap... or a group of folk who wish to remain concealed, but is big enough to fight back intruders?

An internal warning cautioned him against seeking out the cooks in hopes that they'd be generous. Skreekuzz had been relatively compliant under the threat of daylight, but there was ample shade below the forest's canopy and trolls were known to trick unwary travelers and wind up as part of the meal they'd hoped to partake from.

Despite his hunger, Remy put his feet back on the road and turned back towards Cathair Dé. Somewhere near the tree-line came a whistle. A bare-chested man wearing clothes made from animal hides stood waving at him so that Remy would see him, and then the man hurried towards the road.

As he drew closer, Remy realized he was woefully unprepared if the man meant violence. Remy was without any weapon—even his dúshlán. That fear lessened somewhat when he realized the man approaching him was exactly that: a human male.

He arrived just a little out of breath and he rested his hands on his knees sucking air as he introduced himself. "Greetings, Adam. My name is Madadh." Madadh turned his head and pushed his ear forward so Remy could see it and verify the man's species.

Remy bowed as much as was polite. "I am called Remy," he replied. "I'm just on my way back to the city."

Madadh's face pinched with confusion. "Cathair Dé? It is a dangerous place for a human."

"All places are dangerous places," Remy countered.

"True, true," Madadh replied. "Our scouts spotted your approach and we thought to offer you a spot at our table."

Remy squinted shrewdly and touched his headband to ensure his ears were covered. "How did you see I was human?"

Madadh touched the side of his nose. "There are more senses than mere eyesight. Come, come." He urged Remy to follow.

The venison smells urged Remy forward. Madadh *was* a human. That didn't make him trustworthy, but Remy hoped it would at least buy him enough hospitality for a quick meal.

He followed Madadh to an animal run that broke through the underbrush and entered the forest. Madadh was a little shorter than Remy, perhaps of a similar age and a little more lightly muscled. He was, however, significantly more hairy. His chest sprouted thick, curly growth and his grizzled beard hung off his chin.

Half a league into the trees a clearing opened. Makeshift structures of lashed poles and stitched together animal hides dotted the perimeter. Racks hung out freshly killed hides for scraping and drying.

Men and women meandered about the camp in addition to children who dashed around each other in play, mostly unwashed and many undressed. Eyes watched Remy as he moved; he especially felt the piqued interest of female eyes as they looked him over like a prize to be won.

"Welcome to the Fianna," Madadh said, leading Remy to the central fire were several folk worked to cook a community meal. He motioned for Remy to sit on a stump.

Remy took a seat across from him. "This is a human settlement?"

"Not a settlement. Not exactly," explained Madadh. "The Fianna are, by necessity, nomadic. The sidhe," he whispered, as if that was explanation enough.

Remy squinted his confusion.

Madadh told him, "The elves, really all the fey, they are vicious thieves, takers, predators. They collect human stragglers and abuse them. And worse—they steal even their own."

Remy was still confused.

"The Hell Tithe stopped millenia ago. The fey are no longer forced to pay the infernal forces a tribute of stolen children taken from the realm of man. And yet they still sometimes take our children if they have some dark purpose." He leaned forward and spoke in low tones. "And they even prey upon their own. These are evil creatures, Remy."

Remy shrugged and then bowed his head gratefully to the young woman who handed him a plate of food with a broad and lusty smile. "I think they are just people—pointy eared, prone to magic, and native to Arcadeax, but people nonetheless. I've met all sorts of folk—and most of them are terrible. But a few are worth putting up with the rest for," Remy said.

Madadh half smirked. "It sounds like you are an enemy to all."

"Or maybe I'm a friend to all… if they want it," Remy said. "I am very sincere where my friends are concerned."

Madadh chuckled and accepted a plate from the serving girl. "Then I very much hope that we can be friends."

After eating, Remy asked more questions about Madadh's community and their purpose. They were a cluster of families and other collected humans that neared one hundred bodies. Many of the were skilled hunters, hence the venison, and they operated on a kind of pack mentality.

"Our purpose is fairly straightforward, at least in the short term. The Fianna is larger than just us. But we, our group, exists to invite humans into our fold." Madadh concluded a very short loop through the clearing showing him their camp.

Everywhere Remy went, the eyes—especially of those younger females—followed him. He saw the optimism on the faces in the community, and not just the kind of pre-glow lust one expected from horny youth. Each person there saw the Fianna as a better way of life.

"I'm sorry," Remy told Madadh. "But I must return to the city. I have friends there, too. They need me—and I have commitments."

"These friends—they are elves, or other fey?" Madadh looked confused.

Remy nodded slowly.

"And they accept you?"

He nodded again.

"Then caution I warn for you," Madadh said. "A day is coming soon, a day of retribution, a day when humans will repay the sidhe and the Frith Duine monsters for their abuses—for impoverishing us and stealing our children—"

That part caught Remy's ear. "The Frith Duine, the human haters? Do you think they are responsible for the disappearing children at the orphanages? I have heard of that and I am fighting against it in Cathair Dé. What do you know about it?"

"What is there to say?" Madadh asked. "Children make compliant slaves and they keep the longest."

"You have a plan to stop this?" Remy asked. "Maybe we can concentrate our efforts and—"

Madadh shook his head. "I am sorry, friend. We do not discuss Fianna business with those outside our number. We would welcome you to join. Come, help us fight the evils of Arcadeax."

Remy raised a brow, "But if I joined you, I'd never be able to go back, right?"

Madadh inclined his head. "That is the agreement. We need men like you: strong men who can help make our stock stronger—those ones make the strongest..." Madadh trailed off, realizing he nearly overshared.

Remy looked at him quizzically. "The strongest what?"

"Children," Madadh decided he could share, though Remy felt certain there was more to it than what Madadh said.

"The Fianna will fight, regardless of whether you join us. But you may still count us as a friend, I hope. Perhaps someday you, too, will see the weakness of the fey, even of the aes sidhe, and then you will join our ranks," said Madadh.

"Thank you, friend," Remy said. He took the key from his pocket and turned it over to Madadh. "Take this."

"A key?"

Remy explained where to go in order to use it. "I stole the riches from a group of sidhe who did evil. Use it to protect and sponsor as many children as you can."

Madadh nodded and thanked him as Remy stood to leave. "You are sure you will not stay? We have much to offer you."

Remy realized every eye was upon him. All the females studied him intently. Some had partially removed their leathers or furs, others stood in suggestive poses in their attempts to lure Remy into their number.

"You could have any female here. You could have *all* the females here," Madadh said. "The Fianna do not understand attachments as others do. *We are a pack*. What belongs to one, belongs to all." Madadh caught the desirous gazes of the women in his camp. "Though, that does not mean there is no such thing as desire, I suppose."

Remy tore his eyes away from the obvious desire of the women and focused on Madadh. "I thank you, friend, but I must go. I am certain we'll meet again."

Madadh bowed. "Then, until that time," and he let Remy depart freely.

ANYA HELD THORANMIR'S HAND as they stood at the graveside. It was not a cheap plot, as had been reserved by the city to bury transients and unnamed corpses in. He'd dipped into his savings to give Eldarian a proper plot, complete with engraved headstone and a plot of flowers.

Thoranmir had to guess as to which his favorites were. *We can always dig these up later, if Odessa thinks he'd have preferred something else.*

"I'll write to Odessa's family, soon," Thoranmir said. "Just as soon as the contest is over. They'll want to visit, I'm sure."

Anya released his hand. "Don't tell me you're still planning to compete in that barbaric thing... even after all this?"

Thoranmir did not meet her gaze, but he figured he owed her some kind of respite from her worry. "The contest has been informed already that I planned to withdraw." It was the truth of the matter, as he'd stated it.

Anya visibly relaxed. "I'm going to do my best to find out who, or what, has been stalking and stealing the aes sidhe."

Thoranmir nodded, grateful to have such a powerful aithermancer looking into it, but then he remembered the elves who'd jumped him in the alley. *To stop Remy, I might just have to compete, after all, if that can be arranged. Unless there is another way...* The wheels began turning in his mind.

He stared at the open grave and the simple wooden box which held Eldarian's remains. *I refuse to stand here again and watch them bury Anya or Remy, next... not while I still have the opportunity to stop it.*

Only Anya and Thoranmir stood vigil over the open grave. Two fauns, each carrying shovels, approached and waited for a signal from Thoranmir.

He nodded, and the two fey grave keepers shoveled scoops of dirt into the hole from the nearby fresh mound. The first several echoed painfully against the hollow casket, and then they quieted as the hole began to fill.

Thoranmir took Anya by the hand and they turned, leaving for home.

Never again, Thoranmir told himself. *I've got to protect Anya from whoever those hooded freaks were... and I've got to keep Fuerian from Remy. I won't see any more of them die.*

He glanced back one more time where the fauns continued with their tools.

Why am I the only one trying to keep all my friends alive?

DARKNESS FELL ACROSS THE city when Thoranmir strode up to the gatekeeper at the exclusive pub. The elf stood stalwart outside the Thistle and Barrel. He was the same guard who was missing half an ear and who had let Thoranmir and Anya pass a few days ago.

Pausing to present himself, Thoranmir asked, "Do you remember me? Anya the aithermancer, my sister, forgot her satchel here the other day. She told me Chechey would likely have it. I just need to go in and ask him. I'll be in and out."

The guard looked at him with his squinty eyes, glancing back through his stack of waivers.

"I'm sure mine is still in there. I know the drill—hand chopping and all that. I'll just be a couple of minutes. I promise."

"Make it fast," the big guy growled.

"Thank you," Thoranmir nearly stuttered. "In and out. I promise." He was so nervous as he stole inside the lounge and searched out his target. *Fuerian Vastra.*

Thoranmir knew he was inside. He'd watched from the streets all afternoon. He'd had a hunch that the braggart would report in and build himself up to his peers on the days preceding the dueling event. Thoranmir had been correct—but that had not made him brave.

He withdrew a flask from his breast pocket and took a sip. He started to screw the cap back on, and then thought better of it and downed the remainder of its contents.

Thoranmir knew he had promised the ruffians in the alley that he would not talk to any of his friends about what had transpired earlier in the day. *Gods, has it only been the one day?*

He suddenly felt very old and thin.

Knowing that his sister's life hung in the balance, he had decided to rely on his enemies instead.

Thoranmir set his mind, remembering that he must take care not to over-share. He assumed at least one of those sidhe attackers had magic abilities and had possibly cast some sort of glamour, which would let them eavesdrop. Caution was a high priority—but he also assumed that they could only hear what he said... and perhaps they could also hear what he heard. Spells were always very specific, and he assumed something as powerful as activating *all* of his senses would take a great drain upon any aes sidhe who cast it, limiting its effectiveness—but spying on one sense, like his hearing?

That must be it, he convinced himself. *I'd hear my own words spoken, plus any spoken to me. It is what I would do, if I had any magic to command.*

Thoranmir approached Fuerian and took the seat directly adjacent to him. "We need to talk," he said boldly, encouraged by the liquor. "I'm ready to help you out—Remy must not win this contest."

CHAPTER FIFTEEN

— · —

L ONG SHADOWS STRETCHED ACROSS the road and the fields
that dotted the landscape beyond the city. Lamplight burned
in the distance where the edges of Cathair Dé rose in the distance.

Remy knew it would be night by the time he arrived. He quickened his gait and hurried on tired legs.

On the furthermost outskirts of the city, still several leagues from
its actual boundary, small pockets of buildings rose up to catch
the interests of travelers. A few sandwich board signs advertised
various sundries including akasha, traveling foods, and the like,

Remy nearly hurried through the road except that he smelled the
odor of dead things and the three oil lamps present along the short
stretch of highway remained unlit. He slowed his gait, searching
for signs of a trap.

He spotted a marking on a door, instead. A symbol had been
painted upon a simple plank entry: a symbol that Remy knew, but
which did not belong in the seelie. It was an unseelie sign with a
singular meaning. *Refuge.*

Without advancing further, Remy paused, certain he was being
watched. He pulled down his headband to show his ears and called

out in the tongue of unseelie, [Folk of winter, send me your representative.]

A few moments passed in silence, and then a short creature emerged from behind a crate. He was about half Remy's height and looked like a grey-bearded dwarf, but for his diminutive size and his slouched, red hat. He carried a spear which he held at the ready, gripped by overly long fingers indicating he was some breed of goblin.

[Identify yourself, ddiymadferth,] the redcap commanded.

Remy stiffened. He was not in the mood to let some surly redcap threaten him. [I am Aderyn Corff, of the warlord Rhylfelour's forces, and I am in no mood to suffer insults from some uppity powrie.] Folk of the unseelie knew both the reputation and the name which he'd been given by the warlord Rhylfelour. Remy earned fear and respect of the unseelie in the life he'd lived but fled before becoming bound to the winter crown.

The goblin wilted beneath Remy's words. He whispered back to the rest of the fey hidden nearby. [It is really you... the Death Bird... the human who escaped Rhagathena's clutches?] He spat after speaking her name.

"Yes. It is I," Remy switched back into the common tongue.

[We, too are refugees, fleeing the Spider Queen who controls the Rime Throne, ever seeking the forgotten king. Something is amiss in the unseelie. The air is far too foul and the queen is mad.]

Remy looked at the goblin. "Fleeing was wise. But you must go elsewhere. This is not the place to set up a safe house for your fellows. Not anywhere so close to the city. I spotted it immediately

and suspected something was amiss even before seeing your sign."
He pointed to the sigil written upon the door.

"If you stay, you'll soon find yourselves facing Oberon's forces.
I already smell the stench of death. How fresh is your cap, foolish
powrie?"

The redcap grimaced and hedged away from the human. Powrie
were a goblin race, and they had a penchant for soaking their hats in
the blood of their victims. They claimed they'd die without doing
so, but Remy had never known a truthful powrie, except when
speaking the olde tongue.

"That's what I thought." Remy turned to continue the road to
Cathair Dé. "The choice is yours, but you should move further,
beyond even the troll and his bridge in that direction." Remy
pointed towards where he'd met Skreekuzz.

[We thank you,] the goblin said, bowing so low that his hat
touched the ground. [Tell us what you know of the war? Wulflock
may yet be lost, but has the seelie fared well against Rhagathena?]

"I am not in her service... I neither know nor care," Remy explained his take on the great war between the Summer and Winter
Courts. It had been going on for generations prior to his involvement and he'd grown tired of it years ago. "But I will tell you what
I know: Summer still holds sway. But if you're hoping Oberon
will overthrow the Winter Queen, you should find a new savior.
He's too entangled with his own court's politics to take any serious
action against his enemies."

The redcap looked disappointed, but not surprised. He bobbed
his head. [We thank thee all the same.] He barked at his compan-

ions and they hurried out under the cover of darkness, crossing the fields nearby as if nothing more than a flitting shadow.

Remy would have barely noticed them if he did not know what to look for. The unseelie refugees fled into the deeper darkness at the edge of his sight and hoped they would not share with any of Rhagathena's hunters that the Aderyn Corff had moved to Cathair Dé.

He slipped a hand into his pocket to touch the earring there. Remy turned and hurried back to the road leading to the city. *Jaira's city.*

He wouldn't return to the unseelie under any circumstances—not for any promise of wealth. Not so long as Jaira remained a member of Oberon's court.

Remy sucked in a deep breath and held it as he jogged past the buildings which stunk of decay, and then hurried back towards the city.

"I F I HAD MY way," Thoranmir insisted, "Remy would not even compete. So, yeah, we need to talk."

Fuerian did a double-take, thrown for a loop by the elf's curious position against his friend.

"Do we now?" Fuerian chuckled. "How did you even get in here?"

"That's besides the point. I'm here now. And I'm bound not to say certain things," Thoranmir told him.

[So, you have made a foolish vow,] Fuerian accused in the high tongue.

[Something like that,] Thoranmir responded, grinning. "Here's the deal. I don't want Remy in this contest, either. I probably want him to drop out even more than you do."

Fuerian raised an eyebrow. "You are a betrayer, then? How interesting." He sipped from his goblet.

"No! No," Thoranmir insisted. "Well..." *I have to protect my sister* he almost blurted, but managed to keep it inside his head. "Let's just say that there is more happening than you know about. But I think Remy would be willing to drop out under certain circumstances. I... I just need him to quit.... to back down this one time."

"And what's in it for me?"

Thoranmir stiffened, surprised his enemy needed more than a safeguard for his pride. He offered some of the usual reasons. "Power. Influence." He mustered all his courage and stared into the eyes of his enemy and insisted on what he *could* offer. "A guarantee. You and I both know that Remy is maybe the only one you've met who has the ability to actually beat you. If he's gone..." Thoranmir trailed off and refused to blink.

Fuerian turned aside and took another drink. "Let's say that you're right. Let's pretend that I might have an interest in convincing him to turn aside. What would that look like?"

Thoranmir knew he had Fuerian. *He's trying to sweeten the pot. He wants Remy out, too... and if he doesn't see that right now, he'll figure it out pretty quick once the contest begins.*

He took a napkin from the bar and then produced a leaded stylus. He began to draw on it as he spoke. "I'm not going to do your job for you, Fuerian." He finished a sketch: what he remembered of the red, intertwined antlers he'd exposed on his attacker's chest and turned it over. "Just answer me with a yes or no. Does this look familiar? Do you know it?"

Fuerian sucked in a sharp breath. "I do." He clutched the piece of jewelry that hung at his neck as he muttered a few curses at the bottom of his voice.

Damn it... it's so familiar, why can't I place it? I'm sure I've seen it at least once before.

"Then I'll just tell you to look into it. You'll find a way to convince Remy to relinquish the challenge, something you can offer him in private." He jabbed a finger into the drawing and it thumped on the bar top below. "Look into it. You've got the means." Thoranmir stood and then walked away.

Behind him, Fuerian chuckled as if this whole ordeal was beneath him, but from the corner of his eye, Thoranmir saw him put the napkin in his pocket. It was then that he knew he had Fuerian. He was banking that the antler sidhe were either so scary that their vague mention would motivate Fuerian to act and provide Thoranmir some kind of opportunity.

The wealthy fop was working towards Thoranmir's end goal, now. *But will it be enough to protect my sister?*

As Thoranmir hit the exit, his tightly wound nerves practically unraveled. "Sorry. Chechey didn't have it," he told the guard, and then he headed out into the night.

R EMY GOT BACK TO Cathair Dé, wandering the twilit streets as dusk drew deeper. Dull street lamps glowed and warmed the intersections with orange and yellow hues. Some were oil lanterns that required lighting each night, while others were powered by the akashic magic supplied by the city's guild of mystics.

The contrast reminded Remy of the kind of stakes involved in the upcoming duel. Fuerian had to feel like his world had been threatened—not only was some human coming for his betrothed, but ways of life were changing in Arcadeax. If House Vastra didn't find a new business, they'd soon find themselves displaced by a brighter light.

Remy passed by the mostly empty market, which had cleared out by this hour. Most vendors packed their wares and left before night overtook them. A few stragglers still broke down their stands and Remy passed through the square unmolested except by two elven children who pretended to be duelists and did battle with each other.

One of them circled around Remy as he walked, using the human as a shield against his brother who tried to slap him with a sword. A stray blow flashed out and rapped Remy's hand with a sharp crack.

He snatched the child's wooden sword and threw it over his shoulder, leading his brother to pounce on him. Shaking out the bruised knuckles, he left the children behind as they carried on. Remy grinned when he heard one of them—probably the one who'd smacked his hand—start crying.

"Boys are all the same, regardless of the species," he mused, rubbing the red spot where the child had landed a blow. It stung, but less than the wounds he'd taken from Fuerian's thugs.

Finally, Remy arrived at Anya's apartment.

She wheeled herself toward him as he entered. "Ew. You look like crap."

"And you're lovely as ever," Remy said with a lilt in his voice, noticing she looked like she'd been dragged through an emotional wringer that day.

Anya sighed. "You *sound* like a man in love. More's the pity. But *you look* like you got jumped by a pack of highwaymen."

Remy merely shook his head. "It remains to be seen, but I may have gotten the better end of this particular engagement." He pointed to the welt that burned red on the edge of his temple.

Anya steered her chair to the cabinets and retrieved a bottle for Remy. She tossed it to him, and he opened it. The contents had a strong antiseptic odor. He applied the ointment as she said, "You spoke with my brother, didn't you? You got him to drop out of the contest?"

"I did. He promised he'd do so… and he promised to tell you if he hadn't done so yet. And you were right about Fuerian being dangerous." Remy pointed to his wounds. "He's like a spoiled brat who did not mature along with his body."

"This just happened?"

"Last evening. I went to see Jaira at her invitation. Fuerian and his gang found me first. His duelist had warned me to stay away. Words were had. And then his boys beat me up when I challenged Fuerian's honor. This contest… it's supposed to be for sport, but mark my words, there will be blood. It *will* be a duel."

Anya rolled her eyes. "Boys. You always get like this. Especially when there's a pretty girl involved."

"Where is your brother?" Remy asked.

"He went out in search of more wine," Anya said, explaining his absence, though her tone seemed to indicate she thought the wine was some kind of excuse. She explained the day's events and noted that they'd just interred Eldarian a few hours prior.

"He's been acting… strange. Like something's got him rattled," Anya concluded. "It's not the search for some random lover's brother that's got him bothered. Something happened since returning to Cathair Dé that's got him acting odd… more oddly than when you both first arrived."

Remy rubbed his chin. "*Many* things have happened since our arrival—we've had more excitement this past week than in all the prior days I'd known your brother, combined." He sighed, "But I'll keep an eye on him. If something is amiss, I'll try to set it right."

Anya gave him a melancholy smile, thanking him. And then she pointed out where she had some ice in an insulated locker.

He chipped off a few pieces, wrapped them in cloth, and then pressed them against the flesh before retiring to his mattress.

T HORANMIR CREPT INTO HIS sister's apartment late. He saw her sitting in her chair, propped up in the corner nearest her work desk. The chair was tethered to a port by a thin tube which recharged the akashic energy it used to operate.

A kind of helmet with a solid visor lay on the counter of the desk. Ethereal lights flashed from it and painted the furniture in shifting hues of colors. Anya sometimes wore the metal halo device that was connected to wires and jacked into some apparatus that Thoranmir knew nothing about.

He wasn't familiar with the aither, but he knew his sister was a master at it, and he'd seen her in action earlier that day. He also knew that she was inside the aithersphere even now.

Her mastery of that realm was such that she did not need the visual cues the halo provided, which was why the visor was raised. Anya's eyes were closed, but she did not sleep; Anya had mentioned before that she preferred to do most of her work late at night.

The aither does not sleep, he mused, *so she can work from anywhere and at any time.* Thoranmir knew almost as much about the aither as he did about crafting magics like the Aes Sídhe did. But just like the street lamps that helped guide him home, he knew that he could still benefit from the aither's effects, even if he couldn't articulate how.

Somewhere in the distance, Thoranmir heard Remy's snores, and he crept through the low light in search of a bed.

Anya did not open her eyes as he passed. But she asked, "Where's my wine?"

"Uh, excuse me?"

"You said you were going out for wine." Still with her eyes shut, she lifted an empty goblet from nearby and gave it a gentle shake. "Top me off."

Thoranmir sighed. He'd forgotten about that. "I, uh, drank it all," he said, wishing he'd slurred his words a little. He felt pretty certain Anya had seen through his lie.

"Then get me a fresh bottle from the pantry," she told him and waited until she heard the cork pop before opening her eyes.

Thoranmir filled her glass and then his own, which he'd snatched from a cupboard while in route to the pantry. He took a sip and enjoyed it as he sat down.

The day was filled encountering the red circle elves, finding and then burying Odessa's brother, and instigating the worst sort of betrayals. He was more than ready for sleep.

"How are you doing?" Anya asked.

"I'm fine," Thoranmir lied. "Never better. Just happy to be back in Cathair Dé."

"Mm-hmm." She studied him as she took a long sip. Her eyes were lucid and her mind seemed explicitly present, so Thoranmir assumed that she'd pulled her consciousness fully out of the aither to focus on him. He kept a straight face, but cursed inside. Thoranmir was not good at lying, especially to his sister.

"Are you *really* fine?"

Thoranmir paused. He asked instead, "What do you know about the Vastra family?"

Anya took a drink and chuckled. "I know plenty. And they're full of shit. The whole lot of them."

He raised a brow. "I don't know what you mean."

"Well, they cut corners and hire second-rate hacks like Trishana Firmind."

"Should I know who that is?"

"She's my biggest competitor: another aithermancer. Trishana has stolen a few of my better clients and undercut my bids. But she does a second-class job and leaves her clients exposed, and they don't even know it. The Vastras hired her a long while back. She set up their presence in the aither and just kind of abandoned it."

"I still don't get it. Pretend I'm an idiot and explain."

"Oh, sweetie. I don't need to pretend. But think of the aither like a dream realm. Trishana built a castle for them there, but she doesn't maintain it or set proper guards up for it, so folks with any amount of skill might be able to poke around the grounds and sometimes find things they should not see," Anya said. "Let's just say that I *have poked*." She grinned through her glass of wine.

Thoranmir still felt confused.

Sighing, Anya explained to her clearly confused brother., "The Vastras are putting on airs. And the reason I know they're dangerous is that, well, in *my* experience, people with big secrets become ever deadlier the larger their secrets grow."

"And you know their secret?"

Anya nodded. "They're broke. It's all fake. Their entire lives are phony. Little more than gusto glued over with a glamour of smoke and mirrors: akasha and aither. They have everyone fooled. There is no real wealth, only the perception of it."

Thoranmir tapped his lower lip as he mulled that information over, wondering how he could best use it.

"You shouldn't tell anyone," Anya told him. "Not even Remy."

"What do you mean?"

"Knowing what I've just told you can't bring you anything but harm. It won't matter to your friend—he's too in love with this girl to hear anything more about Fuerian—he already thinks the worst of him and this won't change that. It's also a secret Fuerian, and with the backing of his entire family, would kill in order to keep—and maybe even come after me for good measure. While I think Trishana is a shoddy excuse for an aithermancer, she is not without skill. If word got out about their overextended credit, someone as vengeful as the Vastras would wonder who peered behind the veil and got information from the aither."

Thoranmir frowned. He knew the answer. "You're that good, huh?"

"I'd be one of maybe four folks they'd look at first."

He rubbed his chin and drew some assumptions. *If the Vastras didn't attach their name to a prominent, wealthy family, and soon, their credit might dry up. That would make Fuerian incredibly reluctant to release his hold over the Morgensteens... and anyone who got in his way would end up dead. No wonder he hates Remy so much!*

Thoranmir's face fell. That knowledge meant he might be far less likely to work toward Thoranmir's goal of getting Remy to drop out of the contest, and more likely to use his findings to simply harm Remy—to have him killed before the contest ever happened.

"Is Remy okay?" he asked, with alarm in his voice.

"Some of Fuerian's goons worked him over last night... guess he wasn't with the Morgensteen girl after all."

Thoranmir cursed and drained his glass, feeling like a bad friend. The new revelation meant he had limited options for moving forward. He liked none of them, but he'd die before he let someone harm his sister, and Remy could probably take care of himself.

Thoranmir stood. "I think I've had enough wine." He moved to slip away and find his bed, but then realized he'd likely spend the whole night restless. His mind wouldn't let him rest without something to help calm it.

There's only one way I'm sleeping tonight.

Once Anya closed her eyes and resumed her journey through the aither, he grabbed the wine bottle and took it to bed with him.

REMY THANKED ANYA FOR the warm bread and honey butter he ate for breakfast. The morning had dragged on pretty late and Thoranmir still remained in bed, snoring loudly. With an empty bottle of wine nestled in his crooked elbow, his completely catatonic state hadn't surprised Remy much.

"Really, a genuine thank you. You don't really have to do all this for me. I'm just some guy who's been hanging out with your brother for the last couple years."

"Oh, I know that," Anya said with a wink. "I'm just here waiting to cash in on your future success. This contest is just the beginning of your rise to fame and fortune, right?"

He smirked at her joke, but couldn't help detecting a look of pity hidden deep in her face. *She thinks Fuerian is going to kill me, or that I'll fail at the very least, and probably become like any of the other destitute humans in the dregs of Arcadeaxn cities.*

"I dreamed of her last night," Remy said.

"Jaira?"

Remy nodded. "I've got to see her. Today. I know the contest is soon, but..." He was interrupted by a particularly loud snore from Thoranmir.

Anya pointed to his still marred face. "You didn't learn your lesson the last time?"

"But this time, I have a plan," Remy said, tying his headband over his brow to hide his ears. "And this time, I'll be unexpected." He glanced back. "How is your brother? You spoke with him last night, I assume."

She sighed. "Still acting a little weird. He said he wished you wouldn't compete in this thing, either. Everything surrounding the duel is getting dangerous for anyone involved."

He nodded, but his eyes glimmered with resolve. "None of that has to do with the competition, though. Fight or not, all the danger swirling around us right now isn't related to the contest. It's all connected to Fuerian Vastra, the duel is tangential. It's been about Fuerian since the beginning. Even my rescuing the Morgensteens more than a week ago was all because *Fuerian* was the target of an assassination attempt."

Anya remained silent. She could only attempt damage control at this point. Remy was committed to his place in the duel.

He grinned and picked up another slice of bread as he headed for the door. "But weird is a fine state for your brother. It sounds like the only Thoranmir I've ever known. I'm heading off now to do something that's probably stupid, but I would regret not trying it."

"Good luck," she spoke as if it was a platitude with no real expectation.

He winked at her, "I'm in love. I don't need luck."

As he closed the door, he barely heard her mumble, "That boy's going to get himself killed."

R EMY PEEKED OVER THE neatly manicured hedge rows that the Morgensteens' landscaper had just trimmed. The garden was large, and it was also immaculate. Remy watched the elf work with clippers and shearing blades as he crept through the gardens and memorized the layout of the place—in case he needed to make a speedy escape.

Finally, Remy cleared his throat. "Excuse me, sir? Might I have a private word?"

The gardener stood, flashing a pained look as he straightened his bent back, and then focused on the unexpected guest. He brushed stray twig clippings away, which hung off his long, pointed ears. Once he looked Remy over, his stiffened, formal posture slumped. "Oh, it's you. I've heard of you."

That can't be good, Remy thought. "I'm sure it's all positive."

The gardener gave Remy an askew look that indicated otherwise. "You shouldn't be here. Sir Morgensteen would not be pleased to find you here."

"You might be right," Remy admitted, "But I have an errand of some urgency."

The older elf raised a brow.

"Okay," Remy admitted. "It's more of a personal mission." He stepped closer and asked the elf, "Have you ever been in love?"

"Aye," he replied. His eyes glossed over with a faraway look. "Most beautiful gal I ever met. I knew that very moment—the minute I met her—that I wanted to marry her."

"Then you must understand how I feel about Jaira Morgensteen," Remy said. "And she feels the same for me. I think about only her all the time, and I must tell her. We were supposed to meet recently, but Fuerian had other plans." He pointed to the red mark on his face where the welt was still visible.

The gardener winced.

"I'm certain you feel strongly, but have you considered that her father would never accept a human as the spouse for his only daughter and heir?"

Remy blushed. He undid the bandanna tied around his head. "It's that obvious, is it?"

"Afraid they been talking about it since yesterday. A lot of folks have gibbered on and on about you. The whole house, Fuerian included, knows you two are quite taken with each other." He waved to a young she-elf further down the lawn. "Work on the roses next," he called to her.

She nodded and began cultivating the soil where a new row of flowers would eventually be planted. Remy recognized her from the other day: she was the girl Fuerian had used as a distraction to lure Remy close.

The girl flashed Remy an apologetic frown. It was the same sorrowful glance she'd given him before Remy earned the bruises on his face.

"Not everyone feels such animosity toward humans," the gardener said. "I think you'll find Jaira an impossible match, given her status and her family's prejudices. Perhaps you and my daughter, though?" He wriggled his eyebrows and bobbed his head to the girl working the rose beds. "Liara is of marrying age and her family is not particular."

Remy glanced at her only momentarily. She was rail-thin and her eyes seemed too wide for her face, but they drew attention away from a pronounced underbite and ruddy complexion. Liara was not a classically pretty girl.

"I am sure Liara is very nice, but I must follow my heart. You said you were in love and I'm sure that Liara's mother was a..."

The gardener guffawed. "Oh, no. Liara's mother wasn't the one who stole my heart. No... but she was the only one who would have me. And that is the point I've been making. You can't go pruning buds in gardens where ye don't belong, son." He flashed him a grin and showed off where he'd had several teeth knocked loose and then pointed at the gap and again at Remy's swollen face to indicate he'd endured something similar... only *he had taken the hint*.

Remy flashed him a conspiratorial look. "But what if that girl had said yes to you?"

The old elf paused and, for a moment, wordlessly worked his mouth. Finally, he said, "I... I can't say. I never mustered up the courage to ask her before another suitor did. Had too much fear of crossing her father again."

The human fixed him with a judgmental look. "Shouldn't I be allowed to at least ask my maiden?"

Meeting Remy's gaze, the gardener sighed. "Aye, I suppose if you've got the courage to ask her, then it's only fair."

"Then you will help me? Summon Jaira to the garden. That is all I ask. I simply wish for her to know my affections."

He stiffened. "I can't risk my job." He looked aside at his daughter. "But perhaps Liara could help. She is only here to help me for a time. She's not an employee of the family and has been here helping me for free, just trying to learn the trade."

Remy brightened.

"But on one condition," the old elf said. "If Jaira rejects you or if you come to your senses, you'll take my daughter out and get to know her. Just one night. You'll make her feel special."

"Agreed," Remy said, digging into his pocket and grasping for the earring. "Now here is my plan: have your daughter pick a rose for me..."

F uerian Vastra stood outside the small shop. A hanging shingle sign read: *Aithermancy.*

He glanced aside at his personal protector, the elf duelist named Naz Charnazar, and instructed him to wait outside. Then Fuerian walked into the office of Trishana Firmind.

He'd been here before. The Vastra family had hired her on a few previous occasions. He passed a few tables and banks of stacked equipment used to ply her craft before arriving behind a partition wall. There, Trishana sat nestled among myriad wires and pieces of more equipment he did not understand.

"Mister Vastra, how can I help you?" Trishana asked. She closed a book, but not before Fuerian got a glimpse of it. It was a bookie's ledger. Trishana was using the aither as a neutral meeting space to collect bets and leverage what she knew about each of the fighters in the upcoming contest. It looked like she'd created an elaborate betting system and stood to profit tidily.

"I do hope you are betting on *me*?" he asked.

She smirked. "But of course. You're the one outcome that is practically a certainty. It's all these other ones out there that have zero promises. Many of the other contestants are unknowns, so I am creating information about them in the aithersphere to shift the odds and create favorable margins. Half this stuff I've got to fabricate from scratch—doesn't anyone keep records these days?"

Fuerian narrowed his gaze. "Aren't the daily and weekly journals putting out a dossier?"

Trishana nodded with a vicious grin. "They are. But, at least with some of the contenders, the information is scant. Naturally, they needed an aithermancer to harvest the data for them."

"Naturally."

She continued. "I was able to skew things a certain way to provide the gambling scenarios I want. At the end of the day, it's all about the math."

"And if you lose those bets?" Fuerian asked.

"I'm also acting as the house with one of my shell companies. I feel generous toward my friends and am willing to forgive those debts—of course, about the only company I prefer to keep is my own... as far as friends go."

Fuerian knew she was corrupt, but she'd always been honest about it. That was why he knew he could trust her. "Have you located any information about the contestant named Remy Keaton?"

Her eyebrows piqued. "The human? No. But I'll admit it's just been easier to make up information than to venture down every rabbit hole and locate the truth, unless that information is easy to come by. But there's already some stories floating around out there after the debacle with some hitmen they say were looking for you?"

Fuerian shrugged, indicating the rumor was more or less accurate. "I need as much background on him as you can get. But I need the actual, honest truth about it. Gambling networks aside, you can say whatever you want about him—but I've got other interests in him. There is some dark mystery about this human. I must know what it is. Dive deep, little fish."

She frowned at his indication. "What makes you think that he is anything more than some random ddiymadferth?"

Fuerian withdrew the napkin he'd taken from Thoranmir at the pub and turned it over to her. "Because whoever he is or whatever he is involved in, it has drawn the interest of particular parties."

Trishana unfolded the napkin and looked at the symbol. Her eyes widened. "A high maven. Do you know the color of the sigil?

Fuerian shook his head.

"Then I shall be ever cautious as I do my research."

He stood and turned to leave, hesitating. "While I am putting you to work, let me add another task. This one may be easier, but if I'm committing so heavily to the Morgensteen family, let me do my diligence on them as well. Find me their dirty laundry. I must know it all before I invest my good name into them with a marriage."

Trishana nodded. "Aside from the daughter's sexual fetish for the sons of Adam?"

"Naturally," he said.

"That won't prove too difficult. I will see you when it is done."

Fuerian looked down his nose at her. "Time is short, so make it soon."

"I'll do what I can," she promised.

Fuerian bowed, and departed.

Chapter Sixteen

J aira looked up from where she was seated, spotting a she-elf about her age hovering at the edge of the drawing room. Her father sat at a nearby desk and stationary table where he mused over forms and documents. He made final authorizations and arrangements for the impending activity soon to unfold in the Cathair Dé stadium.

The she-elf, dressed for outdoor work, announced herself with a demure knock in keeping with protocol and the difference in her station.

Harhassus barely looked up from his ledgers to see who had entered. The feather from his quill bounced happily, in stark contrast to the elf's expression, as he worked the tip of his pen upon paper.

"Miss Morgensteen?" Liara asked, holding a rose in her fingertips.

Jaira cocked her head. She did not know Liara well, except that she was the daughter of their gardener and had been helping him all summer. They had spoken maybe twice in passing over a few months' time. With her interest piqued, Jaira stood and went to the girl.

"It is Liara, right?"

Liara nodded. "Yes, ma'am. I thought you would enjoy a rose from your father's garden. They are truly exquisite this year, as are the other flowers."

Jaira glanced out the window, which overlooked the gardens, and thought they looked no better or worse than in previous years. She hadn't given them much attention this year and briefly scanned the hedge rows and blooming shrubs through the glass. When she was a child, she would play and run through them. They felt like they were as tall and as menacing as the labyrinthine forest which guarded sections of Arcadeax from the world of Adam.

But age and maturity had changed her view and those maze-like hedges were now barely shoulder height to her. She smiled at the nostalgic memory. *I think I would like a stroll in the garden again.*

She turned her attention back to Liara and the rose. There appeared a glimmer of precious metal on the bud, catching the sunlight just right. Jaira closed the distance and accepted the flower. She looked closer at the glinting metal.

Encircling the base of the petals, nestled between pink flesh and the green sepal above the stem, rested her hoop earring. *The earring I dropped for Remy.*

A broad smile spread across Jaira's face. *Vennumyn is nowhere in sight, the unseelie nighthag.*

"Thank you, Liara. It is a fine rose indeed."

"How long has it been since you saw the rose bushes up close?"

"Too long," Jaira admitted.

Liara gave her a knowing look. "If you like, I could lead you to them and show you the roses I think you would most appreciate."

"That would be lovely." An excited glimmer sparkled in Jaira's eyes.

The scratching sounds of her father's pen seemed suddenly loud.

Jaira added for his benefit, "After all, I've nothing much to do on this day. Hurry up and wait. I will be happy once this contest has both arrived and ended." *And once Remy has won it... but even if he loses, I much prefer him to Fuerian. Perhaps we could run away—maybe I could live with him in the world of man, hiding my true self there as he does here?*

She suddenly realized she knew very little about him. Could he travel beyond Arcadeax at will? Did he have two lives between the worlds? She only knew that she loved him—deeply and irrationally so—and she thought he reciprocated the feeling.

Liara took Jaira by the hand and led her out of the drawing room.

"Thank you," Jaira said, smiling. "You are a true friend."

Liara's eyes sparkled, as if hearing those words spoken by someone as renowned as Jaira might be the highlight of her life.

But as she felt the waves of happiness roll off the gardener's daughter, Jaira felt her father's suspicious eyes upon her back. She turned to him and found he'd returned to working on his ledgers.

The leather of his fine chair creaked as he leaned forward and plied stylus and ink. For all his love of modern gadgets, Harhassus did not trust record keeping to akashic devices as many of the more progressive fey did.

Jaira stared at him, letting her eyes burn like wood boring beetles against the elf who was too busy to look and grant her permission to leave after his orders that she remain supervised outside of the home's walls. Finally, still without looking up, Harassus waved a hand to permissively dismiss her.

And then, they were through the door and away. Harhassus Morgensteen's pen still furiously scratched ink upon paper behind them as they departed, sharing mischievous, knowing glances.

FOOTSTEPS ECHOED IN THE corridors as Fuerian and Naz walked to a regular assembly of members of House Vastra. Naz stopped at a threshold, as was protocol and stood with the other hired folk. There was a collection of them; a few were duelists and several were familiars of a variety of duties. But only family were allowed within the chamber.

Fuerian Vastra entered the banquet hall in his ancestral home's estate. The facility more closely resembled a fortress than a castle. As much as the Morgensteen home was warm and glowed with burnished woods and familial accoutrements, House Vastra was all bare and polished stone.

A long table stretched the length of the room and two seats remained at the end, near its head. One reserved for him and a second designated for whenever he took a bride.

Fuerian took his seat and glared across the table. As the designated heir, his seat was at the right hand of the family's patriarch who had the final say in all business and domestic issues. Across the table sat Fuerian's rival who he'd vied with for years to retain his position as the next in line to take the mantle and chair at the table's head.

Juriahl Vastra sat across from Fuerian with a pretty young she-elf whose hand he held. Instead of scowling at Fuerian, as Juriahl usually did, he smiled smugly and stroked his new lover's forearm with a fingertip.

"What is *she* doing here?" Fuerian asked.

His rival spat a barb back at him. "I much appreciate the recent moves, Fuerian," Juriahl said, his voice dripping with pride.

Fuerian leaned forward, pressing his point. "Protocol, Juriahl," he hissed. "The chamber is for members of House Vastra only. I do not know this—"

"It seems a marriage was made just last night," said Margrave Vastra, patriarch of the family. He gripped the high back of the formal seat.

All family members down the line stood as he took his place. Margrave took his seat and the others all did likewise. Servants entered with plates and goblets to set places for the meal and over the din of cutlery Fuerian leaned to the head and hissed, "What is the meaning of this?"

Margrave, an elf of sallow skin with dark and sunken eyes that accompanied advanced age, merely shrugged, lifting his shoulders a breadth from his too-thin hair.

"Perhaps I have gone sentimental in my old age," Margrave stated.

There is no chance the stone-hearted old elf has done any such thing, Fuerian thought. *Not after four centuries of such devious manipulation.*

"I guess that, after three hundred and eighty six years, I have given up trying to figure out love," Margrave said.

Filled with suspicion, Fuerian glowered side-eyed at Juriahl, and at his new bride. He was not a handsome elf by any stretch, and he was considerably older than Fuerian which made him immediately mistrustful of the she-elf's intentions.

I will not be usurped from my birthright—not when I am so close!

Even though Fuerian had been given a boon that promised him the spot as heir to Margrave's chair, there was a chance it could be taken from him if Juriahl produced a legitimate male son before Fuerian could. The boon, an amulet which hung around his neck that provided him protection from mind magics, had all but guaranteed his ascension... *but now?*

He clutched the pendant around his neck and noticed that he drew a curious look from Juriahl's young wife. *She's up to some game, for sure... that, or she's just curious about what real power looks like.*

Fuerian momentarily wondered if Juriahl had been manipulated by mind magics, but then realized none such arcana was required. He'd found a loophole and a willing participant to make an end-run at Fuerian's birthright. If it hadn't infuriated him so much, Fuerian might have admired the move.

Margrave's security team swept through the feast hall with one final check and then gave the patriarch an all clear signal. Many of the Vastra family's businesses were less than savory, and they preferred to keep a tight lid on the dissemination of information. That, and industrial espionage was a real possibility.

Juriahl playfully popped a plump grape into his wife's mouth and she bit it seductively, playfully sucking his finger in the process.

Fuerian pushed his plate away, refusing to eat in response.

"Back to this new business venture you offered up to the House," Juriahl spoke to Fuerian loud enough to include Margrave in the conversation. "The cost and income analysis look wonderful, though one wonders about public sentiment coming against any industry that gets involved with apothiks."

"That is why there was an alliance included in the package," Fuerian rolled his eyes. "Dream hallow is wildly toxic stuff. But the payoff could be enormous—especially because its users have to come back over and over again."

Juriahl sneered. "But you want to ally us with House Morass?"

Margrave leaned in. "The Morass Family," he corrected. House Morass had been de-elevated from it's official nobility status by Oberon. They were no longer méith.

"It is risky," Fuerian noted, "but who better to take the fall than the Morass if someone must?"

Juriahl crossed his arms over his chest. "Risky indeed. The amount we've invested in the scheme is already more than I'm comfortable with."

"Then it's a good thing it is not up to you," Fuerian snapped. "The profits far outpace the risks."

Margrave leaned back and stroked his chin. Despite his cloudy eyes, he glared at a few members of the family seated on the far end of the table. "Similar conversations were had before certain members of House Vastra got involved in the slave trade. Luckily, we escaped most of the backlash because the bulk of those stolen children belonged to humans. Still, bribes paid to cover it up some of the more dubious business has put us in a precarious position—one which the apothik business could further indebt us with."

Fuerian's nostrils flared. He'd never known Margrave to find such a lucrative venture to be distasteful. However, Fuerian also so a low hanging opportunity.

By family doctrine, he had to bring all business to the table. *But if the House did not want any part of it...* Gareth and the Morass Family made the perfect patsy if his plans for the apothik trade went poorly. The dream hallow was wrapped up in layers of complicity with Nhywyllwch and his Stór Rúnda... and certain layers were far more profitable than others.

"I request a vote on the topic, then," Fuerian demanded. "Let us each voice support or objection to the risks and rewards."

Margrave nodded, calling for the vote on family business.

"Fine," growled Juriahl. "But, by right, my wife also gets a vote."

The patriarch acquiesced. "This is true." Margrave shot Fuerian a look of warning—there could be no discussion on the matter. He looked at the young woman and told her, "Loitariel Vastra, I will provide instruction for how we operate. Your husband may give you further details as is convenient."

Loitariel grinned and leaned against her husband.

Picking up his goblet, Margrave drained it and then held it high. All the family members at their seat did likewise. Juriahl instructed his wife to do the same.

Margrave instructed, "Place your cup upright in support of the apothik trade, and invert it if opposed. Lay on its side to abstain."

Cups clattered and echoed as the family members up and down the row placed their votes at the same time. The patriarch had abstained and both Juriahl and his wife's votes were against the measure. At the final count, it passed by a single vote.

Fuerian looked up and down the table, assigning votes to family members. They had each aligned with the measure exactly as he had assumed.

For his part, Juriahl did the same, sending menacing glares and scowls of disapproval at specific sidhe who he'd wanted to follow his lead.

"I bring another business matter, as well," Fuerian stated, pressing another issue.

Margrave raised his brows.

"I have a second opportunity to bring to the family. I have received from my future father in law a parcel of land which I now own free and clear and offer to House Vastra, as required."

"What kind of land?" someone called out.

Juriahl steepled his fingers with rapt interest.

Fuerian knew his rival had connections in the land office and would be familiar with the transaction.

"It is a mine. I intend to look into reopening the plot which initially made the Morgensteens their fortune."

Juriahl cackled. "The Morgensteen mine?"

The entire room went quiet. All forks and eaters fell silent. Every diner watched and listened to the exchange.

"Harhassus has always had a good business sense and wanted me to have the parcel as a token of good faith," Fuerian defended.

"Then you have been duped by a man with better business sense than you," Juriahl accused. "That mine, if it can even be called that, is a poisonous liability. It is ferrous, toxic: filled with iron. You might owe this to your future family allegiances with the Morgensteens, but do not bring such an insulting acquisition to House Vastra!" He sat back, grumbling. "As if we should assume someone else's liabilities, and for no gain. Ha!"

Margrave looked to Fuerian. "Do you wish to call the vote at this time?"

"I certainly wish it," Juriahl insisted before Fuerian could answer.

"Then you shall have your vote," Margrave said, lifting his goblet.

The votes came down in quick succession, aligning against Fuerian's offering by a fair margin. Juriahl and Loitariel led the vote against accepting the ferrous property into the family's holdings. Margrave had also voted in this matter, siding against the measure.

"Let Fuerian personally hold this liability," Juriahl said, sitting back and signaling for a servant to refill his wine.

Fuerian sat back as well, keeping a placid expression on his face. *Exactly as planned,* he congratulated himself as he recognized the glances from Juriahl's wife. *Definitely up to something... I will have to keep an eye on that one.*

The patriarch leaned towards his chosen heir to provide counsel. "Like with your dueling, timing can be everything. One can not push too hard in either business or family politics," Margrave cautioned him. "I thought I had taught you better than that."

Fuerian leaned even closer so that only the patriarch could hear him. "Oh, *you did*. And all went exactly as planned."

Margrave's eyes twinkled with a knowing gleam and he masked his grin from all but those fey who knew his tells. "I should have guessed as much."

Fuerian sat back. His hunger finally returned and he pulled his plate closer, finally ready to enjoy the feast.

REMY'S FACE BRIGHTENED AS Jaira, led by the gardener's daughter, stepped around a hedge and met him by the rose bushes.

Jaira rushed to him and put her hands on either side of his face. She leaned in and placed her forehead against his chin, averting a kiss at the last moment.

Curse the Arcadeaxn magics and vows, Remy thought.

"What did they do to you?" she fretted, turning his head and looking over his facial wounds.

"I think the bruises will be mostly gone by the time the contest starts," Remy said.

She embraced him and sank into his arms. "I'm sorry I missed you the other day. Fuerian and his goons stopped by and so I could not get to the forest. I think the housemaid knew of my plan and told on me—she's always wanted to serve in the biggest house in Cathair Dé, which most believe is the Vastras. I'm forced to marry Fuerian..." She pressed the earring back into his hands. "Keep this. For luck."

He looked down at her. "Then you *do* love me?" Remy bent his neck and touched his forehead to hers. His nose filled with her scents, like the aroma of flowers. "I must confess that I am consumed with thoughts of you."

"Of course I love you; I want to kiss no other. My heart shall be broken if you do not win this contest."

"So, this competition is a fight for your affections?"

She screwed her eyes up. "Of course not. But my father is not an easy sidhe to please. He has arranged my betrothal to an elf I have nothing but contempt for. I would love you in a hovel or in a palace. It matters little. But if you win this competition, it could be the first step on your rise to prominence, letting me break away from Fuerian and cling to you. My vow ensures the blessing of the Dagda, and by extension, all Arcadeax."

Remy did his best not to blow a raspberry of disbelief as he held her in his arms. "Dagda is a myth, and the blessing is little more than a luck charm, if anything at all." He could see from her response that she was taken aback by his comment.

"I mean to say," Remy said, "that *this*, you right here and right now, is what I most desire. Your touch is better than a thousand blessings from Dagda, Danu, Annwn, and the rest." Their bodies touched, but barely, and she radiated heat through her dress. He smelled the fragrance of her lilac water and the sweetness of her skin.

Their heads inclined toward each other again. Remy leaned in to kiss her.

"No," Jaira snapped, pulling back. "You mustn't. *I mustn't*. You may not believe in Dagda, but do not strip the honor from my vow. Elvish magic is severe, and I made an oath by the magics of Arcadeax. You must first win this contest or you will incur a curse, and me along with you."

Remy leaned in. The breath of his words fell warm on her neck. "But we'd be cursed together, at least."

She furrowed her brow and then realized he was playing with her. "I would not see any true harm come to you."

"Nor I to you," he said.

She pulled back slightly. "I have come to know Fuerian well this last year since the engagement was announced. He is a monster, but he is respected by the elites—the méith, and that carries some weight. But beneath the veneer, he is cruel and treacherous. Tell me you can beat him?"

"In a fair fight and with your love, I believe it with every fiber of my being," said Remy. He looked into her eyes. "When I was very young, I awoke in the unseelie with nothing but a knife and my own wits. I learned to defend myself, how to hide, and fight. I've been battling monsters since I was a child." He put a hand on her cheek, and she pressed into it. "I've always fought to survive before. But this contest is for something bigger than that. Something more. Survival without love means little."

"And a fight it may be. My father is thoroughly committed to his agreement with the Vastra family. But I say let *him* marry Fuerian," she offered a half-hearted smile. "He needs their support. Father's business has not been doing as well as reported, and I am meant to pay the penalty for his failing ventures."

Jaira curled up into his arms again and looked to the window of her family home. There, she spotted Harhassus, her father, watching them from the window. He wore a stern look of disappointment on his face, but also one of resignation—as if he'd been certain of this outcome all along.

She sighed. "I'm afraid our time is about to close."

Remy saw the shifting silhouette of the elf in the window. He interlaced his fingers with Jaira's grip and held her hand for a moment longer. "Then I shall see you again in Cathair Dé."

He kissed her hand and then released it, assuming such a minor action would incur no penalty to her honor or to the old magics.

Remy left, slipping back into the trees like a fox ahead of the baying hounds.

D AY HAD TURNED TO night and back to morning with agonizingly slow speed. Thoranmir could think of no way to compel his friend to quit the tournament, and he'd wracked his brain all night trying to create new schemes. Day finally arrived and Thoranmir departed the apartment with his sister and Remy.

The contest had been on the minds and lips of the entire city. And now, it had arrived at last.

"You're still sure you want to do this?" Thoranmir asked Remy as they walked the streets. The wheels on Anya's chair churned behind them, crunching the dirt and pea gravel of Cathair Dé's streets.

It wasn't the first time Thoranmir asked, and he didn't assume it would be the last time he'd raised the question. Thoranmir *needed* his friend to drop out of the race, but he couldn't tell him why without condemning his sister's life. For now, he could only sow seeds of doubt—as much as he hated to do it.

Anya sighed, wearied by her brother's nagging. "I think your friend's mind is resolved, Thoranmir."

"I'm just surprised to see you out of your apartment, Anya. I've not seen you away from an aither portal. Does the sun hurt your face?" Thoranmir defended himself, ignoring the fact that she'd traveled to The Haunts with him.

"I am not always connected. Just like I know you're not always so petty, Thoranmir. Besides, your friends are my friends. I don't normally take in random strays, you know."

They continued throwing barbs as they moved through the streets.

Aside from the wry grins, Remy seemed to mostly ignore the sibling banter. He walked ahead of them in stoic silence as they continued toward the stadium. His eyebrows raised and his gait slowed when he rounded the corner to the dueling market.

The place sat empty. Not a single booth remained and the only pedestrians in the square moved through it quickly, heading for the same place as everyone else: the stadium. As they stared a moment longer, Thoranmir saw his friend's hand slip into a pocket and clutch the earring, which he knew Remy kept.

Thoranmir picked up a paper which had been discarded to lay like a miniature tent. The headline raved about the contest as the entertainment event of the year and several articles made the story out to be larger than life. Semi-accurate versions of the attack on the Morgensteen family, with little mention of Remy and no note of Thoranmir, built up the excitement. Another article cast Fuerian Vastra, the betrothed, as some kind of local hero. A handbill inside the folds provided gambling odds and information for the two-day event.

A centerfold showed the tournament roster and listed all the names of the first day's fights, which would be randomized on the following day once many were eliminated. Thoranmir scanned it and found where his name had originally been. The slot was re-titled to merely read *vacancy* on all the reprinted handbills.

"Can I convince you to throw the fight?" Thoranmir asked. "We can place a substantial bet upon you and then when you lose, we can all be rich?" *Finally, a sensible scheme—surely this will be the one!*

Remy frowned. He turned the paper and pointed to the probabilities chart. "Nobody thinks I will win. At least not whoever wrote this drivel and set the odds. If I lose, you'd hardly get back more than you bet. I must win for these odds to make anyone rich." He squinted at his friend. "Besides, my honor is worth a lot more than a lump of cash, of which you have plenty after we defeated the sidhe with the dream hallow."

"We... we should have plenty," Thoranmir said. He looked at his friend incredulous. "You spent it already?"

"I gave my half away."

Thoranmir scowled; Remy had said it as if he'd given away pocket change, rather than a small fortune. Thoranmir folded the paper and stuffed it in a pocket.

After crossing to the next street, they found the crowds swelling. The Morgensteens' contest had taken on a life of its own.

"This event has certainly gotten huge," Remy said.

Thoranmir stepped to his side. "Does that make you nervous? Because you know you can still..."

Remy glared daggers at him, and Thoranmir snapped his mouth shut.

Bells rang in the air, echoing somewhere in the distance. The reverberations bounced from building to building in an oddly ethereal manner, making their location difficult to pinpoint.

"Do you guys smell smoke?" Anya asked, rolling forward. Remy sniffed a few times and opened his mouth to speak.

They rounded the corner at the edge of a building where the hustle and bustle of the streets reached its apex. Vendors and hawkers lined the roads. Some lit kindling in their firepots and others who had been there longer stoked coals and turned skewers of meat as they roasted. The marketplace had moved to create an impromptu market. They'd each set up to service the needs of the spectators, who turned out in droves for the amateur dueling contest.

"You know the saying," Thoranmir said. "Where there's smoke..."

"There's fire?" Remy concluded.

"No. Smoked meats." Thoranmir licked his lips. He rummaged in his pockets, searching for a few coins so he could purchase a snack, but they were empty. And he wasn't about to beg any money off his sister so soon after they'd traded snark.

"We can't get distracted," Remy said. "I'm sure Jaira is already at the stadium, and we must get there early. I'm sure there is catering at the event."

Thoranmir nodded and followed as Remy and Anya cut their way through the crowd, heading to the gates as quickly as possible. A security team barred their path, but Remy explained he was a competitor and that his friends had special tickets granting them access.

The guards checked their names against the registers and allowed them to pass. A short elf directed them where to go. Thoranmir recognized the contest director who he'd seen several days prior when he'd quit the competition, right before being attacked by the mysterious third party dead-set against Remy's victory—the ones who were willing to kill to ensure it.

Seeing him, the director scowled at Thoranmir. The elf gave a sheepish, frowning grin in return, realizing he'd likely made extra work for the director when he'd abandoned the competition. He absentmindedly touched the folded paper in his pocket. *Probably had to reprint all those fliers at the last minute.*

The director escorted Remy to his private quarters, where he could prepare for the day. There, he would be briefed on all the rules and expectations.

Another elf sent Anya and Thoranmir to the spectators' area. A special box had been set aside to accommodate Anya's chair.

Thoranmir helped get her into place and then glanced at his sister. She looked happy to be out and about, even if the contest was still hours away from beginning. Anya took out a book and opened it to pass the time.

He did not know a lot about the aither, but if it was anything like the real world, he assumed it was nice to escape from it within the pages of a good book. *Too bad escape isn't an option for me.*

Only a short hop down from the viewing platform and the box seats was the arena. The fighting grounds had already been set up below. Thoranmir spotted Jaira and her father walking across them, doing a final visual inspection. A pinch-faced servant who Thoranmir assumed was a governess of some sort, followed Jaira.

With a heavy sigh, Thoranmir realized he'd run out of options for getting Remy to exit the contest. Ever since returning to the arena, the words of his attackers in the alleyway rang fresh in Thoranmir's mind. *Get Remington Keaton to quit this contest... If you don't, your sister will pay a price*

Stuck in the viewing box, he would have no chance of rescuing his sister from them—whomever they were, and he didn't trust Fuerian to help dislodge his friend from the tournament schedule.

He withdrew the printed info he'd retrieved from the street. Based on the paper chart, Fuerian and Remy wouldn't even meet until the second day of the event.

"Excuse me," Thoranmir said, locking his eyes on Jaira. "I've got to go say hello."

Anya barely lifted her eyes from the book as her brother vaulted over the edge and down to the main floor. He jogged over to the Morgensteens.

Harhassus's face did not appear enthusiastic to see the ditch digger. Thoranmir ignored what might have been a slight and withdrew the tournament sheet from his pocket. He pointed to it and said, "I hope I'm not imposing too greatly to ask a favor of you two?"

Jaira's face was kind and accommodating.

Her father's gaze was stern and narrow. "Again? I already signed off on releasing you from the competition, and now you want something more? I had to pay to reprint all the materials, you know."

"I'm so glad that you were willing to risk your lives for us back on the road," Jaira said, flashing her father a look meant to shame him. "He meant to say that he knows it would have been more convenient if you'd kept digging the ditches instead of coming to our aid. So grateful."

Harhassus looked down at his feet with a dour expression. Jaira's words proved effective.

"Yeah, uh, sure." Thoranmir's cheeks reddened as he pointed to the slot listed as vacant. "I've got just one embarrassing request."

CHAPTER SEVENTEEN

J AIRA MOVED ASIDE TO meet Thoranmir. Vennumyn stepped in between them.

Tilting her head indignantly to her father, Jaira called out to him. "If Vennumyn wishes to remain alive, you had better reel in her leash, Father."

Thoranmir seemed to stiffen at the cold tone of Jaira's voice. Jaira meant every word of the warning. She'd had enough of the she-elf's meddling. Her father wasn't about to let Jaira out in a public setting where the human could be lurking—not without a chaperone—but Jaira wasn't going to let Vennumyn interfere with her life, either.

Harhassas motioned to the servant and Vennumyn backed off, though it clearly irked her to do so.

Jaira pulled Thoranmir a few steps aside from her father and looked him up and down. "You are sure you want to do this?"

It had brought Jaira much relief when Thoranmir had dropped out of his own volition—now that he wanted back in, all the extreme outcomes of her varied visions were back as potential outcomes. *The shadowy elf must be at work!*

"Circumstances have changed," Thoranmir told her. "I *must* re-enter this contest."

Jaira half hid behind the elf so that she would not draw Anya's gaze. She may have appeared to be reading a book, but Jaira felt certain the shrewd aithermancer was keeping an eye on her brother.

There is his stubbornness, again, Jaira thought.

"I'm afraid for Remy," Thoranmir said in a low voice. "And I have... *other* concerns, too." He looked Jaira in the eyes. "Please. You have to let me take the open slot."

"Let him have it," Harhassus interjected, obviously eavesdropping. "The slot is open, and there'll be complaints about somebody getting an easy pass without an even roster."

The older elf looked Thoranmir over. "Not that he won't already be an easy victory, but if he wants the spot. Let's give it to him. At least it will *seem* fairer."

Thoranmir sat back on his heels, obviously insulted to a degree, but he looked Jaira in the eyes, obviously willing to suffer the insult in silence in order to get satisfaction.

Jaira's face fell. There was no way she tell Thoranmir about her talents as a seer... but she also could not guarantee that he'd have any of the dire outcomes she'd seen for him. She was more concerned with her own.

A GAROGOL LOOKED UP AS his master entered the chamber, Mithrilchon the red. The sluagh, Agarogol's night thrall, was no respecter of person or position and barely paid the maven any mind.

Mithrilchon paused near Agarogol. "Word from the White Lord of the tower," he said. "I've received a letter. Suíochán Naséan would prefer if the human did not compete. At all."

Agarogol gave him an inquisitive look. "It will be difficult to put him out of the contest, now, so close to the event."

"I have engineered an alternative plan in an effort to put him out without drawing suspicion." Mithrilchon scowled. "It appears that Thoranmir failed. Is your sluagh prepared to enact retribution upon his crippled sister?"

The apprentice nodded. "At your command. But, if I may, Loitariel and I have engineered our plans against Remy Keaton and the delivery of the fetiche curse. The sluagh is a part of that plan."

Mithrilchon crossed his arms. "Are you advising mercy?"

Agarogol shook his head. "No. Merely that we afford him more time. The human could still lose the contest, which would render the entire thing moot."

"This is true," Mithrilchon admitted. "Your energies are set against the human; Loitariel is meant to foil the Vastra."

Agarogol nodded. "Suíochán Naséan will be satisfied. Our plans are good. They merely require more time to unfold. Loitariel's fetiche will coincide with my plans to eliminate the human."

"Explain."

"We put pressure on the Morgensteens to require that only fey compete, but Jaira was opposed to the measure and unwilling to disqualify the ddiymadferth. But if Jaira was out of the picture..."

"Miss Morgensteen must not be harmed," the maven reminded him. "She bears the blessing of the Dagda. There would repercussions if we were responsible for her demise."

"She need not be hurt," Agarogol promised. "Though, if it came to pass, or if our hand were forced, the sluagh would bear any consequences, magic or otherwise, and provide a buffer to us. Meanwhile, we could hold her until the family signed on to prohibit any sons of Adam from competing. That would remove any consequences to the rules of magic and we'll cast suspicion on the human-haters to allay any suspicion."

"The Frith Duine?" Mithrilchon asked.

Agarogol tipped his head. They'd been the only vocal dissenters to Remy Keaton's inclusion on the fight roster. They were a small group, but very loud—and their influence was growing.

The maven grinned. "I find that acceptable."

An elven worker led Remy to a small, private locker room. It was no bigger than an economy-sized bedchamber at a rural inn; there was barely enough room within for a cot. He'd stayed in many rooms like it.

"You may wear this chain shirt if you desire," said the elf, who had introduced himself as Adawar. "And we'll need you to sign these forms which state you understand that even in an amateur fighting competition, death is a possible outcome. We are using the same rules as are common to the dueling guilds and these ensure that every party has agreed to abide by them. A chain shirt might prevent a lethal wound, but injury is still very likely."

Remy scanned the document. *The fey and their love of contracts,* he mused. The agreement also insisted that no competitors fight each other outside of the tournament, at least not until the winner was declared. The last paragraph was written in the olde speech which would bind the signing party by the Arcadeaxn magic, in addition to the law, and threatened penalties for violating the rules.

Adawar offered him a stylus and Remy signed it.

"Weapons?" Remy asked him.

"Someone will be by shortly to present some selections for you to use. We require they be left inside your quarters here, except for when you are called to the fighting floor. We believe that helps keep the tournament results clean and free from outside tampering."

"Has that happened often at these sorts of events?"

Adawar frowned. "We once caught a guild-house attempting to enchant their members' weapons. Another was caught visiting an apothecary and known poisoner. Ever since, it has been standard that all combatants use the house weapons, aside from anything natural such as fang, spike, or claw that some fey possess—we can't exactly confiscate a faun's horns. Of course, there are sometimes bound weapons that fighters are allowed to use, as they are resistant to such tampering."

"Like a dúshlán?" Remy asked.

"Yes," said Adawar, blinking with surprise. "I suppose that would be allowed. Do you own a dúshlán blade?"

"I do," said Remy hesitantly.

"May I see it?" Adawar asked more out of curiosity than a matter of protocol for the contest.

"No," Remy stated matter-of-factly. "Not right now." He didn't feel like disclosing the fact that Fuerian had stolen it from him.

"Very well." Adawar shrugged, making a note of the blade on his forms. They were not especially common, nor were they overly rare. The dúshlán were said to be forged from the vengeful nature of Arcadeax itself, and they were not especially different from one to the next. "An armorer will be in this morning to present the weapon options for you. This is a melee competition, so there will be no range weapons, though I think a whip is one of the options: no arrows, bolos, slings, bows, muskets, etcetera."

Adawar handed him a scrap of paper detailing the options he could choose from. The list was long but weighted to provide options while also trying to keep the field relatively level.

"Also, you can expect a few visitors in the next couple of hours. There are several scouts from the various dueling guilds and at least two gambling networks who wish to interview competitors, each for their own purposes. You may choose to speak with them or not," Adawar told him before moving to the door.

"Thank you," said Remy, and then he was left alone in the room. He wasn't sure if the butterflies in his stomach were due to his thoughts about Jaira or of the contest.

He laid back and rested in the meantime. *Definitely Jaira.*

H ARHASSUS EXAMINED THE BOX seats where he planned to watch the event from. As much as he enjoyed the dueling games, he was more intrigued by the prospect of the Innovation Fair as he was calling it.

He and Jaira would watch from the viewing box. Harhassus wished that Eilastra, his wife, would join them, but she'd expressed the desire to be anywhere else. She'd had her fill of violence upon the road when the human and his elf friend had saved them.

But the event was not all combat. Aside from the contest, which he knew would draw massive crowds, he'd also invited several inventors and other entrepreneurs to display their creations, businesses, and investment opportunities.

Harhassus prided himself on discovering new advancements and becoming an early adopter; whenever possible, he also tried to be an early supporter and financially back such innovation—usually in exchange for shares of royalties.

A number of those entrepreneurs had begun setting up in their designated areas beyond the combat zones and he was eager to see their offerings. Before he had the chance, Oberon's delegates stepped into the viewing box.

Two elves, both in dark cloth and cloak entered.

"Mavens," Harhassus gave a stiff bow. "To what do we owe the pleasure?"

A maven melted into the background. He was obviously second to the High Maven who stood next to Harhassus with the crimson crest emblazoned upon his breast only partly visible under the folds of his cloak.

"Greetings. I am Mithrilchon," he introduced himself, "and I am here as the sanctioning agent from Suíochán Naséan. I am sure you were expecting us?"

Harhassus nodded. "Anytime magic is involved or a blessing from Arcadeax is carried on Oberon's behalf, I expect the Radiant Tower's involvement... though I didn't quite expect to entertain a *high maven*."

Mithrilchon inclined his head, accepting what appeared to be reverence for his position.

"We are here to ensure the Dagda's Blessing is delivered to the worthy contestant and to help run the contest on behalf of the duelists' guilds," Mithrilchon continued. He produced a tournament roster and turned it over to Harhassus.

A few scribbles and adjustments had been made upon the paper and Harhassus raised an eyebrow. "What's this?"

"For your consideration," Mithrilchon stated. "I would like to suggest a few changes."

Jaira stepped forward. She looked over the form and scowled at what she found. "Maven?"

Mithrilchon had struck Remy Keaton from the list and then moved his opponent, an elf named Deohecha, into the spot which she'd just authorized be granted to Thoranmir Shelton.

"The tournament was uneven with the open spot," Mithrilchon said. "We thought it best to make a slight change in lieu of the unrest surrounding a human contestant."

Jaira began an objection, but Harhassus stayed her. "What unrest?"

"There is a group of fey who *hate* humans. Have you heard of the Frith Duine? They have gathered outside the stadium gates and begun a protest."

Harhassus nodded. "I've heard of them. Loud-mouthed troublemakers, is all."

"There have been some violent, anti-human displays from chapters nearer Daonra Dlúth and the Radiant Tower," Mithrilchon noted. "Simply prohibiting this Remy Keaton fellow from competing would ensure safety and easy operation of the—"

"Out of the question," snapped Jaira.

Her sternness caught the maven off guard and he blinked.

"My apologies, High Maven," Harhassus said. "My daughter is—"

Jaira cut him off. "Is capable of speaking for herself and authorized to speak on behalf the Dagda's Blessing and Oberon's interests regarding the prize. That is how this works, is it not?" She held Mithrilchon's gaze.

Harhassus shrugged and mumbled, "This is what meant to tell you."

Mithrilchon blinked as he inclined his head. "Yes. You have the authority, as the bearer of the blessing. I merely wished to point out that are certain risks regarding civil unrest, and there is a simple solution."

"Thank you for your concern, High Maven," Jaira took a more polite tone, "but my father once told me 'Simple solutions are the frequent paths of vagabonds.'"

"You are adamant on this point?" the maven asked.

"I am." Jaira's voice was resolute but not rude.

Mithrilchon bowed. "Then so be it. We shall try to enhance security against any plans the Frith Duine may engineer beyond voicing simple protest."

"Thank you, High Maven," Jaira said.

With her words dismissing him, Mithrilchon and his follower turned and departed to make final arrangements for the duels.

ONE OF ADAWAR'S STAFF escorted Remy to the stadium, where he waited in the tunnel that opened onto the fighting grounds.

Remy had attended the feast arranged for the contestants to partake in as one of the perks for tournament participants, but he had only taken a light lunch while waiting, making sure not to overindulge. He'd hoped that Jaira would be present, but none of the Morgensteens had attended, and so he did not stay long.

As he had suspected, many of the amateur entrees spoiled themselves as they prepared for the contests, especially on the wine.

A few bouts had already passed, warming up the crowd to the idea of bloodshed.

Somewhere, a horn blared followed by the announcement for the next fighter. The crowd cheered for an elf named Deohecha, who Remy was soon to face. He waited for the announcer, who used some kind of akashic device to amplify his voice's volume and broadcast it across the stadium seating.

"Deohecha will fight Remy Keaton, the human!"

Remy emerged from the tunnel to take the field and a hush seemed to fall over the crowd, followed shortly by a murmur. He could tell by their expressions that they did not have much interest in seeing a human fight. Or perhaps their opinions had been swayed against the idea of seeing a human fight an elf—the Frith Duine's presence in the city had made at least some kind of impact.

Having selected a simple broadsword with a long cross guard to protect his hands and gauntlets to shield his forearms, Remy carried them into the arena and took his place. He bowed respectfully to Deohecha.

The elf sneered at him, clearly irked that he should be forced to face a human. Deohecha held a curved longsword lackadaisically. "Ddiymadferth," he growled before spitting on the ground.

A referee entered the field. He was a runty little faun who carried a buckler in each hand in case he had need of separating armed contestants while fending off stray blows from weapons. The faun stood between them to announce the match. He held his hands up and then someone sounded a gong to signal the competition's start and the referee scrambled back from the space between the fighters.

Remy held back a few paces from Deohecha. The elf made no move, but he watched him with unnerving eyes and active disinterest.

"You might want to get ready," Remy told him.

"I don't need a human to tell me my place," Deohecha hissed.

Remy stalked around him, trying to figure out the elf's strangely passive approach.

Deohecha's eyes followed him, but he didn't even turn his head in response.

Finally, Remy found an angle he liked and rushed forward with his sword ready. Deohecha leapt back and out of the way, keeping the distance between them.

The crowd gasped and then applauded, as if the elf was fighting a massive cù-sìth: waving a flag to draw in the feral beast and then leaping out of the way at the last moment.

Remy lashed out with his sword and then elf side-stepped out of the way, keeping lithe and limber like a snake. The tip of Remy's sword passed through the air where Deohecha had just stood as he parried slightly, taunting the human.

The crowd went wild. Fey loved a good sport. They loved it even more when it turned humans into the butt of good jokes.

But Remy grinned along with them. He'd figured out Deohecha's entire style in those few seconds. Deohecha relied on evasion—but he overly relied on it. Remy could use that.

Dodge then move. Draw blood when the opponent is overextended. Staying slippery as an eel, Remy knew he could use Deochecha's wriggling, offensive moves against him.

Remy made no indication he'd figured his opponent out. Instead, he pressed another attack, and then another—slashing, stabbing, thrusting—ever so slightly telegraphing his intentions.

Deohecha will be talented enough to pick up on the breadcrumbs I give him.

Remy made his actions predictably and stiffly, as if going through a fighter's movements as an exercise on forms. Had Deohecha not moved, those forms would have skewered him, all the same—but a fighter of any skill would have seen them coming. Remy made the elf fall into a pattern without even knowing it, and together, they went through a series of synchronized dance steps.

Finally, Deohecha sidestepped the human's blade and moved exactly to where Remy wanted him. Deohecha could step neither left nor right against his next motion—he could only go backward.

Then Remy made his move. He slashed to one side, and then the other. Instead of coming in with an overhead spar that was the anticipated next maneuver, Remy freed his gauntleted hand from the restraints that held it firm. He punched, relaxing his hand so that the metallic glove flew off his hand and smashed right into Deohecha's face.

The surprised elf brought his blade to bear, and barely in the nick of time, knocking the gauntlet aside. As soon as he'd cleared his field of view, he found Remy close behind the dislodged piece of armor. Remy knocked Deohecha's sword wide and then swung with a bare-fisted left hook, breaking Deohecha's nose and knocking him to the ground with a mangled nose that gushed red.

Deohecha scrambled backward, frantic to relocate his weapon, but the gong sounded, and the faun jumped in between them. "Blood is drawn by Remy. Do you dispute?"

Still lying on his back and without a weapon, Deohecha touched his fingers to his nose. Slowly, he pulled them away. They were slicked with crimson that flowed from mid-face and down his chin.

"I yield to the results," Deohecha said disdainfully.

The faun bowed and motioned to Remy. Again, the gong sounded, ending the match. The announcer proclaimed the human as the victor.

Remy extended a hand, and Deohecha grudgingly took it. He human helped the elf to his feet. The crowd cheered in response to the lively bout.

Money changed hands as viewers watched and pointed. Some who had bet on Deohecha cajoled him for the loss.

In the viewing box, Jaira sat next to her father, beside the gong. She watched the events—looking like some kind of prize to be won.

Even still, she smiled at her favored fighter, and Remy smiled back at her.

Remy looked away and searched the crowd. He spotted the box where Anya sat; Thoranmir was not with her. He locked eyes with Anya, and she gesticulated with a big shrug.

The announcement interrupted their silent conversation. "The next competitor is a local elf named Thoranmir Shelton."

Remy and Anya locked eyes, and he saw his worry reflected in them. "Damn it, Thoranmir," he grumbled, before looking around in search of his friend.

He's going to get himself killed!

CHAPTER EIGHTEEN

T HORANMIR COULDN'T BRING HIMSELF to look either Remy or his sister in the face when he took his place on the stage. His face and ears were flush, and he hadn't even heard the name of his opponent.

He gulped when he looked across the platform at the elf. His opponent wore a nasty snarl as he pointed at Thoranmir while bouncing from foot to foot, waiting for the gong and ready to explode with offense. His enemy was cocky and ready.

I thought I wanted to be here, but I definitely do not, Thoranmir thought. *But I* need *to be here.*

Glancing back, he spotted Remy watching from the sidelines near the tunnel leading to the coliseum's interior halls.

Thoranmir hardened his resolve and drew his sword. The opposing elf drew a short blade in one hand and unfurled a whip in the other. He rolled it over a few times and made its sinewy length seem to come alive. Giving it a sharp crack, the crowd reacted with a roar of anticipation.

The faun approached, signaled, and jumped back just as the gong crashed.

Thoranmir leapt aside as his enemy rushed forward and the whip snapped the air. He dodged a second time as the whip thundered close enough to his face that he felt the air break near his cheek.

His opponent whirled the coil into the air a third time, and Thoranmir knew that he could not keep jumping out of the whip's range if he wanted to stand any chance at winning. *And for Anya's sake, I have to keep going.*

Thoranmir could feel the elf's eyes upon him, picking out his legs, as if he thought to snare Thoranmir by the feet and then fall upon him with his blade. As the whip streaked toward him, Thoranmir leapt into the air. He held his blade low so that the whip's end had something to grab hold of.

It snatched his sword and then Thoranmir landed feet first on the thongs of the whip. His weight stomped down on the taut length of it and yanked the whip free from the enemy's hands. Its handle clattered at Thoranmir's feet. Without thinking, he snatched it up. The momentary slack had been enough that the whip released Thoranmir's weapon.

Thoranmir snatched the whip's handle and whirled it, snapping his wrist so that the tip's arc sliced across his opponent's chest, leaving a crimson line across his neck and collar bone. The wound puffed instantly with a lash of angry, welted red that dripped blood at its crest.

His opponent winced, surprised at the sudden turnabout. Even Thoranmir stood stiff and somewhat dumbfounded as the gong sounded. The faun rushed in and confirmed that the match had concluded.

"Thoranmir wins," came the announcement to an applauding stadium.

Reality came crashing back to him all at once and he watched the loser walk gingerly away from the arena's central dais. With every left step, the elf winced, the whip's sting reminding him that he'd failed the combat challenge.

The faun approached Thoranmir.

"I'm keeping the whip," Thoranmir insisted as he retrieved his sword.

Pointing, the faun sent him back toward the lockers. *He didn't care if I wanted to eat the whip*, he thought, still somewhat in shock, but there was another contest soon, and he needed to clear the floor.

Thoranmir kept his eyes down so that he wouldn't accidentally see the disappointment on his sister's face as he hurried back to the hallway. But he had to pass by Remy, who fell into step beside him. They stopped just short of entering the tunnels.

"What are you doing, Thoranmir?" Remy asked. His voice came off like an accusation.

"Winning. Didn't you see it?" He shook the whip at him.

"You got lucky," Remy insisted. "I'm afraid for you, my friend. You might get paired up against someone who's really dangerous."

"Like Fuerian Vastra?" Thoranmir kept his gaze cool.

"Yes. And there are others. My opponent fought with more style and grace than you'd expect from an amateur."

Thoranmir recognized the worry in Remy's voice. He considered telling him why he had to fight, especially after promising that he'd quit. *I could tell him; he's always been the smart one. Maybe he'll know what to do. They can't have possibly put a spell on me that would last this long... right? Surely they're not listening anymore.*

He glanced back and caught a glimpse of the Morgensteens seated near the gong. His heart sank when he spotted a guest with a crimson circle embroidered upon his chest. It looked like thorns or interlocking antlers.

All the pieces suddenly fell into place in Thoranmir's mind and his heart sank. *It's the mavens!* He and the embroidered elf locked eyes momentarily.

Remy barred his path and Thoranmir faked a bout of self-confidence. He had to maintain the façade of cocksure hubris. *Especially with those bloody cheating bastards here—they're surely keeping an ear and eye on things!* "Don't worry, buddy. You know I'm not trying to steal your girl's kiss from you—even if I *am* going to win this thing."

Before Remy could argue, Thoranmir pushed past his friend, shaking his head and ignoring the rapid drum of his heart.

"I know that," Remy called after him, exasperated. "Damn it, Thoranmir. It's not about a kiss."

An idea struck Thornamir, *the solution—I've figured it out.* "I will quit the contest if you do too. See? A nice compromise."

"I *can't*," Remy growled. He leaned closer. "You don't know—I haven't told anyone—Fuerian stole my dúshlán and he and I have made a wager. I cannot exit the contest without losing... *it's all I have of my past,* Thoranmir."

"You idiot," Thoranmir said. "Who cares when you have such a huge future to work towards? Jaira will still love you—maybe even more so—if you refuse to continue. You have nothing to lose but pride. And what's pride ever gotten a man except dead?"

"I... can't," said Remy. "And you should follow the same advice you give. Dueling is dangerous, and its filled with dangerous folk. And there are worse fates at play here than whip lashes and stray cuts."

Thoranmir shook his head and walked away. He didn't turn back for fear that Remy would begin to ascertain the truth of it all if he met his gaze—and here, under the surveillance of the mavens, he had too much to risk.

"It's like you think I can't win—or that just by competing, I'm going to get myself killed," Thoranmir argued. *What am I going to do? Without getting him killed or beating him, myself, how am I supposed to get Remy to quit this thing now?*

He stormed into the hallway, but heard his friend say behind him, "Yes. That is exactly my worry."

It was Thoranmir's worry, too.

FUERIAN WALKED THROUGH THE faire-like atmosphere surrounding the dueling contest. An intermission had been declared so that folk would go and see demonstrations, visit vendors, and learn about new products.

He chuckled, realizing this was perhaps the real reason Harhassus had decided to put on the event. *Harhassus is either pitching a new venture, or seeking one out.*

Fuerian paused, considering a third option. He could have been trying to build in-roads with a future son-in-law who had a love of the dueling culture.

The haughty elf scoffed. It was nice to think that family ties would operate that way, but it was not something he had ever experienced. House Vastra was as political as Oberon's court.

Fuerian rounded a corner and then froze. He saw a familiar figure in the distance: Hymdreiddiech—the mage who was in league with Nhywyllwch. Fuerian was also in cahoots with the business elf, but that did not mean that Fuerian trusted the arcanist... or Nhywyllwch, for that matter. But Fuerian understood the game they all played, and their roles in it.

Hymdreiddiech wore a dark robe, much like the mavens—the same as any number of travelers, in fact. Fuerian noted the creature's distinct body language and recognized him by the paleness of the skin, though his eyes seemed somehow different at a distance.

It could be a trick of the light, he wondered, and then watched, following. *It's him, all right.*

Hymdreiddiech did not appear to notice him, and Fuerian kept a healthy distance as he observed in secret.

And then Fuerian spotted Juriahl's wife.

Juriahl Vastra had been the only sidhe devious and ambitious enough to vie with Fuerian for the rank of Margrave's successor to House Vastra. Fuerian hadn't expected such a drastic move on Juriahl's part and it had been the first time in years the elf had surprised him.

Fuerian also considered Juriahl to be ugly. Sure, wealth bought the affections of beautiful females for a night, *but a marriage?* That was why he'd memorized the visage of the pretty she-elf who had taken vows with Juriahl. And it was also why he found Loitariel Vastra to be so suspicious.

Even more suspicious was the fact that she and her husband were crossing paths with Hymdreiddiech in a very public space and making every attempt to make it seem their meeting was not premeditated.

Fuerian cocked his head when Loitariel pointed to something in the distance and sent her husband to fetch her some inconsequential item. Fuerian scowled as he watched Juriahl scamper off like some befuddled imbecile on his leash-holders errand while Loitariel pretended to be interested in some demonstration at a vendor's kiosk.

If Fuerian was good at anything, it was reading body language, and Loitariel had engineered this meeting... *and* her husband's absence.

Fuerian picked a heading and walked forward through the crowd, focusing his attention and inclining an ear to try and glean whatever he could from the conversation as he passed by, like one face in the crowd of passersby.

He only caught one sentence as happened past, and he recognized Hymdreiddiech's voice.

"It happens at dusk—so be prepared..."

And then Fuerian was out of range. The crowd noises drowned out any ability to eavesdrop and he found himself face to face with Juriahl who carried two fried treats: one for him and one for his wife.

Juriahl gave him a short, familiar bow. "Greetings, cousin."

Fuerian returned the gesture. "Greetings to you."

"Good luck," Juriahl said, sounding as sincere as possible. "May your performance bolster House Vastra's fame."

They had that in common, at least.

"I think none of the offerings will give me pause for concern," Fuerian said.

"No," Juriahl said. "Likely not. Your skill is with the blade, to be true. Your real concerns are likely elsewhere." The elf lifted the two fists full of snack food. "The vendor promises his special recipe increases fertility, so if you'll excuse me... I have big plans for tonight."

Fuerian scowled as he watched Juriahl push through the crowd and head back for his wife. Loitariel stood there, and Hymdreiddiech had since disappeared.

F UERIAN SAT COMFORTABLY IN his locker. He had the best quarters, and he'd had a servant furnish it so that he could spend the day there. His fight was not until much later and the day was spaced out with many leisure attractions, like the intermissions meant for meandering through the innovation fair, which spaced out the duels.

Several inventors and other clever arcanists had set up a kind of expo at the Morgensteen's bidding. Fuerian knew that one of those was likely Harhassus Morgensteen's next business venture. Harhassus always had an angle, and this entire event was part of some larger business scheme to lure Fuerian in further.

For his part, Fuerian put out of mind what he had seen when touring through the expo. He had little desire to think about whatever designs Hymdreiddiech had upon Loitariel, the newest member of House Vastra. The secretive sidhe spell caster was in league with his business partner, and was a critical part of the plans to build an empire meant to exploit the akasha. But if he meddled in Vastran affairs?

Fuerian could not afford the mental energies to ferret out potential reasons for his connection to Juriahl's wife. He wanted to know, and badly, but he could not dwell on that right now. So he compartmentalized his feelings and decided to look into it, later.

A knock sounded at the door and Trishana, his aithermancer, entered. She walked past Naz, Fuerian's guard, and closed the door behind her, leaving Naz in the hallway.

As Fuerian waved her in, she produced a leather binder. Trishana tossed it to him. "It's all there, in all its damning glory."

Squinting as he read, Fuerian's eyes lit like the sun. The files contained it all: Remy's history, his heritage, and most importantly, why he owned a dúshlán. "This... this is the kind of information that gets a sidhe killed."

Trishana nodded. "I pulled it from the aither and printed it with my auto-scribe. And then I destroyed it, burned it to a crisp. Sometimes akashic equipment retains a kind of memory shadow when it interacts with aither, so I took drastic measures and used it as kindling." She looked at him with a severe expression. "Where I went to get that... those kind of folk do not take kindly to intrusion. They will know it was accessed. And now, you hold the only copy."

"So, this information no longer lives in aither?" Fuerian confirmed.

"Not anymore. It was locked away in secret to begin with. Practically forgotten about, except by a few whose steps I followed to gain access." With her finger, Trishana drew the antler crest upon her torso to indicate how and where she'd found the data. "I destroyed it all and made sure I had the only copy in the aither." She tapped the packet. "It only lives in there and in here," she tapped her head, "and within any of those who already know the truth."

"Good. Let's keep it that way. I'm sure neither you nor I want trouble with the Council of Mavens or their enforcers... or *who had this information hidden away.*"

Trishana blanched and shook her head.

Fuerian asked, "And what of the other files I wanted? Did you find the Morgensteens' trove of secrets?"

"Yes... but no."

He looked down his narrow nose at her as if he found particular disgust at hearing the word *no*. "What do you mean?"

"That information might prove less deadly to possess, but it was well protected. I had to do some *things* to get it that may bring me future trouble."

"Such as?" Fuerian pressed.

"Burning down a crippled woman's home," Trishana admitted. "The Morgensteens' aitherspace was reinforced by my competition. I had to destroy the physical seat of her power to drop those defenses."

Fuerian crossed his arms. "And what do you want in return, then?"

"I need a favor."

Fuerian only studied her in silence.

Trishana continued, "You know of my gambling ring. This Remy Keaton was supposed to have lost to Deohecha... Deohecha was supposed to be the second-best contender on the fight roster. You told me he was tough. Anyway, he and his friend Thoranmir are wrecking the under-card matches and obliterating my standings. I'd rigged them a certain way so that I'd earn a tidy profit, but they're interfering by winning. The crowd seems to like them, but I can't change the standings and odds now, or the whole system will fall. People won't bet if they know the house is playing against them."

"It is," Fuerian pointed out. "It always is. That much is common knowledge."

"Well, yeah. But once folks talk about it, that's when it becomes real." Trishana put her hands on her hips and looked at Fuerian. "How worried do I need to be about this Remy Keaton person?"

Fuerian set the file down on a table and placed the stolen dúshlán atop it. "Deohecha was supposed to have eliminated the human with ease; that's why I got Harhassus to have them meet so early in the contest. Dagda knows that even *I* had trouble landing a blow on him. That he beat the elf with such seeming ease does have me a little concerned."

Trishana scowled and paced the length of the room while growling. "You've got to get him to drop out. Bribe him, threaten him, whatever. I don't care. But his winning could ruin me."

"He won't win." Fuerian looked offended she'd even considered the human could beat him. He spun the dúshlán knife by its handle. "And he won't quit. Not now. He made a vow, and he would have to leave behind his need for vengeance with this blade if he quit." He tapped his finger to his lips. "I'll come up with something. Just get me that file."

Trishana sneered. "Well, I'll need a new auto-scribe first." She muttered curses beneath her breath as she left the room with Fuerian close behind her.

He glanced back at the file and the dúshlán. Fuerian left them there. If anything, Remy and his friends would be outside to watch Fuerian compete, probably hoping to glean some information about tells or techniques they think would help them overcome the cocky duelist. "Naz," he ordered, "go keep an eye on Remy Keaton. Make sure he doesn't come anywhere near that knife."

Naz nodded.

"Oh and send Gareth and his new crew to take care of the cripple and her brother when they return home tonight."

He grunted an acknowledgment and headed out.

Fuerian buckled his dueling belt and then exited, heading for his appointment in the fighting arena.

REMY AND THORANMIR STOOD on the field and watched Fuerian Vastra emerge to fight. The elf grinned smugly as they announced his name, waving at friends and admirers in the crowd.

Dusk had not yet fallen, but the sky would darken soon. It was about to be the last fight of the evening, which had been given to Fuerian, as he was considered the main event. Between the afternoon start time, the additional expo demonstrations, and the large number of bouts, each fighter had only one engagement on the first day. The second day would allow for multiple matches until a grand champion was declared, and a kiss was earned.

Fuerian drew his rapier, an elegant, light weapon with a basket-style hilt, and took his place on the stage, awaiting the first gong. The young elf who stood opposite him looked terrified to be facing down the highest competitor.

"This doesn't look like a fair fight," Thoranmir muttered.

"I'm not sure anybody expected that this event would be fair," Remy said. "The path of a duelist requires grit, above all else."

"Yeah, but we're not *dueling*," Thornamir said. "It's supposed to be a kind of exhibition, right?"

Remy fixed his friend with a surprised look. "What are the rules for this 'exhibition?'"

"The same as the duelists, but..."

"And what is the expectation, kiss aside, for the champion?"

"That he'll become a duelist and gain a sponsorship from one of the guilds." Thornamir's brow furrowed with recognition.

The gong crashed and signaled the match's start.

Fuerian stepped forward aggressively, and his opponent practically wilted. He stiffened so badly that Fuerian could have ended it right then and there. But the affluent elf was too cocksure and too much of a braggart to simply put his opponent out of his misery. He turned his back and walked away, throwing his arms up to the crowd and getting them to cheer before turning back quickly to defend against the blows of the inexperienced fighter who tried to seize an opportunity and clumsily rushed forward.

The crowd was electrified at Fuerian's bravado and screamed their approval even as the elf beat back his inexperienced opponent and knocked the sword from his hand. Fuerian walked casually to the far side and gave the whelp space, motioning for the younger elf to retrieve his sword.

"This is just embarrassing," Remy said with a scowl. "Half of the folks they added to this roster shouldn't have been accepted." He tried to keep from giving Thornamir too obvious a look. Thornamir had already insisted that he would not depart the contest unless Remy did likewise. *Jaira will still love you—maybe even more so—if you refuse to continue. You have nothing to lose but pride. And what's pride ever gotten a man except killed?*

Remy knew that his friend was likely right, but he'd hitched his future hopes to the contest and even bet his dúshlán against Fuerian. He was honor bound to the competition, but his friend seemed incapable of understanding that.

Fuerian engaged the crowd again and their cheers seemed to shrink the elf's opponent, who had already lost the battle in his own mind.

And then, Fuerian rushed forward for a glorious victory. He knocked the whelp's weapon aside and spun around him in a whirlwind of quick slashes. Before the faun referee could rush in and the gong could sound, Fuerian had given his opponent five cuts: one on each arm and leg and another across his back.

Each wound had been just deep enough to draw blood, but the realization of how badly he'd overwhelmed and beaten the younger fighter came with a quintet of bloody streaks. Fuerian's opponent collapsed to his knees, trembling with adrenaline and barely able to move from injuries.

The lad didn't respond when the faun asked if he yielded the victory, and the goat-like creature waved his arms for the final gong, declaring Fuerian Vastra as the winner.

Fuerian turned to Harhassus Morgensteen, his daughter, and the other honored guests and bowed, which made the crowd thunder even louder. His body respectfully dipped to the hosts, the announcer, and the maven who oversaw the contest, but his eyes remained fixed on Remy and Thoranmir.

INSIDE THE STADIUM DAY one of the event ended with a brassy chime of the gong. Fuerian had barely broken a sweat in the contest and he walked the area, searching for the shifty she-elf, Loitariel. Whatever her plans had been, or whatever her involvement in Hymdreiddiech's schemes—and which might or might not involve Nhywyllwch—they were supposed to involve something at dusk.

Fuerian did not see her or Juriahl anywhere. Neither could he spot Hymdreiddiech.

As the crowd dispersed, Fuerian watched an exhibitor struggle with two very large batteries that were each the size of a child. They looked as if they weighed even more. The things seemed to glow and crackle with akashic energy. This fresh set of batteries would allow the demonstrator to pilot it home.

Fuerian had watched his earlier presentation of the hover carriage. It was like the kind Harhassus was fond of, but this one required no horses and boasted twice the speed of a stallion. Even if the batteries drained extremely fast, the contraption could represent a promising new tech—but not for decades until it was perfected.

Between some of the day's earlier matches, the elf had zipped several laps around the stadium's inner floor at impressive speeds. Fuerian's future father-in-law had watched with great interest, and Fuerian hoped this was not the elf's next planned venture; it looked like an overly expensive toy to him. Fuerian did not think the invention practical so long as horses were readily available.

Harhassus Morgensteen finished speaking with another exhibitor on the stadium floor before walking toward a waiting carriage, the standard horse-drawn kind, where Jaira leaned patiently. Vennumyn, the maid who had provided Fuerian with information in the past, stood a step behind.

Fuerian's eyes watched the older elf with rapt interest. The event's outcomes were a delicate balance and Fuerian felt he could control the outcomes better by being in the middle of it all.

Naz, Fuerian's private duelist had become something of a valet for him, and he had followed Remy back through the tunnels like a shadow. There, he would be Fuerian's eyes and ears in places where Fuerian could not be.

"Stay with the carriage," Harhassus told his daughter. "I have one last minute piece of business to attend to."

Jaira sighed and seemed to comply, but Fuerian knew her well enough to spot the little signs she'd hidden in her body language. He had seen her do those same things to *him*: an eye roll that wasn't quite an eye roll, a stiffened posture that was a hair shy of rebellious, and a defiant pout of the lips.

He couldn't help but grin. His betrothed had made impudence into an art form. Fuerian appreciated it when it was directed at

Harhassus, but he knew he'd have to break her of it once they were wed. The Vastras wouldn't tolerate such temerity within their family, especially from one who had entered in by vow instead of blood.

I wonder if Loitariel will be allowed grace, or if Juriahl will have to break her, too? Fuerian assumed the new Vastra's attitudes were of a similar stripe to Jaira.

Harhassus stalked off toward one of the halls leading to the lockers and Fuerian felt he could accurately guess his destination. As Fuerian had come to know Jaira, he'd also figured out Harhassus; he probably knew the father even better than the daughter. Harhassus's neck had blushed all the way up to his ears.

He's angry. Remy Keaton was supposed to lose and same goes for the human's friend, Thornamir. Harhassus is going to see the human.

He chuckled, thinking it all inconsequential. Fuerian still planned to win this contest, despite Remy's seemingly easy victory over Deohecha, who Fuerian had dueled before. He didn't care so much about the Dagda's kiss and the blessing that Jaira's lips promised to bestow upon the victor. Fuerian didn't believe in luck charms and had always thought the Dagda was more of a parable or creation legend than a true story... but he *did* care about his pride and reputation. Letting a *human* publicly kiss his fiancé would damage to that.

The lights popped on, some ignited by lamplighters under Vastran employ, others sparking to life from akashic luminary fixtures. The sun crept lower and lower. As shadows began to creep ever so slightly across the stadium, Fuerian walked back toward his locker to gather the materials Trishana had collected for him.

But what about Thoranmir? he wondered. *He seemed almost desperate for his friend to not emerge victorious when we met at the Thistle and Barrel... and now he's in the contest again? Does he think he can beat Remy? How is he tied into the mavens?*

Things didn't add up in Fuerian's mind, and he did not like that. He turned a corner to the corridor that would lead to his room and found Naz Charnazar, one of the best duelists in Cathair Dé, lying dead on his back with his arms splayed in a pool of blood. The crimson puddle still grew, indicating the fresh kill.

Fuerian ran closer and found a short sword still protruding from Naz's chest; Naz still clutched his rapier in his hand. A kind of black ichor instead of blood slicked the tip of Naz's blade. He'd at least scored a blow against his attacker, but Fuerian did not know what kind of arcadeaxn creature bled like that.

And then he found out.

An elf burst out of Fuerian's room, clutching Remy Keaton's stolen dúshlán. The elf was shrouded in black, and his skin appeared pallid, with hair that hung limp, as if someone had recently hauled the thief from his grave. A puckered scar crossed his face that looked neither healed nor bleeding.

It's a shade! Fuerian realized. *A night thrall made by necromancy.*

Before he could put a hand to his blade, the thief dashed past, shoving Fuerian to the ground and then sprinting through the halls.

Fuerian scrambled to his feet and pursued. He got to the dueling floor just in time to see the carriage horses scrambling away from the wagon.

The Morgensteen's driver had cut the horses free to save Jaira; without horses, the kidnapper could not steal both vehicle and girl. The driver paid for his quick thinking with his life as the night thrall slashed his throat.

Screeching and shouting for Jaira to flee, Vennumyb tried to slow the thing down. The attacker slammed Vennumyn into the side of the covered wagon, breaking her neck with the ferocity of it. She flopped into a heap with her head twisted at macabre angles.

He dragged Jaira into the akashic-powered hover carriage. With the stolen dúshlán pressed against Jaira's throat, the elf-like creature fumbled at the controls, and then ignited it, making the car hover on a bed of mystic air.

With the blade still against the girl's neck, the shade glanced back and shot Fuerian a look of warning with those cold, dead eyes. Fuerian stopped in his tracks.

Where have I seen this elf before?

And then, he remembered. He'd seen him previously. Fuerian had killed this elf once already in an illegal duel; Gareth and his cronies had buried the body. *Glenric, he'd been called...*

Someone had exhumed and reanimated him. Fear gripped Fuerian—not the fear of the dead, but of whomever controlled him. *Glenric is a sluagh—made by magic!*

Mavens primary duty was to work on behalf of Oberon's court-they were here to do more than mediate a contest. *All mavens wore an embroidered patch depicting two stags' antlers locked in combat to form a circle.* Fuerian finally realized he and Thoranmir shared the same trepidation about the mavens.

Thoranmir may have stumbled into their web first, but as a méith Fuerian knew far more about them and their capabilities than some ditch digger from the slums. That knowledge held Fuerian's feet to the floor—despite having handily beaten the undead elf previously, and despite the fiend kidnapping his betrothed.

Was this the work of Loitariel and Juriahl Vastra? No—impossible, Juriahl would never violate internal family accords, and necromancy does not necessarily indicate this is the mavens.

Glenric—or whatever he was, now—sneered at Fuerian whose blood ran cold.

The creature hit the accelerator. He—it—fled the stadium in the strange flying contraption, with Jaira screaming for help as it sped away, leaving Fuerian, and anyone else who cared about Jaira, behind in its wake.

CHAPTER NINETEEN

—— ❖ ——

H ARHASSUS MORGENSTEEN FLUNG OPEN the door to Remy's locker without knocking and shoved his way inside without an invitation.

"Can I help you, Mister Morgensteen?" Remy still tried to act politely.

"I'm going to level with you, son," Harhassus said, keeping a stiff demeanor and making pointed eye contact. "I'm going to ask you to drop out of this event."

Thoranmir would be tickled to hear of this, Remy thought. *Friend or not, he's been trying to push me out for days now. He'd be amused to know he's not alone.*

Thoranmir and Anya had left for their apartment shortly after the last match, with Anya giving her brother an earful as they departed. But Remy had recognized the look on his friend's face: Thoranmir was committed to seeing the contest through, as foolish as that choice was.

Harhassus stood there looking at Remy, not amused at all that the human hadn't given him his full attention. He maintained a kind of threatening body language that Remy assumed he'd used to intimidate lesser folks.

But Remy merely chuckled. "No. I don't think dropping out would be in the interest of a spirited and honest competition." He winked at the older man, expressing how little he was coerced by the elf's bluster.

The older elf's face reddened. "You cannot possibly hope to beat Fuerian Vastra. Surely you know this—why would you force my daughter to watch her rightful fiancé gut you like a... a human stuck on the slopes of the Maighe Tuireadh?"

"Yeah. People keep saying things like that." Remy played it cool. "I'm not sure if you are all so badly underestimating me or if you're grossly overestimating Fuerian. I guess we'll soon find out."

"I can see it clearly," Harhassus said. He wagged a finger uncomfortably close to Remy's face. "Do not think I am fooled. I see that you have developed some kind of juvenile crush on my daughter. And what could you hope to accomplish here *human?* Even if you did manage to beat Fuerian, what then?"

Remy ignored the finger and let the father vent to his anger.

Harhassus continued, "What if you win and become a duelist—an actual professional instead of some child pretender—which is all I see before me now? Would you marry Jaira? Could you *actually provide* a better life for her, or would her life be of a worse quality than what Fuerian could provide her?"

The statement stung for a moment. Remy hadn't thought any of the elf's barbs could sting. He'd been wrong.

"Firstly, sir. Nothing I have seen convinces me that I will lose. And I'll confess that even a successful duelist might provide only little means compared to the riches of a wealthy house, but can money purchase everything that matters in life? Can gold buy love? I think your definition of a *good life* needs reconciling."

Harhassus's face verged on a snarl. "You would bring shame to her name? Don't you know how they talk of elf women who consort with humans? You talk about love, but you remain willing to sully her reputation by merely being a *possibility*."

Remy did not flinch. "At least I love her."

Harhassus stiffened. "I love my daughter."

Remy continued, "Then how dare you sell her into a relationship with a mate she does not love, or even *like*, like some kind of whoremonger—you call that love?"

Harhassus balked, and then bared his teeth. Everything in him poised to physically strike Remy.

And then Fuerian burst into the room. Both Harhassus and Remy turned, shocked to see him.

The elf had blood smeared on both hands and stained on his tunic.

"They've taken Jaira. She's been kidnapped," Fuerian said.

T HE AKASHIC SPEEDER SKIFF crashed through carts and vendor wagons as it caromed through the streets leading away from the stadium where the dueling contests were held.

It came to a sudden stop in a designated area and, even though the sluagh had a firm hand on Jaira, she managed to wriggle free. She'd nearly leapt from the vehicle when its strong hand shot out and grasped her.

Jaira refused to relent. She'd nearly gotten free again when a woman stepped out from the narrow alleyway where her abductor had stopped.

She wore a dark cape and cowl which hid her face, but she was undeniably feminine. "Hold her," she ordered, producing a dagger and threatening Jaira with it until the thrall grappled Jaira into submission.

The fiend clamped its grip tighter and restricted Jaira's ability to move. She could barely even breath with its arms around her.

Her captor retreated a few steps back into the darkness of the alley and the place where she'd prepared her reagents.

Jaira could feel the energies of the universe being pulled into it like some kind of vortex. *She is a spellcaster! Has it been a she all along... the shadowy elf?*

The arcanist mumbled a string of words below her breath, chanting the verbal components of the incantation and gathering the energy of her will and the magics of arcadeax.

She returned a moment later and pressed a thumb to Jaira's head, invoking her will. Then, she pressed it to the dirt to invoke the power of arcadeax itself. She touched her heart next, binding her desire to the spell's outcome.

Jaira had her secret magic talents, but she was uneducated, by and large. However, she knew some about spellcraft. Whatever this spell was, it was not the normal sort eldritch practice she was familiar with. Whatever *this* was, it was older—some kind of rite that she knew nothing about.

As the final act, the strange elf touched her thumb to Jaira's lips and smeared the dirt across them, making a muddy smear. And then she bowed back into the shadows and the thrall yanked Jaira back into the akashic speeder.

Before Jaira could try to flail her way to freedom again, the skiff took off, crashing through anything that stood in its way, and the dead-eyed driver returned Remy's dagger to her throat. Those eyes had no emotion, no life to them. But they communicate one explicit threat: if Jaira moved, she would die.

AGAROGOL AND MITHRILCHON EMERGED from the deeper shadows and surrounded Loitariel.

"The rite is completed? Your spell was delivered?" Mithrilchon asked.

Loitariel nodded. "The spell has taken root. At her next kiss, she will deliver our curse, the Kiss of Daggers—whether to Fuerian or to Remy, we shall see."

Agarogol chuckled. "It would still amuse me if it turned out to be some random sidhe warrior we could not predict."

"Or if she kisses her father upon return after being ransomed?" Mithrilchon said dourly. "We can only prepare for what outcomes we can anticipate. No plan is foolproof. We must each remain vigilant until we are certain that the seer's prophecy has been averted."

Agarolgol cast his eyes downward and nodded. His master was not in a mood for mirth.

"Each of you," Mithrilchon said, "you have jobs to do. The prize is out of play for the moment, but that does not mean the game has ended."

Loitariel bowed and then turned and hurried away and into the dark. It was far more than a game to either of them. Loitariel's marriage may have been a sudden ruse to stymie Fuerian's power—but it was also very much real, not that love had any part to play in it.

But she still had to abide by the oaths of her wedding vows—and if she produced a legitimate male heir before Fuerian could, she could gain considerable power and influence in order to help the Tower.

Mithrilchon had to stay to oversee any maven obligations to the contest and provide guidance for what to do in the absence of the Dagda's Blessing.

Agarogol watched them both go, and then he hurried off, too. He had to direct the sluagh, and he had to watch over the prisoner once she arrived at a safe house well beyond the city. His thrall would grow somewhat weaker and slower with the dawn and he had to get there by then to ensure that Jaira did not escape.

H ARHASSUS WORDLESSLY WORKED HIS jaw and blinked at Fuerian. Finally, he managed, "What?"

Remy's eyes burned and he asked, "Who?"

"They were a… a shade of a person," Fuerian insisted. "Someone took her. Someone with magic—bad magic. An elf controlled by the Aes Sídhe." He turned and almost cringed, knowing it slighted his own honor to admit the last detail. "He also took your dúshlán."

Remy rolled his eyes with a growl.

Harhassus turned to Remy. "You've got to save her. You've saved her once before!"

"Why are you asking me instead of Fuerian?" Remy crossed his arms and stared down the old elf.

Fuerian practically scoffed. "Mess with the Aes Sídhe? Surely you jest. She was taken by a night thrall, a shade, that is not magic to be trifled with and is no mere product of akasha—this is the creation of a dark and talented mage."

Remy's jaw dropped, flabbergasted that neither of these two were doing anything to rescue Jaira—who they both claimed to be protecting *from Remy!*

"I would not interfere with the Aes Sídhe, not for anything," Fuerian concluded. And then, he leveled an accusatory gaze at Remy. "But I know *why* they have taken her. It is because of the human."

"How do you know this?" Harhassus asked.

"Because the shadow took the dúshlán. *Remy's* dúshlán. Surely you see that he is connected to all of this at the center?"

Remy snatched a fistful of Fuerian's shirt and snarled. "Coward! You didn't stop them—you've no right to claim her. Which way did they go?"

Fuerian's eyes widened and he nearly fought the human back, but instead, he pointed in the direction he had taken her. "The shade stole that new levitation car they demonstrated earlier. You'll never catch them; he was certainly fleeing Cathair Dé."

Remy released the elf with a shove and snatched his gauntlet and sword, disgusted that nobody else was even trying. He moved toward the door.

"It was a sluagh. Folk call them night thralls because they grow stronger in the dark—and it will be immensely powerful until the dawn," Fuerian informed him.

Remy pushed past the other dueling contestant and muttered, "What a craven bastard... it's like you've never seen a shade before. They're not completely uncommon in the unseelie." The human rushed out from the room, leaving the two elves to gawk at his heroism and wonder exactly what his life had been like before he'd found his way into the seelie side of Arcadeax.

After sprinting from the stadium, Remy located the first horse that looked fresh and leapt onto its back. Its owner shouted at him, but Remy was already away. He called over his shoulder, "Harhassus Morgensteen will pay for your horse!"

The animal responded to Remy's commands and surged through the streets, which were fully awash with evening luminaries that bathed the avenues in golden hues. Hoof strikes echoed through the road and announced to the crowds they ought to move aside if they hoped to avoid being trampled.

Already, Remy spotted an overturned cart and three demolished vendor stands. Their owners still picked up scattered produce and damaged goods and the sluagh had blazed an easily tracked trail of destruction. *The fiend must have come this way and plowed through the crowds.*

He hunched down and let the charger gallop as fast as it could toward the main road leading away from Cathair Dé.

Minutes later, the mount burst past the city limits like a quarrel from a crossbow. It ran with reckless abandon and seemed to know the way: *follow the road as fast as possible.*

The winding highway out of the city stretched into the distance, leading to the inner parts of the Summer Court; the seelie kingdom controlled by King Oberon and Queen Titania. It was arranged with its capital, Faery Cairn, located at the center.

With the stars and moon shining brightly overhead, Remy could spot the distant vehicle. It glowed faintly with an oddly arcane sparkle where the mechanized contraption traveled into the distance. It was far off and still moving quickly, but its speed was relatively the same as a horse set at an urgent gallop.

Remy had watched the machine's exhibition and noticed that it seemed to slow after several laps through the stadium grounds. It could not maintain its charge with extreme speeds. *I will catch it,* Remy promised himself, *and I'll free Jaira or die trying.*

With his head still ducked and bobbing in rhythm with the horse's strides, Remy pursued it hotly. The galloping seemed to stretch and twist time along the familiar road.

I've been this way before!

Past the banks of heather and grassland was the copse of trees where he'd been fed by the Fianna. They closed range slightly as they drew nearer and Remy's hopes mounted. *Perhaps Madadh and his kind will come to my aid?*

They came and flew past the nearest point where the trees encroached upon the road, but there was no more odor of smoke. The Fianna had already departed and moved their camp of rovers.

Remy growled, wishing they had been an option to provide assistance. *I'd even take help from that cluster of unseelie redcaps,* his thoughts turned dark. *But they, too moved on—and at my insistence.*

With labored breathing, the horse increased speed. It somehow seemed to understand that the goal was to catch the odd vehicle ahead of them on the road.

The wooded region where the Fianna had once been broke and opened up into large flats of grassland and low hillocks and shallow vales. From his position atop the mount, Remy could see for leagues and leagues. Near the furthest edge of the meadowlands, a river cut through, followed by a massive forest which sprawled for at least ten thousand acres.

If Remy did not catch them prior to them reaching the sprawling woods, he might never recover his beloved. It was simply too much land to run and hide within and Remy was just one man.

My horse seems to be gaining—perhaps I will catch it yet! The machine also slows... it's akashic batteries might be dying.

He tried to stay optimistic, but knew that they might make it into the forest first. Then, they could disappear into the acreage where the night thrall could ambush him, or worse, become lost forever and escape into the forest.

Remy tried not to think about the other possibility: that the shade might kill Jaira. He had to hope that the thing had taken her for a reason. Night thralls were slaves to their master's wills—to the desires of the mage who created it, and this thing had taken Jaira for some larger purpose. That meant he or she wanted Jaira alive. The shade would not kill her unless there was no other choice—and that meant Remy could still attempt a rescue. Provided he could catch up to them before the forest.

Damn it, that thing is fast.

It slowed more noticeably than before as it crossed the stretch of open land, just not as quickly as he'd hoped.

Remy's horse grunted as it tried to maintain the sprint, but it, too, had finally begun to lag. The human could only hope to fully close the gap and make his move somewhere on the other side of the cold, rushing waters, but before the dark line of tall trees and menacing bracken.

T HE WHEELS OF ANYA'S chair crunched to a stop, grinding upon the blackened gravel. Nothing was left of her apartment but ashes and the smell of smoke. The dwellings on the floors above were less affected, or untouched, even.

Her eyes narrowed to slits as she looked over the charred and hollow husk that was the remains of her home. The damage pattern seemed to indicate that someone had burned *her* place in particular—and no others. *Her home had become a target.*

An elf wearing the uniform of the fire magistrate spotted her. "Are you the owner or occupant of this apartment?"

Thoranmir stepped forward as if to open his mouth, but then melted beneath his sister's scathing glare. He shrunk back as Anya turned to the inspector.

"Yes. I am... or *was* the occupant. What happened here?

"Fire," he said matter-of-factly.

Somehow, despite her short height while seated in the chair, she managed to look down her nose at him.

The magistrate elaborated, "I mean, looks like arson. You got any known enemies?"

"Many," she said. "I am Cathair Dé's most well-respected aithermancer—depending on who you ask. I live—*and work*—here."

"You think someone burned you out so they could weaken your presence in the aither?"

Anya nodded. "It's the best way... the *only* way to defeat some of my defenses. But only someone who lives near here would be able to discover where I live. I keep that information secret."

"So who knows you personally—or maybe professionally?"

Anya inclined her head to confirm.

"And are there any *other* reasons your home could be a target—maybe not aithermancy related? Maybe a husband or lover... do they maybe have enemies of their own?"

Anya shot Thoranmir a sidelong look. "My brother. He's got more than a few, and he's got a particular talent for pissing people off." She said it with enough fire that it was clear she was among them."

The elf in the uniform took notes and then thanked her for her time. He slipped away before Anya could ask what she was supposed to do next.

"Great. Just great," she cursed at the sky. At the ashes. At the blackened and wrecked slag that had once been her instruments. She could barely move her chair around and through the debris.

"Anya, I'm so sorry," Thoranmir said. "If there is any—"

She held up a hand. "Not another word. I'm still mad at you for unrelated reasons. But, well, *this* doesn't make me any less angry right now."

After a few more minutes spent sifting through the wreckage, she finally spun the chair and sent the vehicle crawling away from the destruction. It didn't make it out before the battery died. The nearby charging port that connected to the lines of akashic energy was melted and useless so she could not recharge.

She growled, shook her chair with rage, and then breathed deeply, forcing her rage under control. Anya called to her brother, "Don't speak. Just push."

Thoranmir obeyed. He dutifully pushed the wheeled seat out and down the lamp-lit streets.

R EMY SPURRED HIS STEED onward, encouraging it to keep up its pace, quickening it, even. They were gaining on the enemy's hover car and had gotten close enough that Remy could confirm Jaira's identity as the prisoner. He could see the terror in her eyes.

The gap shrank, and then closed further as the horse pushed itself. It was so close that Remy could nearly reach out and grab ahold of the fleeing car.

And then the horse shrieked as if it had been stabbed. Its speed dramatically flagged and it continued to howl with a pained trill, It was lamed by some unseen ailment, and exhausted and out of breath. It spat flecks of spittle as it cried and hopped lightly whenever its wounded leg touched the ground.

No, no, no—damn it! Remy, hunkered low so it could not buck him off as the things gait shifted into an unruly gallop. *I'm lucky the thing didn't pitch end over end.* He kicked his ailing horse in the flank, trying to get whatever speed out of it that he could.

Jaira looked back. The terror in her eyes spread across to her entire face. The whites of her eyes shone under the starry sky, and she tensed to leap from her kidnapper's vehicle. Without looking, the night thrall laid the sharp edge of the stolen dúshlán against her soft neck. She stiffened and wilted beneath the enemy's threats.

"Hie!" Remy shouted, kicking his mount's flank again and coaxed a little more acceleration out of it. They very nearly closed the gap, and then the horse howled again with a renewed, pained equine cry, and completely lost its speed.

The kidnapper pulled away as Remy's horse went fully lame, barely at a run. At least one leg had stiffened with cramps. It neighed again, scattering foamy spittle and threatened to topple every other step.

"No, no, no!"

The terrified look on Jaira's face would forever haunt him, he knew. Her face shrank into the distance as the akashic powered vehicle pulled away at something only a little more than a human's typical sprinting speed.

In moments, it would reach the bridge, and afterward, it would hit the straight-away and have a clear shot to the forest. Without a healthy horse, there would be no catching them. He wouldn't even regain enough of the lost distance to track the vehicle.

Remy's chest tightened, and he screamed as his beloved grew smaller and smaller in the distance. The hovering contraption went around the curve and over the river crossing, soon to be gone forever.

T HORANMIR HEARD THEM BEFORE he saw them. Still pushing his sister's wheelchair he quickened his steps, drawing irked comments from her.

Shadows darted through the side streets all around them as they headed towards a local hotel. Thoranmir was pretty sure that he recognized at least one of the young sidhe who trailed after them: the young sidhe who had been the leader of the gang that sold dream hallow—the ones responsible for killing Eldarian. The ones who he and Remy had beaten to a pulp before robbing.

Remy's not here, now... and I'm guessing they're deciding our warning not to return to business in this neighborhood no longer applies.

Hairs on the back of Thoranmir's neck rose. He could feel them gathering behind them. And then they made it through the doors to the closest inn and Thoranmir pulled the entry shut behind them.

Their pursuers did not follow.

The entrance to the inn was a large lobby with a wing on either side where people sat and ate. It was a traditional place, not like the fancy hotel Thoranmir and Remy had stayed in at the last encounter with the gang. The lobby was filled. A crowd of people waited for the host ahead of them.

Anya looked up at her brother from her seat and finally realized he'd been genuinely rattled. "What was that about?"

Thoranmir leaned against the wall for a moment and caught his breath, trying to slow his rapid heart.

"That fire... does it have to do with whoever is following you?"

Thoranmir tried to keep a neutral expression, but could not help but break into a frown.

Anya cursed below her breath. "Well, tell me about it, then."

Thoranmir did.

He explained that they had been responsible for supplying, and killing, Eldarian. Then he told her how he and Remy had roughed them up and warned them not to do business in the neighborhood around Anya's home, and how they'd been followed on at least the first night.

"I recognized at least one of the sidhe stalking us. He was one of the same who tracked Remy and I to the rich part of town."

Anya scowled and spoke flippantly. "Well, you're the fighter, aren't you? So go and fight them."

Thoranmir stood silent for a moment, weighing his odds.

"No. Don't," Anya sighed. "I don't need to bury another elf this week. Let's just hope they were satisfied with burning my house down and let this be the end of it."

Thoranmir squeezed his sister's shoulder.

She brushed his hand off. "I'm still pissed at you for numbers of reasons, though."

"Fair enough," Thoranmir held his hands in front of him and shrugged. *She can't stay mad forever... I can make it up to her after the duels are over... after I've saved her life—maybe then I can finally explain all of—*

"Sorry," a voice called out from the front of the crowd, interrupting Thoranmir's thoughts. "We are at maximum capacity. Everyone willing to double up on a room has already done so. No more lodgers for the night."

Thoranmir pushed his way through the grumbling crowd as they all exited the establishment and headed out in search of other places. "Please, ma'am," he pleaded with the woman at the front. "My sister just had her apartment burned down."

The she-elf shook her head, unmoved. "Not my fault. We haven't been at full capacity in four years, and then this contest comes in and boom. We're already well over what we can handle and likely to be so until the duels are done."

"Do you know anyone else who might have a room?"

She shook her head. "Good luck to you. The duels are quite a draw."

Thoranmir grumbled and turned back to his sister. "We'll have to keep looking." He turned her chair and pushed her to the door,

350 CHRISTOPHER D. SCHMITZ

wishing he'd gone out with the dispersing crowd. That might have masked them enough to lose their pursuers.

Thoranmir took in a deep breath and held it against the unexpected and then pushed through. Then his heart sank.

A big elf stood there with the apothik peddlers who Thoranmir and Remy had assaulted days ago. Their wounds had healed. Adjacent to the big elf stood the leader of the gang and Thoranmir recognized the scrawny kid in the flatcap who'd stolen Jaira's earring from Remy.

Apparently the kid graduated to full-blown asshole. The chubby one must be the sidhe who's holding the gang's reins, including their leader? For all I know, this might be the guy who supplied them with dream hallow.

"You owe my boys some money," Chubby said, pointing a club at him. "Both for what you took and for product you ruined. How about you come over here so we can have a little chat about it."

CHAPTER TWENTY

A S THE NIGHT THRALL began crossing the bridge, Remy's
mind flashed with recognition. He had been here before.

Remy shouted at the top of his lungs, using the unseelie tongue.
[The bridge—the bridge! Stop the enemy of Wulflock, the true
and rightful king, from crossing!]

The akashic vehicle crested the crossing, and then the bridge
exploded. Stones scattered through the air and the levitating car
broke in two. Remy watched as Jaira went flying over the edge and
plunged into the river while Skreekuzz the troll snatched the sluagh
in one massive paw.

The necrotic elf kicked and thrashed, trying everything it could
to free itself. It slashed and stabbed at the troll's thick skin with
Remy's dúshlán until the blade lodged itself into Skreekuzz's forearm. The troll dangled the shade high in the air by one foot and it
wriggled free, falling through the air.

Skreekuzz caught him before he could hit the ground and attempt any escape. Not chancing it again, the troll bent the shade's
legs with his superior strength, bending them backward at the
knees so that they cracked like fresh-broken carrots.

The troll turned and waved dumbly to Remy as his lame horse finally arrived nearby, panting and barely able to take another step. Remy scrambled off his mount and dove into the water.

He emerged a few moments later with Jaira in his arms. She clung to him, wet and cold, but her body felt warm against his, and her heart pounded. She coughed and spluttered, but she was otherwise all right.

Skreekuzz watched them emerge with curious eyes. [I recognized your voice,] he said in the unseelie tongue.

[Thank you for helping, Skreekuzz,] Remy said as he and Jaira collapsed onto the familiar riverbank. [I feared my enemy would escape with the woman I love.]

Skreekuzz cocked his head at him and then looked at the broken creature in his grip. The troll stuffed as much of him into his mouth as he could fit and then crunched, chewing rapidly. Sounds of broken bones and rending flesh filled the air with grotesque noises.

Making a revolted face, Skreekuzz bit down hard and then pulled the lower half of the body away, snapping it in two and spilling blackened organs down his broad chest, slicking it with dark and viscous fluid. [Disgusting. Something is wrong with this flesh.]

He threw the lower half night thrall into the distant meadow and spat up the mashed remains of him into the river for the fishes to devour.

[It was already dead,] Remy said. [It was a sluagh, made by Aes Sídhe magic.]

Skreekuzz bent at the river and sucked in as much water as he could to wash the flavor from his mouth. He spat it out with a great gasp, and then turned his hungry eyes to the lame horse, who limped pitifully nearby.

[Your horse is injured, friend. Will you sell it to me?]

Remy remembered their earlier conversation, and that the troll had preference for horse meat.

[What do you have to bargain with?] Remy asked, already knowing how the conversation would end. The troll could take it from them if he wanted, but Remy thought he had already bought enough good will from Skreekuzz—and transactions were extremely important to the fey. Even those of the unseelie.

Skreekuzz pulled the dúshlán from his arm as if it were a mere splinter. [I have this. Perhaps it has value to you?]

[A most excellent idea. We shall call it an even trade,] Remy said, accepting the knife back from the troll and sliding it into his waistband. He motioned to the horse.

The troll's eyes brightened, and he leapt after it. The horse protested and tried to flee, but it had not been faking its lameness. Skreekuzz bounded after it, easily snatching it.

[I am sorry for your home,] Remy said, glancing at the busted crossing.

Skreekuzz shrugged and snapped the horse's neck as casually as if cracking the shells of a nut, ending the animal's frantic protests. There was no malice in it; to it, the troll was hungry and the horse was food. [There are plenty of other bridges.] The troll did not seem worried.

Jaira recoiled from the sight. Remy turned her head and took her by the hand. "Come. We must return to the city. It will be safer there," he muttered in the language she understood.

"Safe?" she exclaimed, doubtful. Jaira winced at the grisly sound of the troll taking big, slurping bites of horse flesh. "Nothing, *nowhere* is safe."

Remy leaned into her and pulled her along the way. "It's safest by my side. I will protect you."

She put her arm around his waist and then walked with him.

With night well underway, they headed toward Cathair Dé at a leisurely pace. The return distance would take much time, and they were more than willing to let Harhassus and Fuerian think the worst had happened to them both, and that was sure to happen.

Remy had already made this trek by foot once before, and knew that he and Jaira would spend at least one night alone together.

THORANMIR STALLED. "I DON'T know you. Why should I even bother to—"

"You may call me Cú Chulainn," the portly elf said whimsically.

"Right," said Thoranmir with his hackles high. "A hero's name for a bastard who poisons poor mages and burns down the houses of cripples. Listen here, fatty—"

Cú Chulainn's nostrils flared and he bared his teeth. He and his henchmen began walking towards Thoranmir with menace written across their faces.

Thoranmir raised his hands. "Hold up. I have a proposition for you." His heart raced and he tried to stall. *I've got to think of something, and fast!*

"You've been causing trouble for these kids," Cú Chulainn growled. "They've just been trying to make a little coin while making folks' dreams come true, and you and your human friend put the screws to em—and to *me* by extension."

The group surrounded them. Even if Anya could run, they'd have no place to go. The look of terror on his sister's face made Thoranmir's blood run cold.

"Here's how it's gonna be," Cú Chulainn hissed. "Those threats you and your ddidymadferth friend made are null and void. We're going to travel the apothik to whomever we want, wherever we want, and you're not going to do a damned thing about it. Further, my boys are going to rough you and your crippled sister up just so you don't go thinking this could have gone any other way."

Thoranmir crossed his arms, suddenly emboldened by an idea. "That's it? You think you're going to stay below the radar of the constables by assaulting a crippled woman? What in the fey are you thinking? You might be holding that kid's leash" he pointed to the street-level leader who he and Remy had thrashed before, "but clearly there's got to be someone holding yours. This move? It's not smart."

Cú Chulainn cocked his head and frowned. Thoranmir's heart almost skipped a beat. *That's it—I hit the target on that one!*

Before the big elf could lose any face by having to ask, which would admit he hadn't thought the plan through, Thoranmir explained it.

"The fire marshal and the investigators are already looking into the arson. If they find us beaten up, there's sure to be an inquiry, and the news? Journalists are going to come asking questions and print a whole story. Lots of people suddenly asking *why would a bunch of thugs beat up a legless she-elf?* You can bet your ass that someone will find out *something*."

Cú Chulainn scoffed, "There ain't no talking your way out of this. It's too late for that." He turned aside to the thugs. "Maybe we just kill em?"

"Thoranmir?" Anya hissed with trepidation. She clutched the grips of her chair until her knuckles turned white.

Thoranmir's heart thumped a million beats per minute, but he pressed ahead, unsure what else to do. "I will make a wager with you, Cú Chulainn."

That got the big guy's attention. "I'm listening."

"The duels. I am in them. Let us bet on an outcome and settle the dispute."

Cú Chulainn laughed. "There's only one outcome. Fuerian Vastra will win the whole thing."

Thoranmir shook his head. "Impossible. Remy Keaton will win... or I will. I'm not quite decided on that yet. I might let him sweep the contest," he bluffed.

"Impossible," Cú Chulainn roared. "There's no way a son of Adam wins."

"Fine. I will wager that Remy beats Fuerian, or at least advances further than him in the tournament."

Cú Chulainn balled his fists and shook his head. "Too many variables. That is not a bet. Fuerian could get sick, or quit on a whim. And where would that leave us?"

"Fine. I bet Remy beats Fuerian."

The elf shook his head. "No... you must bet on the outcome. It's the only wager I'll play the odds against."

Thoranmir looked at his sister and remembered the red circle crest of the enemies who'd sworn him to silence. *If I bet that Remy wins, I've as good as lost—and Anya pays the price!*

"Then I bet I will win the whole of the contest. Jaira Morgensteen's kiss, and the Dagda's Blessing will go to me," Thoranmir said.

Cú Chulainn's eyebrows rose. The whole gang broke out laughing. "A runt like you? *Win the duels?* What if you die in the process?"

"What if I win?" Thoranmir countered. He did not wait to offer terms. "When I win, your gang will leave Cathair Dé alone. No more dream hallow—not anywhere in the city—not in The Haunts, not within a day's walk of the city limits."

"And when you fail?" Cú Chulainn asked.

"I'll repay the sum we took with interest. If I die in the arena my sister will deliver the money. It's under lock and key, currently," Thoranmir said. "Either way, if I don't win, one of us will meet you where this all began: in the alleys where my friend and I beat the shit out of your thugs the first time."

"No police. No reports. And no duelists..." Cú Chulainn mulled it over. "Swear it to me in the binding language."

[I swear that one of us will meet you there if I do not win the dueling contest,] Thoranmir said in the olde tongue.

Cú Chulainn nodded once. He whistled and signaled his crew with his head. They backed off and followed the big elf into the shadows.

Once they were gone, Thoranmir pushed his sister's chair by its handles. They headed out in search of lodging.

Anya looked at her brother. "I hope you know what in the fey you're doing."

Thoranmir frowned. "So do I..." If anything, Thoranmir felt a kind of creeping doom in his stomach. "*So do I.*"

REMY AND JAIRA HAD been walking for hours by the time the adrenaline high had worn off and made their bodies desperate for rest.

It would take the better of the night and following day to complete the return to the city, unless they happened across a caravan or a wagon which could give them passage. Despite the energy crash, they walked and talked, holding hands under the moonlight until they became too tired to physically continue.

Staggering sleepily, Jaira stepped off the road where a small grove of trees provided some cover. She stomped through the tall grasses and made a kind of nest. She plopped down on it and slapped the fluffed grass, inviting Remy to share her space.

He took his spot next to her. "No funny business," he joked. "If I wake up and you're smooching me and giving me all your curses, well... that'd probably be just fine."

She laughed, and they held against each other for warmth. "We will start again early in the morning."

Remy agreed. And though he found it difficult to rest so close to Jaira, breathing in her scent, he soon drifted toward sleep, though every time he'd almost drifted off, Jaira wriggled her hips, or some similar action, and he was fully awake again.

She mumbled sleepily, "You know, my father already thinks you and I are lovers."

Well, I'm wide awake now.

"Oh, really?"

She let out an amused giggle. "It apparently does not matter what the truth is. Public perception is everything. I guess folks are talking about you know... us."

"What are they saying?"

"The obvious things," she said. "My father hopes that I'll outgrow how I feel about you. He thinks its some perverse fascination with humans. He's mostly worried about the perception from folk at court."

Remy hadn't thought about how a relationship might affect her standing with Oberon. The seelie king's wife, Titania, was notoriously set against proper sidhe consorting with sons and daughters of Adam. *Set enough that any high standing at court might be impossible if the higher fey castes at court knew about her love of a human.*

"My father hopes that I'll just... kind of outgrow you," Jaria admitted.

On some deep level Remy understood Harhassus's desire to shield his daughter from any political embarrassment. He asked, "How does your mother feel about it?"

Jaira sighed. "She's more open minded. Although, she's at least somewhat involved in a plot to see me married off to Oberon's heir, which would put our family that much closer to the throne."

Her words drifted in and out as Remy slipped closer to sleep. Jaira explained the dynamics of their family, who regularly drove her crazy. She admired her mother, who had learned to steer her father's stubbornness through the years.

A mother... mother... Remy had only vague flashes of having a mother—like faded recollections of old dreams or the strange inverted light in the vision after looking too closely towards the sun. *I cannot remember my mother.*

Jaira knew her parents genuinely loved each other—and that her father didn't approve of his daughter following the same path. He wanted a strong alliance for her, rather than a loving one, and that had created a division between them.

"Eilastra, my mother, might be the more sensible of the pair," Jaira finally said. "Though she's not particularly good about taking risks, not even measured ones. Father might have a reactionary temperament, but he's at least willing to roll the dice."

Remy sucked in a deep breath, and tried to make it not sound like a tired sigh. "And they are both set against us?"

Jaira yawned, her body finally admitting its weary state. "They will both come around. I know they will. It will just take time."

Remy shifted his body against hers. He put his arms around her and melted into her warmth. They both drifted further towards the inevitable draw of sleep.

Finally, before drifting off completely, he mumbled to her, "I don't want to forget about it, but your father's got to pay for that horse."

She responded with a pained chuckle.

Remy smiled at her. And then sleep came.

"**W**HAT DO YOU MEAN the tournament is postponed?" Thoranmir practically yelled at Adawar.

Adawar squinted at Thoranmir. He'd obviously not forgiven the elf for all the extra work he'd caused him with over these several days. "The lady Jaira Morgensteen has been kidnapped."

"What?" Thoranmir exclaimed. His heart plunged into his belly. "What do you mean—what steps has the family taken?"

"Right now, they can only wait until the offending party sends a ransom demand. I am told the human duelist contestant has gone after them."

"Them? Them, who?"

Adawar shrugged. "I only know what I've been told."

Thoranmir cursed as he left the manager's office. Upset crowds had gathered outside the stadium. They'd shown up wanting to see bloodshed, but would have to settle for whatever was spilled in the minor altercations outside upon the courtyard as tensions ran high after the postponement announcements.

If one of the fighters had failed to arrive the tournament standings would be adjusted and the event could continue mostly as normal—but with the bearer of the prize being abducted? With Jaira gone, they *could not* continue.

If it was over—did that mean he was free from those red circle bastards?

"Damn it," Thoranmir growled. *No. Not free... just delayed.*

He'd just bet his life on this contest to the apothik pushers. Even if the one group of his enemies were satisfied, the others would not be. His bet had been very specific: *he had to win*. Canceling the event might satisfy one party, but not the other.

Once again, Thoranmir's life was falling apart and Remy was not there to help him pick up the pieces.

Thoranmir found Anya waiting for him nearby. He explained what had happened and she sighed. "I'm not spending another night outside under the stars," she said.

"If they'd canceled the whole event we'd maybe be able to pick up a room for the night," Thoranmir said.

Anya pointed. "Well, let's get back to my apartment now that we've got the daylight and see if we can salvage anything."

A N UNEVENTFUL DAY STRETCHED on and on. Luckily, Remy and Jaira had been able to flag down a traveling wagon as it carried a load of hay and straw to the city.

Remy picked the stray pieces of heather from Jaira's mussed tresses as they approached the edge of Cathair Dé. They sat balanced on the back of a wagon. Barely minutes after nodding off, the distinct clopping of hooves on highway jolted Remy awake. Horseshoes clacking against cobblestones provided a distinct audio marker.

Evening was drawing close as the cart arrived in front of the arena. The generous farmer had been kind enough to deliver them directly to their location. He'd gone to the city in the hopes that the festival market would have a demand for his products. And, in his words, "With no prize, there is no contest, and with no contest, there's no point in my venture into the city."

At least he had understood the symbiotic nature at play.

Remy helped Jaira out of the wagon and escorted her inside. Someone spotted them and took up the call, announcing their return. A runner sprinted away to fetch Harhassus and Fuerian. Both of them arrived at about the same time.

Remy kept a neutral expression. Jaira, not so much.

"You! Both of you are *bastards!*" Jaira accused Fuerian and her father equally after she and Remy met them at the stadium's interior. She belted off on a string of complaints, some embellished, but many complaints were valid.

Fuerian did little but shrug. He let Jaira yell herself out, though Harhassus tried to reason with her—to no avail.

"I'll be staying in my locker area tonight," Remy told them.

"And I'll be staying with you," said Jaira, much to the protest of both the other men.

"He is the only one I feel safe with," Jaira snapped at them. "Besides, one can hardly complain now that this would not be the first night we've kept each other's company."

Harhassus complained, "But your honor, and the pledge regarding your kiss! You vowed to Oberon—"

"Oh, please, Father. You think so little of me? I'm not ruining a chaste vow and risking a curse." She grabbed a fistful of Remy's shirt and pulled him close enough to taunt the other two males. "Not *tonight*, anyhow. But I am staying closest to the only man who seems to care about keeping me alive."

Jaira released Remy, and the human tugged at his shirt to circulate some air, which seemed suddenly warm to him. "I'm going to head down, then," Remy said.

He left Jaira still bickering with her father, though Fuerian slipped away as well. Fuerian followed two paces behind Remy. Irked, the human glanced over his shoulder.

"There's only room for the two of us in my room," Remy told him.

Fuerian followed Remy up to the door of the small chamber. He jested darkly, "Then where will Jaira sleep?"

"You can't stay with us." Remy stopped and turned to face him, remaining in the corridor. "What do you want?"

Fuerian's eyes flitted down to the dúshlán which Remy had recovered and wore again at his hip. Each dúshlán had a unique and distinct appearance. "How did you defeat the night thrall and rescue her? I must know."

"First, I decided not to be a coward," Remy spat. "Second, I'm good at killing monsters."

Fuerian's brows knit as he tried to understand the human's subtext. Finally, he gave up. "I daresay, it seems odd you could be so adept at it, I mean, because of your background... your heritage."

Remy cocked his head. His neck stiffened. "What would you know about it?"

"Plenty," Fuerian's grin stretched like the lips of a hungry viper. "I have done my research on you, Remy Keaton. There are places, dark recesses of the aither, where secrets and information about people like you are stored. And I have plundered its secrets and then destroyed the storehouse so that no others can learn them."

"As if I would ever trust the word of Fuerian Vastra," Remy retorted. "You know nothing."

Fuerian ticked off points on his fingers. "You are a child of Adam, a human from the Earth realm. You were stolen and delivered to the unseelie as a child, where you were abandoned."

Snorting through his nose, Remy shook his head. "All common knowledge. I told you that you were a liar. If there was really information that explained how I got here and who I am, I would have found it long ago."

I know more than is common, Fuerian said. "You spent most of your time as a youth working for the orc warlord Rhylfelour, and even did a job for Rhagathena, the unseelie queen." The sidhe ticked off points from his fingers. He said, "You are the famed Aderyn Corff, the corpse bird of the unseelie realm—an assassin who has claimed lives when your masters demanded it."

"None hold my leash now," Remy said with a tone of warning.

Fuerian continued. "You possess a dúshlán demonstrating how greatly you were wronged in your early life. You found your way out of the Winter Court's reaches and into the seelie side of Arcadeax some years ago."

Remy bit his lip. His enemy had said enough. Remy had a past which he was not proud of—though it was far from information that defined him.

"A pity you do not even remember your mother's name," Fuerian said. "Perhaps the shock of parting the veil and entering the feylands as a child made you forget it. Saoirse is such a pretty name, even if it is a human one."

Remy stiffened, as if struck by lightning. Hearing her name spoken aloud triggered something deep in him—unlocked a memory. Mental pictures of his mother surged back to him and his eyes threatened to well up as they threatened to overwhelm him.

"How… how do you know… what else do you have?" Remy tried to keep his voice neutral, but he did a poor job of it. "There's no way that—"

"I hold all the keys to unlocking your past, Remy Keaton. And the information I possess is not anything you can find elsewhere. You don't want to know what had to be done to locate it. Your heritage is bound up in suffering and conspiracy. This plot reaches all the way up and into Oberon's court. It is an intrigue that is much bigger than you, child of Adam. Whether or not the fey King is culpable is anyone's guess, but he is loath to let secrets of the court slip away without consequence. And all in his court are untouchable. But you may have all the knowledge that I possess. For a price."

Remy tightened and relaxed his hands before asking, "I can only imagine the price is too terrible to pay."

"My terms are simple. Leave Arcadeax. For good. I will even help you by providing escort and safe passage to the borders. You may go to Earth or return to the unseelie, I care not which, but I will make every effort to help you journey elsewhere. You must only pledge to never return."

Temptation played at the edges of Remy's thoughts. His mind reeled at the possibilities. He could scarcely remember his home realm, except for brief, unreliable flashes from his childhood. And now, they intermingled with those few images of his mother that Fuerian had unlocked, memories he could never quite access before.

"Why? What does it even matter?" Remy asked. He looked up and caught movement on the far side of the hall.

Fuerian also turned to look. Thoranmir pushed Anya through the T-shaped corridor in the distance. Jaira walked alongside of them, having finally dismissed her father. Remy's eyes sparkled once he saw her, and then, his face set with resolve.

[Resign this contest and I shall give to you all the knowledge about your past that I have in my possession,] Fuerian spoke in the olde tongue, using words that would bind him by the magic of Arcadeax if Remy accepted his offer. He continued more insistently, [I shall further help you reach a new home of your choice as you quit the seelie realm.]

Remy grinned, thinking, *I've got you now, you sneaky bastard. He needs this deal, as his pride is on the line.* That *is what Fuerian Vastra values most.*

Jaira slipped away with Remy's friends, walking further down the hallway.

"You have an angle," Remy accused, turning the tables on him. "You don't particularly care for Jaira, beyond the fact that she is a pretty face and belongs to a prominent family. So—what do you stand to lose by me beating you?"

"Beat me?" scoffed Fuerian. "The Morgensteens and the Vastras have feuded in trade wars throughout the years—a situation that has hindered both houses from reaching their true potential. Your interference disrupts the peace a marriage could bring us."

Remy's lip curled with amusement and his eyes took on a flinty light. "You can't beat me, and you know it. *Night thrall, ha!* You could've never defeated it, either."

"Either?" Fuerian's eyebrows raised slightly at Remy's slip of the tongue.

"You make such a big deal about being unbeatable in a duel," Remy accused, "that *now I know* that I can do it."

"You'll never know your history, your heritage! It will all be lost," Fuerian threatened, as if he still had some power over the human.

Remy looked him in the eye. "I'm far more interested in forging a future than in dwelling on my past." He stormed away, heading in the direction of Jaira and his friends.

He pretended not to hear Fuerian's final threat: "Then your entire world is going to fall, Remy Keaton, and I shall be there to see it."

"JUST LEAVE ME RIGHT here. I've got it," Anya insisted after her brother stopped her chair at the edge of the cot in Thoranmir's room.

Prep rooms for the competitors had been doled out on a first-come, first serve basis, and Thoranmir had been the last to the roster. His room was a lot like the rest, only worse in every way. It was a simple, utilitarian room meant to prepare athletes, gamesmen, contestants, or whatever kind of folk and events the arena was hosting. Except that Thoranmir's room was small, squat, and had obviously been raided of any spare furnishings.

Using her hands, Anya lifted her body and tried to grab the coiled length of cable spooled beneath the seat. Thoranmir stepped forward to help her.

"I said *I've got it*," she barked, making him recoil. Anya crawled back up, using the weight of her chair as a counterbalance, and then pulled herself into the cot.

She'd been without power for a couple days now, and her emotions were on edge. In addition to having recently lost everything she owned in a fire, she still worried for her brother—*and* for whatever he'd gotten mixed up in when they'd been shaken down the previous evening.

The two bickered like a tired, old couple, and the heavy, cloy aroma of smoke wafted off them. Thoranmir's fingers and were blackened by fresh ash, as was his feet up to his knees, and his hair was sooty and disheveled. Anya's face was darkened by the same stuff as they'd sifted through the wreckage of the apartment for most of the day.

Remy arrived shortly after they'd gotten settled. He found Jaira standing in the doorway. "What happened?" he asked.

"Arson," said Jaira.

Anya hung over the edge of the collapsible bedding and jacked her cord into a port where a pipe rose from the ground and nestled along a groove in the wall. The cable fed into her chair's akashic battery, which had died long ago.

"Is everyone okay?" asked Remy.

"It happened during the morning when we were all away," Thoranmir said. "We tried to get a local room, but all the inns and hostels were booked because of the tournament. After spending last night outside, we finally decided to just sleep here."

Remy's face soured. *The bells yesterday morning,* he realized. *It was the fire alarm.*

Anya flopped backward onto the most uncomfortable cot she'd ever laid upon and tried to find a position that she could tolerate. She fixed her brother and Remy with an irritable gaze. "You two. It's you boys and your foolish duels that have plunged my life into such disarray."

Thoranmir also tried to find appropriate bedding. "I guess I'll just sleep on..." he trailed off and began looking for a place to lay out anything soft he could find to sleep on. Someone had stolen his room's chair and the towels that had been on a shelf when he'd first re-entered the duel.

Anya scowled at him. "Why don't you go bunk with your friend and think about what you're doing to my poor nerves? You two got us all into this. Now you two go figure out how to fix it."

Thoranmir bobbed his head sheepishly and then headed for the door, pushing Remy out into the hall where Jaira hovered just far enough away to avoid any of Anya's wrath.

"So," Thoranmir asked. "I, uh, guess I'm bunking with you two?"

CHAPTER TWENTY-ONE

O N SOME DEEP LEVEL, Remy knew he was dreaming—that
he'd left his body behind, and his mind and spirit ventured
through the dreamlands. Many believed it was possible to enter the
aither while dreaming; Remy had known that was true. He'd done
it on rare occasions, though there were often deadly risks associated
with untethering one's spirit from the body that anchored them to
reality.

Becoming unbound was not particularly dangerous... except
that it sometimes unlocked parts of the mind: and unbound by
time and reality, that often showed a person hidden things. Truth
a person had denied. Facts overlooked. And on rare occasions, it
showed a person the future.

But often enough, dreams were just dreams. It took a talent to
discern when a dream was actually much more.

Even aware that he was dreaming, Remy watched Jaira. They'd
been married, but Remy could not remember how long ago that
had been.

Sometimes time felt as if it moved too fast or too slow in Arcadeax, and Remy had always wondered if it was an anomaly that

only he, an outsider and non-fey, could sense. But this felt like a different sensation as he watched his wife plucking vegetables from the garden in a shimmering, dream-like haze.

Jaira was on her knees, harvesting the meager bounty from a row of cabbages. Gone were the extravagant dress and symbols of her wealth. Instead, she wore a tattered frock to protect her more sensible house dress while in the dirt. But her eyes still sparkled, and her face remained happy to see her husband returning from the forest.

Remy held two eiders by the neck and a long-eared coney in one hand. His bow hung off his other shoulder. The river had produced a better haul of ducks than fish as of late. He raised the animals for her to see, but it wasn't the food that had made Jaira's eyes twinkle like that.

Beaming back, he crossed the glade that made up most of their yard, adjacent to the woodland cottage where the Morgensteens had put away their daughter privately, hoping her fascination and attachment to a human would eventually pass.

In the meanwhile, they'd opted to hide her from proper civilization until she tired of him. Stashing the newlyweds on a small property just far enough from Cathair Dé would help the disgraced Morgensteen daughter become an afterthought in polite society. Remy knew the father wished to someday restore Jaira to Oberon's court and all the political standings and trappings of the feys' higher castes, but he knew Jaira had made her decision.

Jaira had lost all taste for such nonsense. She'd shown Remy as much every night since their secret marriage. *If Harhassus only knew, he'd tear his own ears off.* Remy grinned.

She rushed to his side and kissed him deeply, melting into his embrace. It felt like a year since he'd last seen her, though that couldn't be right.

When the two finally relaxed and separated, Remy felt a bulge pressing against his abdomen. He looked down and found Jaira was with child, and so far, advanced that she could go into labor any day. Suddenly, they were inside their cottage by the fireplace. It was a sufficient, one-room building constructed out of logs.

It's definitely a dream, Remy noted, realizing he didn't remember moving from the garden to house. *I hope to never wake.*

Harhassus, along with Jaira's mother, Eilastra, puttered nearby. They looked apathetic, but more supportive than Remy had seen them before. *Probably Lady Eilastra's influence*, he thought.

Jaira doubled over with a scream. The labor pains had begun.

Harhassus and Eilastra held hands and their faces belied them: they were more invested in the young lovers than Remy thought, especially with a grandchild on the way.

Remy looked down. He still clutched the ducks and rabbit. Jaira still held the head of cabbage. Only now, as he looked more closely, it was a child which she bounced in her arms. Remy held out a finger, which the child clutched as it yawned.

The infant, a boy, had a cute nose like its mother, and its ears were somewhere in between Jaira's long, pointed tips and Remy's shorter, rounded ones; they identified the boy as a changeling. A pang of worry lodged in Remy's gut. The child would experience the same persecution that he had endured from the sidhe. Potentially more.

Remy knelt and tied a bandanna around his son's head as the child stood waist high between him and his mother. *How did he grow so fast? I've missed so much already. Soon I must take him into the woods and train him to hunt.*

Jaira bounced a second child on her hip. A toddler, their daughter. Harhassus and Eilastra were gone, back to their own home.

"You should always wear this and cover your ears when there might be company. People do not understand what we are, and their hate makes them powerful and dangerous," Remy told his son.

"Even Pappa and Grammy?" the boy asked.

"No. They have finally come to understand," Remy told him. "But no one else has. There has been much anger in the city lately and we should take care to protect ourselves and each other."

Jaira put a hand on his head and tousled his hair. "Come, child. Help me and little Saoirse in the garden while your father hunts."

They went outside and Remy smelled smoke on the breeze. It was not the clean aroma of burning firewood. The breeze carried the faint aroma of lamp fuel. A fire raged somewhere, and then, he spotted the mob. *Torches... oil rags hastily wrapped around wooden handles... they've come for me!*

Angry elves clutched weapons in addition to the torches. They poured out of the forest, several hundred at least. Their eyes burned with malice and ignorance.

"The Frith Duine have found us—they said they would never allow us to bring children into this world." Remy scrambled into action.

He yelled to Jaira, "Run! Flee to your parents; I will draw them off."

His children screamed behind him as he ran into the fray and loosed an arrow, trying to take all the mob's attention so that none would pursue his family. Jaira scooped up both kids and fled as several thrown torches landed on their thatched roof.

Flames lapped at the air from their cottage; fire fully engulfed it within seconds. The angry horde trampled their gardens and killed their livestock as Remy staggered to the pasture. He could not outrun them all, and he suffered from multiple wounds.

He collapsed to his knees and blood ran freely down both sides of his neck. The zealots had cut the ears off his face. One of the Frith Duine laced a lanyard through the cartilage in order to wear them around his neck as a trophy.

It took twenty elves to hold Remy down even with a busted spear lancing through his chest and puncturing his right lung. He couldn't move, forced to watch the enemies pursue his family.

The female elves in the mob caught and beat Jaira with sticks, but Remy could not scream. He didn't have enough air remaining in his one lung to vent his rage.

His son lay dead near Jaira with three arrows in his back. The child had tried to run, but the crowd's persecution knew no boundaries.

An older elf woman yanked the youngest, Saoirse, from Jaira's arms and squeezed her by the ankles. As the others beat Jaira with their clubs, the old woman dashed the child against a stone wall over and over.

Remy finally found the strength to inhale and let out a wail of sorrow.

"Gotta cleanse the land of you and your filthy half breeds," growled an elf who stood near Remy. He placed a wicked, curved dagger against the human's throat. "Now, the hidden legion of Fianna will finally be smashed into disarray."

"I—I don't know what any of that means," Remy sputtered.

The elf paid him no mind as he cut Remy's neck wide open, killing him.

Remy seemed to drift in darkness and despair. He didn't know for how long.

And then, he saw Jaira emerge from the misty woods, bruised and limping; she'd barely survived. Her beauty was marred; one eye was swollen shut and burns dotted her skin. Her hair had been ripped out of her head by the vicious mob, all while mocking her and calling her *ddiymadferth harlot, human lover,* and *whore of Adam.*

Harhassus sat on his hands and knees, weeping over the dead body of Eilastra. The mist wasn't a fog at all: it was smoke. The mob had visited the Morgensteen estate first as it looked for the human.

Eilastra's bones lay among the wreckage where she'd tried to escape. They were just as charred as the wooden beams. Nothing had survived the hatred of the Frith Duine.

Remy somehow knew that he, too, was dead. His neck no longer hurt, and his ears had returned; all that pain had instead lodged in his heart.

Jaira collapsed atop her mother's body, sobbing with her father. Harhassus looked up and directly at Remy, who could only observe as an ethereal specter. "None of this would have happened if that human had listened to me and left you alone."

Together, father and daughter cried, bleeding from wounds which may yet prove fatal. And Remy saw a glimmer of something in the ashes. He stepped closer and spotted the hard scaled form of an egg. A dragon's egg.

I don't know what any of this means, the apparition said again.

Remy suddenly awoke with a ragged gasp.

Jaira was nestled in the crook of his arm. He lifted her head gently and squeezed his hand, flexing to chase away the pins and needles.

It took Remy a moment to realize they were both still alive, laying together in the too-small cot in his room at the stadium; it had proved even less comfortable than the grassy bed he and Jaira had nested in along the road.

Thoranmir snored gently on the floor opposite them with his head propped up by a pair of boots.

Remy looked at the beautiful sleeping elf. He wanted Jaira more than ever before. Only now, his heart hurt from the truth of it.

Their relationship would bring about only sorrow, bloodshed, and death.

F UERIAN AWOKE WITH A start to find Trishana standing over his bed. He scowled at her and rubbed the sleep from his face.

"How did you get in?"

"The maid," she said.

Fuerian frowned. He didn't have a maid, but he'd had a female caller late in the evening, one of Madam Holworth's gals. Fuerian kept a healthy rotation of pretty she-elves on his roster of bedmates. The mistress had already left, and likely was the one to let her in. *Maid is a much better cover than the truth... not that anyone believes it, or that a cover is necessary.*

But a female staying most of the night irked him somewhat. Usually, Naz made sure that... *Naz is dead*, he remembered and then fell back into his pillow. He laid there for only a moment before he dragged himself out of the comfortable blankets and dressed himself.

"Why are you here, and so early?" Fuerian asked sleepily.

"It's not *that* early," Trishana insisted. "And it's getting on late enough. Less than two hours before the first gong. I've got to get back to my business."

Fuerian cocked his head, still half asleep, and then he remembered. *Jaira is back—the contest resumes today.*

She held up a file. "Did you uphold your end of things? Did you get the human to quit?"

Fuerian muttered a string of curses. "No," he admitted. "There was an incident after the contests..."

"Yes. I heard about it—so did half the city. Suddenly, this *son of Adam* is a hero? Folks won't shut up about him. It's going to kill the betting structure. He's going to look like an undercard hero"

"Just change the odds," Fuerian said. *If he's ranked super low in the standings and he starts to win, the house will take a bath.*

Trishana glared from the corner of her eye. "Obviously that's what I'll do. I'll call it an adjustment. But some folks made bets on him before anyone thought the human could win. *Those* are the bets that will eat all my profits."

"Well, if a few thought he could beat me," Fuerian said, buckling his belt and hanging his sword. "Those people are fools."

He beckoned for the file, but Trishana clutched it tight, refusing to give it up.

"I have a lot riding on you winning this thing, Fuerian. It's big enough now that my earnings on the undercard fights won't cover my losses if it comes down to you and the human. Especially if the human prevails."

"He will not drop out, and so I must win. It is that simple," Fuerian said, as if his words somehow made it true. "Now show me the dirt you found on the Morgensteens. I must know everything there is before I fully commit myself to this investment."

Trishana chuckled. "I don't think you understand how transactions work. But I will make a bargain with you. I've seen the contents of this file, so I know how important it is that you see it. I'll give it to you, but you will owe me a favor."

Fuerian raised an eyebrow.

She pressed, "Any favor of my choosing and I may call upon it at a later date."

"A free wish of me?" he scoffed.

She leveled her gaze at him. "Trust me. You will thank me for letting you off so cheap after you've read it."

He frowned. But he opened his hand and beckoned for the data.

Trishana handed them over. "Just win this contest for me... and for you. Afterward, consider the findings in this envelope." She released her grip on it and then headed for the door.

Behind her, Fuerian greedily tore open the packet and sifted through the bank documents and ledgers, liens, mortgage statements, business holdings, private transactions, and more. Fuerian stared at the bottom line in the Morgensteen accounts and the state of the family's wealth.

"This can't be right," he complained aloud, feeling betrayed by the findings. "Cheating bastards... the Morgensteens are as broke as the Vastras!"

J AIRA HAD GOTTEN UP and departed by the time Remy returned from a visit to the lavatory and prepared for his day. He knew he had one of the first fights. No doubt, Fuerian had arranged for the human to endure as many possible trials as possible. He would make every effort to wear him out before the elf dealt with him.

He eventually found Jaira waiting in a hallway. The corridor opened into the archway that exited the arena where their fates would be decided on this day.

Remy could see what she was watching. Jaira's father had just arrived. *She must be a swirling storm of emotions.*

Staring into the distance, Jaira seemed touched by melancholy, but brightened when she spotted Remy. "My mother is here this day," she noted. "Father talked her into coming... he probably hopes she'll help keep me under control."

Something hurt in Remy's gut. Last night's dream still haunted him in his waking. It had been all too real and still remained all too possible. Every footstep shook his guts with a quiver of anguish that churned in the pit of his stomach.

He knew what he had to do, for Jaira's sake. But every step he moved toward her felt like a walk to the gallows.

He arrived and his face felt hot. "Can we talk?"

Jaira laid a hand on his cheek. "I will make time."

Remy took her hands in his. "I *will* win this challenge. I shall become a duelist; I swear it. If not the greatest duelist ever, I'll be the greatest human duelist, at least. But..." he trailed off.

She furrowed her brow and searched his eyes. "But?"

"But I think we can never be together," he said. Speaking those words felt like he'd ripped his own heart from his chest.

Jaira balked, blinking rapidly.

"I—I don't want you to suffer. The people of Arcadeax will persecute you for loving me. They will take out their hate for humanity on *you*... and on any children we might bring into our life." Remy's voice cracked as he spoke, and he barely held his tears in check.

Jaira managed her emotions better. She'd learned diplomacy, a benefit of growing up in one of the wealthier houses. "You did not think to consult me on this? You're going to unilaterally make this decision without me, as if I have no say in the matter?"

She stared him down. Remy didn't know how to react.

"I refuse to accept your one-sided decision. It is not for you to decide that we cannot be together, especially if you are making this decision *because of them*. Who even are they? They aren't here."

"All of them," Remy pleaded. "I can't protect you from all the fey who hate humans—"

"The Frith Duine?" Jaira growled. "You're going to let the fucking Frith Duine win? They're barely more than a cluster of impotent, angry old elves."

The pain in her eyes reminded Remy of the anguish she'd endured in his dream. "But they aren't alone, and what can I do about their hate? I cannot bear that you will suffer on account of me."

Jaira held his gaze, and her eyes were kind despite feeling the pain Remy's inner conflict had brought between them. Still holding his hands, she spoke almost in a whisper, "Then you must change their minds. The sidhe are born to love. Make them all love you, just as I have come to do."

They were so close that her lips moved barely a hair's breadth away. She nearly leaned in to kiss him.

Damn that vow she took, Remy lamented as Jaira pulled back. Instead, she put her fingers to her own lips and then pressed them to Remy's.

"Win your freedom, my love. Take this world by storm and subdue it—create the chance to choose your own destiny. And win my heart, Remy Keaton." Jaira let her hand fall from Remy's mouth.

She turned and headed out to find her father and resume the day's duties.

Remy stared after her, blinking. He spoke softly, making a vow of his own, "I will."

CHAPTER TWENTY-TWO

⸺ ⁕ ⸺

THE STADIUM CROWD ROARED with a low ambient hum. It had packed out to maximum attendance.

As Remy emerged from the stadium's interior halls, they announced his competitor: an elf named Velaris who won his contest the previous day without breaking a sweat. He had traveled in from one of the inner cities, Daonra Dlúth, a community much closer to Oberon's capital city of Faery Cairn.

Remy stepped onto the fighting platform as the announcer used his akashically amplified voice. "You all know his opponent. I heard all the buzz in town about him this morning. This human, Remy Keaton, rescued our host, Miss Jaira Morgensteen last night. I hear he may have foiled a plot from unseelie invaders."

A mild applause went up from the crowd watching with rapt interest. The human had gained a sudden reputation, and at least three writers for the yellow rags milled about the arena floor asking other competitors and officials about him, not quite taking the initiative to actually interview a human.

Remy brandished his sword and wrapped his gauntleted left hand over his naked right, sizing up Velaris. His opponent had a kind of grizzled look about him. His eyes were stony and hard, and he had the fighting stance of someone with dedicated training and years of hard living.

The faun stood between them, ready to signal the match's start. He waved his arm in a slashing motion as the gong chimed. Then, he backed away quickly.

Velaris rushed to the center and attacked with a powerful thrust.

Remy blocked it as he sidestepped, only to find a second blow aimed at his face. The human reeled backward just in time for the stroke to go wide.

Spinning and ducking, Velaris whirled his blade around like an akashic cane chopper, aiming for Remy's legs with a swing that could sever limbs.

Remy leapt over the low stroke and then disengaged by two steps. He sized Velaris up. *Whoever this fighter is, he is experienced, and he means business.*

Velaris, too, stood and walked in a slow circle, eyes keenly observing the human's footwork as he searched for weakness.

With a high slash, Remy tested Velaris's defenses.

Velaris blocked, parried, and then rolled aside, proving as adept as he was at offense. He counterattacked with the exact same moves Remy had displayed.

Remy copied Velaris's defensive maneuvers, and the crowd cheered him on.

The combatants each stepped back, calculating their next attacks. And then, they rushed together like two stags with freshly-shed velvet, locking horns with thunderous ferocity.

Slash, thrust, parry, evade.

They traded blow for blow, each fighter countering the other's moves with the precision of a rehearsed dance.

The crowd erupted with cheers and applause. Excitement rippled through them. Howls of worry and fear of loss rang out from those with money riding on one party, screaming encouragement for their chosen combatant.

Remy stepped back, tempting Velaris to overextend, but he feinted and then recoiled, recognizing the draw.

In his spare moments of freedom, Remy risked a glance at Jaira, who watched the combat with expectant eyes. He looked across the side and saw Anya in her box with power radiating through her chair, finally recharged.

Instead of hopeful interest, Anya's face was full of fear. Remy saw his friend yank her cord jacks free from an aither connection. She'd somehow managed to get a link wired at her location. *Probably Jaira's doing?*

Anya threw the cables aside and spun her chair in place, driving it from the box as fast as he'd ever seen it move.

Velaris stole Remy's attention back by pressing a new offensive. He slashed overhead with two looping, fast arcs, each of which Remy turned aside with his blade, before following up with a thrust that the human again sidestepped. The elf turned the sword and spun a full circle, trying to slash the tip across Remy's skin to draw first blood.

Remy leapt back, just beyond reach of the weapon, but the sharp point glanced against Remy's gauntlet with a loud *spang!*

The noise echoed through the stadium and the crowd found its feet. Their cheers drowned out the sharp noise of sword on armor as the two warriors circled each other. Each breathed heavily from the exertion.

Remy spotted movement in the corner of his eye and saw Anya emerge in another part of the stadium. She rolled through an upper-level promenade, angling for the announcer's stage. It sat only a little nearer to her than the box seats where the Morgensteens were, along with a collection of VIP guests, some lower members of Oberon's court, and the maven overseer whose presence validated the contest in the eyes of the dueling guilds.

Velaris came in for another attack as Anya argued with the security there. She pushed her way past, yelling something at the announcer.

Remy could not watch her—he could barely speculate as to what had motivated her. He was too busy defending himself when the gong suddenly rang, and a hush fell over the audience. The faun scrambled in between the two fighters to keep them separated. They kept their eyes locked on each other, their weapons readied. Neither wished to risk giving his opponent room to breathe.

"We've just received word and confirmation of an offense worthy of disqualification," the announcer spoke. The crowd roared with both anger and disappointment. They had come to see blood.

The announcer continued, "Velaris Neauvoah is not who he claimed to be and a search of the aither confirms that his real identity is Siralev Neauvoah."

Remy narrowed his gaze at the liar.

Siralev's face fell.

"Siralev is already registered as a duelist. He is in violation of guild rules by concealing his identity and fighting amateurs in a sanctioned competition." The announcer grumbled something unintelligible. "Simply spelling your name in reverse isn't exactly the peak of clever thinking."

The crowd both booed and laughed at the announcer's jab.

Remy glanced up at the announcer and spotted the maven making his way toward the announcer, whose akashic speaker box could relay his words for all to hear.

Looking them over, the maven stared at the competitors with disappointment on his face. Remy looked from Siralev to the maven and then back to Siralev. Something familiar twinkled in the elven fighter's eyes.

They know each other! Remy thought, wondering how deep anti-human sentiments ran in the upper courts. *Was the maven involved? Did he put Siralev up to it to take me out?*

Something Fuerian had said about Remy's lost history bounced around in his thoughts. *This plot reaches all the way up and into Oberon's court.* Remy hardened his resolve—still adamant that he would win this contest, cheating opponents or not. He'd suspected from the beginning that the fight would be unfair and stacked against him.

The maven took a seat next to the announcer and made his decree that he agreed with a disqualification.

Remy grinned. But Jaira's words also came to mind. *Make them all love you, just as I have come to love you.* He shouted, "No! Let him fight."

The crowd's dull noise dropped to nil, as if every member of the crowd, thousands strong, held their breath.

"Professional fighter or not, I will beat this elf," Remy declared. Holding his sword at the ready, he cockily motioned for Siralev to approach and reengage.

The challenge visibly raised Siralev's hackles, and the crowd erupted. As it died down, the maven asked, "You are sure?" His eyes were locked on Siralev, though, instead of Remy.

"This crowd wants a spirited duel—then they shall have it," Remy yelled; he barely caught sight of his opponent also nod his acceptance.

After conferring with the announcer, the maven made an official declaration. "This shall be Siralev's final fight of the contest. Win or lose. But we shall give Siralev something to fight for. If you win, you shall only be subject to penalties from your guild. If you lose, your dueling credentials shall be stripped—forever banning you from wearing the badge and ribbon."

Siralev bowed to the maven to accept the judgment; he had no further choice in the matter. The crowd's enthusiasm only escalated. They were eager to see if the human could overcome a certified professional.

Noting the shift in sentiment to support Remy, the maven tempered their excitement. "We will also remove the option for Siralev to escalate the duel beyond first blood. The human may still choose as he pleases."

The maven sat back and relinquished the amplifier.

Remy and Siralev began circling each other again. Remy stepped gingerly, taking delibcrate, slow steps, and Siralev responded by mirroring him. The crowd's noise swelled in support of the human.

Siralev lunged in hard, and with wild, powerful strokes. Gone were his carefully precise, calculating moves. His livelihood was on the line, and so, he gave into the temptations of his rage and zeal. With Remy's skillful performance, Siralev had to utilize the unpredictable nature of overpowered blows and hope to overwhelm the human.

Remy deflected and ducked. He got out of the way, as if avoiding a charging animal with a one-track mind. He hoped the beast would burn himself out. Instead, Siralev recognized Remy was wearing him down and visibly reined himself in.

The older, experienced duelist shifted back into the precise patterns of maneuvers. He slashed and then sparred again, followed by a thrust.

Remy sidestepped. He'd seen the elf try this twice already.

Siralev spun like a whirlwind, attacking faster and fiercer.

Warning bells rang in the back of Remy's mind. *It's a trap! He's baiting you.* This time, Remy planted the tip of his sword in the ground and caught Siralev's blade against his own.

The elf sneered as he leaned on his blade with his full weight, raking the razor edges against each other, blunting them, as he pushed forward just enough to stomp a foot on top of Remy's weapon and pin it to the floor. He leaned in and shoved forward, trying to get his blade close enough to catch the human's skin with the cutting edge.

Siralev's face was close enough to Remy's that he could feel the elf's hot breath as they grunted and struggled for position, more like wrestlers than sword fighters. The stags had locked together, vying for dominance.

The crowd's noise erupted like a volcano.

Remy clamped down on the blunted sword with his gauntlet-shod left hand to prevent the elf from dragging it across his body and bleeding him. Releasing his neutralized sword from his right hand, Remy reached over and snatched Siralev's dagger from his belt.

With a victorious shout, he stabbed it through the elf's forearm. A spray of blood shot out. Though the weapon missed any vital parts which would cripple him permanently, the fight was decided. *He'll need that hand if he hopes for an illustrious future career digging ditches*, Remy thought.

Siralev staggered backward and fell on his rump, roaring at the pain of the blade lodged in his flesh. He relinquished the sword, letting it clatter to the ground as the faun leapt in to prevent the human from doing any further harm to the beaten enemy. It didn't matter; Remy had no intention of further violence. He had won. The gong chimed twice to end the match with Remy standing victorious.

The crowd had returned to its feet, cheering for a contest that they were certain they would one day describe to future children and grandchildren. Remy turned to the crowd with his arms raised and pumped his fists into the air.

And then, Siralev was back on his feet with the dagger in his hand. He shoved the faun aside and lunged for Remy's back.

As a collective unit, the audience gasped, alerting the human gladiator of the danger. He whirled away in the nick of time and slashed his sword downward, severing the dagger arm at the elbow. The dismembered appendage flew off to the side as Siralev staggered.

The faun charged and rammed the disgraced duelist, knocking him off the fighting stage and to the dirt where security grabbed the rule breaker.

Cheers resumed, their volume reaching new heights. Even Jaira was on her feet, clapping with her hands. Her eyes sparkled like polished emerald. Though she sat next to both her parents, Remy blew her an unabashed kiss. She blushed but didn't look away.

Bowing, he then spoke, though he knew his words were drowned by the crowd's applause, "I have made them love me... nothing will stand in our way."

Remy stepped off the dais and walked toward the exit. He caught Anya's eye as he went. A look of relief spread across her face, and she nodded to him. He nodded back, thanking her for the assist, and tried to calm his racing heart and heaving chest.

He'd just cleared the stadium floor when he heard the announcer call the next competitors. "Next up will be Fuerian Vastra, facing off against Thoranmir Shelton."

Remy's heart sank into his gut. He shouted a string of curses and then turned, sprinting back to the main floor of the dueling ground. A whole new paradigm of dangers presented itself.

They were certainly going to cheat against me—I hadn't even thought they might do it to Thoranmir...

CHAPTER TWENTY-THREE

R EMY BURST BACK ONTO the stadium field shortly after the gong crashed.

Thoranmir attacked Fuerian with every kind of attack he knew. He swung overhead and Fuerian parried. Thoranmir thrust and Fuerian deflected and spun away; Thoranmir slashed and Fuerian blocked.

Fuerian is playing with him!

Remy turned to look at Jaira, who gave him an apologetic look; she had no control over the match pairings. But when Remy looked to the crowd and met Anya's eyes, she looked crestfallen. She, too, knew that her brother was greatly overmatched—both in skill and ego.

The human hurried further toward the combatants, but security, on high alert after the recent incident with Siralev, blocked Remy from getting any closer. Members of the crowd noticed and began to stand, intrigued by whatever drama was unfolding *outside* of the match as much as what was inside.

Thoranmir's frustration visibly mounted as his skilled opponent proved too talented to overcome.

Fuerian concentrated very little on Thoranmir, who he dealt with easily. When Thoranmir let up, Fuerian took a step back and leveled his gaze at the human, grinning maniacally and taunting him. He even pointed a finger at Remy with a sneer.

And then, with Fuerian's gaze turned away and with eight paces between them, Thoranmir unfurled the whip bound to his belt and cracked it, lashing the cocky elf across the cheek. It drew a long line of crimson from jaw to ear. The crowd erupted in a cheer just as the gong crashed.

Incredulous, Fuerian touched his cheek and pulled his fingers away. His eyes went manic at the unexpected sight of blood.

Remy's face blanched. "No, Thoranmir, you fool—"

The faun rushed in between them, announcing, "First blood to Thoranmir Shelton." And then, he looked to Fuerian.

Time felt as if it stood still for Remy, as if he knew what would happen before anyone else did.

The horned adjudicator asked, "Do you wish to—"

"Yes, I wish to contest," Fuerian snarled. He turned his full attention to Thoranmir. His eyes narrowed to slits, and his nostrils flared as he pointed at his opponent with the tip of his blade.

Wide-eyed, Thoranmir turned to his friend. He paled when he saw the worry on Remy's face, and when he looked to Anya, who stared slack jawed with watery eyes.

The crowd's noise fell to a dull roar of both excitement and morbid curiosity at how the contest would play out.

Anya's eyes turned to fix on Jaira, as if she had any control over the situation. Jaira's eyes remained on her feet.

"By duelist rules, the wounded participant chooses to escalate! Fighters, prepare yourself," cried the faun. He produced a black cloth of shiny silk and threw it into the air.

"Wait a second," muttered Thoranmir, clearly confused and forgetting that duelist rules allowed such a provision. "What's the rule?"

"This is now a fight to the death," yelled the announcer. As soon as the black cloth floated to the ground, the gong crashed.

Fuerian rushed across the open space before Thoranmir could even think about using his whip again. He swung his blade with violent ferocity.

Thoranmir dropped the whip and placed both hands on the hilt of his sword. Even with his full grip, he barely withstood the other elf's strikes. Thoranmir stepped back, turning his feet and trying to angle away.

Fuerian struck again and again. His opponent lost a step each time and Thoranmir seemed to shrink, instinctively clamming up into a purely defensive posture. Fuerian's blows were merciless, and he shouted with each stroke of the blade, scattering flecks of spittle and sweat. His normal coif, too, had lost its composure and his hair flung just as wild as the elf's attacks.

Finally, with Thoranmir turned and backed into the middle of the arena, Fuerian shifted away from the powerful, animalistic blows and returned to his precise, rehearsed form. He stabbed Thoranmir in the left shoulder and then again in the left thigh.

Thoranmir howled and tried to return with another offensive, but the wounds made him sluggish.

Fuerian sidestepped and then stabbed again, puncturing the opposite shoulder and leg. With an upward slice, he cut a long slit from waist to collar bone, and then another across his left thigh, the last wound gashing deep.

Thoranmir's knee buckled, and the crowd gasped.

Fuerian spun around, keeping well clear of his opponent's flailing weapon, until he stood fully behind Thoranmir. He grabbed a fistful of the elf's hair.

Thoranmir spluttered. Fear and surprise were clearly written on his face. He stared at his sister in the audience and mouthed the words, *I'm sorry.*

Anya wept openly.

At this distance, Thoranmir couldn't hear her words, but he could read her lips. *Thoranmir, you foolish elf.*

Snarling behind his enemy, Fuerian looked over Thoranmir's shoulder and locked eyes with Remy. He lingered for a half second, smirking, before plunging his blade up through Thoranmir's back. His bloody sword tip emerged through Thoranmir's chest.

Fuerian leaned in and spoke to the elf who had drawn first blood against him. "Do not worry, Thoranmir. I will still honor your request and make sure your friend does *not* win this event. *Just like you asked of me in the pub.* You will see him again soon."

Thoranmir's eyes widened, and he looked down, seeing the blade protruding from his torso. Slowly, he glanced up at his friend.

It took four security guards, two holding down Remy on each side, to keep him from charging the stage and murdering Fuerian.

The crowd was torn, equally intrigued by the violence on the dais and at the drama to the side of it.

Fuerian twisted the blade, tearing the puncture wound wide open with a violent motion and a cracking sound as it widened the gap between ribs.

Thoranmir cried out as his killer jerked on the blade, slashing through sternum and sliding its razor-edge through internal flesh. He turned his face to Remy; shock and worry beset his features. His hand seized the key that hung around his neck, the key to a small treasure trove Thoranmir had stashed after he and Remy had broken up the dream hallow gang.

"Forget the bet, give this to Odessa," Thoranmir insisted, even as Fuerian ravaged him. Thoranmir clutched the key and yanked it free from his neck, snapping the thin, leather thong it hung from.

Remy had no idea what he was talking about.

Fuerian jerked his blade and, finally, it nicked his heart. Blood poured from the wounds as Fuerian withdrew his sword and Thoranmir fell face first to the ground, stone dead.

THORANMIR'S BODY FELL TO the floor with a sickly, wet thud and Remy rushed to his friend where he collapsed to his knees. He roared with a guttural rage that welled up from some primal part of him churning deep within.

With trembling hands, he reclaimed the key and tucked it into his pocket, tearfully promising to deliver it to the she-elf who his friend had cared for more than Remy had understood... until now.

Fuerian turned back to his enemy and bowed for the crowd as if he expected applause for this display of brutality. Their enthusiasm was more muted than Fuerian would have liked.

Shaking with emotion, Remy gave vent to his fury and roared like a lion, *"I will end you, Fuerian Vastra!"*

The crowd in the stands had gone silent.

Fuerian remained standing on the killing floor as the faun and a few of his comrades dragged Thoranmir's body away, trailing a long streak of red in their wake. "Many have tried and failed, human. You will be just one more conquest whose name I shall soon forget." He pointed at the body that the fauns hauled away and snapped his fingers, as if conjuring a thought. "Just like, oh... what was his name again?"

Remy nearly tore himself free from the guards who again restrained him. His chest heaved, but he relaxed in the enforcers' grip. "I *will* see you in that arena."

The guards allowed Remy to stand. And then, the human backed away, retreating several paces.

The crowd murmured. Its noise had lulled enough that Remy, snorting angrily as he paced, stared across the grounds to his enemy and shouted, "I will avenge you, Thoranmir!" He screamed his vow loud enough that it could be heard anywhere in the stadium.

A dull roar picked up in volume in support for Remy. The crowd cheered for *him*. Fuerian had the backing of the people before the competition had started, but it shifted to the human as every elf who'd ever felt disenfranchised or bullied now sided against him.

On one side of the stadium, Fuerian stood, awaiting his next bracket. An elf child took Fuerian's blade from him, wiped it down, and then took a sharpening stone to it to freshen its edge.

Remy continued pacing on the opposite part of the facility. Their hatred for each other seemed to fill the entire coliseum like a palpable fog. He barely glanced away when young elf approached. The sidhe wore a flatcap and asked him, "Sharpen your sword, sir?"

The human handed his weapon over and the young stropper took it. He carried it to the side of the stadium grounds where he could service it.

A pudgy elf claimed the sword from the child and set it on his table. He withdrew a pouch of tools and took out the sharpening stone, along with a file. He used the stone to refine the edges, leaning over the weapon and working it for a few seconds with all eyes turned aside; the next two fighters had emerged from the tunnels.

Minutes later, the child returned the blade to Remy before scrambling away.

The next two contestants took their positions, but neither of the elves readied their weapons. Before the gong could crash, they each turned to face Harhassus and Jaira. They bowed, and both declared an unwillingness to continue, forfeiting the contest.

Harhassus asked the first one, "You are sure that you refuse?"

He nodded.

"And you accept his forfeit?"

The other contender bowed to agree.

Then, the announcer addressed the other elf, "You win and will advance."

The elf glanced at the fury still boiling out of Remy and then at the murderous grin on Fuerian's face. "I withdraw without advancing," he said, and they both exited the arena.

As the next two contestants were announced, they also yielded, both quitting the fight. A noise swelled in anticipation as the announcer called Remy back to the field.

The human walked toward the center as a plump elf caught Remy's eye. Remy immediately recognized Gareth and touched his face near the eye, remembering the bruise from the metal-knuckle-punch Fuerian's goon had delivered in the woods near the Morgensteen home. The skin was still tender to the touch.

Gareth had just walked a circuit on the stadium floor to stand near Fuerian. He didn't catch the exact words, but Remy got the gist of it through body language and reading lips. *It is done.*

Whatever Fuerian put Gareth up to was likely bad news, but Remy couldn't do anything about it until he knew more—maybe it wasn't even related to the duels.

Remy took his place on the fighting arena, glaring at his grinning enemy the whole way.

"Next up to face Remy Keaton will be Vuloir Magestys."

A minute passed, and the announcer called Vuloir again, but he refused to emerge from the tunnels.

"I don't quite know what to say," he announced. "I guess we have lost another competitor to forfeit."

The gong rang and Remy, never taking his eyes off Fuerian, returned to his side, still pacing like an anxious animal.

"Next is Waesley Amiir."

An olive-skinned elf stepped very nervously onto the field. He swallowed a big gulp.

"He will face Fuerian Vastra."

Waesley's face fell as Fuerian rushed into the arena and flashed Remy a wink. "Let us get this over, then, shall we?"

"I wish to yield," shouted Waesley. "I want to forfeit!"

The announcer asked, "Fighter Fuerian, do you accept his resignation?"

Bloodlust permeated Fuerian's face. "I do not!"

The crowd muttered as audience members asked each other about the protocol.

Fuerian turned to the announcer and then aside to the maven. "If the fight is accepted, and the field is taken, it cannot be ended without satisfaction of the opponent."

The announcer looked to the maven, who nodded, confirming Fuerian's point. The maven pointed to the faun, and the faun waved his arm, signaling for the gong. As soon as it chimed, Waesley drew his dagger and slashed himself across the arm. He held his bleeding arm aloft to show the blood.

Again, the gong rang, before Fuerian even knew what had happened.

The announcer looked visibly confused, and he turned to the maven, who shrugged. This scenario existed outside of the written rules. "First blood is drawn against Waesley... by Waesley. Uh,

Waesley—the bleeding party—cannot escalate per dueling rules as he is wounded."

Fuerian turned and stared at Remy. His face had darkened at being outsmarted by a younger lad whose blood he wanted.

The maven shuffled some papers and consulted with the announcer. Finally, the speaker said, "We have two remaining contestants. Fuerian Vastra will face Remy Keaton."

Remy slowly approached, and the crowd fell as silent as teenage voyeurs hiding outside a bathhouse peephole. Silent enough that everyone could hear the singing of Remy's blade as he drew it.

Both enemies stared at each other, glaring daggers. Remy turned and looked up at Jaira, who nodded her approval at the fight.

"Let us finish this," Remy growled.

Chapter Twenty-Four

R EMY APPROACHED THE ARENA. The human seethed as he
walked toward Fuerian. His opponent bounced from foot
to foot, eager for the conflict, his eyes locked on Remy.

Pausing before he set foot on the fighting floor where the elf and
the faun waited for him. Remy's shoulders calmed. He turned back
to look at Anya who still remained in the viewing box near the
announcer and not too far from the maven.

Anya's glare was hard. She nodded at Remy, signaling she wanted
him to kill her brother's murderer.

Remy's gaze shifted to Jaira, whose face remained neutral. *She's
masking her concern,* he thought. *Doesn't want me to worry or lose
myself inside my mind and risk a mental defeat.* Jaira bowed her
head.

Remy returned the gesture and turned back to his enemy. He
stepped into position and readied his blade, clutching his gauntleted hands around the weapon.

There was no crowd noise this time. The audience sat riveted
on the edges of their seats and Remy vaguely heard the speaker
make his announcements, but it was drowned out by a sound

like rushing wind as blood coursed through his ears. It carried adrenaline and other endorphins with it.

Time seemed to slow like a stretched bowstring. Remy tensed his muscles and attuned his hearing to the tune of the gong.

When the cymbal crashed, everything snapped back to regular speed—making everything feel even faster. Remy and Fuerian both launched themselves like arrows toward the middle, meeting each other in a flurry of blows.

Blades crossed and metal screeched against metal as razor edges raked across one another.

With blades locked, Fuerian reached across and grabbed Remy by the hair. He yanked him back, baring Remy's neck.

One dirty move begs another! Remy twisted his head and leaned in, trying to bite Fuerian's forearm.

The elf pulled his arm back and Remy's teeth snapped shut on only air. Parting a few steps, the two fighters circled each other, growling like mongrels fighting for survival.

Fuerian flew at Remy. Swords flashed again, and both sides pressed their weight against their blades as the tips angled upward and the quillons crossed in the physical struggle, tangling under the pressure like thumbs in a dvergr finger trap. Remy clamped a hand on the pommel of Fuerian's weapon, and the elf did likewise as they wrestled on either side of the blades.

Hand over hand, with both wrenching, the swords flung free, and the two contenders pummeled each other with their fists. Fuerian's landed first, bruising Remy's eye.

Remy struck with a jab cleanly to his opponent's face and knocked Fuerian back a step. He seized the opening and surged ahead, swinging from his hips. He landed a powerful hook to Fuerian's face and sent him sailing to the ground.

Fuerian's head bounced with a nasty *crack* where it hit. He looked up with a snarl as Remy lorded over him. Blood dripped off Fuerian's chin, leaking down his cheek from where Thoranmir had lashed him with the whip.

The faun interrupted them and signaled for the gong even as Fuerian snatched up his blade and roared defiantly.

FROM HER WHEELED CHAIR Anya surveyed the stadium grounds. Her eyes were still hot and wet from watching her brother die her lips had locked into a snarl as she fixated on Fuerian—her brother's murderer. She could not remember how to relax her face.

Then her face went slack when she recognized someone on the stadium grounds near Fuerian's side of the dueling platform. A young sidhe wearing a distinct flatcap. He stood next to a larger, portly elf.

Anya's blood chilled. It was him: Cú Chulainn from the two nights ago. He watched Fuerian fight with glee.

She tapped one of the aides in the box who had been posted to help her after she'd stopped the cheating. "Is there an inspector anywhere? I need to report a crime."

"I'm sorry," said the sidhe. "Your brother... it wasn't a crime. It was unfortunate but was all completely—"

"Not that, you idiot. An inspector? Is there one here?" Anya pressed.

The elf scowled but scanned around the stadium seats. They were in the nicer part of the facility. "The captain of the city guard is right over there."

"Well, fetch him—before it is too late."

He frowned. "Now? In the hottest part of the action?"

"Now!" Anya growled, just as Remy sent Fuerian sprawling to the ground with a hook.

The aide scurried away as the gong crashed. He brought the captain up as the announcer began making his proclamations.

Introductions were hurried and Anya knew she only had seconds to capture the he-elf's attention. "Captain Ochara, do you know anything about the dream hallow?"

"I do," Ochara said. "Stuff's a plague on the city, but its mostly contained to a few of Cathair Dé's darker spots."

She pointed to the elf she only knew as Cú Chulainn. "Do you know that sidhe, there. Next to the kid in the hat."

Ochara squinted. "Gareth Morass? Yeah, well, by family reputation. They used to be méith until Oberon dropped their favor."

Anya's guts twisted. "Captain, I think we need to talk a few moments longer."

And then a new gong rang, recapturing their attention and pointing it back to the battlefield.

B EFORE THE ANNOUNCER COULD make a statement for victory, the maven leaned in to speak with him and pass on an official ruling. "The human seems to have opened a cut Fuerian received from a previous opponent. While blood has been drawn, the wound does not belong to Remy and so does not count to press a victory. The fight continues at the chime."

Remy bent and retrieved his weapon. Fuerian did the same. Neither took their eyes off each other. The gong crashed loudly, and the two crossed sword again. Slash, dodge, thrust, parry. Remy lunged and cut only air as Fuerian reeled back.

Both made attacks meant to deal lethal, or at least serious, blows. There was no mistaking what it would take to make this fight end.

One of them would have to die.

Something glinted strangely in the light as Remy swung the blade. That fell light seemed to glimmer in Fuerian's eyes as well—he also noticed it: a horizontal line across Remy's blade like a hairline fracture, only too perfect to be natural. *More like a file mark... that's what Gareth was doing!*

Fuerian sparred low and Remy had to use his blade to block, but the elf wasn't trying to connect metal with flesh. He drew the response and then stomped on the flat of Remy's sword, snapping it at the line.

The crowd gasped as Remy whirled, still clutching half a blade.

Fuerian pressed his offensive, spinning his sword in deadly arcs.

Remy ducked and deftly leapt out of the way, tucking into a leaping roll over a move meant to cut through his legs. He came up onto his feet in a low crouch and turned his damaged weapon into a reverse grip, drawing his dúshlán in his free hand.

Using both like daggers, he leapt back toward Fuerian, cutting and slashing with reckless abandon. His range was shorter, but his blows were faster, and Fuerian struggled to keep up with the sudden hail of strikes.

The human snuck a lucky blow and punched Fuerian in the nose. With his fist closed around the hilt of his broken blade, he added its mass to the impact. It landed with enough force that the elf soared off his feet for a split second, raised as if held by a giant. Then, Remy plunged his dúshlán into his opponent's shoulder, his thigh, and his other shoulder, in that order. Finally Remy spun, slashed with his busted blade, and cut Fuerian across the remaining thigh.

As the gong crashed, the faun ran to intervene, but Fuerian had shoved him away and already begun raining back retaliatory blows, ignoring the fact that he'd been blooded. The elf made it clear he wanted the human's head. The crowd roared and began to "boo" Fuerian as he tried to kill Remy outside of protocol.

The faun carried a buckler in each hand for a reason. He used them to knock down the elf's blows and back him up a step even as Fuerian tried to reach over and cut Remy with his sword. Three times the gong chimed until Fuerian finally got a handle on his emotions.

By now, the crowd was on its feet, hotly anticipating what would happen next.

"Remy Keaton drew first blood against Fuerian Vastra," the announcer called. "Do you wish to contest?"

Fuerian sucked in a breath of air and held it for an uncomfortable length of time. He glared, looking up at the Morgensteens and then back to the human. His eyes flitted down to the dúshlán.

"We require an answer," the faun demanded.

Fuerian slid his sword back into the sheath and turned his eyes aside to where he knew Trishana sat.

She gripped the chair in front of her with white knuckles, desperate for Fuerian to win this fight. Trishana slumped as she watched his body language. She knew the answer before it was given.

"No. I do not contest," Fuerian said. "I accept the defeat."

The crowd, all except for Trishana, went wild.

Over the din of the cheering, Fuerian yelled at his enemy, "I'll be keeping my secrets; I shall forever know more about you than even you do. And you can keep the Morgensteen girl. It won't be hard to replace her, especially one of her standing."

Remy cocked his head, not sure if Fuerian was threatening Jaira or impinging her honor.

Fuerian grinned at him. He still had to yell just to be heard. "Another secret I just learned: the Morgensteens are flat broke. And besides, I had no intention of becoming a duelist. This exhibition was never about that for me." He turned on his heel and headed the opposite direction, limping slightly and ignoring the blood that stained his ruined clothing.

Remy turned and looked at Jaira as she stood near her seat of honor. Her eyes were wide with both wonder and curiosity. She stared at the blade in Remy's hand.

He looked down, startled. The runes and sigils engraved upon his dúshlán blade glowed.

Whomever else it was linked to stood close by—in the stadium, for sure!

Remy turned in a bewildered circle, searching the crowd, desperate to know who it was and what great wrong he or she had done to him, but there were thousands of people in attendance. *Fuerian knows! What does he know?*

The crowds were moving, heading to collect on bets or gather in groups. Jaira ran down to the arena floor. When Remy saw her, he resolved to put the dúshlán out of his mind. *My future is more important than my past,* he reminded himself.

He dropped the knife, and it stabbed into the ground. Remy opened his arms, and Jaira leapt into his embrace.

Chapter Twenty-Five

⸺ ⁂ ⸺

T HE CROWD NOISE HAD muddled to a dull roar of ambient sound. An occasional cheer went up as Jaira and Remy squeezed into a tight embrace at the center of the fighting platform

Harhassus followed quick on his daughter's heels, pulling her back from the human. Eilastra, her mother, knew better than to intervene where her husband's blood was concerned—though the look on her face meant she'd likely straighten him out later.

"This is not how this was supposed to turn out," Harhassus groused. "You were supposed to kiss Fuerian—you were supposed to wed *him*, Jaira. Now, because of... this, this *son of Adam*," he motioned to Remy and visibly restrained himself from harsher vulgarity, "the Vastras have broken off the engagement!"

Harhassus turned on Remy. "You don't have the slightest inkling of what you've done—what plans I'd laid for Jaira, plans which you've disrupted."

"Good." Jaira looked her father squarely in the eyes. "I've been telling you that this is what I wanted all along."

Her father exploded with exasperation, "Eilastra, can you believe that?!"

He trailed off when he finally noticed her withering glare. Once he'd finally shut up, she spoke.

"Our daughter must follow her heart. And she is following the contest rules as they were written. Her heart happens to align with them in this endeavor. You should be proud that your daughter's strong will and clear mind has seen her through this trial." Eilastra turned to look at Jaira. "At least one of us is keeping level-headed."

The announcer and the maven had come down from the bleacher box to join them in the fighting area.

Wearing a black cloak and robes that covered his feet, dust graying its edges, the maven's breast was embroidered with a misshapen, circular red sigil. Two stag's antlers interlocked to form a bony, horned crown. More importantly than the cloak, however, was the aura of authority which clung to him like a mantle.

A second maven, dressed just like him, stood a few steps behind. He was obviously the high maven's second.

Carrying the object that projected his voice, the announcer commented, "The winner of this contest, sponsored by the Morgensteen family, is Remy Keaton who—"

Jaira didn't wait for him to finish. He had already been announced as the winner, and so, Jaira grabbed Remy and kissed him. Their lips locked, and she pressed into him, deeply—passionately.

Remy melted into her as if they might merge into one flesh in that very moment. Electricity seemed to surge through the emotional emptiness that hollowed him out through the course of the duels and filled him with hot vigor.

She finally pulled away only after the maven cleared his throat.

The maven bent at the waist and picked up Remy's dúshlán. He turned it over to the victor. "This belongs to you, I think. I'd hate for someone to trip on it."

Remy bobbed his head and accepted the blade, sheathing it at his waist. The runes on his dúshlán had stopped glowing.

"Remington Keaton, I represent the Circle of Mavens. We enforce Oberon's will and authority on all things related to dueling, as well as arcana, and many other interests."

The maven turned over a duelist's pin to Remy. [You are now recognized as a Duelist,] he announced in the olde tongue, which made it somehow more official. "And you are the first of your kind. There has never yet been a human duelist, though our ranks are filled with many kinds of fey."

"And the guild or house I should belong to?" Remy asked.

"You are *ina aonar*. Until a guild offers you membership, you are house-less. But I am certain that it is only a matter of time before one reaches out to you." The maven bowed and then took his leave.

Jaira recoiled from him slightly, as if something about the maven gave her a creepy feeling, but she tried to maintain a proper level of politeness. Once the maven had gone, she relaxed and pinned Remy's dueling badge to his chest before kissing him again. She let this kiss linger long enough that the audience took note.

A few more cheers rose from the dwindling crowd, mostly leers and catcalls. It concluded the drama that had unfolded in the arena. Except for where Thoranmir was concerned.

As the crowds petered out, security waned, and nobody blocked the entrances to the stadium's floor. People trickled down and formed a mass outside.

As folks clustered closer to the winner and his prize, the meandering crowd parted slightly, and Remy spotted Anya Shelton. She drove her akasha-powered chair at a slow amble. Her face appeared pained and proud all at once: a special kind of melancholy.

Remy walked to her. His face mirrored hers.

"I—I'm glad you won," she said. "But I'd have rather you killed him."

"Me too," Remy said. "Thoranmir deserves justice. And I'm sure that, *someday*, he will have it." The words resonated with powerful meaning, feeling almost like a vow spoken in the olde tongue.

Anya wiped her eyes. "If anyone can make it happen, Remy, it's you. I see why my brother followed you."

Remy's eyes reddened with moisture. *It may have been the other way around—I would not have even headed for Cathair Dé and met Jaira if not for him.*

"Thoranmir was like a brother to me," Remy told Anya. "That makes you family. And family always has each other's backs."

She tearfully nodded, thanking him. "Family is in short supply for me these days."

Remy bent down and hugged her. "Yeah. For me, too."

"And you're going to need me," Anya said as they broke their embrace. "Something tells me we haven't seen the last of Fuerian Vastra." She turned and pointed across the way where Chief Ochara and a crew of his loyal sidhe wrestled a chubby elf to the ground. "But we may have seen the last of Gareth Morass. At least for a little while."

Remy cocked his head. "How do you... what is he—"

"Arson, at the very least," Any said. "They might still pin more on him. Thoranmir had a deal with his thugs—but his death complicates it... but Fuerian. He's the real enemy."

"And he'll get his due in time," Remy said, taking Jaira by the hand. "But right now, we're not going to think about him—we won't let him take any more time from us... not until *we decide* to take everything we lost back from him."

Jaira nodded her agreement, leaning forward and squeezing Anya's hand sympathetically. "Right now, there is only us." She turned to fully face the human who had won her heart, and then she kissed him again. A comforting shiver ran down Remy's spine as he gave into it.

Another face pressed through the crowd. Donnalia Fyndrolker, the she-elf child, stood a short distance away. She held a sack. Remy caught sight of her and grinned broadly. He knelt. The young girl rushed over to him and hugged him. He looked up to see Odessa Cócaire standing nearby. He embraced her, too.

Odessa's eyes were ringed with red. She'd obviously been crying.

"Thoranmir... oh, I'm sorry," Remy said, remembering their burgeoning romantic connection, and then Odessa's tears broke out anew.

Donnalia tugged on Remy's shirt and when she'd gotten his attention, she gave him a sack filled with coins. *Lots* of coins. High value amounts.

"What... how?" Remy floundered.

"It's what my father owed you and Thoranmir for the last day of labor. I took it from him, and I bet it on you... and some on Thoranmir, but..."

Remy nodded.

"I made Odessa bring me. I'm sure father is freaking out right now." She put the money pouch in his hands. "It's yours. Use it to start your new life... with her." Donnalia looked at Jaira with envious eyes.

Another elf approached, a regal-looking male. Remy cocked his head and bowed to address him.

"My name is Xander Kent." The elf handed over a paper card with his name and address on it. "I own several businesses here and abroad. Come see me soon. I'd love to hire a duelist of your caliber." He glanced down at Anya and gave her a card, too. "I've also heard rumor of your prowess as an aithermancer. I think I will have need of a new one soon. I heard just this morning that my local contact is headed for trouble."

Kent bowed. "I look forward to a future meeting." After a friendly wink, he departed, leaving the new duelist to his revelry.

Remy wiped his eyes free before any tears could fall. He addressed those gathered around him, keeping Jaira close. "Today, I lost my best friend to an enemy who I shall forever hate," he told, with a gentle nod at Anya. "But I also found a family of my own," looking to Donnalia, "wealth," and kneeling before Jaira, "and the love of my life."

Jaira looked down at the man she loved. "Is this a proposal?"

"Be with me. Forever?" Remy asked.

"Yes. Absolutely, I will." Jaira took Remy's face in her hands and kissed him again. And again and again, until the crowd, and everything else, drifted away.

Chapter Twenty-Six

R EMY AND HIS FRIENDS had departed the stadium in a close knot. Other teams of friends meandered away from the event as well. Mostly they consisted of other fighters or staffers at the building which had nearly emptied by this hour.

Jaira took several steps over to Anya and put her hands on the chair's handles, manually piloting it a pace away from the others. "We must speak," Jaira said in a low voice.

Anya addressed her with red-ringed eyes. The pain was still fresh on her face and she kept her words quiet. "This was one of the outcomes you'd foreseen?"

Jaira blinked as she nodded. "It is. I am sorry—if I could control the fates..."

Anya nodded solemnly. "What is it?"

"You are the only person who knows my secret. I... I need your help."

The way she'd said it, the terrified tension that cracked like rosin on horse hair, got Anya's attention. "I will help. Of course."

"I... I saw him. In the stadium. He was there."

"Who?"

Jaira's face looked at her. It had filled with gray worry and she could not remember if she'd even given Anya all the details of her horrific visions. She said, "The shadowy elf."

They both quieted when Captain Ochara approached with two dozen of his soldiers, dressed in armor and carrying saps. "Pardon me," he told Jaira. "Miss Shelton is oathbound to return with us to help clean up a part of our streets."

Remy, Jaira, and the others who accompanied them, stared at the soldier. Donnalia hid behind Odessa obviously afraid that they'd been sent by her father to locate and retrieve her.

"I'm just fulfilling one of my brother's last desires," Anya explained. "He promised to meet the thugs selling apothiks and make good on a debt if he failed to win the competition." The last few words came out more difficult than the rest. "And he did not win. That means I must meet them... but it does not mean I have to go alone."

Remy gave her a melancholy smile. "He's gone and still cleaning up the city streets."

Anya nodded, and then let the captain wheel her away.

XANDER KENT, REMY'S NEW employer, had put up Remy in one of his lavish apartments in the city. It was twice the size of Anya's and he'd moved in quickly, putting up Anya in a spare room and also homing Odessa and Donnalia in the meanwhile.

Remy's duelist pin shone brightly on his breast. Its out edges were trimmed with white fur to indicate he was currently a member of no dueling houses.

He leaned back in his chair and sipped the hot beverage from his mug and grinned at Jaira over the top of it. Below the table, his foot playfully tapped hers.

"You must both come to the wedding," Remy insisted to Odessa and Donnalia.

"I don't think father would be happy about it," Donnalia said.

Jaira took the young girl's hand. "Let me worry about that. House Fyndrolker would not refuse a direct request from the Morgensteens."

Remy nodded. "I do not have an abundance of friends." He pointed to his ears and gave a wry shrug. "I never really have, and so you must come. Anya will need the company on the groom's side of the aisle."

Odessa nodded. "If Jaira can make the arrangements, then yes. Absolutely."

Remy handed her a key. "Before I forget, Thoranmir wanted you to have this."

She gave him an inquisitive look.

"He wanted you to be cared for in his absence," Remy said. "Thoranmir was a sidhe with a mission, I think. He lived in the now... but he was always looking ahead, and trying to help."

Anya nodded. "Every problem was one my brother thought he could solve." She looked at Odessa. "Your brother's killers, the ones who fed him that poison, were brought to justice. Captain Ochara rounded the whole bunch up and that garbage excuse of an elf, Gareth Morass, is scheduled to go before a magistrate soon."

Remy looked to Anya. "Do you suppose there is a connection between the disappearing arcana students at the universities and the missing humans?"

Odessa's eyes narrowed. "There are *more* gone missing?"

Remy nodded. "Many students have simply disappeared from the nearby academies. But even more humans have gone missing... mostly the very young or very old."

Anya tilted her head. "Those most unable to protect themselves."

Remy nodded. "Exactly. "Thoranmir and I were looking into it. Do you think there is any sort of a connection?"

"Not that I can see without looking into it in greater detail," Anya said. "But if there is one, we'll find it."

"You'll help take up Thoranmir's last cause?" Anya asked.

"Of course. We were working on it together before he was taken from us," Remy said. "I guess it's one mission that remains incomplete."

Anya nodded. "I will look for any connections evident within the aither and then we can compare notes."

Jaira sat back. "But *after* the wedding."

Remy smiled and agreed. "After."

C ALITHILON GRUMBLED AS HE entered the main chambers of the Suíochán Naséan. Mithrilchon waited there for him along with his apprentice Agarogol.

"Trouble?" Mithrilchon asked. "You look as if you've come from a bad meeting."

"The local Frith Duine," the white maven said. "They're pissed because you sanctioned a human duelist." He looked down his nose at the maven. This will cause us problems later. If not the human's status as a duelist, then the Frith Duine will be a pain in our collective ass."

Mithrilchon had already given a report to his superior and so he knew what actions he'd taken and the curse of daggers which they'd assigned as a way to eliminate Remy Keaton in the future.

"You are absent a maven, are you not?" Calithilon asked.

The red high maven nodded. "Loitariel is appointed elsewhere and will be for a long while. She remains behind in Cathair Dé to keep an eye on developments."

Mithrilchon asked, "What news from the seer?"

"None," said Calithilon. "She has quieted. We will not know if our efforts to avert cataclysm are successful or not until she will speak again on the topic."

"What does she speak of now?" Mithrilchon asked.

"Only one word," Calithilon said. He looked at them both and said it. "Dragonfire."

EPILOGUE

REMY LOOKED ACROSS THE garden and then back at the crystalline statue in the center of the room; he sat by its feet and finished his reminiscence with a sigh. With a finger he spun the dúshlán knife so that it rotated in circles on the tip of his finger. Perfectly balanced at its hilt, it turned a lazy circle on its fulcrum as it looped around.

The silence of the room was deafening.

"I really wish you could talk to me, Jaira." He turned his eyes to Jaira's likeness. The statue was in her image.

Moreover, Jaira *was* the statue.

She was frozen in the same posture as she had been since the curse claimed her, petrified her. A layer of crystal encapsulated her, locking her in time and stasis—undying and yet unliving. Remy was forced to age and live without her, withering away as he searched for the cure to free his beloved.

Finally, the dúshlán stopped rotating and Remy snatched it by the handle and sheathed it. He stood to his feet and staggered.

Blood dripped off his fingertips. Both *his* blood which flowed from the wounds on his body, and the slightly pinker blood of sidhe warriors which had splattered his arms and now intermingled.

He clutched the earring into his fist and squeezed, pushing the thick, red fluid out as he clamped his hand around it. With blazing eyes, Remy limped a circle around her.

Sidhe bodies lay strewn around the floor, arms and legs splayed in mangled repose. *So many bodies! They came for me again, but I will not stop—not until Jaira is restored to me.*

Remy stepped over one of the attackers who struggled to crawl away. He ignored the elf's miserable thrashing and groans; the creature wouldn't get far before Remy dealt with him. He touched Jaira's face, leaving behind a few blood-smeared fingerprints, and looked into her eyes. He wished for a blink, a flit of her eyes, anything to demonstrate she was still present.

He pulled his hand away, leaving a red hand print. *I will see her restored if it is the last thing I do!*

Remy stalked after the would-be assassin and grabbed him before he could reach the exit. The attacker was a he-elf and had all the appearance of a soldier with training and allegiances to the seelie court.

The wounded soldier gasped as Remy seized him and kicked the elf over and onto his back. His blond hair flew in a tousled mess as he flipped.

Remy dragged his enemy close, leaving a smear of red across the ground.

The human pulled his dúshlán and brandished it. The blade's edge was as keen as it was the day it was formed.

Pressing the knife to his enemy's flesh, Remy roared in a jagged, raspy voice, "Where is he? Where is the Black Maven?"

What Comes Next?

I first explored the world of Arcadeax in an overlapping multi-verse of interconnected Urban Fantasy books: *Wolf of the Tesseract, The Casefiles of Vikrum,* and *The Hidden Rings of Myrddin the Cambion.* The paranormal investigator Vikrum Wiltshire, who connects the worlds falls into Arcadeax and has to flee the spider-queen, Rhagathena.

The world is ever expanding. Parts of Remy Keaton's back story is told in *Origins of the Fey Duelist* and also in other prequel short stories including *The Crow and the Troll*. The sequel is forthcoming, *Of Mages, Claw, and Shadow.*

Keep up to date and stay in touch with the author at this link: https://www.subscribepage.com/duelist

and add your email to be added to the newsletter list!

ALSO BY CHRISTOPHER D. SCHMITZ

More in this series! Also check out:

Curse of the Fey Duelist: Origins of the Fey Duelist
Curse of the Fey Duelist: The Crow and the Troll
Curse of the Fey Duelist: Of Mages, Claw, and Dagger

If you like *A Kiss of Daggers*, you should also check out my urban
fantasy series,
Wolves of the Tesseract
1. Wolf of the Tesseract
2. Gate of the Multiverse
3. The Architect King

The Casefiles of Vikrum Wiltshire

GLOSSARY

Aes sidhe – a class of magic wielding seelie fey

Aes sith - the equivalent of aes sidhe, but these fey are all wildfey

Aderyn Corff – "the death bird," a feared unseelie assassin who disappeared after defying the unseelie queen

Akasha – "magic in a bottle," a magic-based power source available to non-casters

Anansi – the title given to the ruler of the unseelie giant spider-folk known as N'arache; Queen Rhagathena, ruler of the unseelie, is the current Anansi

Aither – a spiritual realm composed of pure thought and power

Aphay tree – a tree whose fruit erases memories

Arcadeax – the world of faerie-kind which coexists with Earth, the Infernal Realms, and many others

Bruscar – low class tier of Arcadeaxn society

Changelings – half fey, half human

Coroniaids – often mistaken for dvergr who are the subterranean version, these are dwarves

Cù-sìth - a kind of hellhound

Cupronickel – a common metal alloy used so that no iron is present

Dagda – the chief deity of Arcadeaxn religious thought

Ddiymadferth – the chief insult among the fey: a derogatory word for human

Dream Hallow – a type of drug that causes euphoria and sends its users into the aither

Dúshlán – a kind of fetiche item given by Arcadeax itself, it is a boon for its recipient to right a great wrong with an act of vengeance

Dvergr – often mistaken for coroniaids who are the above-ground version of dwarves

Ellyllon – a wildfey variant of the sidhe with a slightly more feral appearance, typically thinner limbs, and longer, more narrow ears

Faewylds – any part of the world not claimed by the seelie or unseelie courts

Fetiche – Arcadeaxn magic that predates the aes sidhe; it is the magic of the gods

Fey – a word used to describe anything with Arcadeaxn origins

Frith Duine – a fey alliance dedicated to the eradication of humans living among them

High speech – also called the Olde Tongue and denoted by [brackets] when it is being used... oaths and commitments made in this language cannot be broken

Ina aonar – a house-less, ronin status for duelists who belong to no specific guild

Maven – politically aligned mages who govern factions of magically gifted citizens

Méith – the elite class of the Seelie society

N'arache – the giant spider folk of the unseelie; they live mostly in the Spinefrost Ridge mountains and have elf-like bodies fromt he waist up and giant spider bodies on their lower half much like centaurs

Olde Tongue - also called High speech and denoted by [brackets] when it is being used... oaths and commitments made in this language cannot be broken

Oibrithe – middle class of of the Seelie society

Powrie - a goblin-like race of tiny unseelie creatures who wear red caps and have generally murderous intentions

Saibhir – upper class of of the seelie society, but not méith

Seelie – the summer court: one of the kingdoms of elves ruled by Oberon and Titania

Shade – a kind of animated corpse under the control of a necromancer

Sidhe – members of an elvish species of the fey folk

Teind – the "hell tithe" which rulers of Arcadeaxn realm must pay to infernal forces to keep shut the gates of hell

Trow – beneath the seelie and unseelie realms are subterranean kingdoms of under-elves which make up the autumn and spring courts

Tuatha – creatures or "people" native to Arcadeax; includes the sidhe but also other sentient beings such as fauns, dvergr, etc... can be a synonym for fey in certain contexts

Tylwyth Teg – a type of elf from the faewylds and considered uncivilized and barbaric by their seelie and unseelie counterparts; looked down on by other sidhe

Vantadium - a metal alloy made of vanadium and titanium so that no iron is present

Wolfranium - a metal alloy made of tungsten and titanium so that no iron is present

Wulflock – the long-lost rightful king of the unseelie

The Faewilds

Te Sástacity

Solstox Cliffs

Raidhse

Saibhir Gaoithe

Cathair Dé

Vail Carvanna

The Selvages

ACKNOWLEDGMENTS

I would like to thank my amazing kickstarter partners and super-fans.

ABOUT AUTHOR

Christopher D. Schmitz is an indie author from the fly-over states who dabbles in game design. He has published award winning science fiction, fantasy, and humor. He's written and freelanced for a variety of outlets, including a blog that has helped countless writers on their publishing journey. On any given weekend, he can be found at pop culture and comic conventions across the USA or playing his bagpipes for people. You can look him up at:

www.authorchristopherdschmitz.com.

Made in the USA
Monee, IL
04 October 2023

43834100R00261